A Tainted Dawn

The Great War

1792–1815

Book I

A TAINTED DAWN

THE GREAT WAR

1792-1815

BOOK I

BY

B. N. PEACOCK.

Fireship Press
www.FireshipPress.com

ISBN-13: 978-1-61179-212-6 (Paperback)
       978-1-61179-213-3 (e-book)

BISAC Subject Headings:
    FIC014000   FICTION / Historical
    FIC032000   FICTION / War & Military
    FIC043000   FICTION / Coming of Age

Address all correspondence to:

Fireship Press, LLC
P.O. Box 68412
Tucson, AZ 85737

Or visit our website at:
www.FireshipPress.com

1.0

ACKNOWLEDGEMENTS

It would be impossible to thank all those involved in publishing this book, but I would like to pay tribute to the major players. First on the list is my editor, Jessica Knauss. She was invaluable in guiding me through the publishing process. Likewise, the rest of the staff at Fireship Press. Many heartfelt thanks to Penny Sansevieri and her team at Author Marketing Experts for getting the word out about my book. Kudos to Ann Robson, former interlibrary loan librarian at Culpeper, for obtaining the many arcane historical sources I requested. I cannot list all the many friends who cheered me on during the writing process, but their worth is more than gold.

Finally, I wish to give special thanks to the late Tom Grundner and his widow, Mary Lou, for making my dream of publication possible.

Important as all these people are, Daniel Peacock was my guiding star. My husband's faith, love, and patience sustained me every step of the way. My children, Dan and Stephanie, also gave unstinting support. And last, to my mother, who longed for, but never lived to see this day.

To Daniel

He never gave up on me, nor let me give up on myself.

CHAPTER ONE

Bliss was it in that dawn to be alive
But to be young was very heaven!

William Wordsworth, *The Prelude*, xi. 1, 108.

Even in August, London streets could be clogged. Two drivers had locked the wheels of their dray carts, blocking the turn from Piccadilly to Old Bond Street. Hoping to profit from the stalled traffic, boys hawked broadsheets along the way. *Bloody mayhem in France!* Not to be outdone, others shouted that the National Assembly had drafted the *Declaration of the Rights of Man and the Citizen. Liberté, Egalité* (both badly mispronounced) for all! The bloody mayhems won.

When the carts finally separated, a lacquered carriage with a coat of arms turned down Bond Street. Arrived at its destination, a footman jumped down from his rear perch and opened the door for a petite lady in a black riding-style dress and black beaver hat. She walked purposively to the shop of Monsieur Saulnier, tailor. Head down and biting his lower lip, a youth followed. With his standing collar, superfine wool frock coat and Demerara shirt and jabot, he possessed the requisite taste and status required for Monsieur's clients. But the dark brown hair resting on the stiff, grey collar was too short for a queue and too long for a child's cropped cut. He was at that awkward stage, neither boy nor man.

Lady and youth ignored a street player with a square fiddle. After all, London teemed with beggars. Inside the shop, two men gesticulated in French. The more corpulent was Victor Saulnier, the proprietor; the pale copy, his brother Jean-Claude, who managed their Parisian branch. They stopped mid-sentence to pay homage to the entrants. A fifth figure pinched wool broadcloth between his fingers. Tall, blond, and blue-eyed, he was dressed *à l'anglais*, the height of fashion in both Paris and London. His continued preoccupation was a gross breach of etiquette, one which didn't go unnoticed.

Victor's body immediately paralleled the floor. "A thousand padons, Milady. My nephew, he understands not the English ways." In French, he hissed, "Louis, your manners!"

Louis shrugged. He did not like England. He did not like the English. He did not like his English clothes. His wearing them was the result of a heated exchange between him, his father, and his uncle. Victor Saulnier prevailed then, and he prevailed now. His temper was legendary.

The French youth inclined his head slightly. "Madame." That was all.

Victor Saulnier grew red red with fury. "You will now greet the young monsieur!" he hissed.

The lad's struggle to comply betrayed itself in his tightened mouth. The English boy's mouth also betrayed his thoughts. His lips' amused upward twitch rankled.

"I have nothing to say to that brat."

The English boy eyed Louis top to toe. "Clothes do not make the manikin."

It was the French, true Parisian, not the retort, which stunned Louis. Victor Saulnier seized the moment – and Louis. The shop bell clanged loudly. His offending nephew ejected, Victor wrung his hands. "Milady, the rioting – in Paris. It has affected his reason."

"Enough! Edward requires two mourning suits, delivered to Evington House tomorrow."

"*Mon dieu*, that is –"

"You cannot?"

"No, no, it shall be done! The second fitting?"

"We haven't time. There will be a bonus, though, for the haste. Now see to my son."

Monsieur's journeymen were skilled. Edward soon was absently accepting his coat and preparing to leave.

The young fiddler greeted the re-emergence of mother and son with a lively air. Louis also waited. Enraged by his treatment, he hurled French insults at Edward. When Edward kept walking, Louis rushed him. Edward landed a swift uppercut before footman and coachman pulled them apart, knocking the fiddler down in the process.

Held at bay, Louis spat, "*Aristo!*" at an equally hostile and impotent Edward. Neither youth could bypass the burly coachman or muscular footman to get at the other.

Satisfied all was well, Elizabeth Deveare gathered her skirts. "Edward, come."

Edward bit his lip and helped the fiddler to his feet instead. The beggar dusted off a shabby jacket which ended at the hips. Long pants and hobnail boots marked him a country lad, an impression reinforced by a tanned face, a face totally lacking London sharpness. A decent face. "Here," Edward said, handing the red-haired lad a coin, "and don't let *him* take it."

The street player gaped: a gold piece. Gratitude aside, two things impressed him about his benefactor: the dark blue intensity of his eyes and the black arm band.

"Do not be deceived. He is an oppressor!"

The country boy intuited menace in the foreign gibberish and clutched his fiddle. The young gentleman, however, pointedly ignored the Frenchie. The fiddler admired his coolness. He was a true Englishman.

An impatient "Edward" issued from the carriage. Edward still lingered. "What's your name?" he asked the fiddler.

"I... be called Jemmy, sir."

"Jemmy."

"Edward!" The lady's third summons allowed no gainsaying. Edward returned – slowly – to the carriage. Footman and coachman resumed their places. The entourage rattled away, leaving the musician and Frenchman behind.

All three went their separate ways, but all three retained the memory of the others.

CHAPTER TWO

It is the fate of those who toil at the lower employments of life to be rather driven by the fear of evil than attracted by the prospect of good...

Samuel Johnson, Preface to the *Dictionary*

Birds twittered in the morning air. Sunlight streamed through a curtained window. Jemmy's mother smiled down at him. Happiness, deep and overpowering, bathed Jemmy like the sunlight. Home. Albury. Everything was right again.

The blissful feeling wavered as he struggled awake. Jemmy clung to it for all he was worth, but it was no use. Sunlight indeed streamed through a window, but the panes were grimy and curtainless. If any birds sang, it was impossible to hear them here. Albury was miles away, his mother long dead. He was in London.

Jemmy groaned and rolled off the straw pallet. Rents were dear, and carpentry work sporadic. They couldn't afford a house, only a room. But then, they hadn't lived in a house since Gran died last winter. Jemmy sighed. Foolish Gran and her dreams.

He took care not to wake Nan. Dad always let his young sister sleep late. It wasn't fair. He sighed again, but let it go. Nan was only five; he was thirteen, and more responsible.

His coat hung from the chair where he'd laid it the previous evening. A florin. He'd never gotten as much for playing his fiddle.

Perhaps that young gentleman would return and give him more. Jemmy dressed quickly.

James Sweetman's carpenter tools lay untouched in a corner. He'd brought his family to London after Gran died. Dad worked here a little, there a little, and Jemmy with him. At first they'd earned sufficient for lodging and food. Jobs, though, had dwindled. Dad had once worked for himself; he didn't take orders well.

If London hadn't proved a city of gold, it had shown itself a city of cheap gin. Jemmy warily checked his father. He sat hunched in a chair, clad in shirt and trousers. That didn't bode well. Dad wasn't going out to seek work.

Dad finally noticed his stirring. "Where you be going?"

"With you, if there be a job carpentering."

"Take the fiddle down to the docks. Sailors be generous when they come off ships. Might be, you'd do better than a florin there."

So he'd found the money. The light was dim, but Jemmy thought his father looked bleary. And his voice was hoarse. He must have visited a gin house late last night, after Jemmy and Nan had fallen asleep.

"I thought to go where I'd been," Jemmy said. "There might – "

"You don't think nothing! You go where I say, down by the docks, and play there. We be needing food."

Jemmy knew better than to sass his father when he was hung over, but the waste of the florin galled him. "Sailors mostly be drunk this time of day." Reckless, maybe, but he wisely backed away.

Whatever his state, Dad caught the inference. "Why can't you be like Nan? Get you out and be damned!"

Jemmy's eyes stung. Nan, always Nan. It didn't matter how many times she strayed, or how much trouble she caused. Everything she did was right; everything he did was wrong. Grabbing the square fiddle, he stormed out of the dingy room. It wouldn't take him long to reach the docks, not from their Wapping lodgings.

Despite what Jemmy claimed, the streets were already filled with men who either made their living from the sea or from those who sailed it. Carts wheeled by men and larger ones pulled by horses crowded the alleys. Jemmy inhaled deeply. There were fascinating scents here, from faraway lands. He quivered trying to name them, to guess their origins. Scents of things brought here by the ships whose masts rose out of the Thames like a forest of ancient oaks. Might there come a day when he'd sail away on one of them?

Jemmy leaned against a lamp post. His head swirled. What if he strayed, like Nan, only further? Would Dad care? Would he even notice? No, Jemmy decided stonily, he would not. He'd never let their father learn how many times his sister wandered away, nor how many times he'd fetched her back. Dad would have blamed him for her faults – and beaten him. Only now it was Jemmy who contemplated straying, not coming back.

"Gi' us a tune, lad!"

He turned this way and that to see the speaker, a difficult task given the crowd, the mountains of bales, boxes, barrels, and hogsheads, and the mist. It was only when the request was repeated that Jemmy was able to trace their source: a common sailor determined to hear a song.

Months on London streets honed Jemmy's ability to gauge his audience. He tucked his fiddle under his chin and began a spirited rendition of "Britons, Strike Home." One or two other passersby stopped to listen. By the time Jemmy finished, his audience had expanded to six. He reached for his cap, but to his dismay found he'd left without it. The lack of a coin catcher didn't deter his audience. First one, then another threw silver pennies at his feet. Not much, but it was a start. He'd barely stuffed them in his pocket when a muscular tar in a short blue jacket, open shirt, and blue-and-white striped trousers asked him to play "Black-eyed Susan" for his "lady." Jemmy bobbed politely at his companion, a frowsy woman all too obviously a street walker. While he played, the "lady" melted against her man. At the song's end, her admirer flipped Jemmy a coin. A gold crown, twice the amount the young gent gave him yesterday! Pocketing the coin and smiling broadly, Jemmy put bow to strings again.

"Here, you, take yer cock-eyed fiddle and clear out! This here's my spot."

The speaker sported a peg leg. Working it rapidly, he planted himself in Jemmy's face. Before the astonished Jemmy could react, Pegleg shoved him.

Jemmy beat a quick retreat. He hadn't known another musician had already claimed the spot. He wouldn't have played if he had. He knew the street rules.

"Where're you bound, lad?"

Someone was following him. Jemmy tried to outdistance his pursuer.

"Avast there, I'm not giving chase."

The tone was well meant for all the voice was loud and gruff. When Jemmy slowed down, an older man in a blue coat with brass buttons and a glazed black hat drew abreast. The face underneath the hat was sun-burnt and creased but kindly. Still...

"I'm not the press, if that's what you're thinking. Me name's Brighty, bo'sun of the King's ship, *Amphitrite*. I owe you somewhat for that fine fiddle playing. How are you called?"

Perhaps the man was alright. "Jemmy, sir. Jemmy Sweetman."

"Well, Jemmy Sweetman, what say we set our course for The Three Anchors. A pint and a bite never hurt no man none."

Jemmy missed the breakfast he'd never had. He nodded and fell in with Mr. Brighty. The Three Anchors lay in easy walking distance. Although sparsely patronized this time of day, it appeared to cater to men like the bo'sun. Jemmy relaxed and took a seat in a high-backed booth opposite his new friend. The bo'sun called for two porters and a plate of pasties.

"Ever been to sea?"

"No, sir. But I think on it times."

"Do you now? Well, my ship sails fortnight, and we lack a fiddler."

"You said you weren't the press."

The bo'sun laughed. "I'm not, but that don't mean I can't ask." A waiter offloaded their food and drink from a tray. Jemmy attacked a crusty beef pasty and gulped beer while Brighty watched. "Three square meals a day. Can you do aught besides fiddle?"

"Carpentering."

"Carpentering? At the shipyards?"

"My Dad, he's a plain carpenter."

"And what would your Dad say to you going to sea? I could get you on the books as a landsman. Upwards ten pound a year, and an advance to sweeten his yea."

To go to sea. Jemmy started to open his mouth, to say yes, when he caught himself. What if this man knew Captain Finch? If Finch were *Amphitrite's* captain? One of the quality, Captain Finch had driven Dad out of Albury. The bo'sun watched closely. Jemmy regretted his naïveté.

"I've fouled my anchor, right enough," Mr. Brighty said, as Jemmy rose. "But think on my offer, Jemmy lad. You wouldn't be the first to go to sea without a father's consent. Nor the last, neither, I'll be bound. And though I might not swing my hammock aft, I'd see to you."

Jemmy avoided the bo'sun's eyes but accepted his hand. If only Dad hadn't struck Captain Finch's man. "I, I be thinking on it," he managed at last.

Mr. Brighty built on Jemmy's wistfulness. "If a berth aboard *Amphitrite* sounds right to you, I'll be here. And if I'm not, wait for me. Mind, though, I ship out on the morning coach."

Jemmy left hurriedly, determined to go back to that fancy shop. Whichever way he went, however, the docks bewitched him. How he'd longed to go on board a ship, to sail to unknown lands. But something always held him back: Dad.

Ashamed, he searched for excuses for his father's surliness. Misfortunes had made Dad drunk and angry. He hadn't always been that way. Once, he'd been happy. They'd all been happy, back in Albury. The crown. Jemmy almost cried out with relief. Dad would relent once he showed him the crown. Jemmy's fingers searched eagerly, then desperately, in his pocket. In the end, the only thing they found was a silver penny.

His brain stumbled over the recent past. Pegleg had shot out both hands, but Jemmy only recalled one touching him. He realized why: Pegleg had picked his pocket with the other.

If Dad had been surly before, he'd be furious now. The August day warmed, but Jemmy shivered. What had Mr. Brighty said? About going to sea without permission?

"Get you out, and be damned!"

Dad didn't care about him, only about the money he earned. He couldn't go back. He wouldn't go back. Dad had Nan, and he was welcome to her.

Jemmy roamed the docks. He was right to do what he wanted. It was Dad who was wrong. He was old enough to fend for himself. And so it went, until finally, his mind hardened, his heart sick, Jemmy's faltering steps gained a momentum which carried him to The Three Anchors. Mr. Brighty sat at the same booth, but someone else sat with him. Jemmy's breath stuck in his throat. Had he found another fiddler?

The waiter who'd earlier tended them dashed past. He noticed Jemmy standing uncertainly in the doorway. "Ho, sir," he shouted, "he's back!"

The newcomer twisted around. He wore a uniform similar to Brighty's. Jemmy's breath came out in a relieved rush.

The bo'sun also turned. Booming so all could hear, he said, "Welcome aboard, Jemmy lad."

CHAPTER THREE

It was a day which changed my life forever.

Evington Papers, 7759/9,
Surrey History Center, Woking, England

Edward gazed out a bow window. Portsmouth. A confusion of water and air. A muddle of salt, cockles, and cod. A jumble of tea, tar, tobacco, and spice. A Babel of peddlers' cries, women's shouts, foreigners' bubblings, and sailors' cursings. A tangle of masts and rigging afloat; carts, cargoes, carriages, and peoples ashore. Madness and more. And yet, coherence overall, and order in the form of officers dressed in blue and white.

A loud "Ahem" recalled him to where he was and why he'd come. Mr. Charles Peris, Esquire, was about to begin. With one long, last, lingering look out the window, Edward took his place behind his mother's chair.

"In the name of God, Amen."

Mr. Peris' monotone sent Edward's mind wandering. The attorney was a sallow raven who, Edward speculated, just might fly away if he clapped his hands and shouted. The better known quantity was his mother, Elizabeth Deveare, Lady Elizabeth, per her courtesy title, a rigid figure draped in the total black of first mourning. Many said Edward resembled her. True, he had her brown-black hair and vivid sapphire eyes, but that was as far as it went. He was his own person. Then there was the older man, a stranger whose height and breadth dwarfed Edward, his mother,

11

and the attorney taken together. His baked-clay face had deep-set eyes of either light blue or grey; Edward couldn't say which. When Edward arrived, those eyes had raked, then cut him. His mother pretended the man didn't exist, and he returned the favor, studiously ignoring Edward and his mother thereafter. Who was he?

"I, William Bryson Deveare, of High Street, Portsmouth, parish of Portsmouth, Hampshire, being of sound and disposing mind make this my last Will and Testament in manner and form following (that is to say), if it is God's good will…

Just days ago, a messenger delivered a letter informing Edward and his mother of his father's death and requesting they journey to Portsmouth for the reading of the will. He hadn't cried. Edward worried, though, about his continuing numbness, proof to him that he wasn't a good son.

A good son. Why hadn't his father – No, not that, not now. He studied the stranger, a quaint figure in a collarless black coat with wide cuffs, throwbacks to fashions a decade or so ago. Equally outdated were his black breeches, buckled above the knees. In contrast to this head-to-toe black, he sported a white Ramillies wig. Old Ramillies Wig, that's what he'd call him. Whoever he was, he was no one's servant, not the way he authoritatively overran his chair.

Peris waded through a series of small bequests to his father's friends and relations, none of whom were present. How odd to have the reading of a will in an attorney's office and not a home. Odder still, there were only the four people present.

"Lastly, I do hereby nominate, constitute, and appoint my esteemed father Benjamin Alan Deveare, Rear Admiral in General Terms, of Southsea, parish of Portsea, Hampshire, to be in life the sole Executor of this my last Will and Testament, to whom I bequeath…"

Admiral Deveare? His grandfather? Edward gave Old Ramillies Wig his full attention. He sat as he had from the start, head down, knees apart, hands overlapping the head of a cane positioned exactly midway his feet. The possibilities. Edward's mind teemed with them.

"…and to my son, Edward Evington Deveare, of East Dene Manor, Surrey, I give, devise, and bequeath my house on the High Street, No. 143, Portsmouth, parish of Portsmouth, Hampshire, and the bulk of my Estate, both possessions and monies…"

His father *had* remembered him. Yet the old hurt resurfaced. Edward blurted, "Is that all?"

The Admiral raised his head, but it was the attorney he challenged, not Edward. "By God, what else does the whelp want?"

Edward's mother also spoke through the attorney. "After the payment of the Captain's debts, what could remain except –"

"Tell that jade –"

"Sir! My lady!" In his efforts to curtail hostilities, Peris knocked a sheaf of papers off his desk. Neither combatant acknowledged the attorney's awkward retrieval. Faces set resolutely forward, mouths indignantly clamped shut, they squared off.

Never mind the insult to his mother. Edward didn't want to alienate his newly discovered grandfather. Anyway, his mother was more than anyone's match verbally.

"A letter, a note, that's what I meant." He'd never told anyone he'd written many times to his father. Or that his father had never written back.

Peris faltered, "Was there any –"

"No!"

The Admiral had a magnificent set of lungs. Edward's ears were still ringing as the attorney gripped the papers he'd retrieved and raced through the rest of the will.

"And in conclusion, I commend my son Edward to my father, Benjamin Deveare, whom I name his Curator until such a time as he, Edward, attains his majority. I hereby revoke all former and other Wills by me made and do ratify this for my last Will and Testament, by way of Testimony whereunto I have set my hand and seal on this the Third day of March, in the year of our Lord one thousand seven hundred and eighty-seven."

Edward struggled with the dates. 3 March 1787. Today was 11 August 1789. He'd been thirteen when his father made the will.

The attorney stuffed the papers into a cardboard portfolio and handed it to the Admiral. "Take these," he said. "They and your grandson are your concern now."

His mother's hat brushed Edward's cheek as she rose. Her skirt pressed against the chair's edge. He got the impression she had her back to the wall.

"Edward is mine."

Hers, as if people were something to possess. Edward crossed to his new guardian. "Your servant, sir."

The Admiral aimed a death's head grin at Elizabeth Deveare. With a speed Edward never thought possible in one so old, he laid hold of Edward's upper left arm. Edward glimpsed his mother's bloodless face in passing, but her parting shot absolved him of any guilt he had in leaving.

"I'll have him back before this week ends. I swear it!"

Edward checked the street behind him. Neither coachman nor outriders stirred. Because of the Admiral's haste, that was as much as Edward saw or cared to see. The possibilities. The life he'd craved was his for the asking. Edward would have stretched his legs three times their limit to keep up with his grandfather.

He didn't complain until they came to a puddle of anything but honest rain water. His grandfather straddled the muck. His legs too short to jump it, Edward ploughed through the muck. Shoes oozing, he protested, "Let go of me!"

The old man broke his stride. Tightening his hold, he hit him with the fist holding his cane. "You speak when you're bespoken!"

A bitter taste invaded Edward's mouth. Blood. No one had ever treated him like this, not even at school. When he tried to wrench free, the Admiral retaliated with full force.

Edward reeled from the pain. Bright specks filled the air. The street became a kaleidoscope of shapes and colors, which gradually settled into a row of flint houses with doors fronting on the street. Old Ramillies Wig dragged him to one of them, entered without knocking, and shoved Edward into a room filled with people in black. Their collective stares made Edward aware he was disheveled, bruised — and dressed in grey.

A sandy-haired lady with a pinched nose greeted Old Ramillies Wig with a kiss. Looking from him to Edward and back again, she asked, "Papa, what is this?"

The Admiral shook his cane. "See him! He fair makes my blood boil! Hasn't even the decency to wear proper mourning. Even *she* did that."

Edward flushed. It wasn't his fault Monsieur Saulnier failed to send his mourning suits. His grey frock coat was weighted down with black armbands and cuffs. He even wore black buckles on his pumps. But these were just second mourning. First mourning required a black suit, like everyone else. Like a good son.

14

A good son. Edward tugged his coat over a shoulder and searched the surrounding faces. Of the room's occupants, three stood out from the rest, men with tawny hair framing strongly delineated faces, faces similar to the Admiral's. Disapproving men in unrelenting black, his father's family, the family he'd never known.

"He's...William's son, isn't he?" asked an unseen person.

"He's *her* son!"

"Papa, why is he here?"

Old Ramillies Wig punished the carpet with his cane. "Will must have been mad with fever. The whelp, not you, gets this house, and I am become his guardian."

The same person who'd puzzled out Edward's identity spoke again. "You could always return the boy to his mother."

"And please the jade? Damme, Daniel, but you speak like a fool!"

His mother not present to defend herself, Edward took up her cause. "Were you not such an old man, I'd challenge you to a duel!"

Benjamin Deveare snorted. "She taught you well, didn't she, whelp? You're as much like Will as a dwarf is a man. I always said she played him false."

Edward's face went hot. He was short for his age, that was true, but he was growing. Moreover, his father had acknowledged him as his son. "Not only does your age prevent me from dealing with you as you deserve," he said, "but your manners as well. A gentleman may only duel with another gentleman."

The old man leered down at him. "A bastard isn't a gentleman."

Edward lifted his head and looked down his nose. His father had openly named him his son.

A lady his mother's age rustled to the fore. "Shouldn't we allow our friends to go home to their dinners?" she asked the Admiral. "And go in to our own?"

She'd spared him another confrontation with the old man. Edward, however, wasn't grateful. He welcomed the opportunity to show Old Ramillies Wig he wouldn't be cowed. The guests, however, took the lady's hint. One by one, they came forward,

15

expressed their condolences, bid their farewells. One by one, they stared at Edward, the oddity of the hour.

Nine people remained. Two ladies stood uneasily by themselves, probably his uncles' wives. His father's brothers and sister formed a group around the Admiral. The plain lady spoke in an undertone to a middle-aged man who'd joined her. Edward stayed to himself.

The daughter led the ladies into the dining room, the Admiral the men. The middle-aged gentleman was the last to leave. He gestured toward the dining room. Edward went in to dinner solely to show his contempt of Old Ramillies Wig.

The Admiral took the seat at the foot of the table. His daughter took her place at the head and instructed a maid to set a tenth place. A serving girl wedged a chair on the pinched-nose lady's left, the female side of the table. Edward pushed it out of line.

The servant bustled out and re-appeared carrying a tureen. She placed it at head of the table and ladled cold garden soup topped by hot cheese pastry into ten bowls. The pinched-nose lady passed them down the table. Edward didn't touch the summer soup. It was begrudged him.

The old man hailed the arrival of the next course. "Red mullet, as fine a fish as can be had. You set as good a table as ever your mother did, Flora. Daniel, you should be thankful for what you have to wife."

Flora evidently was the tall woman, the Admiral's doting daughter, which made her Edward's aunt. Her fondness for her father ensured her Edward's dislike. Daniel, her husband, was the man who'd escorted him to the dining room. A colorless sort of person, like the fish.

"Is he to stay here, Papa? I can't think what I'll do with him if he is."

"Do with him? I know what I'd like to do with him, by God."

"*Amphitrite* sails soon. Her captain owes the firm money."

The uncle who commented was the pinch-nosed equal of his sister. He sat opposite the lady who'd spoken with Daniel. Plain as she was, Edward decided she deserved a better mate.

Old Ramillies Wig poured himself a glass of hock. "Go on."

"We could visit him after dinner, you and I. Captain Neville's generally to be found having a steak at Parade Coffee House this time of day."

"You're a son worthy of me, Bob, for all you didn't go to sea." Wine glass in hand, Ben Deveare leaned forward. "So you don't like our food, eh? Take the whelp to the gable room, Daniel, and lock him in. He'll run if he gets the chance. He's got the look of a coward, by God."

The cumulative insults broke Edward's frayed self-control. "This is my house now! The devil with you and your food! *You're* nothing but a guest here, an unwanted one at that."

Daniel's hands clamp downed on Edward's shoulders just as the old man threw down his napkin. "That's quite enough, young man," he said.

Edward recognized the voice as the one who'd suggested the Admiral return him to his mother. He tried to shake off his hands, but Daniel's calm determination transmitted itself through them to him. In the end, it was that calm which induced Edward to leave.

When they reached a narrow staircase illumined by a skylight, Daniel's calmness gave way. "You young fool, what were you thinking?"

"That man is a lout, a –"

"He's your grandfather and guardian now as well. You'd do well to remember that — unless you want him to knock you senseless. Up those stairs, before you do yourself any more harm."

A door stood at the end of the hall. Edward glanced toward it. He could escape.

"Would you give him the satisfaction of calling you a coward?"

No one was going to call him a coward. Edward marched upstairs.

Daniel opened a door off the third landing. "Temporary accommodations only."

Beyond the door was a cubbyhole containing a pine chair, a rope bed with a frayed quilt, and a small chest of drawers with claw feet. A chipped washbowl rested on top the chest; a chamber pot sheltered underneath. A servant's room. This was what Old Ramillies Wig considered suitable for *her* son.

The door closed; the key clicked in the lock. Edward went to the sole window, wrenched open the sash, and stuck out his head. He judged the distance to the alley below around twenty feet. He'd risk breaking a leg or worse if he jumped. Bending backwards, he studied the roof. It had a sharp, sooty slope. Still, if he held on to the top of the gable, he could balance on its frame and climb up. He'd get his bearings and a better idea of how to escape. Struggling, slipping, scraping, he fought his way to a safe footing adjacent the chimney.

On the roof, a multitude of gulls gave him the welcome his father's family withheld. The buildings on either side, though, limited his view. There was no seeing around them. Looking up again, he noted the house on his right had a flat roof and the stones in its wall were irregular. To scale it would be tricky, but up there perhaps he could determine where he was. When he'd hauled himself onto the adjoining roof, he found he'd done better than he'd hoped. He recognized the massive wall with the sally gate in the distance. His father's house was on the High Street, not far from where they'd stayed last night. Then Edward looked over the wall.

Like a scene from an enchantment, the panorama unfolded. The afternoon sun gilded sails and masts, transformed simple sprays of water into rainbows, made ordinary men heroes. Boats rowed by one man or many glided over the water. One and two-masted skiffs plied their way from ship to shore, from shore to ship, from ship to ship. They ferried men and supplies to the great ships, ships of the Service, ships of the line. Man-of-wars at rest until such a time as war summoned them. Until such a time as war summoned him.

Pennants rose and fell in the wind. Other ships lay at anchor also. Ships painted blue and red or black with ochre stripes swayed gently at their moorings. Ships flying the flag of St. George and St. Andrew. Ships flying foreign flags. From his command point on the roof, Edward reached out his hand to grasp them all.

The ships, oh, the ships. He had to get to them. Old Ramillies Wig was plotting something to do with a ship, a way to get rid of him. Edward stiffened. Never would he cooperate. A large sail billowed free in the wind. The ships. Did it really matter how he went to sea as long as he did?

He stayed on the roof until shadows outran the sun. Shortly after he scrambled back through the window, the maid brought his supper tray. He sampled, then consumed cold tongue and pudding. He was scraping the last of a gooseberry tart off a plate when the latch lifted.

Uncle Daniel burst into the room. "Hurry! The *True Blue* leaves for London posthaste."

Manners trumped grievances. Edward rose. "Indeed, sir."

"It's the London coach. You're leaving on it, to go back to your mother."

"I'm not a coward, and I'm not leaving my house."

Uncle Daniel's fingers ploughed his hair. "Forget what I said. He'd send you to the West Indies, a pestilential place. Do you wish to follow your father to the grave – and soon?"

"Not everyone who goes to sea dies."

"For God's sake –"

"I'm not going."

Daniel's hand abandoned his hair. "Very well." He thrust it inside his coat and produced a small silver-framed oval. "I meant to give you this before you boarded the coach. Perhaps it shall prove your talisman."

A miniature portrait of a naval officer done on ivory dropped into Edward's hands. He had no need to be told the subject. He devoured the watercolor face of his father, the first he'd ever seen of him. Yet the more Edward studied the likeness, the more disappointed he became. He'd always imagined William Deveare a copy of the Velásquez at Evington House: a dark-haired, intense gentleman with a vitality that made him seem ready to walk out of the canvass. This man was a younger version of Old Ramillies Wig.

Convinced his father hadn't been anything like the old man, Edward forgave William Deveare his face. He closed his fingers reverently over the miniature, his sole connection to his father, his talisman. He'd prove he was a good son.

CHAPTER FOUR

Man was born free, and everywhere he is in chains.

Jean-Jacques Rosseau, *The Social Contract*

A Paris breeze fluttered loose overblown petals of Provence roses. Louis Saulnier flicked them off a painted table and re-arranged the bouquet. Still critical, he moved the blue-and-gold Sèvres vase forward an inch. His peace offering must be shown to its best advantage.

"I was wrong to send you to England to watch over your father. I should have sent someone to watch over you!"

Louis' stepmother dismissed the maid who'd unrolled her thick, chestnut hair from rag curlers. Albertine Saulnier could have been a Roman matron of the Republic era: chaste, pious, and industrious. Yet even French copies of Roman matrons could be stern. Louis studied his stepmother's dimples. They still showed in her left cheek. She wasn't truly angry. He negligently sank into a toile chair.

"What I did was an act of patriotism."

"Patriotism? Do you call disrupting your uncle's business patriotism?"

"Plucking the feathers of English *aristos* is more than patriotism."

The dimples disappeared. "You belong to a family of distinguished tailors. Many, if not most, who deal with us, are *aristos*. Victor lives in England; it is only reasonable English *aristos* claim his custom. As for that, need I remind you of your admiration for La Fayette?"

"He believes in liberty."

"Do not try to distract me. My point is your uncle is angry with you, your father is angry with you, and what must I be? I, who must placate them?"

Even the best of women occasionally could be unreasonable. Louis was nineteen, a second year student at the University of Paris, not a child to be scolded. Besides, he'd committed no crime. He'd merely bribed his uncle's apprentices to delay delivery of the English brat's suits.

Louis picked at a worn spot on the chair's arm. "My father acts against all reason. As for Uncle Victor, he's nothing to say worth hearing."

"Ha! I would like to see you tell Victor that."

Mother Albertine's thrust went home. Louis winced at the memory of his uncle's outburst over those waylaid clothes. Nevertheless, he shrugged, "No harm was done."

"No harm? The English milady swore she'd never again patronize your uncle. Worse, she will tell others of her displeasure and turn them against him. Isn't that 'harm' enough?"

"Uncle Victor should have considered the perfidy of the English before setting up in London." It was senseless, arguing over this. Louis placed one boot on top the other, their sheen and suppleness worthy of him. The boots were part of his uncle's gifts, English boots. He'd kept them, but not the English clothes. Dressed in blue and buff, the English repeatedly had mistaken him for one of them. They did well to call themselves John Bulls, for they had the wit of cattle. Did they think every tall man who had blue eyes and blonde hair English?

"Victor pledged his word those suits of mourning would be sent by the specified date. Tradesmen are valued as much for their verity as their skill."

She hadn't lectured him like this since he'd broken a neighbor boy's arm during some childhood foolishness. Then, at least, he'd done something wrong. "I am no tradesman. Besides, it was you who insisted I accompany my father."

22

"So. It is my fault now. I see."

Perhaps it had been. He'd protested he hadn't time to spare from his studies, but Albertine had countered, "Remember who pays your bills." She could be ruthless, Mother Albertine.

"And what money have you of your own," she pursued, "you who profess to despise its source? For your clothes, your studies – or that woman you sleep with?"

To be scolded for a prank was one thing, but to bring his first amour into this was inexcusable. "Your pardon, madame," he said getting up from the chair. "I must go."

Albertine's eyes clouded. "The Queen's friends, the Polignacs, are gone, and with them, much good custom. Who knows who – or how many patrons – will emigrate next?"

The Polignacs. Louis reacted as if he were haranguing the crowd at the Café du Foy. "The Austrian woman beggars France to enrich such trash! It is well they have gone, before the people deal with them as they did de Launay and Flesselles, not to –"

"Peace, I beg you!"

The mention of butchered aristocrats visibly distressed her. He'd been too harsh. Was she not a woman with tender sensibilities? Louis clasped her hands in both of his. "Forgive me, good mother, my passion."

Her hands warmed his. "I will – if you do something for me first."

"You have only to ask."

"Make peace with your father."

"What?"

"You heard me. Go, and restore my tranquility."

Louis withdrew his hands. "He is the stubborn one."

"And you?"

The young English *aristo* had probably whined to his mother about his precious suits. Louis gathered his books. "Do not wait for me. Bertrand may need help with his latest pamphlet."

The dimples disappeared again. "My cousin is too much an 'enraged one.'"

"His passion and mine are to see France a brotherhood governed by free men. Would that all Frenchmen were so enraged!"

"When brothers quarrel, they can be more savage than beasts. Remember that, when your head strays too high among the clouds."

Bertrand Meslier, a former advocate, was Albertine's cousin. He was also Louis' childhood idol and mentor, the reason Louis wanted to be an advocate. "Bertrand and I will never quarrel."

"Return before dark. Many claim to be patriots – and are thieves."

No matter her moods, she was always concerned for him. Louis soothed the hand that touched his arm. "I will try, good mother, I will try."

"And your father?"

"If it eases your mind," he said with a characteristic shrug, "I will see him. If he will see me."

"My terrible child, who brings me so many grey hairs."

Louis relented. How could he not? He had been a baby when his mother died, barely a toddler when his father re-married. Albertine had loved him from the start, and he her. Having no children of her own, their love had deepened over the years to that truly of mother and son.

The lips that brushed his cheeks were as soft as the roses he'd brought her. Somewhat mollified, his university robes swirled around his legs as he left her bedroom. Jean-Claude Saulnier's bedroom was a place he didn't often visit, nor was often invited. But he'd promised Mother Albertine. Louis rapped on the door.

His father's room was as unlike Albertine's as he was unlike her. White and gilt Louis Quinze furniture and red moiré wallpaper mimicked the royal apartments at Versailles. Could his father's aristocratic patrons see them, they'd sneer at his bourgeois pretensions.

Jean-Claude didn't greet him; Louis had expected as much. He fussed while an old servant guided canary yellow, cloth-covered buttons through red-and-blue embroidered button holes in a long, silk waistcoat. Louis' father had begun offering the latest English styles, but like his son, he refused to wear them. Louis sidled next to the pier glass into which his father primped. He got his father's attention by leaning against the mirror.

"Are you here to beg more money for your gaming and your whores?"

"You give me sufficient for both, my father."

"You thank me on behalf of your vices, do you? I am touched."

The servant presented his master with a cinnamon coat. Other merchants might dress conservatively, but not his father. He was fond of ostentation, very much the "little big shot." Louis marveled there had been a time when he'd admired his father as a man of great dignity. But that had been before he'd known Bertrand.

Despite his grumbling, Louis knew Jean-Claude secretly gloried in what he thought were his son's "vices." Gambling and womanizing were aristocratic pastimes.

"And I am touched by your munificence, my father," Louis said. Fortunately, his father didn't catch the sarcasm.

"I've no time for your nonsense. Had not madmen destroyed the Bastille, I would demand a *lettre de cachet* to send you there. You disgraced me before Victor, not to mention wasting my money on English whores."

What would the old man do if he knew that instead of studying law to support injustices such as the *lettres de cachet*, Louis sought to overthrow them? The apology Albertine had wanted him to tender would have been an insincere one at best.

"You wrong me, my father," he said silkily. "Now, had there been some French –"

"Begone!"

Aping the flunkeys sent to his father's shop, who in turn aped *les grands*, Louis' arm traced cascades in the air. His father did not live over his shop, as lesser tailors did. The Saulnier establishment fronted on the rue Sainte-Honoré, adjacent other similarly exclusive shops. His family's home with its airy balcony was in the Immeuble Montholon, a new building composed of identical apartments wedged at Carrefour de Buci, a crossroads where many streets met. Louis jogged down some flights of stairs before erupting into the rue de Four.

Waiting at a fountain, servants cradled their pitchers. They lifted their caps as Louis passed. Pathetic creatures, they were as deluded as the men they served, men like his father who reveled in groveling before fools. Like the English street musician who'd fawned on that English brat.

The aroma of freshly brewed coffee enticed him. Louis traced its source and handed a vendor some coins. In return, he accepted a cup of thick, black, sweet liquid. He sipped it and surveyed the familiar territory fondly. Summer had carried its hot brightness into September. Deliverymen pulled broad-brimmed hats down over their eyes. French voices greeted one another, their cadences falling and rising like singers. Wood smoke left a pleasant tang in the air. How Paris shone after the sooty, coal murk of London, the new Carthage.

Members of a newly formed National Guard regiment paraded past, the red, white, and blue of their uniforms inspired by the colors of Paris and constitution, totally unlike the white of many regular French units, uniforms patterned after the Prussians. Louis dreamed while they disappeared into another street. 14th July. An army of citizens, Louis among them, racing through the streets of Paris. Black powder and anointing by blood. The somber black of the Third Estate, the people, which Louis wore under his robes, no longer seemed desirable.

Someone jiggled his elbow; coffee spilled over his robes. Louis turned to tell the fool who'd bumped him what he thought.

"Bertrand!"

Albertine's stoop-shouldered cousin, Bertrand Meslier, pretended to be scandalized. "Not at your classes? What an advocate you will make."

Bertrand's thick hair, so like Albertine's, escaped its ribbon. That much was unchanged. As for the rest, he lacked a neck cloth, his waistcoat was disordered, and his linen looked as if he'd been born in it. Although Bertrand had always been pale, now his veins showed through his skin as if illuminated by a candle. He'd been working too hard and eating too little.

"Let me buy you a coffee," Louis said.

"No, I –"

"Yes, not no." Louis grasped Bertrand's hand and led him to the vendor, where he paid for two cups. Despite Albertine's occasional threats and his father's constant complaints about wasting his money, Louis had an ample allowance.

Bertrand gulped the steaming liquid. Louis had been right. Bertrand lacked money for food. Louis bought another cup and some rolls.

In the short time they'd tarried, the streets had become clogged with people. And not only people, but vehicles and animals as well. He let Bertrand lead him in the direction of his college. They dodged a hired carriage, its driver shouting imprecations at them. Louis caught a glimpse of a lady in a modest straw hat and print muslin gown inside. Some respectable merchant's wife likely on her way to do charitable work, like Mother Albertine. *Aristos* lay abed this time of day.

Wishing to assure Bertrand he was serious about his studies, Louis said, "Last night I read Tacitus' account of Nero's matricide. If only d'Orleans would –"

"Hsst!" Bertrand glanced around, his own voice barely audible above the hum of activity around them. The mention of the King's brother, a liberal who curried the people's favor at the King's expense, neither vindicated nor minimized Louis' hint that d'Orleans should assassinate the Queen. "The Austrian's spies are everywhere."

Bertrand might hate the Austrian, but he still feared her. Because of a pamphlet he'd written in 1785 proving the Queen had indeed authorized the purchase of a fabulous diamond necklace, Bertrand had had to flee Paris. The former advocate couldn't forget his days of hiding and nights of running before he ultimately escaped to England. Nor could Louis. In a voice bitter with indignation for Bertrand's wrongs – but a low voice nonetheless – Louis said, "We've not come far enough if we cannot say what we believe."

"It will come, it will come," Bertrand said. "And you shall have your part. Have you time to spare this evening?"

"Yes. And afterwards, the Palais-Royal?"

"Perhaps."

"Perhaps?" Bertrand, forgo the excitement of the Palais-Royal, with its never-ending throng of patriot orators? "Have you nothing left of the money I gave you?"

Bertrand hid his hands behind his back. "Your father detests me. I will not accept any more money from him – through you."

"Take it," Louis said, retrieving one of Bertrand's hands and forcing a leather pouch into it. "My father thinks me another Mirabeau." Count Mirabeau was an *aristo* who, though siding with the people, maintained aristocratic interest in women and cards. Louis found his funding of Bertrand all the more pleasurable because Jean-Claude Saulnier, a royalist, condemned the patriot Bertrand, an innocent who blushed if a lady looked at him and frowned on gambling. The older Saulnier, on the other hand, downplayed Mirabeau's follies. The Count's brother bought his court clothes at *La Maison Saulnier*.

Since his return to France earlier in the year, Bertrand contributed to Simon Linguet's paper. He also wrote and distributed pamphlets, popularly known as "black butterflies" because of the way they fluttered around Paris. Linguet paid him little; as for the pamphlets, Bertrand had to pay, in advance. He was currently working on a tract arguing France should become a republic. He might be employed by the liberal Linguet, but Bertrand was of Camille Desmoulins' thinking. He scorned those who wanted France turned into a parody of England, a monarchy with a nebulous set of rules. Bertrand wanted the monarchy overthrown. Louis agreed wholeheartedly – and funded him.

His latest gift sat limp in Bertrand's hand. Not for long. With a convulsive gesture, Bertrand embraced him. "I'll repay you one day. I swear it!"

"But of course," Louis said, laughing. "Principal and interest."

Bertrand's mood lightened a little as he stuffed the purse inside his coat. "If you come early, we may yet be able to deliver my piece to Desein. He is busy these days, the printer, but he takes all I give him." For a moment, some of Albertine's mischief glinted in his eyes. "And if we accomplish all this, then, yes, we will visit the Palais-Royal. If, that is, you finish your studies."

They parted with a last embrace. Bertrand hurried toward the Faubourg Saint Marcel and his garret, a hole in a poor section of Paris. Louis didn't hurry anywhere. The Buci crossroads were convenient to his college. Even so, unless he moved faster, he'd be late for a lecture on Cicero. He smoothed his robes. It was well and good to read the ancients, but he'd rather read French law, the better to be able to reform it.

His mind, however, seemed unable to dictate to his feet where they should go or what pace they needed to set. Around him, the streets were littered with packing crates bristling straw and barrels, large and small, daring one to navigate them. Children shouted and played hide-and-seek among them. Men, women, and students streamed in and out of shops for which the deliveries were intended. A horse pulling a wagon loaded with wine barrels stopped to relieve itself in the middle of the street. Louis gathered up his robes to avoid being splattered by urine. He held them there and thus avoided a sizable pile left by another animal. The street cleaners had been lax.

Some women loitered outside a baker's shop, complaining about the price of bread. Four to six sous above the usual eight or nine for a four-pound loaf, depending on the honesty of the baker. "Good weather and a bountiful harvest must surely drive prices down," one argued, "else there would be more beggars starving in the street, and they and their families among them."

A citizenness whispered loudly that she'd heard from a porter at les Halles, the chief market in Paris, that the millers connived with the Queen to starve the people. A young clod, the baker's assistant probably, adjusted a heavy wooden shutter above a display window. The whisperer ceased whispering and spoke for all to hear, "The porters of les Halles know whereof they speak." The Austrian woman. Louis ground his teeth. No harpy of ancient lore was more rapacious than she, no Messalina or Agrippina more lustful or depraved. What had these poor women done that this monster starve them on a whim? France must rid herself of such as she.

The clop of hooves and clogs took on a hollow echo. Louis looked up and saw a colossal equestrian statue of one of France's better kings, Henry IV. He was on the Pont Neuf. No guards pressed the stall owners today for taxes. Soldiers were cautious since the taking of the Bastille. The people saw to that. The Pont Neuf, though, continued to be an endless source of entertainment. Here one could meet any number and variety of persons, from the wealthiest to beggars. Two men, one ragged, the other respectably shabby, greeted one another.

"Little One!"

"Lecluselle! Who let you loose in Paris, you thrice-dead dog?"

"Patriot soldiers, that's who. After you left the regiment, our good colonel locked me up. He said I was impudent for saying the people had done well. But friends let me out, and I ran away. That for Monsieur le Colonel!" The first man snapped his fingers. "And you, Little One, how came you here?"

Lecluselle was a ragged man, his pigtail long as a musket; "Little One," a titan with a nose worthy of a Frenchman. Neither was in uniform, so it was hard to place them. Their swagger was more pronounced than that of National Guardsmen, but their legs weren't bowed like hussars or dragoons. They must have been infantrymen, Louis concluded. Wanting to hear more, he pretended to examine apples in a stall.

"I 'gave my notice' when the Bastille fell," said Little One. "I belong to one of the new Guard's regiments now, a sergeant."

"Good for you! I only hope someday patriots will remember our officers and chop them to pieces like they deserve. Do you know the Colonel fattens his rabbits on the bread he denied us?"

Little One scowled at a carriage with sleek bays threading its way across the bridge. "When they do, I wish to be among them. We starve while they feast, the bastards! And in a year of good harvests, too!"

The two soldiers lowered their voices. What he'd already heard, though, provided more than enough for another pamphlet.

"Where're you off to?" the tall one asked, aloud.

"To a baker's, any baker's. Perhaps one will give me bread if I rake out his ashes."

"Come with me. We'll visit the guinguettes of Belleville instead."

"Have you heard anything of Caron?"

"He begs me to join him in the Indies, and become rich, like him."

The crowd swallowed the soldiers as they went in search of the wine shops on Paris' outskirts. The stall owner demanded Louis pay for the apple. Louis tossed him the core.

The sun turned the Seine into a river of diamonds. One day, he'd fight for the people's rights like a Roman tribune of old, as an advocate. An advocate. His classes. He'd better invent an excuse or two for his lecturer. If he went to his lecture, that is.

Under the new order... A white-uniformed officer on horseback pushed through the crowd. *Sacré aristo!* France needed citizen officers, not just common soldiers. An army of citizens, like Republican Rome. He and Bertrand would give Desein two manuscripts tomorrow. The first, Bertrand's; the second, his, a tract demanding the army be led by citizens. On route to the Faubourg Saint Marcel, Louis envisioned one such officer.

Someone who looked just like him.

CHAPTER FIVE

When I think back upon that time, now so very many years ago, with what glad anticipation and beating heart I first scaled those wooden walls... I can only sadly shake my head and conclude, I was a d––d fool.

Evington Papers, 7751/3

"La, dearie, them togs is big enough for the both of us. What say, I get in with you?"

Edward kept walking. The tart's remark about his clothes stung, though. Second hand, bought from a shop with three gold balls, pawn broker's relicts, beyond doubt. The blue wool of the frock coat was worn thin at the elbows, its white silk lining stained, notably under the armholes where yellow arcs radiated outward. It had no lapels, and its blue standing collar was dark where something sewn onto it had been removed. Nine small, scratched gilt buttons adorned with anchors ran down a side, with three more per each cuff and pocket. Waistcoat and breeches might have been white – once. A battered bicorn with a staved-in peak and frayed black cockade completed his ensemble. Old Ramillies Wig had flung the bundle in his face, informing him, "This is your kit, by God, and more than you deserve."

The Admiral's barrel-chested, tub-bellied servant carried his trunk through the sally port, the gate in the wall he'd viewed from the roof. Edward hiked his breeches and hobbled after him.

A shingle beach dotted with boats and people lay the other side of the sally port. The servant grated the trunk bottom on the pebbles. He searched for someone or something, and found them.

"Hoy! This here's to be shipped to *Amphitrite* and left. He's the one who'll pay."

He tugged his hat at Edward, more from insolence than respect, and decamped.

Two women, if women they were, left a boat. Their smocks outlined tree-trunk legs, which ended in booted platters. Amazons would have been dainty by comparison.

"*Amphitrite*, young sir? Tain't a long haul. But it'll cost you a sovereign, up front and handy." The smaller one spoke, her open mouth revealing missing upper teeth.

Edward scanned the available boats. "I'll inquire of –"

"Go to, sir. You'll not do better nor us."

Edward preferred any other boat, but their owners either grinned or looked the other way. If he wanted to get out to his ship – and he did – it was to be this or none. He gave them their price.

The silent one cut a length of rope from a coil in the boat. "Short splice this to your mizzen course," she said, thrusting it at him, "afore it comes loose its yard."

It was incomprehensible, almost. Shaking a hand free of a sleeve, Edward took the rope. Passing an end through the buttonholes of his waistband, he worked it over his neck, into another buttonhole, and tied a knot. The improvised braces held. He let go his breeches.

"Why, don't you look all flash and fine. Here, give us your hand, and we'll push off."

"Flash and fine," now there was a joke. Even with the rope, his breeches reached three-quarters to his ankles and his coat sleeves were half as long again as his arms. Refusing an outstretched hand, he scrambled onto a seat.

They cleared the beach and made for the ships. As anxious to be rid of his companions as he was to get to his ship, Edward pointed to a vessel. "Is that mine?"

"Nar. She's an Indiaman, not long back from thereabouts. Yours lies abaft *Fairy*."

He regretted the Indiaman and her fine lines and gun ports. His curiosity whetted, he asked the same question of every ship.

Starting with what the two wherrywomen styled a "second rate," *Barfluer*, and going through the "third rates": *Edgar, Colossus, Magnificent,* and *Endymion*. Edward learned something from this series of disappointments. The rating system had something to do with the size of the ship and the number of guns: the higher the number, the smaller the ship and the fewer her guns. He also noted the second rate had three decks pierced with gun ports, third and fourth rates only two. "Guard-ships," the Amazons explained. When he asked what that meant, Hercules, the brawnier one, replied, "Ships what sail the length o' their mooring cables with hands what mans the town."

Three ships lay farther out, the smaller one closest. As they rowed past, Hercules noted she was the *Fairy*. Recalling what they'd said about *Amphitrite* laying abaft *Fairy*, Edward strained to see. The larger ship had to be his. But when he posed the question, he was told she was *Adventure*, 44 guns. The last ship – his ship – rested midway the two. Hercules volunteered she was a "sixth rate." *Amphitrite* had a single row of gun-ports, her painting scheme dull black and ochre. Black, the color of mourning.

In answer to Hercules' repeated hailing, a stubbly face shoved through an open gun port. "What d'you want?"

"We's got a midshipmite."

"Already shipped our share. Sheer off!" The head disappeared.

Shouting to be heard above the music, laughter, swearing, and shrieking, Edward swayed to his feet. "I demand to come aboard."

Higher up, a man wearing a glazed black hat appeared, or rather his head and shoulders, for that was all Edward could see. A deep voice boomed, "Boat ahoy."

The Amazons stopped sniggering. Hercules, the spokeswoman, shouted back, "Aye, aye."

"So it's Moll and Poll, is it? What're you tarns up to now?"

"We's got a babe who says he belongs to you, and his chest for to hoist up."

The man peered down at Edward. "Whoever or whatever he be, he must be babe three times o'er to be taken in by the likes of you twin she-devils. Stop sculling about the bow and put him off at the side, where he belongs!"

Edward resented the "Whoever or whatever." Since he was admitted to the ship, though, he sat down on the bench. His escorts pulled round a cable running out an opening in the ship's bow. Leaning over backwards, Edward made out long, thick poles angling diagonally upward. Directly underneath them rode the upper half of a buxom female who wore brightly painted and gilded classical robes: *Amphitrite*, the sea queen who lent her name to the ship. Eyes forward, the goddess ignored mere mortals. Likewise the excrement-caked water beneath her.

The rowers steered clear the sewage. "Please, sir, that'll be an extra shilling apiece for taking you the grand tour way."

"I already paid you."

"Naow, sir, is that a gentlemanly way to use us when we's been so good to you?"

"Yes."

"Well then, if you won't give us naught, we's give you something."

Hercules, she of the beer breath and food-sticky mouth, caught him and kissed him full on the lips. The second wench was all for imitating her, but Edward threw up his arm. The "twin she-devils" cut short their merriment to answer a second hail.

"You there, lay hold the rope. Damn you, jack, fetch up his chest."

A sailor threw down a line to haul up his chest. Edward checked "the side." Narrow rungs ran up the side of the ship. Two ropes, each the thickness of his forefinger and as slick as if they'd been waxed, were attached to iron stanchions. His feet would have liked wider treads and his hands something easier to grasp, but nothing was going to prevent him from boarding his ship. Coat tails flapping in the wind, Edward caught the ropes.

No one met him on the broad horizontal ledge at the top, nor was the sailor who'd hauled up his chest in sight. Taking a deep breath, Edward plunged down into a sea of people.

A man with a grey monkey on his shoulder bumped Edward into large piles of hair-like hemp resting at the base of a large mast. Edward tripped and landed smack against a fat woman's backside. Where a mouse wouldn't have found room to twitch a whisker, she pivoted and screeched, "Mind what you're bloody well about!" Three men shouldering kegs drove her aside. Edward ducked the last keg, his sideways movement knocking him into a second woman, a pretty one carrying a basket of bread. Pretty, but spiteful. She shoved back. Edward nearly tumbled down an opening in the deck. Windmilling his arms, he regained his balance only to be jammed against a cannon carriage. He rubbed a skinned ankle.

An officer went up a ladder to a higher level. Tired of the bedlam, Edward heaved, pushed, shoved, and rammed his way there. The first person he saw stood legs apart, spine stiff, hands clasped behind him. His bicorn was trimmed with thin gold lace, gold tassels either end, a black cockade the left side. His blue frock had a falling collar decorated with square-ended gold lace loops, with more loops on lapels and cuffs. Neckcloth, frilled shirt, waistcoat, breeches, and silk stockings were irreproachably white. As a finishing touch, a straight-bladed spadroon swung from a belt, its ivory grip rising out of a black leather scabbard with silver fittings. The man's expression was as Olympian as the ship's figurehead – until he saw Edward.

"Where the hell did you come from? A convict hulk? And take off that hat to me, or by the God of War, I'll make you sorry for it!"

Edward rid himself of his hat. "Yes, sir. I mean, no, sir. I mean I didn't come from –"

"What's your purpose here? Do you carry messages for me?"

"No, sir. I've come to join the ship."

"In what capacity? Clown?"

"No, sir, I –"

Contempt highlighted an angular face whose chin looked as if someone had pressed in his thumb and left it. "Don't ever appear on my quarterdeck in that ridiculous rig again. Those bruises. Brawling in the hatchway berth already? Answer me, and be quick about it, too!"

"I've just now come, sir. I've no idea of what a hatchway berth is, much less fought there."

"Did no one meet you at the gangway, to direct you where you should go?"

"Someone told me to come aboard, sir, that was all."

"The midshipman of the watch wasn't about?"

"I know no such person."

The glacier green eyes narrowed. "You've a saucy tongue as well as a sorry look, Mr. Scarecrow. I shall take pleasure in teaching you your duty." He left Edward with the same speed he'd pounced on him. "Mr. Reynolds!"

A young officer instantly materialized. "Captain?"

35

"Find where that rascal Mason's gone and have him report to me at once. Mr. Claverall!"

An older officer joined them, more slowly than Mr. Reynolds, but hardly at a walk. "Sir?"

"Get this, this – thing from off my quarterdeck, and see to it he gets settled below. Mr. Fordyce, make ready my barge. And be quick about it!"

A youth in a similar but better-conditioned coat than Edward's, with white patches on his collar, hopped, skipped and jumped. Edward had no problem picturing him as a rabbit.

Mr. Claverall had heavy jowls like a wooden puppet's hinged ones. He scoured Edward from the top of his head to the bottom of his shoes. "Scarecrow's too good a name for you, I'd say. You there!" he bellowed at the nearest sailor. "Find his chest and take it down to the hatchway berth. If the mids'll have him, that is."

Edward was happier to leave the quarterdeck – for that was what he now knew this part of the ship to be – than he'd been to arrive. Going below, he banged his head against an unexpected beam. Edward blinked several times before he realized he'd reached the journey's end. Light was at a premium down here, despite the open hatchway. His next mistake was to inhale. A decoction of carcasses, rotten fish, unwashed bodies, stale cooking, and fresh filth, mellowed by sweated shoes and stockings, moldy cloth, and vinegar hit him. Gasping, Edward sought the ladder. As he turned, he noticed a canvass structure with a door and window on his right. Inside, one person lounged at a table while another stood in the doorway talking to him. The latter, well past youth, wore a natty shirt and petticoat trousers. The former was in his prime and wore part of a better version of Edward's uniform.

The well-dressed youth spoke. "God in heaven. Look what's washed up here!"

"Scarecrow's what the Captain called him. He's a crab," said a voice behind Edward. "He told Neville he didn't know what or where a hatchway berth was."

The first mid stared provocatively in Edward's face. "Johnny Newcome, eh? I'd sworn he was off a revenue cutter. Did Mama and Papa send little milksop off with all sorts of delights?"

The unseen speaker came forward. Edward recognized him as the Mr. Fordyce of the quarterdeck. "Poor children don't have full purses," said Fordyce.

"Open the chest, Scarecrow," said the well-dressed mid.

"No."

"I'll crack it, your honors. For a price." A weasel of a boy said this.

"There's your price, damn you!" said the well-dressed one, slapping the child. "If you open it quickly, maybe I won't kick you as well."

Edward watched the greasy waif produce a slender piece of metal and jiggle the trunk's lock. It clicked instantly.

The mids rifled the contents. Fordyce picked up a bottle, pulled out the stopper, and sniffed. "Lavender scent? Is this all you brought, by God?"

"Let's make him drink the blasted stuff!"

The cry galvanized the other two. They tried to drag Edward into the canvass box, but a tug of war resulted. At first it was a draw, but the two redoubled their efforts. They pulled him inside and hoisted Edward onto the table. Far from conceding defeat, he landed his foot in someone's chest and wrenched up on an elbow. The well-dressed mid pulled Fordyce, for that was whom Edward had kicked, aside and handed him the bottle. Hands emptied, he counter-attacked, driving Edward back so hard his head thudded. Edward dug his fingers into the wrists holding him down, but the mid wrestled his arms onto his breast. Meanwhile, someone lay atop Edward's legs. Someone else grasped his jaw. Edward snaked his head back and forth to avoid the bottle. For a moment, it seemed he'd avoid drinking the scent. Only for a moment.

The bottle was rammed down the back of his throat. Edward gagged and swallowed. Mercifully, it was small and half empty. His assailants satisfied, they released him.

Coughing and retching, Edward hung over the table's edge. To what hell had he come? Eton had been no Eden, but even his first term there had been nothing like this.

When he could trust his stomach again, he struggled to a sitting position, his hands propped behind him on the table for support. Head down, he took several deep breaths. His legs shaky, he held onto the berth's framing. His attackers were gone, but they'd left their handiwork behind. The debris of his trunk was everywhere.

He inventoried the remains. The carriage trunk's top tray had been dumped upside down. Righting it, he found it empty. Gone was his razor. Gone were his silver hairbrushes. Poking in the trunk, he saw his shirts, waistcoats, frock coats – everything the servant had packed for him – looted. All he had now were the clothes Old Ramillies Wig had given him. Old Ramillies Wig, how he'd laugh if he knew of this. But then, he'd planned it.

Pencils, pen, and quadrant lay on the trunk's bottom. And a sword. Edward drew it from its scuffed black leather scabbard. He'd acquired a cursory knowledge of weapons from fencing lessons. Less than three feet long, the blade was thin and straight with one side nicked. He ran an exploratory finger along both edges, then tested its weight and balance. Without bothering to resheath it, he threw it into the trunk. He was about to lock the trunk, but then he laughed harshly. No need. The others would take whatever they wanted anyway.

Above decks, he wandered everywhere except the quarterdeck. Contrary to his first impression, the bustle wasn't entirely chaotic. Half hogsheads were being unloaded from a boat alongside. Men lifted them with pulleys attached to the masts, then carefully lowered them onto the deck and through a second opening, this one forward the one he'd already discovered.

After the sailors finished with the casks, some climbed into a waiting boat and made for a place he'd heard them call "the Hard." Under the crew's expert handling, the wind caught the single loosed sail and sent the boat skimming over the water, heeling to one side. They deftly navigated a passageway crowded with other small craft.

A guard-ship eventually obscured the ship's boat. Edward turned his attention to his own ship. Miles of intricate ropes were strung upward, to and from the masts. That each one had names he deduced from the talk going on around him, a foreign language spoken in a multitude of dialects. Edward vowed he'd break the code.

More than anything else, the masts lured him, their height a challenge to be met and conquered. Edward shaded his eyes and searched for a way up the tallest one. Not finding it, he asked an available sailor. The man pointed to the web leading downward from the mast attached to the ship's outer side. "Mainmast shrouds."

Edward despaired at first because the quarterdeck seemed the only way to access the shrouds, but a closer investigation revealed an alternate route. He clambered onto the ledge he'd scaled coming aboard. Beneath it projected a lip, extending from the outer side of the ship, beginning forward the quarterdeck. That was the way to the top.

Six thick vertical ropes rose skyward. The end two were unattached to the others. The inner four were laced together by a series of thinner horizontal ropes. Edward grasped the two innermost ropes and began the ascent. As he climbed higher, he shifted to the outer ropes.

A third of the way up the mast was a platform built out from it, rigging running around and through it. The platform had an opening. Pleased with his success thus far, Edward opted to go around rather than through the opening. A sailor in a checked shirt and loose, umber trousers watched as Edward dropped onto the platform beside him. In the manner of the common people, he touched his forehead.

"Is it possible to go farther up?"

"You're having one on me, sir."

"Not at all. Can I get up there?"

"Damn my eyes! And you steered clear the lubber's hole." The fellow hooked his thumbs in his waistband. "What say you to a few shillings, to pay your footing like?"

Practicality more than vanity made Edward generous. Servants were more eager to serve if well tipped. "Here," he said, trebling the Amazon's fee, "use this to drink my health."

The sailor swore in admiration. "You're a true gentleman, sir. I'll see to you when you go aloft – or when the lieutenants masthead you. And being cap'n of the maintop, I'll see to it others does as well."

Edward pointed up.

"T'gant mast, sir?"

Edward intuited that meant the very end. "Yes," he said and swung out of the platform after his guide. Past the platform, the mainmast became a series of two stepped masts. A rope ladder with dowels served as a means of access. Edward ended perched on a short yard, not at the tip of the t'gant mast, but close to it.

A hand on the mast and the other on his hat, Edward gloried in where he was until he looked down. Below, people had shrunk to the size of Lilliputians. His vision blurring, Edward hastily switched to the horizon.

"Pity you're for the quarterdeck, sir," said the man. "You'd make a rare maint'pman, you take to it that natural." The captain of the maintop balanced free of hands. "I'll wager you'll be midshipman o' the top after you've been afloat awhile."

If being midshipman of the top meant being up here on a regular basis, so much the better. Edward could stay here forever. His companion couldn't.

"We'd best be getting down now, sir."

The sailor's bare feet negotiated the dowel rungs with ease. Edward made his way down more slowly. He left the captain of the maintop on the platform.

Safe on the deck again, Edward examined his stinging hands. His palms were crisscrossed by cuts the ropes had made, a cheap price to pay for the glory of the tops.

A bell clanged. How many times, Edward couldn't say. The hubbub around him made him lose count. A reedy pipe blew mournful notes. Men and some women traded places with others who came from below. Edward dropped onto the ledge, then the deck. He searched for the goat he heard bleating, but the sound seemed to come from beyond the ship. Sheets of canvass coverings held by nets obscured the view. Edward scrambled from a cannon barrel onto the nets to see what was making the noise. Two boats approached bearing livestock. A Noah's medley of chickens, pigs, sheep and goats clucked, squealed or bleated. A man naked from the waist up eased a sling under a protesting goat's belly. Edward watched, waiting to see what would –

"Ow!"

"Get off them nettings, young gentleman!"

A glazed black hat shaded an uncompromising square face: the man who'd hailed the Amazons. Close up, his blue coat had lapels, cuffs, and falling collar all the same shade, with gilt buttons bearing the same device as Edward's, only bigger. A shirt frill tucked neatly into the top of a red waistcoat, over which hung an intricately worked, curved silver pipe decorated with copper bands. In his right hand he carried the rattan cane with which he'd whacked Edward. Although the man previously had been helpful, Edward numbered him among his persecutors.

"Why, may I ask, is it disallowed?" Edward asked, rubbing his backside.

"Only a lubber who hadn't cut his first tooth would ask such a thing. Because it ain't allowed, that's why! Now off with you, and be thankful I don't make you better acquainted with my 'persuader.'"

So far as Edward was concerned, no thanks were warranted. He got off the nettings, though, his face, not his rear, to the man. A fiddler paused in his rendition of a popular tune. It seemed vaguely familiar, but Edward hurried on to escape further acquaintance with the "persuader." He came to a table chained to the deck with two sand glasses atop it. Behind it stood a red-coated sentry, musket to shoulder. The soldier glanced at Edward, but since he didn't advance, the man did nothing more.

"I recommend, sir, you find some other place to anchor. You've already gotten off on the wrong tack with the Captain. He'll not welcome you near his cabin."

Edward swept off his hat to the young officer he'd seen on the quarterdeck. "I disapprove as much or more of my uniform, sir, but there's little I can do about it."

"Have you no others?"

"Only one, sir, in similar condition."

"Then I suggest you make the acquaintance of the ship's tailor. You've a little money with you, I suppose?"

Concerned who else might be listening, Edward equivocated. "A pittance."

"Bargain with him, then, and see what he'll do for you, Mr. —?"

"Deveare, sir. Edward Deveare."

"The son of the wine merchant, Robert Deveare?"

"My father was Captain William Deveare, sir."

"Is he without a ship, that he doesn't have you with him?"

"He's dead, sir."

"Ah, yes, the armband. I'm Anthony Reynolds, second lieutenant. The sooner you get yourself trimmed, Mr. Deveare, the better it will be for you. Seek the ship's tailor."

The gangly young officer's skeptical frown was the closest thing to encouragement Edward had found thus far aboard *Amphitrite*. Anxious to please, and even more anxious to have his uniforms altered, Edward asked, "Where may I find him, sir?"

"Being an idler and in port, almost anywhere about the ship. Make inquiry. As to your own status as idler today, make the most of it. I understand Mr. Claverall, our senior, has listed you on the first part of the larboard watch. That's my division, Mr. Deveare." Though he tried to sound casual, Mr. Reynolds' pride was unmistakable.

"Mightn't I begin my duties now, sir?"

The second lieutenant smiled with the indulgence of an older boy for a younger. "You can sling your hammock until tomorrow. Make the most of it." He took the ladder to the quarterdeck where he joined four army officers in scarlet. Visitors, Edward supposed.

Edward readily conceded he'd made a bad impression on Captain Neville. As for the other things Lieutenant Reynolds said, he wasn't as sure. What was a hammock, and how was he to sling, or get, one? He did understand about the tailor, but when he asked where to find this "idler," he received the answer, "Below and fore." He had no great desire to go there again, but neither had he much choice. He went down the ladder.

Five had gathered in the hatchway berth for a meal. The weasel toasted sausages over charcoal smoldering in a large piece of ragged metal.

"There's the little sneak who set the Captain on me!" The accuser scraped out of the berth and blocked Edward's progress.

"I don't know what you're talking about. Please let me by."

"Liar! I'll square your yards for you! You told the Captain I wasn't at my station."

So this was the missing midshipman of the watch. Edward had no need to caricature him. As he stood, he was an overstatement. He wore his clothes poorly, shirt overhanging his breeches and waistcoat unbuttoned, more sailor than officer, even apprentice officer at that. Eyes, nose and mouth formed an arresting asymmetry: the failed first attempt of a petulant child to draw.

"Stow it, Mason," said the master of the table. "You're already in the Captain's black book; don't make things worse by fighting. As for you, Mr. Scarecrow, since you're one of us anyway, join in. I'm John Hallard, master's mate and president of the mess, by the way. That's Jeff Fordyce," he said pointing his fork in the direction of the person named, "and Claude Ensley," indicating the one next to him. "The oldster there is Gibbs, alias Grog. The sheer hulk, Mason, but then, you've already met."

Indeed they had. There was Fordyce from the quarterdeck and scent bottle affair and Gibbs, who'd helped manhandle him. Likewise, Ensley, the well-dressed mid. Smiling hypocrites all. His loathing of Edward etched in his face, the "sheer hulk" clumped over to an empty stool.

Edward had no desire to be served at the same table on which he'd been served up. However, he prudently took an empty place on a chest, his back to the door, leg brushing a sack of potatoes.

His second visit to the hatchway berth showed him things the first hadn't: hat boxes, swords swinging from hooks, bottles of ginger beer, half-empty jars of pickled vegetables, dirty stockings, scuffed shoes, tea caddies, and a bag of onions cozying the sack of potatoes. Fat sizzled onto the charcoals as the weasel toasted sausages, sage and pepper the dominant spices. Slabs of brown bread in a basket crowded a dish of pickles.

Hallard helped himself to the sausages and passed the plate clockwise round the table. The other dishes made the same circuit. When they reached him, Edward salvaged a burnt shred of sausage and a heel of bread. The pickles were gone, but some biscuits hadn't been touched. Edward reached for them, but Fordyce stuck out his knife and skidded the bowl to Hallard.

"Thanks for the brushes. By the way, how did you come by silver ones?" Hallard had a devil-may-care air which was appealing. Under other circumstances, Edward might have liked him. But these weren't other circumstances. Hallard had shared in the plunder.

"Think nothing of it. I don't."

The others looked to their chief. He rephrased the question. "Poor clothes on and fancy stuff in your chest. Explain."

Explanations might lead to disclosure of his whereabouts, should tales be told. "Ask those who now possess them," Edward said.

"His father probably nicked them from a debtor."

"Does yours do the same, Mason?" asked Fordyce.

"No matter," Hallard said finally. "All appreciate your generosity. For your kit, that is. However, as president of the mess,

I must ask you contribute to the common fund, especially since you brought nothing eatable or drinkable with you."

Edward stood in danger of being beggared at a time when he needed his money to look less like a beggar. "I have little."

"Your entrance money, or you don't mess here, Scarecrow."

That name. If they wanted what he had, they'd have to take it. Table or no table, they tackled him. His two scent bottle acquaintances pinioned his arms behind him while Hallard patted a bulge in Edward's inner pocket and removed his wallet. Contents emptied onto the table, he offered it back to Edward.

After counting out four pounds, five and tuppence, the remains of Edward's monthly allowance, Hallard said, "Not much, but it'll have to do for now. And don't complain to the lieutenants. Tale bearers don't fare well aboard ship."

Hallard shouted for the weasel to set the glasses on the table, together with a jug and a bottle of wine. The boy poured dark amber liquid into five glasses. Fordyce slopped red wine into the sixth and plunked it in front of Edward.

Hallard held up his glass. "The King."

As much as he hated them, he respected his monarch. One foot on the sack of potatoes, the other searching for the decking, Edward repeated the toast. Hoots greeted him. The others hadn't budged. He sat down, adding disrespect to the King to their already long list of faults.

Edward grimaced. The wine he'd sipped was sour. The others downed amber stuff. Whatever it was, it made Mason belligerent. After the glasses had been refilled, he reached his toward Edward, spilling some on the table as he did.

"You're junior here now. Give the toast of the day."

"I don't know it."

"Did you hear him? A captain's son, says he? Not bloody likely!"

Mason didn't get the appreciative guffaws Hallard had. Meanwhile, the president of the mess stuck both feet on the table, the others both or one. "I go a-cruising one last time tonight," Hallard said. "Going to close with that smart little tender I've had my eye on."

"The bluff in the bow one we hailed Spice Island way?"

"God, no, Jeff. She was a scow!"

They watched him closely. Although he understood neither the literal nor implied meanings of what had been said, Edward refused to betray his ignorance. He yawned.

He must have done the right thing. They went back to their discussion, their talk about what they'd do with their last hours ashore. Edward's mind drifted to more important matter. Below and fore was where the tailor was said to be. He got up to leave.

"Where do you think you're going?" Hallard asked.

"I've business to attend."

"Not without my permission."

"*May* I be excused?"

"He's as thick as two short planks," Hallard said to the smirking faces. "Here's your first lesson in the Service, Scarecrow. Address your superiors as 'sir.' Always."

He had to find the tailor. Choking down his resentment, Edward complied. Only after Hallard made the delay as humiliating as possible did he allow Edward to crouch forward to where the people congregated.

A vendor hawked watches only a fool would believe to be gold. The animals hoisted aboard earlier bleated and mooed at the far end. Edward exhaled. A barnyard would have been more pleasant.

Small chests and bags lay in parallel rows. Crockery was neatly arranged on shelves above them. The people sat, sprawled, or reclined on or against their belongings. Somewhere, amidst the pandemonium, sat, sprawled, or reclined the tailor. Edward asked his whereabouts from two men sitting on chests, their noses buried in tin cups of beer.

The more unshaven of the two wiped his mouth on his sleeve. "Go aft, where you belong."

Edward stumbled over one of Hallard's phrases. "Belay that," he said, but the sailor remained uncommunicative. His companion jerked his head to the right. "Yonder's where the tailor be, sir."

Unable to do anything else, Edward glared. As he left, he heard the second man say, "Be you daft, Jake? Speaking back to the likes of him'll get you a checked shirt at the gangway."

Heading in the indicated direction, Edward found a shiny bald head lolling on a female's splayed lap. The body belonging to the head sported a red and blue shirt, brown velvet waistcoat, and green striped trousers.

"Do you know where the ship's tailor is?" Edward asked wearily.

The man scratched one bare foot with the blackened toenail from his other. "I could might, then again might not. Who does asking?"

"I do. My uniforms need altering."

Pig's eyes winked behind smeared spectacles. "You're carrying enough canvas for main course. Go seek sail maker instead."

"The devil with you! Do you or don't you know where this tailor is?"

"I be he, but I bain't no Elijah. Trouble somebody else." The tailor nestled deeper into his lady's lap and fondled her legs.

Edward had taken all the insolence he was going to take. "Would you like a checked shirt at the gangway?" he asked, taking a wild guess at what he'd just heard.

The man shot from the woman's lap, his opened shirt revealing a chest teeming with moles, not hair. "I didn't mean no disrespect. Truly, sir."

He'd correctly deduced the words' disciplinary meaning. Putting on a scowl for the tailor's benefit, Edward said, "You agree to alter my uniforms?"

"Aye, sir, but I meant what I said about it being a hard job. I'll have to charge you a bit more than the usual for it."

"Put it on my account."

The tailor's bulbous nose changed shape like a soap bubble in a breeze. "I never to do nothing on account for the young gen'lmun. It's all up one hatch and down t' other with them."

"Name your price, then."

The man evaluated his clothes. "A guinea per frock, waistcoat, and breeches. And that don't include no shirts nor trousers."

"A guinea be hanged! I could have a new set made for that."

The man settled back onto the woman's lap. "Maybe new is what you need then."

The boy refused to accept defeat. Either he did what he could for his uniforms, or he would be barred the quarterdeck, the place of officers.

"What would you take in place of money?"

"It's brass or —"

The petticoat-clad female bent over and whispered something in her man's ear. He rolled his eyes. "Ladies always knows best, bless their hearts. Does they give you grog yet, sir?"

"Grog?"

"Grog, sir. Rum and water to drink."

So that was the amber stuff the others had drunk. "I had wine. I'll give you that."

"Don't like wine none."

The man's adamancy was infuriating. "What do I know of your ability as a tailor?"

"I be equal to any afloat!"

"Oh, really?"

"Bring them togs here. I'll show you who's a tailor!"

He'd won. Edward turned to get his clothes.

"What about me pay, sir?"

Edward silently damned the tailor and his greed. "It begins the very next time I have wine."

"Be sure you'll keep your word, sir?" The bubble worried the air.

The revulsion he'd felt when the wherrywoman kissed him crept over Edward. Of having touched something past redemption. Of being defiled. Nevertheless, he made himself say each word clearly and evenly.

"I'll keep my word. I always keep my word."

CHAPTER SIX

Oh! The roast beef of England,
And old England's roast beef.

Henry Fielding, *The Grub Street Opera*, III.iii

Mr. Brighty had indulged him for two days. Today, though, he'd had enough. Sick or not, he ordered Jemmy on deck.

Moaning, Jemmy dressed and crawled up the ladder. He was going to die; he was convinced he was going to die. He deserved to die. Hadn't he deserted his father?

Brighty's "cure," however, proved effective. Fresh air countered the pitch and roll of the ship. Gradually, the mutiny in Jemmy's stomach eased and the drumming in his head ceased. Persuaded he was going to live after all, he took more interest in his surroundings. The last time he'd been on deck one of the ship's boys had pointed out a rock formation called "The Needles." A famous landmark, his companion claimed, the Isle of Wight to larboard, the coast of Hampshire to starboard. Now, the sea was all around them, with nothing else in sight. Jemmy turned aft; the wind met him face on. Looking aloft, he saw further evidence of its power. Myriad sails strained at their lines. He felt a thrill, a heady feeling he'd never experienced before. He, too, wanted to soar with the wind. He, too, wanted to go aloft.

A Tainted Dawn

A shouted order preceded a wailing call. In an instant, men swarmed the starboard side of the mainmast rigging. One was smaller than the others, but he was among the foremost. Jemmy envied him his work and wondered who he was.

More orders followed the seamen once they were aloft. Jemmy labored to hear them, and even more so to understand. Those aloft, however, seemed to understand perfectly. They climbed out on the yard directly above the largest sail, the topmast Jemmy remembered it being called. On the forecastle, a seaman hoisted a long bundle up the halyards. Next, others sent up two yards or spars, Jemmy didn't know the precise terminology, one long and the other much shorter, to the men aloft. They attached the longer one to the yardarm. In no time, the sailors aloft undid a rectangular sail, rigged it to the end of the yardarm extension at the bottom, and at the top to the shorter spar. A new sail soon billowed out. Adjustments made, a final order had all but one descend to the waist and forecastle below. That one, the smallest, sought the quarterdeck. He must be one of the young gentlemen. Jemmy admired his agility and standing.

His study, however, had attracted the attention of the first lieutenant. Mr. Claverall walked to the quarterdeck rail and haughtily regarded him. Jemmy dropped his eyes and backed away.

Behind the mainmast, out of Mr. Claverall's range of sight, Jemmy marveled at the quiet bustle. At Portsmouth, everything had been rush and noise. Here, everyone knew his place – except him. Everyone knew what to do – except him. When a bell clanged, though, even Jemmy knew it meant dinner.

"Found your pins, 'ave you, mate? Proper time, I say."

It was the ship's boy who'd pointed out The Needles. Recalling his seasickness, Jemmy defended himself. "I be that much better, now the storm's past."

"G'won! Why, we's 'ad as fair a wind as a man could ask! But let's go get our share, 'fore the others eat it."

Despite his chagrin, his appetite nevertheless had returned. Mr. Brighty had put him in with the ship's boys, others his own age. Youngsters all, they messed fore surrounded by men. Or rather, they messed as they were able, for three of the boys served table for others. Jemmy found the earthenware plates, the mess's pride and joy, already set. His friend served up his portion and handed it to him. Dreading a repeat of the previous days, Jemmy ate gingerly at first. Finding the rumbling in his stomach came from emptiness, not the desire to empty itself, he wolfed down his share of briny stew, beef the meat might once have been. Not the best food he'd ever had, but an abundance of sorts. Jemmy grabbed a biscuit as it came his way. He soaked it in the stew and took a large bite. Rock hard, he decided to soak it a little longer.

While he waited, Jemmy helped himself to the small beer. They even had a chunk of cheese to finish things off. When he reached for more, however, his guide stopped him.

"That's for the others."

"Don't envy Joe none, waiting on the young genl'mun, no matter how tricky he be," said the Hanway boy. His time at the Marine Society, a school meant to train poor lads for the navy, set him apart. He could read, write, and do simple sums, but it was his practical skills which earned him the respect of the others, including Jemmy, who looked up to him.

Talk of the young gentlemen brought to mind the daring one whom Jemmy had watched aloft. Mention of him brought immediate comment – in whispers.

"Cap'n hates him like poison," said the Hanway scholar. "And the mids take their lead from Cap'n. He's in for a rough voyage alright."

The Needles boy belched. "Officers all think 'e's Bob Deveare's bastard. Shows what they know! Me sister's friend walks out with a lad who carries coal to Dan Tribe's shop. You know," he said loftily, "'im what sells watches and chronometers Lombard Street way, what's married to one of the Deveares. Anyway, Mike was waiting to be paid, see, and 'e overheard Tribe say what a black shame Old Ben means to dun William's son out of 'is inheritance. William Deveare, not Bob. And William Deveare t'were a brass cap'n."

The hushed comments, so like the muted hum of bees, meant little because the people mentioned were unknown. Jemmy leaned on his elbows on the chest that served as their table and drowsed. Dad would forgive him. He'd send whatever money came his way back home. Mr. Brighty had promised to help him do this. As if the very thought of his mentor held certain powers, the messmate who served as the bo'sun's servant brought word Brighty wanted to see him. Jemmy gave his plate a few swipes with sand and a cloth, and put it in a makeshift rack.

He worked his way without trepidation to where the bo'sun messed. Brighty might wield his cane with a will, but he was a benevolent god to Jemmy. He'd seen to it word was gotten to Jemmy's father, after he was gone, of course, as to his whereabouts and how to get in touch with his son. Brighty had advanced Jemmy money, that confident he'd be able to sign him on as landsman, and made good that promise. Nor had he stopped there. In Portsmouth, Brighty had seen to his needs aboard ship, helping him procure the necessary "slops," as his new clothes were called, and mattress, bolster, and blankets. Even his messmates he owed to Mr. Brighty's arranging. Perhaps he'd help him find a way to go aloft, too.

The bo'sun dined with the Master, carpenter, master-at-arms, gunner, and purser. Their table, suspended by ropes from the overhead beams, was weighted down with creamy plates filled with a considerably upgraded version of what Jemmy and the others had eaten. Brighty grunted when he saw him. Overawed by the collection of authority, Jemmy attempted a feeble salute. The resulting chortles made Jemmy wonder if he'd done something wrong.

"Took time enough to get your sea legs. Almost got us both on the Cap'n's bad side because of it, too. And that's a place I damn well don't want to be."

"I'm sorry, sir. I won't do it again," Jemmy said, as if being seasick was something he'd willfully done.

"Til we meet with a gale," Brighty said dryly. "But that ain't why I asked you here. You're to play for the dog watches, starting today. Cap'n's orders. The lads get their exercise that way, so make sure you play lively tunes, hornpipes and such. Understand?"

"Yes, sir."

"As for your other duties, report to the carpenter's mates. On by day, off at night."

The bo'sun's cut and dry manner was at odds with the way he'd previously behaved. Jemmy's throat tightened. Brighty took a long pull from a pewter tankard. The mouth he wiped afterward was more relaxed. Jemmy took encouragement from that.

"Ye—ss, sir. I be wanting to, that is, is there any way I could I, I mean –" If he didn't get it out now, he might never be able to say it, or to have a chance again. The words came out with a rush. "To go aloft."

Brighty guffawed. "Is that all? I thought you was going to ask to cap'n the ship – or bo'sun it. Well, if aloft is where you want to be, go. It's expected ship's boys be familiar with the tops. And since it's dinner, you can't get underfoot."

"Yes, sir. I mean, aye, aye, sir."

Laughter, the amused sort, not the mocking kind, rippled through the warrant officers' mess. As light as that laughter, Jemmy proceeded topdeck. He'd scurry up the ropes like a, like a... At the foot of the mainmast, he tilted his head back until it wouldn't go back any more. The sails billowed out in all their glory. He knew then the way he'd go aloft: like that young gentleman.

Trembling with excitement, Jemmy made his way over to the short ladder leading to where the mainmast shrouds attached to the side. The helmsmen kept the wheel steady. Except for him and one or two others, the decks were deserted. Not even the soldiers they were taking out to Barbados were on deck. Jemmy looked up. The mainmast swayed above, so much higher than he'd thought. The spaces between the ropes were wider, too. Fear overrode excitement.

"You'll be blown out of the rigging if you climb that way."

Jemmy let go the shrouds. The speaker wasn't a particularly well-dressed mid, but Jemmy touched his fingers to his forehead. To do less risked incurring punishment for disrespect.

Some would have been interpreted his silence as insolence, but the slight midshipman didn't. "Do you really wish to go aloft – or are you just going to stand there?"

Had Jemmy been less nervous or more experienced, he might have thought it odd a midshipman bothered about a ship's boy. Or perhaps, he might have suspected he was trying to play a prank. As it was, Jemmy was simply relieved that someone was there to help.

"Yes, sir."

"Good. Follow me."

This time, Jemmy did wonder at his good fortune. He knew him now, the young mid whom Mr. Brighty had whacked in the nettings. Did he associate him with the bo'sun? He glanced with trepidation at the other. He, however, removed his shoes and stockings and motioned for Jemmy to do likewise. Carrying them, they crossed to the windward side of the ship and laid them down.

Certain Jemmy was behind him, the midshipman began the ascent.

He climbed effortlessly. Not so Jemmy. His feet had difficulty reaching the successive ropes at first. Then there was the motion of the ship itself: the forward plunge downward, the surge upward, the side to side roll. All of this had to be gauged on the climb aloft. The various motions took their toll. Jemmy clung to the shrouds.

"Look up. Now!"

The young midshipman no longer climbed ahead; he was beside him. Jemmy drew a ragged breath and looked up. It was so high.

As if he guessed his thoughts, the slight mid said, "We'll only go as far as the top itself, and then by way of the lubber's hole. I'll stay beside you as long as I can. When we approach the top, I'll be behind you. Ready?"

He sounded so matter of fact, made it seem so simple. Jemmy chided himself for his fears. The young gentleman wouldn't let him fail.

He started upward again. True to his word, the midshipman stayed close. It was only when they reached the top that he fell back. Jemmy felt a push on the bottoms of his feet as he went through the lubber's hole. His friend joined him on the platform called the main top.

"You did it," he said, as if it were the most foregone conclusion in the world.

Jemmy believed him. He believed in himself now as well. He'd achieved his goal, been granted his wish. All through the help of the young gentleman. He no longer had any desire to look down. The world went on forever and ever up here. It had no beginning, no end. Against custom, he raised his eyes to the young gentleman's. Their deep blue intensity startled him. He'd seen eyes like that only once before.

"This is more than worth it all."

Jemmy didn't answer. For one thing, the midshipman was talking to himself and not him. For another, Jemmy was piecing together a puzzle. Could this badly-dressed young gentleman be the lordly one of Bond Street? The distinctive eyes aside, the build was similar. He carried himself with the same assurance. But the other boy had been sad. The midshipman moved to the edge of the top, exposing as he did a black armband.

"Dinner should be over soon. We'd better go down now."

The glory had been too brief. Jemmy waited until the other disappeared through the lubber's hole. The descent was easier, quicker than the ascent. Jemmy was still puzzling out the young gentleman's identity. As they exited the rigging, Mr. Claverall gave the answer.

"Mr. Deveare, since when does a captain's son consort with the people?"

Mr. Deveare saluted and went in search of his stockings and shoes. Shy of officers, Jemmy barely remembered to knuckle his forehead. The young gentleman of the nettings, the one who'd climbed aloft so easily, the supposed captain's son, were all one and the same: Mr. Deveare. Only he really was a captain's son, and more, one of the quality. Only one thing remained unanswered: how he got here.

...what a black shame Old Ben means to dun William's son out of 'is inheritance. Someone called Old Ben sent him on this ship to cheat him. According to what he'd heard, Captain Neville despised Mr. Deveare. Be that as it may, Jemmy stubbornly concluded as he joined the carpenter's mates, Mr. Deveare had helped him twice, once in London and now aboard ship. That, in Jemmy's book, counted for everything.

CHAPTER SEVEN

...conscience with injustice ... corrupted.

William Shakespeare, *II Henry IV*, III.ii

Elizabeth Deveare gazed out the French windows. With the mist gathering over the water, a stroll by the lake would be most soothing. On the island, two ducks dove in, one after the other, like children playing follow the leader. Children. Who was that child that trespassed her lake, the one who was so elusive? Strange rumors were coming out of France of manor houses being burned and their owners butchered. Impossible such things could happen in England. There had been the Gordon riots, though, seven years ago. Had she been wrong in reopening East Dene?

Her self-confidence, shaken at Portsmouth, reasserted itself. No. She was in the home of her birth and childhood. Nothing could harm her here.

She left the window. Touching a key on the pianoforte, a mid-register note sounded sweet and clear. Had she not been so cowardly Edward would be here, with her, tonight. The last time they'd been here, he'd been nine. That last time ...

The porcelain clock on the had mantelpiece chimed. One, two... Firm, heavy footfalls. Three, four... Quick, lighter ones. Five. The French tutor delivered her son. Freed of the constraints of a dependent's presence, she waited for Edward to come and put his arms around her neck, the way he always did once they were alone. But Edward stayed exactly where the Frenchman left him. He looked at her steadily, the way only a child can. Perhaps his tutor had punished him for some minor misdeed.

"Come, my darling, we'll sing away your cares."

"I don't wish to sing tonight, Madam."

"Madam? When have I become 'Madam' to you?"

"Monsieur Gilbert says it isn't proper for me to call you Mother."

"What nonsense!"

"He says that when we go to France I must never do so, or the French gentlemen will laugh at my boorish English ways."

"It isn't boorish to show affection. Come, give me a kiss. Forget what Monsieur Gilbert said." She smiled and held out her arms, but the child didn't budge. "Edward, whatever is wrong with you? Do you believe Monsieur Gilbert, or me?"

The expression on her son's face had subtly altered. It was as though time had sped forward, and she glimpsed the man that was to be. Father came to mind; the way he locked onto her eyes when she displeased him.

"I heard the servants talking. How my father came for you, but you wouldn't go. Cook said so, to that man who preaches in the fields. They didn't see me. She said she felt sorry for me. I know she'd never lie to him. Why did you lie to me – Madam?"

Madam. He never called her mother again. Elizabeth Deveare abandoned the room for a once loved place. Opening the door, she found that the sheets had been removed from the furniture. It looked just as it had when she'd left it six years ago.

The painting. It hadn't changed either. The little Edward of long ago, pressed affectionately against her, looking up into her face with love and trust. She smiled and caressed the canvass cheek of her son.

Her Belgian lace fichu rose and fell rapidly over her breast. She ached for the happiness of other days. The will. Her husband had thought to cheat her in death, steal her son from her.

She fingered the cameo fastening the lace. How could she have been such a fool? A chance encounter at Vauxhall, a pleasant laugh catching her ear, an attractive man catching her eye. Love, or so she'd thought, long ago. The hand resting on the cameo tingled: the remembrance of his touch. She dropped her hand. It would be dark soon. She should summon a servant to light some tapers. She should, but she didn't.

The room was cold with twilight. Better to go upstairs where a fire burned on the grate. She hesitated, then stepped back. She'd always been able to deal with William, hadn't she? For a moment, it seemed some of the lake's mist had crept inside. It seemed to swirl into a figure: her husband, just as he'd been when first they'd met, mask dropped to reveal his face. It couldn't be. With a little light....

There was nothing there. How weak of her, how very... feminine. William. She'd pursued and won him. Yet what had she won? A handsome man never at home, and such a home. A sliver of a house on the High Street in Portsmouth. Convenient for him, no doubt, close to the Fountain and George Inns where his friends would stay. Close to the sally port and his ships. Close to Portsmouth Point with its drunken sailors and their drunken trulls. And she alone, everlastingly alone.

Unthinkable to invite her friends there, even had they been willing to come. Invite his relatives? They meant nothing to her. The only thing they had in common was the name Deveare. Deveare, yes, that was her name now – and Edward's.

Alone. She'd known Father would never accept William, a mere lieutenant from a common family. Their secret marriage. A friend's slip, inquiring after her "husband." The ugly scene with Father, his disowning her. The tawdry house in a still more tawdry town.

The air freshened. She released the cameo. A draft, some servant must have left an outside door open, to secret a lover, perhaps?

Women. He'd had his share of them. While she... Alone. Alone to usher two children stillborn into the world – her children. Alone to miscarry a third and so to lose it as well. Elizabeth Deveare shuddered. Why did she stay when she could no longer see?

Her fourth and last pregnancy. Desperate. Writing to Father, begging him to take her back. Repudiating her marriage. Weary of her husband and her life with him. Her laughter hurt her ears. No, her life without him.

Father. His oh, so joyous letter. But he hadn't completely relented. She could live at East Dene, if she chose, the place of her earliest childhood remembrances. The place where she'd been born. The place where her mother had died.

Her child came early, born on Father's birthday, as if that made any difference to him. Her body convulsed, even as it had fifteen years ago in her bedroom upstairs. The long labor, the excruciating pain... No, it hadn't been planned.

The portrait. Had the figures moved? Fear. Worse than any contraction. Fear that it would end in yet another stillbirth. But the child had been born alive. Small and sickly, he survived despite the odds. Her son, her darling Edward.

William. He'd actually come after her, here to East Dene, to claim her and her son. Elated by the triumph of birth, she'd defied him. Yes, she'd named him Edward, after her father and his father before him. He was an Evington regardless of the name Deveare. One had only to look at him. Come back? To what? Portsmouth?

William's voice answered her from the past. Home, to him, to his family. Memories resurfaced, loathsome things from unquiet graves. *He* had been there, gloating in his capture of her son. Her hands shook. The old man detested Edward. She sensed it the moment they entered. That grey suit. Monsieur Saulnier had failed her. Hadn't men always failed her?

The tiredness she'd tried to deny came on with a rush. Lacy would be waiting upstairs to undress her. A warm wrapper and a cheerful fire, that's what she needed. In the corridor and on the staircase beeswax candles flickered, their flames pinpointed in brass sconces. Outside her bedroom door, Elizabeth Deveare focused on a dying flame. Let the past be past forever. She'd go on as she always had. Alone.

CHAPTER EIGHT

I soon came to realize that punishment too harsh was worse than none at all.

Evington Papers, 7752/14

The first stroke of the cat left a red welt. Under the Captain's watchful eye, the bo'sun's mate drew back his arm. His aim and force improved with the second blow. The new welt crossed the other, deeper, expertly engraved between large brown moles on the man's shoulder blades. The tailor writhed and screamed. He'd claimed he'd never been flogged. His unscarred back proved the truth of his words, as did his lack of fortitude.

Edward had been at sea three weeks and five days. That wretch of a tailor had hoarded the wine he'd given him, hiding it in a bladder in his sea chest. Two evenings ago, the man failed to claim his hammock. He'd been "dismasted," dead drunk with Edward's sour wine and his own grog. In a bid to gain clemency, he named Edward his supplier. The tailor now paid the price for his transgression and Edward with him.

This wasn't Edward's first taste of discipline. The lieutenants had mastheaded him several times. Not that he'd minded the punishment at first. Being aloft at the mainmast crosstrees with his face to the wind and nothing to do but stay there until he was ordered down was bearable, even enjoyable, for two or three hours. And true to his word, the captain of the maintop, a crack seamen who oversaw the work there, looked after him. Among other things, he'd taught Edward to lash his leg to a horizontal wood bar at the junction of the lower topmasts – the crosstrees – with his silk scarf to avoid falling. But time spent warming the crosstrees had increased with every trip, and the discomfort with it. What Edward really objected to was the reasons behind those trips. The lieutenants punished him not so much for what he'd done as for what he didn't know, beginning the day they'd weighed anchor. Amid the rush for stations the day of sailing, the bo'sun's mate had told him to "Find them devil carpenter's mates and tell 'em to get the hell up here and plug thar hawseholes!" Edward had indignantly refused.

Mr. Claverall had overheard and demanded an explanation. When Edward repeated what he thought he'd heard, the first lieutenant pointed aloft and bellowed, "Cool that saucy tongue of yours with a turn at the mast!"

It was unfair. The mate had dropped his h's and confused his w's with r's, not to mention mangling his grammar. How could any reasonable person blame Edward for his mistake?

He'd been more careful after that. He watched what others did in response to orders and guessed at those he hadn't previously heard. He also worked harder at understanding dialects. His slip-ups thereafter weren't as stupid, but no quarter was given when he erred. With sideways glances at their captain's pursed lips, the lieutenants sent Edward to the mainmast crosstrees. In the shadow of the Captain, the privilege of the quarterdeck became no privilege at all.

Today, per Captain Neville's injunctions, Edward had "a good view of the mischief he'd caused." One of the marines standing at attention at the break of the quarterdeck moved a fraction; sunlight flashed on his oval shoulder plate. Edward averted his eyes. His new line of sight included the Captain, in full dress, Articles of War in hand. Behind Neville were the lieutenants, also in dress uniform; behind them, four infantry officers, passengers bound for the garrison at Barbados. Finally, the midshipmen clustered in their brushed and polished best.

Edward saw the blood congeal on the tailor's back. The drummer never missed a roll as the bo'sun replaced his mate. Flexing his arm to do justice to the next twelve, the cat hissed through the air. Tied to a grating at his wrists and knees, the force of the lash flattened the tailor. He cried for mercy. What he felt

Edward could only guess. Spread-eagled in the weather shrouds, his arms and fingers had long since numbed.

He'd been seized up since four bells in the morning watch. It was after six bells in the forenoon watch now. He'd been in this position over five hours.

His ordeal had begun the day before. Off duty below, Fordyce, the Captain's aide, had summoned Edward to the quarterdeck. There, before the lieutenants, the lieutenant of marines, some mids, two of the supernumerary infantry officers, and everyone else within hearing, Neville had raked him verbally fore and aft. Scoundrel. Dog. Disgrace to the Service. Edward pushed his legs upward, trying to alleviate his physical – and mental – torment.

With a final flourish, the drum roll ended. The penalty had been served. Twenty-four lashes, twelve for drunkenness and another twelve for speaking disrespectfully to an officer, meaning the tailor had tried to defend himself. The bo'sun's call wailed; the tailor was cut down; the people dispersed. Edward anxiously studied Cudthumper, alias Mr. Claverall.

The first lieutenant queried Captain Neville. Neville looked over at Edward and said for all to hear, "He stays there till supper's piped."

Supper was hours away. If Neville held to his word, Edward would be ten hours in the shrouds all told. He desperately tried to catch Mr. Reynolds' eye, to appeal for mercy. The second lieutenant kept his eyes on his captain.

One of the infantry officers, a Lieutenant McAllistair, walked to the break of the quarterdeck. He was a Scotsman to whom Edward had spoken once or twice. The tallest of the ship's four passengers, his ginger tabby hair clashed with his scarlet coat. The Scotsman frowned up at Edward. What right had a soldier to judge him?

Mason loitered underneath the shrouds, joined by others of their mess. "He's found his niche," the ungainly mid jeered. "Scaring away boobies."

The midshipmen drifted away to fetch their quadrants prior to taking the noon sightings. Edward shifted again. He'd been stretched and re-stretched, positioned and repositioned, until those tying him to the shrouds were satisfied he was as uncomfortable as they could make him. They'd left him with his feet barely touching the ratlines, ankles lashed to the shrouds.

Because Edward had to push up to breathe more easily, the ropes rubbed his ankles raw.

Moments dripped by inexorably, like grains of sand in the ship's glass. Sweat overran his eyebrows and trickled into his eyes. Edward rubbed his face on the salt-spray roughness of his coat. Near to England, the shabby garment had barely kept him warm. Days out of Barbados, it made him sweat profusely.

Eight bells. The watch changed. One bell and the mates piped the people to dinner. They hurried below to the mid-day meal, a handful left to see to the ship. The officers, Neville included, congregated on the quarterdeck to take, practice taking, or pretend to take the ship's position. That ordeal, at least, was spared Edward.

Finished, the officers sped below to their dinner. The suffocating feeling intensified, as did Edward's thirst. He didn't miss his lost wine ration. It was water he wanted; water he craved.

The Atlantic sun minutes north of the equator lacked the magical properties of the one at Portsmouth. That sun gilded what it touched; this sun bleached everything dry. It left one fresh from England giddy, nauseated, wishing to strip. Desiccated, despite the wash of salt water.

Neville had a scuttlebutt of water placed at the foot of the mainmast for all to drink. Edward's eyes riveted onto that cask. He forced his legs up more frequently now, seeking air pockets recessed deeper and deeper inside his chest.

The Scotsman had stayed behind, positioned where he had a good view of Edward. Edward's anger at what he thought was the Scot's censure produced a momentary surge of strength. He straightened his back and lifted his head. But the surge receded more quickly than it came. Deadweight in the standing rigging, Edward took comfort in one of Dr. Johnson's witticisms: "Much may be made of a Scotsman if he be caught young."

One of the fo'c'slmen stepped up to the cask: Jake, the man who'd sassed Edward his first day. Jake went as far as he dared with the midshipmen. With Edward, he went further. Face toward Edward, Jake drank deep. Edward involuntarily swallowed.

The ship's fiddler replaced Jake at the water cask. Edward thought he'd looked familiar that day he'd helped him climb the mainmast. When he heard him play that strange square fiddle, he knew for a certainty he was the beggar boy from London. Although they rarely met, Edward watched him from afar. He felt responsible for him somehow, perhaps because he'd gotten knocked down in that set-to with the insufferable Frenchman. The fiddler peered up anxiously at him, as if what he saw troubled him, or seemed to. Edward fought to retain consciousness. The struggle, however, proved unequal. His head soon lolled against an insensate arm.

"Can you hear me?"

The words floated down. Edward tried to blink, but his eyelids stuck to his eyes.

"Have you any sensation in your arms or fingers? Anything?"

Edward struggled to regain consciousness. He was lying on his back with with two blurs hovering over him. Sweat from one wet Edward's face: his first sensation.

"Where..."

"Thank God, you can speak. Have you any feeling, a tingling or prickling?"

"No."

The larger blur said, "For all you look frail, laddie, there must be something to you to have borne what you did."

The rubbing recommenced. Edward soon wished it had never begun. His circulation returned, and with it an agony of feeling. He closed his eyes, his only way to cope. The pain receded, blood vessel by blood vessel. Breathing was not as difficult as it had been in the shrouds, but his chest felt as if two men sat on it. Edward stared at the one nearest his head. Disorientated, he murmured the saying that had earlier run through his mind. "Much – may be – made – of a – Scotsman – if – he – be caught – young."

The man stopped rubbing. "Your lips are burnt and your reason with them." To his assistant he said, "Get some water."

He slipped his arm under Edward's shoulders and raised him to a semi-recumbent position. "Drink," he said and brought a cup to Edward's lips.

Edward gulped eagerly, but the man only allowed him a little at a time. Even so, Edward quickly finished. When asked if he wished more, Edward nodded. He recognized his good Samaritan now, the same Scotsman who'd scowled at him in the rigging.

He placed the cup in Edward's hand and closed his fingers over the handle. Edward's fingers loosened as soon as the other let go. The cup fell and spilled water over them both.

The Scot leaned Edward onto the deck. He took his right arm and carefully flexed the fingers of that hand, then the arm itself. He repeated his examinations with Edward's left arm. The weight of Edward's body had hung from his arms. Tense and stretched, his muscles burned.

The officer rested Edward's arms gently at his sides. As his mind cleared, Edward wondered why a lieutenant of a regiment of foot tended him. A statement, no doubt, of the Captain's contempt for him. Meanwhile, a boy handed the soldier a second cup of water. Edward dully noted it was the ship's fiddler.

The Scot tilted it again to Edward's lips. "Slowly, slowly."

A piece of canvass had been placed underneath him as bedding. Edward was grateful for its comfort. His voice a hoarse imitation of itself, Edward tried to make amends for his insult. "You don't – much sound – the – Scotsman."

Lieutenant McAllistair sat down on the canvass beside him. "And you, laddie, don't much sound the bastard son of a Portsmouth wine merchant."

"I'm not!"

"Then who are you? Half dead, you quote Dr. Johnson, not one of his wiser sayings, alas, but with an upper class accent he'd approve. You give – or rather repeat – orders with a confidence a brigadier would envy. Who are you really, laddie, and how came you here?"

The ship's fiddler faltered, "He be –" but was immediately cut short by another.

"Who he is doesn't matter. It's when he can resume his duties that does."

McAllistair scrambled to his feet. Of the two officers now crouching in the reduced overhead, Lieutenant McAllistair stooped most. His senses fully restored, Edward realized they were in the fore part of the hold, the section reserved for the sick.

"When he's recovered from your torture, that's when," McAllistair snapped.

"Punishment isn't torture."

"It is when it's overdone."

"Where's the surgeon? The boy has the first dog watch."

"Drunk, most likely. Why doesn't your captain flog him as well?"

Unable to withstand the infantryman's withering sarcasm, Reynolds fled for help.

Alienating the only ship's officer not completely against him wasn't going to do him any good. After he'd gone, Edward challenged the Scotsman. "What do you know?"

"Know? My father's a physician. When I was young, I often went with him on his visits. Poor credentials, I grant you, but even so, they qualify me above your sot of a surgeon."

Edward lay back. Prior to this, he'd had little to do with the surgeon. He'd heard, though, that he drank freely, but freely as compared to what? Many drank freely from what Edward had seen. As long as an officer could stand the deck and give orders, he wasn't counted drunk. If the surgeon showed up tipsy, perhaps he'd at least agree to give him the rest he needed.

"Where's your bonny surgeon?"

Mr. Reynolds had returned alone. The smoky rays of the ship's lantern exaggerated his twitching lips. "Can you get up?" he asked Edward.

"Are you so heartless you cannot –"

Edward intervened before the Scot started a full-fledged argument. "I – think I can, sir." Despite the general un-cooperation of his body, he wrenched up to a sitting position.

One side of Mr. Reynolds' face was badly affected by a tic. Edward pitied him. The Captain must have given him a predetermined time to return him to duty. Lacking the surgeon's ruling, Reynolds' understandably balked at contradicting it.

"The morning watch. He must report to duty with the morning watch." Shunning their eyes, the teenage lieutenant turned his back on them.

The infantryman opened the lid to a box of medications and slammed it shut. He had the fiddler help him get Edward into a cot.

Left to himself, Edward worried over the Scotsman's shrewd guesses. Would the Scot repeat his suspicions to his fellow officers? Or the fiddler boy. Wagging tongues could start rumors, rumors which might find their way into letters home and his eventual recall. His right arm tensed painfully. The contempt the officers and the midshipmen had for what they thought he was, however much it suited his purposes, brought little comfort.

The cot's rocking lulled him. To be in something slung fore and aft alone was a comfort. The sleeping area outside the eight-by-ten foot hatchway berth was cramped. The mids had clamored that the only space for Edward's hammock was athwartships, side to side not front to back, a position that routinely dumped him whenever the seas ran high. In calmer waters, someone, most likely Mason, cut the lanyards – the lines supporting his hammock – to produce the same effect.

Edward turned fitfully. He'd traded his pocket watch to buy a straw mattress, which when lashed to his hammock, barely stood in the nettings. A "greyhound," sailors called such lean things. His silver shoe buckles had been traded one each for a hair brush and sea boots. Only the miniature portrait of his father remained. Edward slipped it out from beneath his shirt. The day of sailing, after all the women had been taken off, he'd found a purple ribbon. He attached the portrait to it and hung it underneath his clothes. Clutching it was the last waking thing he did.

"Out and down there!"

It was the bo'sun's mate rousing the watch. Where were the other mids? Then he recalled he wasn't in the hatchway berth.

Bits and pieces of yesterday floated like flotsam and jetsam. Sick bay. The shrouds. The morning watch. Edward wanted to groan. Somehow, though, he must endure the four hours until it ended. His waistcoat and frock had been neatly folded on the canvass he'd laid on yesterday, and his hat and shoes near them. Edward fumbled them on and felt his way to the ladder. On the lower deck, those coming down jostled those going up. In the waist, he stopped at the water butt. Brackish water trickled down his chin. Breakfast.

His squad of two foretopmen, "loosers" like himself, men who set sails, waited. Mr. Claverall designated each watch as a division, sub-dividing these into smaller units or squads supervised by the midshipmen and mates. Edward oversaw Israel Knoles and John Puddefoote. Barefoot, the topmen had their trousers rolled above their knees. Since the space was small, they worked with "prayer books," small sandstones used to clean to perfect whiteness nooks and crannies, opposed to "bibles," larger stones used for the open decks. His group collected sand and holystones for scouring the starboard main channel or chains, the same projection from which Edward had scrambled into the ratlines his first day.

At the best of times, the chains were a precarious place to be. His topmen took turns, one scrubbing, the other washing. Edward stood on the gangway, just forward of the break of the quarterdeck, hanging onto to a deadeye, a round block fixed to the channels by a chainplate, which in turn, was bolted to the ship's side underneath the channels. Near to vomiting, Edward nevertheless remained at his station.

Water slopped; sand scoured wood. Skin clammy, Edward counted planks to lessen the effects of the sea's heaving. One, two, three, one two three. Obedience to orders was everything.

Their job done, he and his men positioned themselves abreast the weather main shrouds in anticipation of being sent aloft, the same shrouds in which he'd been seized up yesterday. The ship's fiddler froze by his mop. He had that same apprehensive look he'd had yesterday.

Captain Neville crowded on as much sail as he could by day, but furled the royals and flying jib every evening, as conditions dictated. It fell to the morning watch to set them, weather permitting. The evolution could be done in minutes and required only two men. Edward went aloft with them, both as supervisor and trainee. Knoles had commented that Johnny Newcomes generally worked in the mizzen tops, the mizzen being the shortest mast. The mainmast was the highest, the one reserved for the most skilled seamen. Edward prided himself on that.

The Captain looked aloft. If he declared the wind fresh, the royals remained furled; moderate, they came down. Edward prayed Neville would declare the wind fresh. He did not.

The bo'sun's call shrilled. The order to "Set royals and flying jib" was followed by "Lay aloft, royal yardsmen." His hands shaking, Edward began the climb.

Youngsters had to serve alongside the foretopmen, learning seamanship that way. Edward liked to think his scaling the mainmast his first day earned him a place there, rather than in the mizzen. Small and light, he was ideally suited to working on the royals, and he learned quickly. It was a point of honor for the midshipmen to outrace the topmen. Edward could now reach the main royal yard in under a minute.

Today, however, repeated cries of "Cheerly, there," dogged him. He was the one meant; he was the one who lagged behind.

Patches of darkness flirted with his eyes when he switched over from the shrouds to the Jacob's ladder. Edward shook his head to clear it. The gesture slowed him more, eliciting another "cheerly." By will alone, Edward gained the lee end of the yard.

"Lay out and loose."

He eased onto the horse, the footropes running three feet underneath the yard, and let go the quarter gaskets, the shorter sennit lines midway out from the slings, the lines holding the sail to the yard. The higher aloft, the wider the circles the mast made, circles which the stays, shrouds, and backstays, the standing rigging responsible for supporting the mast, couldn't eliminate. Dark spots plagued him, but he followed the sequence of orders up to "let fall" and "sheet home."

In nightmarish slow motion, his feet slipped off the horse. But the arcing of the mast, formerly his bane, now proved his salvation. He fell forward and down, rather than out and back. A scream broke his trance: his. Edward clawed for a hold. One hand gained the horse. The other nothing. The deck lay over a hundred feet below.

"Hold on, sir!"

Knoles worked toward him. He crouched down, trying to grab anything he could of Edward. With a hand anchored on the royal yard, he grasped Edward's left arm above the wrist and tried to lift him. Edward swung with the motion of the mast.

"Pull up, sir! Pull up!"

The spots returned. His arm muscles grew weaker. If he stayed like this much longer, he'd fall. Old Ramillies Wig would rejoice to hear of his death. Edward jerked upward.

A small man, Knoles hauled away like a brawny fo'c'lsman. Edward's knees found the horse. A hand on the yard, the foretopman pulled harder. Edward floundered, then found the footrope. Knoles steadied him against the yard.

The boy clung to it. He'd almost died. But almost wasn't enough. His sense of immortality shaky but restored, Edward found Knoles' hovering irritating. Far below, though, the deck symbolized safety. Edward didn't ask whether the order to lay down from aloft had been given. He clambered onto the yard and edged toward the Jacob's ladder.

Gingerly descending, he humbled himself to go through the lubber's hole. Shortly after, Edward dropped onto a deck slippery with sand and water. Knees naked and bent, rear ends jutting upward, the people swished and scraped their "bibles" and "prayer books" over planking.

"Send those slackers to me!"

Neville had seen them. Via Mr. Reynolds, the officer of the watch, he summoned Edward and Knoles to the quarterdeck. Edward led the way. He reached to lift his hat in salute to the quarterdeck, but found he no longer had one. He touched his hand to his forehead instead.

"This is no bloody merchantman," the Captain shrilled. "You delayed setting the royals! I want a smart ship, and I mean to have one!" He pointed to Knoles. "You bugger, two dozen will teach you your business is to set sails, not save lives."

Edward's partner in sin stood in what the officers considered a properly respectful pose: head bowed, eyes down, shoulders slumped. It did no good to protest the injustice. From experience, Edward knew Neville wouldn't reverse his decision.

But they'd finished their duties, Edward's conscience argued. A quick upward glance confirmed the main royal billowed out as it should, no Dutch pennants – loose gaskets – flying. There was no cause for reprimand, much less punishment.

Neville called Knoles everything from son of a sea cook downward. The wind moaned in the rigging. Was it lodging the protest he, Edward, should be making?

"Sir, the fault is mine. He only did what any man would under the circumstances." The words barely said, Edward realized his blunder. He should have said "anyone" or "one of the people." By calling Knoles a "man," he'd raised the foretopman to the level of the officers, an equality Edward himself disallowed.

"You!" Neville said, spit flying from his mouth. "Always the troublemaker! Small wonder your family wished to be rid of you." He stopped directly in front of Edward and rocked on his heels. Edward fell back.

Rage made the Captain's normally pale lips bloodless. Syllable by syllable, he ripped words from between his teeth. "A man, is he? By whose authority? Yours?"

"I only meant –"

"Damn you, hold your tongue! What do you know of men? You're not one, nor ever likely to be. By the God of War, I rue the day I allowed a rabble rouser aboard my ship!"

Neville hit on both meanings of "man," damning Edward on each. Edward was no radical. He'd never troubled himself over events in France or their meaning for Englishmen, never perplexed himself about the issues raised by the American War. If anything, his family's involvement in politics had made him apolitical. But as to that other meaning...

Perhaps it was his silence which made Neville shout harder. "Master-at-arms, take them below! Clap that one in irons, then see to it Mr. Scarecrow gets two dozen strapped over a gun. Be sure he returns to his station afterwards. He's fond of shirking his duty." Neville's already high pitch shrilled like a bo'sun's pipe. "And be quick about it!"

The master-of-arms came at a run. Knoles would be placed in irons below until his flogging. Edward would go to the gundeck, and immediately there, be tied bent over a cannon and have his naked backside whipped by the gunner. Edward drew a ragged breath and descended the quarterdeck ladder.

As if on cue, precise rows of unshaven men again moved back and forth with their holystones. No one spoke; speaking wasn't allowed while working. No one looked up as they passed by; it was forbidden. Edward squared his shoulders and carried his head high. Let the Captain say what he would, he'd take his punishment without a sound.

Like a man his father would have approved.

CHAPTER NINE

...a hideous dream.

William Shakespeare, *Julius Caesar*, II.i.63

Ship's discipline had been relaxed since *Amphitrite* dropped anchor in Bridgetown, Barbados. With no duties to attend, Jemmy marveled anew at the organized chaos. A woman's teeth flashed white as her sailor handed her his leftover beef, fresh beef from shore. Jemmy stared. He'd rarely seen black people in London. Here, they seemed to outnumber the whites.

"King ships eat good."

"Merchantmen eat better. Treat the crew better, too. No damned monkey jackets neither."

The bare-chested speaker was Jake, the fo'c'slman. His last point referenced a party of mids ready to be taken ashore, Mr. Deveare among them. Jemmy edged away. His messmates had warned him about Jake, a troublemaker in the making. He concentrated instead on Mr. Deveare.

A man, that's what Mr. Deveare had said, a man. Jemmy relived the last few days. The words had reverberated around ship. Not openly, no, for the officers would have seized the offenders and punished them for "seditious talk." But quietly, over the various messes and whispered at night from hammock to hammock. A man. A revolutionary idea. Or not so revolutionary.

Jemmy's messmates boasted, "Aft's the more honor, but fore's the better man." But to hear a midshipman raise a foretopman to his own level, in front of the Captain, on the quarterdeck...

Normal talk lapped around Jemmy. But the whispers. Rights of man. All men created equal. The Americans had it right. The Frenchies were getting it, too. What was he to make of such talk? Or Mr. Deveare. He was either a Frog lover or a rebel lover, like that firebrand, Charles James Fox. On the other hand, Knoles, the foretopman, worshipped Mr. Deveare. Jemmy frowned. Why would someone who'd been flogged for saving a life do that? Jemmy didn't claim equality with his betters. And yet... Dad had been punished for protesting rents deliberately set so high as to force them out of their home.

Jake's woman laughed. The black women here seemed to laugh often, and freely. Jemmy had nothing against her, but that Jake, he hated Mr. Deveare. The Captain did, too. Jemmy stirred uneasily. It wasn't right what he'd done to Mr. Deveare and Knoles. Mr. Deveare had spoken out bravely, not for himself, but for someone else. He was kind. Jemmy had discovered that in London. London. Mr. Deveare was a *somebody*. He'd tried to tell those two officers that day in sickbay, but they wouldn't listen. If they knew, they'd surely treat him better, the Captain, too. The Captain had to be told, but how? The quarterdeck was as distant as London for such as he.

Yet even as Jemmy despaired, he intuited the answer. Mr. Brighty. He spoke with the officers. Yes, that was who he'd tell. Since they were in port, the bo'sun most likely was overseeing the stores. Jemmy threaded his way to the Master Sail-maker's locker. Both the sail-maker and bo'sun were there, waistcoats taking the place of coats.

"Eight yard Canvas number 6, repairing fore and main topgallant sails."

"Good. Next."

"Fifteen yard Canvas number 7, ditto."

The sail-maker's and bo'sun's inventory seemed to take forever. Jemmy chafed in the confining heat of the 'tween decks. Yet he could do little else until they'd finished. Satisfied at last that the accounts were true and nothing had been stolen, Brighty turned to go his way. There were people about, making a hubbub. Jemmy would have liked to talked in private, but perhaps the noise would mask what he had to say.

"Mr. Brighty, it's Mr. Deveare."

"What of him?"

The words were offhand, but Jemmy sensed a subtle change in the bo'sun's manner, guarded and waiting. It was as if he didn't want to hear what Jemmy had to say. Jemmy proceeded anyway. Mr. Deveare deserved that much.

"One of my mess said his sister's friend overheard at Portsmouth someone called Old Ben be going to dun William's son out of his inheritance. And that William Deveare twere a cap'n. Mr. Deveare is William's son. That makes him a cap'n's son, like he says. Not only that," Jemmy said hurriedly, seeing Mr. Brighty was about to interrupt, "I knowed Mr. Deveare from Lunnon, least I met him there. He rode in a carriage with servants and a lady. He be good to me there, an' he be good to me here. Don't you see? Cap'n's got to be told. So he won't be down on him."

It all seemed so lame, the way it came out, not the way he'd wanted to say it. At least, Jemmy thought so, judging from the bo'sun's somber expression.

"Not many fight to get the ship properly outfitted, or get us safe passage out during hurricane season like Cap'n did," Brighty said. "But he ain't one to be crossed, nor forget if he is."

"But what about Mr. Deveare?"

"You can't help him, and you'd only hurt yourself if you tried. Besides," he said less gruffly, "now we're in port, things might blow over a bit. Cap'n's got other things to occupy him."

"But –"

"Leave it, is what I say!"

The order came short and sharp. And final. Jemmy hung his head. He'd done what he could for Mr. Deveare. He began to walk away.

"There, lad," the bo'sun called after him, "take a turn ashore, later today. Things should look brighter then."

Off duty, Jemmy drifted toward his mess. He felt sleepy, the tropical heat to blame. A black woman in a gaudy red head scarf noticed him. Smiling, she beckoned. She tell his fortune, good one, she said. Suddenly uneasy, Jemmy declined.

He noticed an unoccupied spot near a cannon, too small for most, but not him. It was as good a place as any to shelter, maybe even sleep. Jemmy curled up behind it.

He slipped into a place somewhere between sleep and waking. The quiet was unnerving, as if he were suddenly isolated. Then came the mists, swirling, swirling. There were people inside the fog, their forms indistinct. They shattered the silence, shouting, jeering, at someone ahead. Someone Jemmy knew, but couldn't see. So familiar, so like... Then the mists closed in, and all was lost.

He woke trembling. Around him, everything was the same. It was just a dream, Jemmy reasoned, a bad one brought on by the heat. But he no longer felt hot; he shivered. Gran had claimed dreams had meanings. She said the ability to see the future through dreams ran in their family. Jemmy had thought it just the foolishness of the old – until she foretold her own death.

She'd told him before she died he'd know if the gift would come to him. Jemmy had liked her despite her craziness. It was that woman's fault, the one with the red head scarf, wanting to tell his fortune, he desperately tried to reassure himself. Dreams meant nothing. Nothing!

But he'd left Dad. He'd done it to spite him, no matter arranging to send him money. What he'd done wasn't right. Then it came to him, clearer, much clearer than in the dream. Dad was the one the people jeered. Something was wrong. Or would be. Jemmy felt as if Death itself had touched him. Despite what he told himself, he knew the gift had come to him.

CHAPTER TEN

On this side lay Scylla, while on that Charybdis...

Homer, *Odyssey* XII

Elizabeth watched raindrops patter on yellow oak leaves. September was coming to a close. Soon Surrey roads would be quagmires. It was time to leave East Dene.

Servants hurried past in the outside hallway, ants scurrying in the overturned anthill of routine. At her orders, they sheeted the furniture prior to leaving. The gold brocade settee disappeared under one such sheet. Just yesterday, Lady Onslow had sat there, repeating her husband's suspicions as to the young trespasser's identity. The child came and went as it pleased, totally eluding capture. Recently, though, there had been no visits. Elizabeth had felt almost apologetic at their continued concern. Lady Onslow told a tale of strangers occupying a hut near Wescott. She believed the child one of them, sent to determine the best time to break into the house. Arm the groundskeepers and the male house servants, she'd urged. Then, by way of reassurance, she'd added, "No need to worry, though, Onslow will get to the bottom of this." No need at all, for Elizabeth was leaving for Charnworth.

She traced the mother-of-pearl inlay on her secretary. Fox's letter lay in the lower right drawer. Lord Onslow had picked it up at the post office in Dorking and given it to his wife to deliver. Lady Onslow had handed it over with a knowing look. Foolish woman, there was nothing between her and Fox. They shared political passions only, nothing else, and not even that entirely. Fox was too fulsome about events in France. She'd run into him by chance at The Crown in Guildford, he still pale from his last illness. As if that innuendo hadn't been sufficient, Lady Onslow had blundered further, mentioning Edward's absence from Eton, via news from her sister's son. Edward. Elizabeth removed the letter from the desk and smoothed it. Perhaps if she re-read it, it would say something different.

St. Mary's Hill

21st September 1789

My Dear Lady Elizabeth,

Since last I enjoyed our delightful conversation, I've spared no effort on behalf of your son. News of him proves more elusive than I'd thought. The Admiralty clerks checked their most recent muster lists but could find no record of anyone by the name Deveare currently on any of HM ships. That does not mean, of course, he is not on one; if a person joins a ship at the last minute, his name may not recorded until a later date. It is also possible your son might have been entered under another name, which will delay finding him. You will rejoice to know I have not limited my inquiries to the Admiralty alone. It can be said of a certainty no one bearing your son's name or description has been employed aboard any East India Company ships. As for merchantmen, the task of tracing him becomes daunting. Sir Colin Lewes sent a clerk to Portsmouth to make inquiries there. Let us hope he uncovers something soon.

Yours &

Charles James Fox

Post Script: I had a note from Sir Colin this morning. His clerk learned from the attorney who handled the will, a Mr. Peris, that he'd heard Rear Admiral Deveare shipped the boy aboard a vessel bound for the West Indies. Sir Colin is confident his clerk will find out the particulars. Do not despair; all will yet be well.

"All will yet be well," she repeated aloud. So Fox had met with Sir Colin Lewes, Father's friend, a barrister of note. She'd consulted with Lewes also and gotten nothing out of him. Elizabeth supposed she should be thankful Sir Colin had co-operated with Fox, but then, didn't men only trust one another? Elizabeth pressed her hands against her temples. Edward in the West Indies? Anything could happen to him there. It had an evil reputation for sickness. And death.

What to do? There was no use in seeing Lewes again; he disliked women and her most of all.

As for Fox, he'd done all he could. Father. She stared at the blank sheet before her. Should she write him? He'd left her to oversee the estates, and now her brother and his wife accused her of mismanaging them, meaning she'd refused to advance them more money. Better Father should hear her side of the story first. She fingered an ink pot. If she sent a letter by today's post, it might reach Paris within a week. Or longer, given the unrest in France. Then again, writing might be construed as an admission events had outrun her. The lid to the inkpot remained unopened.

Ah, but Edward, alone and sick on some godforsaken island. Elizabeth flicked open the inkpot. Father must be made to return – at once.

Chapter Eleven

When men come to the sea, they are not fit to live on land... and when they come to know it, they cannot escape it.

Dr. Samuel Johnson, 1776

"I will not quit my ship."

Edward challenged Lieutenant McAllistair across the well-picked remains of three courses. Forty-seven days after making sail from Spithead, including short stopovers at Madeira and Tenerife, *Amphitrite* rode at anchor at Bridgetown, Barbados. The Scotsman had been born in Barbados. Serving at Fort St. James, he temporarily lodged with family friends in Bridgetown. He and Edward dined alone; the family that owned the house were away visiting relations. The soldier used every argument in a landsman's arsenal to persuade the sailor to abandon the sea.

A black boy gathered dishes coated with custard and pastry crumbs, the plates clinking as he stacked one atop the other. Most of the servants here were black and slaves.

"Laddie, your decision is nothing less than madness." His birthplace explained his accent, a dash of Scots in a dish of English. "Your Captain's a bastard. I cannot say it any plainer. He'll stop at nothing until he wears you down. Your speaking up to him before his officers and people didn't help your cause either."

The servant brought a decanter of port and two glasses. Annoyed at the lecture, Edward said, "You said you'd made him think twice."

"For a time. He'll worry lest I make good my threat to complain to his commodore. But once he – and you – sail, what then?"

Unconvinced, Edward reached for the wine.

His host's arm got there first. "Your Captain is 'all sugar or all shite,' laddie. Surely you must grasp by now which he means for you."

The welts the gunner's mate had left on Edward's backside hadn't entirely healed. Nor had that queer numbness and tingling in his right arm and hand. Barbados temporarily might have transformed what he'd endured into a bad dream, but the dream had left indelible traces.

McAllistair studied him intently. "Who will fault Neville if another 'accident' befalls you? It would simply be put down to your inexperience."

"I've taken the King's shilling and mean to keep it." This was the third time Edward refused to quit. Perhaps now his friend would believe him.

McAllistair put down his glass. "Does that admiral grandsire of yours know of other – better – captains to apply on your behalf?"

"Were I dying, I wouldn't ask him for anything!"

"Mayhap, laddie," McAllistair murmured, "death will come, do you stay where you are."

Edward's arm twitched. The Scotsman's intervention on his behalf had stayed his going aloft. Even so, he'd had no real rest. The spasm worsened. Edward clamped his arm against the side of his wool coat to hide it.

"You spoke of your father and his family, but what of your mother's? Would they –"

Edward scrambled out of his chair. "I must meet the ship's boat at sunset."

The Scot sighed and shook his head. He was tall, like Edward's uncles, like his father must have been. Edward looked away. Whenever an older man had shown interest in him, Edward had always imagined his father there, in his place. Only now his father was dead.

"I cannot understand what you wish to conceal, but if your mother's people haven't completely disowned you, apprise them of your situation. There's no dishonor in asking for help when it's needed. But come, a wee dram, by way of farewell."

The soldier went to the sideboard, stuck his fingers inside two tumblers, and grabbed a square flask. These he carried to the table, where, straddling his chair, he sat down and deposited the tumblers and flask on the table. "Do you know what this is?" he asked, tapping the flask.

"Brandy?"

"Brandy? This is good Scots whiskey! I share it only with my friends."

It was a tribute, an acknowledgment of the manhood his captain scorned he'd never attain. Edward eagerly accepted his offer.

Lieutenant McAllistair's "wee dram" proved to be a "bumper," a glass filled to the brim. Raising it in salute, the Scotsman said, "To a long and abiding friendship!"

"To friendship!" Edward said, and assuming whiskey no more potent than wine, he drank deep. Eyes tearing, he gagged, choked, then spluttered. The stuff burned like hell.

"Steady, steady."

"Do – you drink this often?"

"Not so often as I'd like. Supply's a problem here." One arm carelessly resting on the back of his chair, McAllistair refilled his glass. "Have you ever heard of Robbie Burns?"

"He's a poet, I think," Edward said, still spluttering.

"A *Scots* poet, laddie, and a great one. Our drinking together brings to mind one of his more tuneful pieces, "A Bottle and a Friend." Do you know it?"

"No."

"Well, then, we must broaden your education." Lieutenant McAllistair grasped his lapel in one hand – he was in civilian dress – and waved his empty tumbler in time.

> There's nane that's blest of human kind,
> But the cheerful and the gay man,
> Fal, la, la, la, la, la, la, la

Fal, la, la, la, la, la, la, la.

Here's a bottle and an honest friend!
With wad ye wish for mair, man?
Wha kens, before his life may end,
What his share may be o' care, man?
Then catch the moments as they fly,
And use them as ye ought, man,
Believe me, happiness is shy,
And comes not aye when sought, man.

"Bravo, bravo!" Edward clapped enthusiastically – and swilled the rest of his whiskey.

"Sing with me, laddie!"

The residual whiskey as fiery as the first, Edward coughed through the first two lines. But he was lusty with the fal, la, las and gleeful with the verses. When they ended, McAllistair turned Edward's glass upside down in response to his request for more. Edward fiddled his neckcloth loose and trilled the chorus.

"It's a pity you cannot stay longer. I'd get you properly drunk, to forget your sorrows."

The room seemed to float. Edward found the sensation interesting.

"Can you find the harbor, or should I send my servant with you?"

"Must I go?"

"Aye. Though I dislike hurrying you, we mustn't give your bonny Captain fresh cause to torment you. Good-bye. And don't forget to write!"

Shaking air, then the lieutenant's hand, Edward said farewell. He dare not miss the boat.

After he'd seen to it that his feet did indeed touch the ground, Edward checked his surroundings. From what he saw, Barbados deserved the title "Little England." Ballast bricks from English ships together with indigenous coral cut from nearby cliffs formed stone buildings with small pane windows, sturdy grey edifices, some dating to the days of the royal Stuarts. Edward stopped in front of a shop window. Its interior melted into a room with a cheery fire, a tester bed, and a wing chair. Home. A bird screeched. The sun was bright, too bright for so late in the day. Farther back, the hills were green and rolling, but gaudy with trees like the poinciana and cassia, brazen things despite their declining clusters of flame and pink flowers. Other flowers abounded apart from trees, their fragrance overwhelming. How could they be otherwise, with such gaping petals? This was not, never could be, England.

The whisky-induced euphoria deserted him. Women promenaded down the other side of the street, one especially lovely. An octoroon, she had skin the color of chocolate richly laced with cream, her dark eyes lustrous. A towering white headdress, a turban sort of thing, hid her hair. Apart from wider nostrils and thicker lips than Edward would have liked, she had delicate features, European, for the most part. Slender of waist and full of bosom, she was a belle by any standard, a frigate, in naval parlance.

Females. Bum boats full of them had swarmed *Amphitrite* before her anchor cable had completely played out in Carlisle Bay. The Captain allowed them aboard. Except for experiencing the act itself, Edward now knew most of what there was to know about cohabitation between male and female. And if he wanted, women were plentiful enough. "Dignity ladies," women who did washing and other jobs, were standard sleeping fare for mids, but after seeing the sailors with those women...

Something crashed inside a nearby doorway. Oaths fouled the air. Edward sniffed. Rum. A grog shop, with a drunken scuffle taking place. Rum was everywhere, and the sailors took advantage of it. If it tasted as bad as it smelled, it must be awful stuff. Whiskey, on the other hand... His stomach churned. He bent over and lost all he'd eaten and drunk.

His outlook as lackluster as his stomach, Edward slogged the last yards to the quay. No boat. He tensed; his arm tingled. Had it left without him?

Worried, he scanned the harbor. Ships' boats pulled for shore – none of them his. Should he try to find someone to take him out to his ship? Island-accents tittered and sang in bad English, the sounds floating down the beach from black sailors unloading cargo.

Water turned white sand into an imperfect mirror. Close in, the sea sparkled turquoise; beyond, it shimmered sapphire.

Merchant ships drifted, their heads pointing ashore. Dark against a sky a stunning palette of reds, roses, pinks, and golds, *Amphitrite* rode easy at anchor. The artist in him ached to capture the scene, glory enough to dazzle an archangel. Then his eyes went back to his ship. Glory but for Neville. Like *Amphitrite*, he was a dark blot on Edward's horizon.

His eyelids drooped, as did his body, but drink wasn't the only cause. He hadn't adjusted yet to the erratic sleeping patterns of shipboard life. Like the other mids, he was on a three, rather than two, watch rotation, which meant every third night he could claim eight uninterrupted hours sleep. But for every one night of unbroken rest, there were two split by a four-hour watch. And such sleep as he got on the third was spoilt by heat.

Edward regretted his emptied stomach. When would he enjoy such an excellent meal again? Not aboard ship. Although he'd paid his mess fee, he only got the leavings; the others had large appetites. Moreover, they threatened to put him out if he didn't pay this month's dues. Dues. Edward unconsciously thrust his hand inside his coat pocket. What dues? He had no money.

The others. Gooseflesh prickled his arms and chest in recollection of the cold cannon, his fingers rigid in re-enactment of clutching iron as stroke after stroke cut his skin, stretched over a gun barrel, fighting nausea and an overpowering urge to faint. The greater struggle after the twenty-fourth stoke: to straighten with the blood rushing to his head and pain burning his backside. Breeches re-buttoned, to hobble to his station pretending nothing had happened. The hush at breakfast when he'd sat down, forbidding his body to flinch. Not even Mason had laughed. For a time. Edward kicked sand upward, startling a land crab. His bottom, at least, was making good progress. But not his right arm and hand.

And the man who was responsible – Neville. Luckily for Edward, the Captain spent most of his time ashore, making official visits and accepting planters' invitations. But Lieutenant McAllistair's warning haunted him. What would happen once they sailed?

With no one around, no one trying to argue him out of his decision to go to sea and stay at sea, the small, still voice of reason made itself heard. Wouldn't it be better if he took the Scotsman's advice and wrote his mother? Fine clothes, all the food he could eat, a feather mattress to sleep on, his own room. He held up the palm of his right hand; a yellowed tab accentuated an angry red patch, whorls visible.

But it had been his choice, he argued, his bad bargain and no one else's. There was no point in writing. His mother would insist he return to England, to Eton, to the life she dictated.

Despite Neville, were things really so bad? What of quiet nights during the middle watch? Hadn't he seen millions of stars in a way he'd never seen them before – distant jewels laid in a case of darkness? Without the smoke of towns to dirty them, or the trees of country estates to hide them? And the moon. It left a path so real he'd been tempted to walk on it: the flam-flew.

And his days? Yes, he'd hurt at first, from headaches caused by the reek of foul fumes and from banging his head against the beams, bruises from losing his footing on the heeling deck, but once they picked up the easterlies south of Madeira, the frigate behaved like some great bird, alive with a life all her own, surpassing even the legendary phoenix for beauty, her sails both clouds and wings. She'd all but sailed herself, rarely needing more than her royals and jib furled at night, or a reef taken in the topgallants. She skimmed the sea, churning the waters white at her prow and jade in her wake.

Then there was the sea itself. Crisscrossed with fine lines like those found on hand blown glass on days with light winds or heaving white-capped peaks when tossed by moderate breezes. Now blue, now green, now gold, now brown. Sometimes lost in banks of clouds, sea and sky one grey mass. Waves carrying the ship upward to the heights and carelessly plunging her down to the depths. The ever-changing sea, reflecting the skies above and the wonders beneath.

The sea. Yes, the sea, his mistress. How could he leave her? Before he'd ever seen her, she'd dazzled him. Looking out at the sea now, as it stroked the sands, it was as if a beautiful woman stroked him. The sea, a seductive woman, treacherous and not easily wooed, one whom he'd never be sure of winning, one for whom he'd already had developed a healthy respect. The wind was her scent, exciting him, arousing him. Coral reefs the jewelry of her undulating body. The waves her touch, alternately playful or punishing.

And her pets. The awe of whales breaching the waves, of dolphins frolicking together. Of the phosphorescent creatures swimming beneath them, making it seem Neptune and his court held a luminous ball below. Of the sailors' enemy, the shark, caught with a fight, displayed in triumph, and eaten. Or the abrupt line of sea and sky, endlessly appearing to end but never ending. It made him feel he could sail on and on for –

"Mr. Deveare. I – be having something to say to you, sir."

"What?" His rapturous reverie shattered, Edward stared stupidly at the boy standing before him. His brain finally re-adjusted to his surroundings, he recognized the fiddler.

"Mr. Deveare," Jemmy said breathlessly, when Edward finally silently acknowledged him, "it be about you, sir. You've got to tell them! The Cap'n, special. When they be knowing who you really be–"

"I don't know what you're talking about."

"Sir, that day we be meeting, back there in Lunnon. You rode in a carriage with servants and all. And that lady, she were a *real* lady, your mother maybe. The officers, they've *got* to be told!"

The beggar-turned-ship's-boy stepped closer, so he stood almost touching Edward, his up-turned face gazing pleadingly into Edward's. The mention of his mother stung like a whip. Hadn't she sworn she'd have him back? Still the worse for the liquour he'd drunk, Edward said, "I don't need a beggar telling me what to do."

"But Mr. Deveare, sir, it be for your–"

Edward grabbed him by both shoulders and all but lifted him off his feet, "I said," he hissed into Jemmy's startled face, "mind your own business! And don't breathe a word of–"

"Catch a turn there, the twain of you!"

Mr. Brighty confronted them. "What the devil's going on?"

He lacked his "persuader," but it didn't matter. Edward hastily let go of Jemmy. "Nothing, sir."

"I be just..." Jemmy faltered. He was visibly shaken and seemed unable to say more.

"What d'you think I am," Brighty snorted, "simple?" He gave Jemmy a shove toward shore. "Wait the boat down there." But when Edward started after him, Brighty stopped him. "I've somewhat to say to you, Mr. Deveare."

Edward's hand knotted protectively behind him. Of course he was going to take the blame. What else could he expect, given Neville's example? He'd be fortunate to get nothing more than a scolding.

Brighty didn't speak until distance formed a barrier between them and the fiddler. When he did, his face had lost none of its sternness. "When I found out you was a Deveare, I wondered which way the wind would blow with you."

The bo'sun was no friend of his. If he associated Edward with anyone, it was probably Old Ramillies Wig. Why didn't he just get on with it?

Brighty, however, turned his attention to *Amphitrite*. "A good night to take a caulk."

"Take a caulk" meant sleeping topdeck. It made no sense. Had the bo'sun been drinking also? Or was he playing with him?

Wanting to be done with it, Edward asked, "Am I to be charged with fighting?"

Brighty turned to him. One eye had a milky film, a convenient excuse to see only one side.

"You said nothing happened, didn't you?"

"You mean you're not going to put me on report?"

"If nothing happened, what's to report?"

"Sir?"

"The boat's coming. Get along with you, Mr. Deveare."

It was unwise to delay carrying out an order, but Edward seized on the grizzled man's original comment. "Sir – you say you knew them – him. Was he, am I, like my father?"

A chink appeared in Brighty's sternness. "You're like yourself, younker," he said somewhat begrudgingly, "Be glad of it. Now haul your carcass down to the pinnace afore she's out oars and away."

He left before Edward could ask more. Not wanting to spend the night ashore, Edward hurried to take his place in the stern. He took great care to ignore Jemmy. He only hoped that Brighty hadn't overhead their conversation and started wondering what the fiddler had meant. Brighty had mentioned taking a caulk. Edward understood him now. It mightn't be such a bad idea to claim a spot above decks, the better to avoid possible contact with the beggar.

Well-trained men at the oars, the small pinnace soon found her ship. Fading light cast rippling reflections on *Amphitrite*'s hull. A loud splash drew Edward's attention. A brig had dropped anchor nearby. She had a long, concave run and a slight rake to her sternpost. Her larboard side to Edward, he saw two three-pounders mounted there. She was hardly man-o-war fashion: in need of paint and riding so low in the water, her hold must be awash. Probably a slaver who'd just made the middle run. Her crew would do well to find a better ship.

A better ship. After he'd gotten some sleep and his head cleared, he'd consider the possibilities.

CHAPTER TWELVE

... but it is patriotism, disinterestedness, and virtue that are needed to seek and defend the interests of a great people ... and be a child of the fatherland.

Guy-Jean Target, *Parlementaire*, 1789

Louis pulled Marie-Rose's sleeping warmth closer. Awakened, she averted his lips and pushed at him. Louis was caressing her to his way of thinking when a wild pealing startled them apart: the tocsin, church bells sounding alarm.

"Is the King sending troops to Paris?" Marie-Rose asked, sitting up.

Louis groped for a tinderbox and a tallow stub. Soon the candle yielded a yellow-blue glow, in which their bodies produced outsized shadows. Marie-Rose's shadow trembled. "No one will harm you as long I am near," he said, gathering her in his arms.

Marie-Rose leaned her cheek against his. "Louis," she murmured, "I, I told the women we're to be wed."

If she'd schemed to find a way to make him keep his distance, she'd succeeded. "What made you say that?" he asked, releasing her.

"They taunted me, called me 'la Du Barry.'"

Each quarter of Paris was an entity unto itself, where everyone knew everyone else's business. The women of the rue Meslay pried into theirs. They'd twisted Marie-Rose's last name, Barré, into Du Barry, the previous king's mistress. Du Barry also was a commoner.

"Let them wag their tongues at those who deserve it!"

"*Are* you going to marry me?"

"What are profane priests who dishonor their vows to us?"

"It is as *la Vinaigre* says. You just want to sleep with me!"

Louis kicked Marie-Rose's shoe out of the way and picked up his shirt from off the floor.

They dressed in angry separateness. Out in the rain-drenched street, the people, or more precisely, the women, were everywhere. It was as if a plague of locusts had descended upon Paris in the form of lean and angry women.

"Citizenness, we go to the Hôtel-de-Ville, to denounce the bakers and demand bread for our families! You must come with us."

Two females, *poissardes*, fishwives, by the smell of them, toke hold of Marie-Rose's arms. Working women who flaunted their earthiness. "Good patriots," Louis said, prying loose one set of hands, "her soft voice will add no weight to your pleas."

"My voice is as loud as theirs, and my passion for liberty as ardent!" Marie-Rose spat at him. "Citizennesses, I am with you!"

Louis' protests were lost in the female tidal wave which washed the streets. They swept everything and everyone before them; not even the alleys were empty. Louis' last sight of Marie-Rose was over liberty hats and drenched hair, then she was gone. *Well, let her be,* Louis thought, angry that she had defied him. He tried to make his way home, to make headway against the waves of women. It was no use. At length, he found himself in front of the Hôtel-de-Ville, Paris's governing offices.

"Bread, give us bread!" The shouts drowned the tolling bells. Soldiers of the National Guard lined the steps of the Hôtel-de-Ville. Soggy in woebegone white, dripping blue, and spattered red, they pointed their muskets at the crowd but broke ranks before the relentless waves of women. Disgusted, Louis started for the Buci crossroads. Marie-Rose could go to the devil.

Numberless throats took up the shout, "To Versailles, to Versailles!" then "Maillard. Citizen-soldier Maillard!" Maillard, hero of the Bastille, would lead them to Versailles.

The rat-tat-tat, rat-tat-tat of a drum punctuated their shouts. Maillard at their head, the cannon of the Hôtel-de-Ville behind, thousands of women set out for Versailles. The temper of the females exceeded the white heat Louis had seen at the Bastille. Given their mood, they would stop at nothing short of the Austrian bitch's head. Louis approved their supposed goal and joined them.

October rain pelted down like angry musket balls driven by an angrier wind. Rain dripped from the brim of his round hat and blinded him. Rain made his greatcoat cling shapelessly to his body. Outside Paris, rain and countless feet churned the road and surrounding land into a slough which turned his buff and black English boots brown. Rain, as inexorable as the people.

Impassioned and wet, they marched on. His body steaming and weary, Louis raised his hat brim. Ahead lay the town of Versailles; beyond it, the Chateau of the Bourbons.

He cursed Maillard for yet another delay. Hadn't they already stopped too often, giving the King and the Austrian time to learn of their coming? Louis lifted his feet carefully, so as not to let the mud to suck away his boots. A plague on Maillard for ordering the men to the rear. Did they need women to shield them from the traitors guarding Versailles?

A wilderness of bodies with dank, disheveled locks could be seen, smelled, touched. "Down with the Flanders Regiment! Down with the Royal Guards! Long live the Nation! Long live the People! Bread! Give us bread!" Suddenly, a hush blanketed them like a shroud. Giddy with patriotic fervor, Louis barely evaded lathered horses dragging the Hôtel-de-Ville's cannon. He watched from a close but safe distance as the woman straddling the barrel of the lead cannon cudgeled her animal because the wheels of the gun carriage were stuck. Wary of the beast – the woman not the horse – Louis asked, "Good dame, where go you?"

The "good dame" wore a mud-encrusted apron over what once might have been a green coat and red skirt, to judge from odd bits of unstained cloth. A matching mud-dotted mobcap adorned by large tricolor cockade trapped her stiff hair. Her nose was hooked; wrinkles mapped her face; gaps took the place of teeth: the quintessence of a *poissarde*. She lifted a leg over the cannon and splatted into the mud, her loud squawk belying her age.

"Who are you to ask, *aristo*?"

So much for politeness. Louis gasped the bridle and ordered two other men to put their backs to the wheels.

"Ha! Now you speak the language of the people." She ducked under the horse's head and seized the other side of the bridle. "Maillard ordered us back." Her calves midway in mud, she simpered and placed a finger under her chin, more gargoyle than grisette. "Smile and sing 'Henri Quatre.' Sacré, sooner would I crawl back to Paris!" With a sound like a hundred children sucking lozenges, the wheels came loose, and the horse lurched forward. Louis released the bridle after the crone remounted her cannon. She raised her cudgel and shouted for all to hear. "If you're any kind of men, you will fight, not sing!"

Louis nodded grim agreement as she beat the horse onward. He, too, plodded ahead with the twisting skeins of women winding their way into the village of Versailles.

Undeterred, they advanced. Of necessity the mob divided into three columns to accommodate the avenues. The townspeople met them with "Long live our Parisiennes!" Soldiers in blue wool uniforms, members of the regiments guarding the Chateau, mingled with the townspeople and the marchers. "We are with you! We are with you," they cried. Were these the men who'd trampled the red, white, and blue cockade and worn the Austrian's black one just days earlier?

Louis had been to Versailles many times. He recognized the street he trod as the rue de Paris, home to the Salle des Menus Plaisirs where the Assembly met. Grunts and a backward kick or two stayed his efforts to approach the Chateau. People, not guards, forced him back.

"Mournier! Mournier and the deputies!"

"They've gained the Chateau! Long live the King!"

Why should a cuckold in a warm, dry palace be acclaimed? Louis shouted, "Long live the people!" and none contradicted him. He almost wished someone had; an argument would have given him something to do other than wait.

He drifted from group to group, asking what was happening, garnering answers anywhere from "They've gone to kill the Queen," to "Mind your own business!"

Thick fog and dying light transformed the Chateau into a palace of ghosts. An other-worldly delegation materialized. The gates opened for some women, then closed. Louis caught bits of words. One prettier and more dignified than the others drew curses from her neighbors. Louis watched several hags grab the girl by the throat. Iron clanged; the grille re-opened. Shod hooves clattered on flagstones. Maledictions spewed like lava from a volcano.

"Down with the traitoress Chabry! Hang her from a lamp post! To the lamp post!"

"Down with the Royal Guards! Down with the Flanders Regiment!"

"We want bread, not words! Make the King promise in writing!"

The clatter of hooves faded; a loud clang told him the horsemen had retreated through the gates. High-pitched howls shattered the ear. Shots rang out and a roar, like the universe collapsing, resounded. Flung headlong against the bars of the gate, Louis yelped: a wolf slashed by the teeth of fellow wolves.

A shriek like nothing he'd heard made him struggle round. Through a space in the crowd, he saw a horse collapse, writhing and twisting, helpless under the pikes of the people. Women landed clumsy whacks on the carcass. Those wielding *ferres* grasped the long sticks in the middle and sliced off the saddle and bridle and slit open the horse. A mist hovered above the blood and body of the dead animal, its life force supplicating heaven.

Sickened, Louis let an onrush of women push him from the gates. A small female, hopping like a crippled sparrow, waved a torch. In the shelter of an arcade, men gathered pieces of dry wood. The sparrow applied the torch. Sparks fizzled, gradually gaining the strength to turn into fire. The odor of blood and burning flesh choked him. Useless hours attending Mass conjured an image; *Dies Irae* orchestrated it. The people. Demons lit by the fires of hell feasting on the damned.

His patriotism shaken, Louis sought refuge in the National Assembly only to discover many assemblymen had gone. Women occupied the chamber. With President Mournier at the Chateau, a strapping poissarde sat in his chair.

"Madame le President!"

"I recognize Therese of the cockle stall."

"Madame, two months ago we fishwives came to greet the Queen, after the manner we do every year. Madame le President, I present you with a new greeting for the Austrian!" Therese of the cockle stall hiked up her skirts. Her bared behind emitted a loud *phhhhttt*. The others clapped and hooted.

"Madame, set bread at three sous a half-pound, and meat six sous the pound."

"Madame, Madame, Madame."

The madness Louis had tried to escape had preceded him.

A Dr. Guillotin returned from the Chateau. He waved a piece of paper over his head to gain their attention. Madame le President gone hoarse, she banged her shoe to restore order.

The doctor read from the paper. "The King proclaims his concern for his people." That brought cackles and jeers. "Let me speak," he cried. "I come direct from the King." It took some time, but they quieted. "Henceforth grain will flow freely; you and your children will be fed. The King has written it in his own hand!"

Scattered cheers rewarded the doctor. Louis' reward, and that of those within the chamber, was more waiting. President Mournier and the rest of the delegation were still at the Chateau. Rumors abounded. Rice, not grain, was to be issued. La Fayette and the Paris National Guard were marching on Versailles to rescue the King. No, to side with the people. The Queen had ordered her carriage and was trying to escape with her children. She was fleeing to Austria. No, she'd already left. No, it was the King who had fled. To Metz. D'Orleans would now be king. Rumors and rumors of rumors filled the chamber. His name heralding his appearance, Mournier entered. The people parted for him. Even at a distance, one could see he blanched at the zoo of women. Louis's eyes narrowed. The cleric was a coward, not fit to command men.

Monsieur le President sent runners to recall the members of the Assembly. A portion straggled back. Louis rejoiced to see men displace at least some of the women. The chamber, after all, was a place for men. Louis easily recognized Count Mirabeau by his pitted face and melon body. Mirabeau hovered near Mournier's chair. A stranger with a fine forehead and large, eloquent eyes paused by Louis's bench. His greatcoat was muddy, like all who'd marched here.

"My God, what times! I wouldn't be a soldier this day for all the wealth of Versailles."

Nettled, Louis asked, "Why is that, Citizen?"

"Because they lack good leaders. Their officers are either hiding in the barracks or the Chateau. Most likely, the Chateau. With stout leaders the soldiers could – Ah, but I see a friend."

The stranger melted into the darkness. A good leader. A good soldier. The soldiers would fight. If Louis were a soldier, he'd not stand idly by, donning the black cockade one day and the tricolor the next. He'd not waste time in useless talks with Assemblymen and lackeys. He'd force the King to accept the will of the people. A good citizen-soldier would do this.

More Assemblymen drifted back to give the appearance of order. It must have been near midnight when distant vibrations made his body a tuning fork quivering to the measured tramp of countless feet. "La Fayette and the National Guard! Long live the National Guard!" Their step, step, step, penetrated the innermost passages of Louis's mind.

Louis fell in with a file of soldiers. "Where do you go, my friends?" he asked.

"To eat and then sleep," said a little fellow. "That damned La Fayette made us stop every ten paces. He must be in league with the *aristos* – and the King."

Louis defended La Fayette, but the man was soon replaced by many others. File after wet file faded into darkness. Soldiers. An army of citizens.

The night a rope wearing thin, Louis gave up trying to find out more. He searched for the nearest dry haven. A stable offered him convenient shelter, and he took it. To his annoyance, he found himself wondering what had become of Marie-Rose.

Voices woke him much later. Louis uncurled from the straw on which he'd slept. The Guardsmen who'd crammed into the building after him were waking. Like them, Louis wondered what the new day would bring.

In the morning, yesterday's rain had turned to a chill drizzle. Louis joined those milling before the Chateau gates. Women, soldiers, and men moved with the uncertain jerks of puppets worked by amateurs. The people, the gates, the Chateau. A shot, a cry, and ... cataclysm.

"Murder! He has murdered Jerome!"

"At him!"

The first barrier crashed open. Two royal sentries, one of whom had fired the fatal shot, fell under the hands of the people. A stalwart man raised a pike and brought it down in a brutal sweep. Louis fought a woman for the bayonet from the headless corpse's musket. He brandished it like a sword. "The Austrian! The Austrian! Let us make her pay for her crimes!"

Myriads took up his cry. At the bottom of some marble stairs, a woman hugged the corpse of a National Guardsman. She cradled the shattered head in her arms, moaning as if it had been her own son. Louis marveled that fishwives could weep.

More shots rang out. From which side, Louis didn't know. A man cried out, "This way, to the Queen's apartments!" Louis raced after him. A Royal Guard blocked the passage to a pair of doors. He shouted over his shoulder, "Save the Queen!" It was the Austrian bitch's apartments.

Men and women attacked with pikes, *ferres*, and knives. The Guard went down. The doors cracked. Swords parried the assorted weapons of the besiegers. Hands pulled a bloodied body out of reach. The doors slammed shut behind it.

A new wave assaulted the doors. Under their united force of the attackers, the doors gave way. Louis swept into the violated luxury of the Queen's bedroom. A magnificent gilt bed, the Austrian woman's bed, perfumed and satin-sheeted, bore the imprint of a body, nothing else. Louis screamed and stabbed a pillow. Others imitated him, gashing and ripping anything they could. When the people finished, a raped room lay behind them.

"The Baker's wife has fled to the Baker!"

"Citizens! Follow me, I know the way!"

The mob ran after the speaker. Though his hatred of the Austrian had not lessened, Louis abandoned the chase because it was led by a woman.

Soldiers gripping bayoneted muskets stormed the stairs. Louis raised his bayonet in tribute. The National Guard, the army of citizens.

The priceless furnishings were tempting. Women – and men – plundered what they could. A fishwife denuded a window. An officer whacked her with the flat of his sword. She clasped moire to her breast and ran away. Louis stared at the man, a haughty, white-wigged *aristo* in red, white, and blue. What had he to do with an army of citizens?

Louis resisted his order to move on, but the soldiers obeyed their officer and chased him away. More Guardsmen ran through the Chateau now, swords drawn, bayonets fixed, pursuing the looters, a deployment entirely unworthy of them. They needed better officers.

People crowded the black-and-white tiled courtyard immediately inside the gates of the Chateau. Louis edged his way there. Heads tilted back, eyes riveted on a balcony. La Fayette, commander of the National Guard he'd help establish, stood behind the King on that balcony. Louis Seize, the sixteenth king of that name. The Fat Veto. Only Monsieur le Veto now bowed to the people's wishes.

"It is Our Royal Will to ratify the August decrees destroying feudal rights, and also to approve *The Declaration of the Rights of Man and the Citizen.*" Cheers answered the King's speech. Prior to this, he'd refused to do either. "Secondly, We shall procure and send all grain from Our Royal storehouses at Versailles to Paris." More cheers. "Thirdly, all Our prisons filled with political delinquents will have judges made available to them. Fourth and lastly," here the King's voice cracked, "lastly, Our Royal Person, together with the Royal Family, will journey to Paris this very day, to dwell among Our people."

The Fat Veto finished amid wild acclaim. Louis cheered – not for the King, but for the people. The people had won.

Shouts of approval gave way to disapproval. The Austrian and her children had appeared. The Queen was composed; the little prince and princess clung to their mother. Louis added his voice to the clamor demanding the children be sent inside.

Marie Antoinette shepherded the Dauphin and the Princesse Royale indoors. In that short time, she transformed herself. She faced the people alone, her face serene, hands folded on her breast. She, playing the part of a martyr, who was a whore! What happened next defied belief. General La Fayette, the hero of Two Worlds – Louis' hero – came out, knelt, and kissed the Austrian's hand.

The answering thunder made Louis wish he had no ears. It was the act of a traitor! Never again would he praise La Fayette. Never again would he believe *aristos* championed the people.

"Long live the Queen! Long live the Queen! Long live the Queen!"

Had the whole world gone mad?

"Long live the people! Long live the people!" Louis' shouts came from the belly of earth itself and not him. "Long live the people!" Those who were sane echoed him. But their shouts were drowned by more acclamation for the Austrian. Louis left them to their folly.

During the three hours they waited for the royals to set out for Paris, Louis learned Marie-Rose had been one of the delegates sent to the Chateau last night. By now, she was already back in Paris, a carriage having been sent to take the delegates there. She had seen the King, and perhaps even the Queen. Louis cursed her.

Multitudes accompanied the royal family to Paris. First, the National Guard, holding high muskets with loaves of bread stuck to their bayonets. Next, a procession of wagons bearing wheat and flour from the royal stores, adorned with more wet loaves. Porters and women followed them, some of the women riding horses or cannon. Some brandished pikes with severed heads. Louis recognized the old witch he'd met yesterday wielding one. Behind these slunk the conquered lines of the Flanders Regiment and the Royal Guards, sans weapons. The royal entourage, strung out in shiny carriages, lumbered after its vanquished defenders. Deputies of the National Assembly and more Guardsmen followed.

Behind these came the people. They danced, sang, shouted, and whirled. "To Paris! To Paris! We bring you the Baker, the Baker's wife, the Baker's son! Long live the King! To Paris!" Near the city, a lone voice began singing a song from Grety's opera, *Richard the Lion-Hearted*. The song was "Oh Richard, Oh My King!" The royalist rallying cry.

> Oh, Richard, oh my king
> All the world abandons you,
> On this earth, there is only I
> Who cares for you.
> I alone in the universe
> Want to break your chains,
> And the rest abandon you.

No one assaulted the singer. There was no need; the mockery was evident. Now all "cared" for the King, the prisoner they conducted to a gilded cage in Paris.

At one of the customs gates to the city, Louis spied an un-spattered man riding a fresh horse burdened with stuffed saddlebags. His feet rubbed raw from his ankles down by the traitorous English boots he'd worn for a day and a half, Louis was in no mood to let him pass. Nor were the fishwives, flush with their victory.

"Citizen, come help us put the Baker to bed in the Tuileries."

"I have letters to deliver. Let me pass."

"Deliver them tomorrow. Come with us today."

"I tell you, I cannot." The man spurred his horse, but five women hung on the reins.

"Who are the letters for?" demanded one.

The man replied by redoubling his efforts to regain control of his mount.

Convinced he must be concealing something, Louis grabbed the saddlebags. "We make it our business, Citizen." He unbuckled the pouches and removed a letter, holding it up for all to see. Not that it did them any good; such women didn't read or write.

"See," Louis shouted, "this letter is addressed to an Englishman. This man is a spy!"

It was the right ploy. Many feared England might aid the royalists. The women dragged the courier from the saddle and clubbed him with cudgels and fists, screaming, "Death to the spy!" Louis shook the contents of the saddlebags, including the man's spare linen, into a gutter of fast-flowing water. The courier collapsed into that same gutter, one arm flung forward, as if reaching for his lost letters. Their work done, the women marched on to the Tuileries Palace.

Louis stayed behind and examined the letter's address. Written in French, it was addressed to *Monseigneur le Comte Evington.* Louis broke the seal. As he'd said, the enclosed missive was in English, a language he recognized but couldn't read. All embassies concerned themselves with the passing of information. The man truly was a spy. Should he take the letter to the authorities?

As if in answer, the man groaned. Both the National Assembly and National Guard had shown themselves helpless before the people. And too many in both were treacherous *aristos*, like La Fayette. Louis shredded the letter into tiny white flakes and let them flutter where they would. Humming "Oh Richard, My King," he headed toward Bertrand's apartment. After he'd washed there, he'd go home, tell his father he'd feared to go out in the streets last night.

"Monsieur Louis!"

Louis recognized the voice, his father's valet. With a certainty, the old prattler would tell what he'd seen. Louis shrugged and kept walking. What of it? He'd concoct a suitable alibi.

CHAPTER THIRTEEN

Black despair succeeds brown study.

William Congreve, *An Impossible Thing*

"Have done with the bloody rake! I told ye it needs a straight jerry."

Jemmy mumbled an apology to the carpenter of the *Scorpion* sloop and fumbled for the jerry. After almost two months at English Harbor, he knew better. *Amphitrite* requiring no extensive overhaul, Brighty and Paul Martin, *Amphitrite's* carpenter, had arranged for Jemmy to be detailed to assist careening ships. He'd even worked under the supervision of the Master Shipwright at the dockyard. Such experience, Martin said, would serve him well toward qualifying as a ship's carpenter one day.

Scorpion, a 16 gun sloop-of-war with a peacetime complement of 60 men, had a small hold, so breathing was barely possible. Her commander, Paget Bayley, didn't think it necessary to use one of Dr. Hale's mechanical ventilators to air out the below decks while she was careened. Instead, a canvas ventilator had been rigged over a hatchway. Jemmy and the other sailors grumbled about the arrangement. Yet it wasn't the nauseous air, so humid one could almost wring the moisture from it, or the wrath of displaced rats which caused Jemmy to use the wrong tool. No, it was his growing obsession with the dream.

Jemmy picked harder at the tar and oakum, as if that could obliterate what was becoming an agony. Yet remembrance seeped unwanted and unbidden into the cracks of his mind. With each repetition the details became more vivid. There was a cart, and Dad was in it. And the people, so many of them, laughing and jeering, keeping him from getting closer to his Dad. What was happening, or why, was something the dream hadn't revealed – yet.

"Gawd's sake, gi' that tool to me! Yer jamming the seam."

Jemmy stared stupidly at what he'd been doing. He still had the rake. Worse, he had jammed the seam, driving the oakum deeper. It was inexcusable, amateurish at best.

"I be sorry, sir. I, I just don't feel right in my head."

"Don't be thinking right none neither. Report to your surgeon, then. Yer no good to me, if ye be nursing a fever."

"Yes, sir," Jemmy said and gratefully scaled the Jacob's ladder suspended through the main hatchway. Above, straddling the hull, he even more gratefully breathed in an unlimited amount of fresh air. He really didn't need the surgeon, but he'd have to seek him because of the carpenter's order. Like most of his mates, Jemmy scorned *Amphitrite's* surgeon, but he had no choice but to report to him now. Since he wasn't really sick, the surgeon might accuse him of malingering, that is, if he were sober. With any luck, he'd likely be drunk, ashore, or both.

Scorpion lay hove down, keel out at the West Careening Wharf. A small part of her lay in the water with the bulk heaved onto the land, her lower masts secured by tackles to the capstans. There'd been no mindless picking oakum aboard *Amphitrite* for him. From his first days at English Harbor, Jemmy worked alongside carpenters and their mates building auxiliary pumps to clear out bilge and excess water seeping into the leeward side of the ship. He'd helped plank over gun ports, covering them with tarred canvass, then plug caulk, pitch, and otherwise secure all other openings or potential openings in the hull. Jemmy had also learned about shores and outriggers, and how to build such auxiliary supports to lessen the strain on a ship's remaining lower masts and standing rigging once she was careened.

Anxiety aside, he was thankful for opportunities like this, where he got to learn more about a ship carpenter's duties. But despite his continuing attentiveness, Mr. Brighty's behavior toward him seemed subtly changed since that day at Barbados. It was as if the bo'sun were holding him at arm's length. Or perhaps, didn't trust him. Jemmy wished he hadn't said anything about Mr. Deveare.

Mr. Deveare. Jemmy turned and regarded his ship, lying quietly at anchor in the still harbor. He'd been so mean at Barbados, so unlike what he had been before. What had come over him? And what had he said to Mr. Brighty that day? Had he called him a liar, or worse? He couldn't know about Captain Finch and Albury, could he? But they both belonged to the quality, didn't they?

Jemmy ducked out of the way of some 'Trites on their way to the provision store. Mid-November and hurricane season over, *Amphitrite* had been transported to a mooring in Freeman's Bay in anticipation of her impending departure. He'd have to wait at the dockyard until a pinnace arrived to take him to his ship.

What would Mr. Brighty think if he saw him standing here with nothing to do? Jemmy stepped aside to allow a detachment from another ship to ready a mast from the mast house. He fretted others also must think he was skylarking. No one challenged him, though. And the only skylarking he could see were some midshipmen boasting what they'd do at St Johns.

Midshipmen. Because of his deployments, he saw little of them. The Captain and officers, including the midshipmen, spent much time visiting the other ships anchored here and sometimes the nearby plantations. But not Mr. Deveare.

Apprehensive, Jemmy checked the harbor again. It might be some time before a boat put out from *Amphitrite*. No one had paid any attention to him yet, but that didn't mean they wouldn't, what with the entire Leeward fleet sheltering at English harbor. Head down, as if to become invisible, he deserted the Capstan House and crept past the Galley, where *Scorpion's* cook was already at work preparing supper for her people, across the yard to the sundial. From what he could tell, it was only around three in the afternoon. Perhaps he should return to work, saying he felt better. That way, he'd be assured of his supper. The tropical sun, though, intervened. With all his worries, Jemmy indeed felt heavy-headed and lacking in energy. He'd find someplace to rest where he'd be out of the way and wait for the boat. Perhaps he go to –

"*Scorpion's* leaks caulked so soon, Jemmy?"

Jemmy scraped off his hat to the Master Shipwright. "Her carpenter, he told me to seek my surgeon. I can't though, till boat comes."

"Too hard a worker for your own good. Well, don't stand mulling about here and risk heatstroke as well. Set your course for the Cordage and Canvass store. Not many quarter there at present, so you can take a rest if you need one. I'll send a Negro when your boat arrives."

Thanking the Master Shipwright, Jemmy lost no time in obeying him. Crossing the yard diagonally, he passed the bo'sun of the yard and *Scorpion's* bo'sun. They exchanged pleasantries with him, and he with them. Because of his relationship with Mr. Brighty and Mr. Martin, Jemmy didn't fear warrant officers. He counted them as friends, unlike the commission officers, whom he avoided whenever possible.

The dockyard a compact space, Jemmy shortly mounted the stone steps of the Clothing, Cordage, and Canvass store. There was ample room above the storage facilities for him. The *Scorpions* housed in the upstairs quarters of the Copper and Lumber store, recently built and redolent of fresh paint and lumber. He'd have the upper storey of the older building to himself.

In the bottom half of the store, a few seamen and Negroes busied themselves with slops. Jemmy absently took the stairs to the seaman's quarters, where he chose a corner near an open window and sat down. The wood planking was hard but clean. Propped against an equally clean white-washed wall, Jemmy yawned. A nap just might do him good.

He eased down onto his side and after one or two turns, pillowed his head on his arm. Jemmy's last thoughts before drifting to sleep centered on the soft crooning of the Negroes working in the yard and the hearty, if not particularly tantalizing, odors escaping the Galley.

A refreshing sleep, however, eluded him. What he slipped into instead was the half-sleep of the dream. He was in England, somewhere. A hill, steep and wooded, lay directly ahead. It was early morning, and there were no mists. Jemmy saw Dad plainly. He was riding in the back of a cart, his arms tied behind his back. He was saying something, but Jemmy couldn't hear. Too many people separated them. Jemmy followed Dad up the hill. Something or someone waited at the top. He tried to push the people away to reach Dad, but they formed an impenetrable wall.

The distance between them lengthened. As Dad neared the top of the hill, Jemmy tried to cry out for him to stay, but no words came. He tried to run to him, but his legs wouldn't move. He could only watch as Dad got closer to the top of the hill.

Jemmy sat bolt upright. Something had happened to Dad, something awful. Forcing himself to breathe deeply, Jemmy tried to remember something Gran once had said. Dreams foreshadow the future. The future. Perhaps, just perhaps, none of this had happened. Yet. That word. He *had* to return to England, to thwart the dream.

Jemmy braced himself against the rough plaster wall. Scraping his hand against the wall, he edged toward the door. Indistinct sounds seeped through from another room. He stopped and listened intently.

"American ships come to St. John's, every year this time...You see him, he take you."

A Negro's voice. The answer came too low for Jemmy to distinguish the words or identify the speaker. The resulting back and forth was difficult to follow. Jimmy caught the words, "You tell," and "I swear," but no more. Footsteps started past his doorway. Someone gave a cry of surprise when he saw him.

Frightened, Jemmy blurted, "You be running." He recognized the man now. Jake Cairns, a fo'c'slman and oarsman. He must have been one of the rowers sent out with the ship's boat.

Jake drew menacingly close. "You know what I'll do if you squeal?"

The words tumbled around in Jemmy's mind. Running. An American ship. Running! A way to get back to England perhaps, if not on this particular vessel, then aboard another. Jemmy lost no time reassuring Jake. "I be saying nothing, for I be coming with you."

CHAPTER FOURTEEN

The underlying premise of equality is that we are equal
to those whom we wish to be equal and superior to
those whom we wish not.

Evington Papers, 7754/11

Amphitrite lay at anchor in St. John's Road, Antigua. The elite
of her people, six of her best topmen, sat finishing dinner. Per
Captain Neville's rules, they'd added a seventh to their mess the
first of the month: Edward.

Hallard had made it plain either Edward pay his monthly fees
or leave. Having no money and happy to be rid of the mids,
Edward left. That had been in October. For the balance of the
month, he'd gotten his own food from the galley. Eating alone had
its benefits. His share was entirely his own. Unfortunately, being
the only one in his mess, there was no one to relieve him of daily
visiting the galley or cleaning his plate and utensils. When Traves,
Captain of the maintop, invited Edward to join his mess Edward
gratefully accepted.

He carefully wrapped his piece of fresh boiled beef in his neck
scarf. While the others yarned and joked, he headed aft toward
steerage.

"Mr. Deveare, sir."

A Tainted Dawn

It was Knoles, the royal yardsman who'd saved his life and been flogged for it. He was one of the mess. Edward paused. "Yes?"

"Sir, I, well–it's your whiskers."

Edward disliked the reminder of how few hairs he had. Moreover, as a "reefer," apprentice officer, he was owed the respect shown to officers. He, not Knoles, should have spoken first. Was messing with the people breeding familiarity?

The yardsman unwrapped the bundle of tarred sailcloth and eagerly offered it to Edward. "I bought this here at the masthead when old Toby died 'board *Barfluer*. If there's anything left of him, he'd be that proud – I'd be that proud, sir, if you'd have it."

It was a razor. "I'm grateful, Knoles," Edward said stiffly, "but I think it best you keep it."

"Please take it, sir. Old Toby looked out for me, just like you."

"All the more reason not to give it away. If you don't mind –" Edward stepped forward, but Knoles stood his ground.

"Blast, sir, I wish I could see to steer a better course in this here thing, but it's this-a way. You took up for me 'fore the Cap'n – called me a man – something no officer ever done. Mr. Deveare, sir, what I done weren't much. Oh, damme, sir, that's not what I meant. Your life *is* worth much. 'Twas my helping that weren't much. Any sailor'd do that for another."

"I appreciate your offer, but the very immensity of the debt I owe you demands my refusal."

Unsettled, Edward resumed his course. Knoles' admiration was more than an annoyance; it was a reproach. Not so much for his having been flogged, though it did bother him, but because he was well aware he'd become a hero to the people because he'd called Knoles "a man." An equal. To repudiate his words meant wounding Knoles and offending the other topmen. And something even more unacceptable – agreeing with the Captain.

An equal. Yet Knoles hadn't been the first of the people to speak to him before he'd been spoken to first. The fiddler also had done so, at Barbados. Edward hesitated. Perhaps he'd been too rough on the boy, but damn it, the fiddler had wanted Edward to tell who he was. Edward's only consolation was that because there had been no change in the way he was treated, the fiddler obviously had kept his knowledge to himself.

110

Edward proceeded slowly to the mids' berth where he slept. In order to access his chest he'd have to interface with his erstwhile "equals."

"Going to Government House, Scarecrow? Oh, I forgot, you're not invited."

Hallard got the usual round of toadish laughter. Technically, Edward had been invited, for it was a blanket invitation to officers of His Majesty's ships in harbor. In the chest were a battered hat and shabby frock coat. Good enough for going ashore, but not much else. Clothes kept him from accepting, that and the fear he'd be recognized by officers from his set, who might write their families in England, who might inform his mother.

The presence of his real equals also kept Edward from visiting the flagship, HMS *Jupiter*, 50 guns, assuming Commodore Parker would see him. Edward had taken Lieutenant McAllistair's advice about asking for a transfer. To date, he'd written one letter and had a reply from the Commodore's secretary. The secretary advised Edward to find a willing counterpart on another ship and have the exchange approved by both their captains. Apart from *Jupiter*, there were *Sybil* and *Maidstone*, 28 guns respectively; *Scorpion*, 16 guns; and *Bonetta*, 14 guns. *Amphitrite*, 24 guns, would be a step down for mids from larger ships, so it was useless to ask there. As for the smaller ones, Edward had his pride. Anyhow, those he'd approached from *Bonetta* and *Scorpion* had declined his offer.

The smell of fresh beef reminded Edward he'd laid his ration on top of his chest. He set it aside. As for the other smells, he was resigned to them by now: sweat, stale food, staler grease, animals, grog, the updraft of bilge, tobacco, urine, dung, mold, and mildew, all well-fermented by heat. If the Captain made the people wash themselves and the 'tween decks more often, perhaps it wouldn't be as bad. And perhaps there wouldn't be as many sick. Not that it troubled *Amphitrite's* surgeon. He preferred spending his time sampling the island's inexhaustible supply of rum, and they had no surgeon's assistant.

Edward opened his chest and removed a shirt of better days. Demarrara cotton, but its cuffs were soiled beyond the aid of urine and salt water and the neck now frayed. Edward used his coat sleeves to hide the cuffs; the lieutenants considered them unworthy of a smart turnout. Edward had come to have a certain fondness for his checked shirt and trousers. They were cool and practical. Even the lieutenants and mids wore trousers when doing duties like taking off cannon or masts. The slops also helped save the wear and tear of his "better" uniform.

Edward considered his duck trousers as he removed them. They and the checked shirt had appeared with his laundry one day. He made inquiries, but no one claimed them. Charity. He loathed, yet desperately required it.

He slipped out of the cool looseness of shirt and trousers and into the itch and confinement of wool and silk stockings. The lining of his coat needed stitching, but the hole provided a good hiding place for his father's portrait.

Relentless sunshine blinded one above deck. Edward squinted to see if the blue peter flapped at the fore-topmast: the square blue flag with a smaller white square dead-center, signaling an end to liberty and imminent departure. Not yet.

A pinnace was made fast to the ship's side by her painter, coxswain in place and crew laying on the oars. Edward started for the side. Two seamen idled in his path: Jake Cairns and Jemmy, the ship's fiddler. Jemmy edged back, but Cairns refuse to budge. He typically sailed as close to the wind as he dared with the midshipmen but saved outright disrespect for Edward alone. Taking the Captain and officers as models, he correctly reasoned he'd get away with it.

Brighty, persuader in hand, moved purposefully forward. As slowly as he could, Cairns gave way, and even more slowly saluted. His sullenness was typical, but not the fiddler's. He, too, moved aside truculently, unlike his usual eager self.

Edward had no time to dwell on the cause. Brighty, less curtly than usual, remarked on his going ashore, and Edward politely responded. But that was all. Edward descended the side into the pinnace. Since he was junior to all the officers, he didn't need wait to see who else was going. Protocol, however, didn't matter, as he was the only occupant in the stern sheets.

After the boat put him off at the wharf, Edward lingered. The horizon showed mare's tails, a cloud formation said to presage a change in the wind. For good or ill? Edward felt inside his coat for the beef and groaned. In his haste to leave the hatchway berth, he'd left it behind. He withdrew his arm and massaged it. The spasms which had troubled him ever since his near fatal fall from the shrouds came and went. They generally occurred when he'd overused his arm, but sometimes also in times of stress.

B. N. Peacock

A sea breeze refreshed him. It was cooler now, particularly the nights. But the weather continued dry. Antigua and the surrounding islands of St. Christopher, Nevis, and Montserrat were drought stricken, Antigua suffering the most. In his forays around English Harbor, Edward had seen slaves collapse in the fields and animals dying from thirst.

He wandered through the streets of St. John's until he came to the market square known as "The Parade." Blacks hawked vegetables, fruits, meats, fish, and innumerable other items from stalls. Hucksters called to him and pointed to their wares: sugar cakes, parched groundnuts, calicos, yams, ginger beer, and more. Edward smiled sadly and walked away.

Noticeable for its difference, a refined female voice rose above the din. A young lady scolded her slave for not holding her sun umbrella correctly. Intrigued, Edward located the source. Blonde curls sheltered underneath a straw hat tied with a pink ribbon. The lady's complexion was exceptionally fair, the result, no doubt of many a well-placed shade. Bright eyes, a pert nose, and a shapely figure completed the vision, a planter's daughter out for a turn round the market. Edward had found his ideal of beauty – and lost his heart.

The day was proving one of deepening despair. Given his shabby appearance, no well-bred lady would give him a second thought. Even so, before she could turn his way, he dashed down a side alley. Short of breath and hope, he finally paused behind the Scotch Church, his only solace a leather bucket with an emblem marking it as belonging to the Friendly Fire Company. Some volunteer must have left it here after a drill. Edward looked inside it; water darkened its bottom. He stuck a finger into it and sampled the result: brackish but not salty. He scooped out a handful or two. It couldn't hurt him.

Instead of allaying his thirst, the tepid water increased it. His stomach growled protest. He should have eaten his meat after all. To give him his due, Neville supplemented the ship's rations with fresh food. Bullocks from Barbuda, slaughtered on ship and served weekly; melons, mangoes, lemons, and star apples, the latter particularly abundant and cheap. And even the occasional basket of soft tommy, fresh bread, not hard tack. Edward had to admit he was better off messing with the topmen. He got more than he had in the hatchway berth. Yet even so, his stomach was never really full. And he stooped more now between decks. He was growing.

113

The sun was lower on the horizon. Edward reluctantly headed back to the wharf. With nothing else to do, he inventoried the ships. There was the coastal schooner, *Sally*. She carried letters as well as goods between the islands. In a circuitous way, he'd had a note from Lieutenant McAllistair. The Scotchman, intuiting Edward lacked the price of receiving a letter, sent one to him via an acquaintance in the 67th Hampshire Regiment, who sent it via messenger to Edward.

Beyond *Sally*, a two-masted snow, a merchantman much like a brig, loaded barrels of rum. Edward studied her with careless pride. Her boom-mainsail traversed the triangular-sail mast, so unlike that of a brig's, which hooped it. He not only could distinguish merchantmen but knew the rating system for men-of-war to a fault. His ship, *Amphitrite*, was a sixth rate: carrying twenty-two nine-pounders and two three-pounders, not to mention four twelve-pound carronades on the one quarterdeck and two on the forecastle. Her peace-time complement supposedly numbered one hundred and forty men, of whom twenty were marines. Her actual complement, though, was one hundred and thirty-three, attrition due to sickness. So far, no one had attempted to desert.

As Edward walked by the snow, he was surprised to see Cairns conversing with someone aboard. The fellow was mate, jack-tar, or master, depending on how one took him. Edward was even more surprised to see *Amphitrite's* fiddler hovering beside Jake. Annoyed the two saw but didn't acknowledge him, Edward ordered them to take off their hats.

Cairns spit tobacco juice near the Edward's shoe. "You ain't naught but a horse marine."

"Horse-marine" was derogatory slang for a green hand. Edward snapped, "I'll have –"

Cairns' stained teeth showed in a jeering grin. "Have what? Cap'n don't give a damn for 'e, no more than officers. Nor me."

The truth, and it stung. Edward turned on Jemmy, the fiddler. With the same hang-dog expression he showed aboard ship, he looked away. The last of the trio met his glare head on. "Some jest ain't cut of the right cloth to be an officer." He spoke with a twang. A Jonathan, an American, probably trading in violation of the Navigation Laws, which stipulated all ships conveying goods to and from His Majesty's possessions be British built and owned, and their crews three-quarters English. Not that Captain Neville seemed to care.

Hot with indignation, Edward strained his face into the requisite mask. Gentlemen did not betray emotion before inferiors. "We'll see about this," he said.

The Jonathan laughed and herded the 'Trites below. Edward was left fuming on the quay. To make matters worse, the pinnace was late coming, and when it did come, it had to wait for Mr. Reynolds. On their way to their ship, Edward tried to catch the second lieutenant's eye to tell him what he'd seen, but Mr. Reynolds ignored him.

Supper passed uneventfully. Likewise the dogwatches, for the ship's fiddler wasn't required to play for these when the ship was in port. The night watches went by quietly also. Only Edward was in turmoil. What possessed the ship's fiddler to take up with Cairns? It was totally out of character, or what he felt was his character. In truth, Edward knew little about him. He was just there, like the others. Cairns, on the other hand, deserved to be flogged. And that Jonathan, the snow needed her papers checked. But who to tell? Who would listen?

Early next morning, the blue peter flapped at the fore-topmast. Neville mustered all hands for one of his surprise inspections, the better to catch any absentees. On the quarterdeck, Edward skirted Mason and the foot he shot out to trip him. Each name called out by the Captain's clerk drew a corresponding response until –

"Jacob Cairns."

No reply.

"Jacob Cairns."

Silence.

With a worried frown, the clerk went down the list until he came to "James Sweetman." When no one answered again, Captain Neville beckoned Mr. Claverall. Even from where Edward stood, he could feel the first lieutenant's tension.

"Search the ship from top to bottom! If you can't find them here, send a party of marines ashore. I'll have those beggars flogged senseless if they've tried to run!" Neville waved toward the muster book. "See to this, Mr. Claverall. Have my barge readied, and be quick about it, too!"

After two months of relative calm, the Captain was having one of his rages. His orders were conflicting: finish the muster and detail two boat's crews plus marines. Without wresting the muster book from the flustered clerk, Claverall called out the names of the Captain's oarsmen and demanded the lieutenant of marines muster and send his squad throughout the ship. The deserters must be found.

The muster continued for those not otherwise employed. Edward hugged the taffrail after it ended and the people were dismissed. An hour later, the jolly boat was lowered and a party of marines was rowed ashore.

Running – desertion – was a serious offense, covered by Article Sixteen of the Articles of War. An offense, which, if pursued to its bitter end, spelled death for the offender and punishment for any aiding him. Or them, meaning Edward, if he said nothing.

The people returned to their work. Some mindlessly got up junk. Their faces blank, they unraveled old cable and re-wove it into points and gaskets. The wind died to nothing. Sounds aboard ship died to even less.

Edward plodded to the sailing Master's cabin for his navigation lesson. For the others, it was mostly review: for Edward, fit was a form of crucifixion. He'd been given a gentleman's education. Latin, some Greek, French, Italian, Spanish, history, literature, drawing, singing, and dancing, but little mathematics. Mathematics counted here.

However, he could and did hold his own in fencing. None bested him in single stick practice. He'd also learned some new techniques. No gentlemanly taps on the breast and "Touché." Slash arm or leg muscles to disable an opponent. Better yet, go for the throat. Kill or be killed.

Navigation went worse than usual. Edward's preoccupation with the deserters won him innumerable reprimands from the Master and sniggers from the others.

The search party came back empty-handed. Later, furious as a black squall, Neville stomped aboard. A tomb would have been more cheerful than *Amphitrite* that night.

Edward heard the early bell and rolled out of his hammock before the mate's "Turn out," and "Show a leg there!" He was tired; he'd not slept.

All hands were turned out before breakfast and the muster uselessly read anew. When the deserters' names were duly read and no response made, Neville summoned their respective messes.

Edward watched as the Captain stamped up and down, first before the fo'clesmen, then before the ship's boys. When no one provided any answers as to their whereabouts, Neville seized a speaking trumpet from the binnacle and struck a fo'clsman. Blood flowed from a cut on the sailor's head. Edward shut his eyes.

Neville dismissed the messes. Hands resting on the railing, he glared down at the people. "You dogs, someone knew of this! When I find who, I'll flog him till he drops!"

Mere feet from the Captain, Edward saw his hands clinched until they resembled the talons of a bird of prey. He nearly jumped when Neville snarled, "Weigh anchor."

Two ladders descended the quarterdeck, one at each end. In the general rush to man the capstan and prepare to go aloft, Edward ran at oblique angles toward the weather shrouds. Mr. Claverall chose that moment to position himself in front of them, the better to give his orders since he lacked the use of the speaking trumpet. Edward's swerve to avoid him placed him directly in the Captain's path.

"Mr. Deveare."

If he wasn't trembling, he didn't know why. His back to Neville, Edward removed his hat. Mr. Claverall shouted orders. Brighty blew his pipe. The people, well-trained crew that they were, had already fitted the bars into the capstan and rammed home the pins. Absent fiddler notwithstanding, they heaved in time. Noise and movement abounded, yet Edward quivered to each of Neville's footfalls.

"Face me."

Edward's feet could have used the capstan's assist. With a supreme effort, he obeyed.

"You went ashore yesterday, did you not?" Neville's voice slithered like a snake over silk.

"Yes, sir." Did he really sound so calm?

"You heard what I said to the ship's company just now?"

Edward kept his eyes level with the frill on Neville's shirt. "Aye, sir."

"Have you aught to say about those buggers?"

"I, I went ashore, sir."

"I know that! And afterwards?"

Neville had been ashore most of yesterday. Had someone told him about Edward and the missing *'Trites*? This was a heaven-sent opportunity to save himself and simultaneously square accounts with Cains and the Jonathan. As for the fiddler, much as Edward regretted his behavior to him, he'd get the punishment he deserved for deserting.

"Look at me."

Edward winched his eyes upward, to Neville's chin, to his lips. The Captain smiled a devil's smile, as false as sunlight filtering through an unfinished storm. And as cruel. Neville enjoyed seeing others cringe. Twice before, Edward had fallen back when Neville pulled his trick of abruptly stepping into the face of his prey. This time, Edward held his ground. His effort not only drove out thoughts of avenging himself, it served as the impetus to a half truth.

"I went about my business, sir, and I suppose they did theirs."

Neville's pupils turned to dirty ice. "Liar! You wish to defy me, do you? You, with your great experience at sea? The very next instant you commit one of your puerile blunders, I'll have you flogged and dismissed my ship! Do you understand?"

The Captain stomped away as quickly as he'd pounced on him. Edward crammed on his hat and hastened to his station. The whites of Brighty's eyes showed the bo'sun had caught every word. Even Mason looked subdued.

No mistakes. He could make no mistakes. He was much improved but –

Dear God, no mistakes.

CHAPTER FIFTEEN

They change their sky, not their minds, who cross the sea.

Horace, *Epistolae*, I.xi

After months in English Harbor's millpond calm, Jemmy became hopelessly seasick in the North Atlantic. With no Brighty to indulge him, *Liberty's* first mate hauled him out of his bunk with a "God damn you, get on deck!"

The substitution of bunks for hammocks wasn't the only difference. No Saturday washday. No Sunday muster. No officers looking down on high, like so many heartless gods.

Amphitrite had two lieutenants, *Liberty* two mates. The similarity ended there. When not cursing or pummeling slackers, the mates were more relaxed, more accessible. The break of her quarterdeck, which terminated just forward her mainmast, was one foot, one inch. Lacking the need to man cannon, *Liberty's* total complement was just thirteen men, lending to a much greater sense of comradeship.

All told, Jemmy liked his new ship. The brig was trim and small, with moderately fine lines. Oak and timber, she was a good sailor, fast with a deep hold. *Liberty* was registered out of New York, although her Master, Jedidiah Philpott, carried an alternate set of papers claiming she was Halifax built and owned. Then there was the crew, a cosmopolitan lot. Five Americans, two Frenchies, two Dutchmen, ostensibly from New York but whose thick accents argued Amsterdam, and four Englishmen. The Englishmen, like the alternate set of papers, were insurance against possible challenges to *Liberty's* trading in English waters. Jemmy was one of the four Englishmen chosen.

A curse from the second mate ended Jemmy's reverie. He'd signed on as a ship's boy, thankful to get even that. Jemmy sighed and emptied the slop bucket over the side. He had to stand watch now, four hours on and four hours off. Jemmy missed *Amphitrite's* unbroken sleep.

The bucket replaced, Jemmy mulled over the past weeks. Their escape had been so simple. Jake had cultivated the friendship of a free Negro at English Harbor. Through him, Jake learned of a Master predisposed to aiding deserters. The Yankee had been reluctant to take them both, until Mr. Deveare arrived. The Master had spent time in a British prison during the American War. He loathed British officers.

Jemmy hugged himself in the aftermath of a wave breaking over the deck. It was late in the year to cross the Atlantic. His messmates said the ship's owners didn't fear God nor man, only lack of profit. Money. He and Jake had been foolish, standing there on deck in plain sight, bargaining with the Yankee Master. Had Mr. Deveare come upon them by chance, or had he shadowed them, wanting vengeance for Jake's disrespect aboard *Amphitrite*? Or was it because of him, because he knew who he was and had told Mr. Brighty? Mr. Deveare been good to him in London, and had helped him his first days aboard ship, but he'd changed. One day, according to Jake, he'd strut the windward side of the quarterdeck, a bloody bastard like the rest of them.

The British navy has a long arm. *Liberty's* first mate had thrown that out one night when they'd shared the watch. Jemmy hadn't told anyone he'd served in His Majesty's navy, but somehow the mate had guessed. Or perhaps he was used to signing on deserters – cheaply. Jemmy anxiously scanned the horizon and squinted past *Liberty's* wake. No sign of a ship, but that didn't mean that one wouldn't follow, perhaps *Amphitrite* herself. Mr. Deveare surely told what he knew, that he and Jake had run.

The heightened wind cut through him. Except for the clothes on his back and his fiddle, Jemmy had nothing else from *Amphitrite*. He and Jake had gone ashore at St John's ostensibly for a day of liberty. Liberty, an odd choice of words. Jemmy headed into the wind, toward the mates' berth. He was free, wasn't he? *Amphitrite* was bound to the Leeward station. No ship had trailed them to New York either. Even so, Jemmy had looked over his shoulder many times in that city where everyone walked so fast, as if in pursuit of some special destiny. He never stopped dreading someone would recognize him. *The British navy has a long arm.* Jemmy knocked at the second mates' cabin before entering. Would he ever truly be free again?

With difficulty, he closed the cabin door. Despite the rough seas, the men said *Liberty* was making good time. Liberty. That was the subject of many a lively discussion over dinner. Liberty and equality. All men were created equal, the Americans claimed, or mostly so. A man was what Mr. Deveare had called the foretopman. Did he mean what he'd said? Jemmy took down the mate's best coat and brushed it vigorously. The Frenchies proclaimed liberty loudest of all. Liberty. Equality. A man. Was that what that Frenchie had shouted at him in London?

Jemmy savaged the coat. None of this had anything to do with him. He was going home to find his father. That was all that mattered.

CHAPTER SIXTEEN

The appetite grows by eating.

François Rabelais, *Gargantua*, I.v

"Monsieur Louis, I am a poor man. Your father pays me little."

"I get nothing more until next month. You know that."

"True, true, but you kept back a bit for Monsieur Bertrand last time. I saw you give it him. And I think you do this month as well. Your esteemed father would be most angry were he to know – as he would of the October Days."

When had his father's old servant turned into such a fiend? He'd caught Louis returning with the triumphant marchers bringing the royal family from Versailles during what had now become known as "the October Days." The price of the servant's silence initially had been modest, only half his month's allowance. That had been in October. In November, he'd demanded Louis' entire allowance. Louis assured him he'd given all. In actuality, he kept back some for Bertrand, who as usual, needed funds. Now in December, this monster insisted Louis not only hand over all, but five *livres* more.

"I have not that sum! You must wait until next month."

"Next month will be too late, Monsieur. Your father –"

"*Sacre*! What do you want – blood?"

Louis glared down at the man, but for all his show of anger, he knew there was little he could do. If his father discovered his revolutionary sympathies, well... He had no means of support, no where to go. There was Bertrand, of course, but without Louis' money, they would both be out in the street.

"I'll see what I can do. I promise nothing more."

"I attend your father this evening. Shall I enlighten Monsieur as to his son's true sentiments?"

Cursing him silently, aloud he promised he'd have the money. Sick of the sight of the old valet, he ordered him out of his room. A rash thing, perhaps, an act of senseless bravado, but it soothed his vanity nonetheless and his growing sense of impotence.

After the door had closed, Louis vented his sentiments aloud. "*Aristo.*" The term had taken on a wider meaning. Going beyond its original intent, the nobility, it was now the insult of choice, increasingly hurled at those whom one disliked or disapproved. Louis savored the momentary relief. His need for cash was more lasting. He inventoried his room. Pastoral prints hinting his Rousseauan sensibilities. Not much there. Furniture? He'd attract immediate attention trying to get it out of the building. Books? He required them for his studies. Clothes? Good quality and the latest cut, he loathed to part with any, all the more so because of his father's laments about declining patronage. Replacements might be slow in coming. Louis dug his fingernails into his palms. There must be some way he to raise five *livres*.

One hand inadvertently brushed against the back of a book. Books, they were the only thing he possessed in abundance. If he sold those he used least, perhaps no one would notice. And if he did need them again, he could lie convincingly that his lecturers insisted he have them. He collected volumes from past lectures, little regretting their leather luxuriousness, even less the knowledge they'd imparted. Truth to tell, he was sick of his studies.

His took down his coat, a high-collared garment of thick blue wool lined with shot silk, from the wardrobe. His father, for all his recent economies, hadn't stinted here. Louis slipped into its fashionable warmth before gathering up the texts he'd decided upon.

The December day was overcast. The wind gusted, threatening rain or snow. Louis judged it best to keep close to buildings; nevertheless he was still forced to put his head down against the wind. He hugged his books to him and set out at a brisk walk for the bookshops of Saint-Germaine-des-Prés. The wind cutting into the warmth of both coat and body, he dived into the first one he encountered. Without intending it, he'd entered one he often patronized. Its owner greeted him affably and listened to his request. He checked each book carefully. Three *livres*, Monsieur, no more. See, there are marks on this one and that. Louis gathered up his books and tried an adjacent store. The shopkeeper there offered even less. Didn't Monsieur see he was overwhelmed with Tacitus and Horace? Paris was filled with starving students – and priests. Priests because the renegade Bishop of Autun had successfully transformed the Church into a paying partner of the revolution. The reforms Louis once welcomed now worked against him.

So it went until Louis had exhausted his options. No one offered the amount he needed. At the end, no one offered anything at all. In the street again, the afternoon was wearing on, and with it, such pretense to warmth as existed. Uncertain what to do next, Louis looked doubtfully down the street. Other students, not so fortunate or perhaps more profligate, often mentioned shops whose proprietors took anything they had to sell. Louis racked his memory to recall even one such a shop, but his efforts produced no names. He'd been too well-off then to pay attention.

Where were such shops most likely to exist, he demanded of himself. Where the poor lived, do doubt. For lack of a better answer or direction, he started toward the Faubourg Saint Antoine.

The lot of the common Parisian had not improved since October. If anything, the sansculottes were more meagerly clad and hungry than ever. In the grudging light of a sunless day, haggard men in ragged pants, raw feet, and threadbare jackets hovered in peeling door frames. One begged alms. When he protested he had no money, the would-be beggar hissed, "*Aristo.*"

Louis tightened his hold on his books and hastened on. With every stride, he chided his fears. Hadn't he often walked among the people, alone at that? Hadn't he often proclaimed his love for them, both by voice and written word? Surely, the people were his friends. Reason, however, had little to do with reality. His weren't the only footsteps he heard, nor were there only one set following him. What seemed to him a thousand whisperings shaped themselves into a final loud curse, "*Aristo.*" Louis broke into a run.

In his haste to escape his pursuers, he turned into an alley. Two men stopped him, one tall, one short. They wore blue coats with crossed white belts, white breeches and gaiters over their white stockings and carried long muskets slung over their shoulders. Louis could have cried for joy. They were National Guardsmen, most likely of La Fayette's corps from their dandified uniforms. He didn't hold that against them now. Their purpose was to maintain order.

"What do you here, Citizen?" the taller one asked.

"My books – I wish to sell them."

"Not many can read in Saint Antoine."

"True, but –"

"Go back! Before you are robbed, and your body thrown in the Seine."

"I tell you, I *must* sell my books."

"Eh, Little One," said the shorter one, "he seems desperate."

The pair seemed oddly familiar. Emboldened, he said, "I cannot return home without money."

"Why?" asked the first.

"My father gives me no more."

Both Guardsmen broke out laughing. "So," the tall one said, "it is as bad as that! Women or wine? Or a little of both?"

"*Le patrie.*"

"Ah, a patriot. Come then, *Monsieur le Patriot*," said the tall one, clapping him on the back, "we will show you a place that takes what one has to sell. But do not expect its owner to make you rich. Were that the case, we would be kings."

Louis willingly let the men guide him. The short man proved loquacious. His friend was Sergeant Jacques Beldoque, son of a schoolmaster from Orlean. He was Corporal Henri Lecluselle, son of a laborer from Soissons. Young and idealistic, they'd enlisted in the King's army during the American War, fighting the British in a place called Virginia. After the war, they'd returned to France and remained in the army for a time. Not so idealistic, they left the army. After the fall of the Bastille, they'd enlisted in one of La Fayette's National Guard units, largely composed of seasoned soldiers like themselves. Their uniforms were paid for, and their arms. Other than that, they had little. Like Louis, they derided La

Fayette as more braggart than soldier. Rochambeau, Beldoque claimed, was the true hero of two worlds.

They left him no opening to talk about himself. Soon, the two opened a heavy door to a dingy shop in a nameless cul-de-sac. The owner darted out to meet them, first this way, then that. He ducked a cobweb to face them behind a kind of counter. Louis regarded the quivering form with horror. Lecluselle spoke for him. Monsieur has come to sell his books. Boney fingers not unlike pinchers grasped Louis' bundle.

Repelled, Louis watched the pinchers crawl over each volume, page by page. One *livre*, in *assignats*, was the final assessment.

Assignats were the new paper currency peddled by the government. His father claimed they were worthless. "Five *livres*, and no assignats," Louis counter-bargained.

"Does Monsieur doubt the peoples' government?"

"No, I am a loyal citizen." Louis wavered. Should he accept the assignats? Then he studied the man's greedy face. "One *livre? Mon dieu*, the lot cost ten times that new!"

"Ah, but they are no longer new. Monsieur can take the offer or leave it. However..." Pinchers reached over the counter and fingered Louis' sleeve. "Such fine wool, one does not often see its like. How much would Monsieur take?"

What light the grimy shop window couldn't block had dimmed noticeably during the transaction. Louis thought quickly. His father was known to discuss business of an evening, perhaps in hopes Louis would take some interest. He hadn't. Therefore, he'd no idea of the coat's true worth. "Five *livres*," he blurted finally. "Coins, not assignats."

His movements a series of quick jerks, the shopkeeper disappeared. He reappeared with a box. Looking suspiciously at the three, he opened it and counted out five *livres*. "No, Monsieur," he said, as Louis held out his hand. "The coat."

Louis felt that although he'd gotten his price, he was still the loser. The coat became him and kept him from the cold. It was of superior quality. Did he really want to see it in the hands of this creature? But then, what choice had he? The shopkeeper lovingly stroked the garment Louis handed him.

Beldoque emptied the ashes from his pipe on the floor. "*Mon ami*," he said, "I know a wine shop owned by a compatriot. We will stand credit for a bottle, to warm you on your way."

"I have not the time," Louis said, gathering his books.

"Shall we meet again?" asked Beldoque, hard on his heels out the door.

"If you wish."

"Where, and when?"

"Outside the Café du Foy," Louis said, running down the street. "I no longer have the money to go inside."

"No more than we. When?"

"Tomorrow, at noon."

The Guardsman's assent was barely audible. Anxiety and exertion denied the biting cold. Or perhaps it was stubbornness and pride. At length, Louis bounded upstairs to his room. He flung the money at the feet of the man who waited there.

His father's servant retrieved the coins. Louis saw his lips move as he counted them. He despised him for the effort. He hated him for his satisfaction.

"*Bien*. Since Monsieur had no trouble obtaining this, next month I require double."

CHAPTER SEVENTEEN

And in the lowest deep, a lower deep,
Still threat'ning to devour be opens wide;
To which the Hell I suffer seems a Heaven.

John Milton. *Paradise Lost*, iv.75-78

Hammock-cloths whipped and crackled, the men pulling them off the railing nettings along the quarterdeck, waist, and fo'c'sle. Tonight the lines of sailors weren't quite so straight or silent, the result of an extra ration of grog to celebrate Christmas Day.

A snuffler, a light wind, rippled the surface of the sea. The bo'sun's mate piped Edward's division. After a sailor handed down the doubled bundle, Edward hove it over his shoulder. The fresh breeze enticed him. He discounted the superstition that sleeping in the moonlight harmed one. He longed to take a caulk in either the waist or fo'c'sle, using his blanket for warmth and his hammock for a pillow. Sleeping above decks, however, was prohibited at sea.

Christmas had been a mix of work and saturnalia. Earlier, Edward had overseen the hoisting out of the launch. He and its boat crew had ferried empty water casks ashore at Nevis, filled them, and returned them to the ship, after which they'd been struck into the hold. They'd no sooner gotten in the launch and taken down the tackle, when the order to get under way had been given. At five in the afternoon, the pilot had come on board. It was nine now, and *Amphitrite* had long since cleared Charleston Roads on route to St. Kitts.

The dogwatches had been especially merry, the more so since the Captain replaced the original ship's fiddler with a black from Barbuda. Edward's mess loved singing. With an extra ration under their belts, the choruses had been robust. Seeing Edward's foot tapping, the topmen invited him, boisterously but respectfully, to join in. To his surprise and theirs, Edward did. The people to a man appreciated a good singer. They stomped their feet and clapped at his polished renditions of "Hearts of Oak," "Lord Anson and Hawke," and "The Royal Sailor." When the choice of songs became too lewd, Edward excused himself.

All this past, Edward made his way with his bedding to the hatchway berth. He unwound the turnings securing his hammock and spread out a canvass bed. Not trusting to flickering pusser's glims, tallow candles stuck in rum bottles, he ran his fingers over the clues, the series of small lines either end of the hammock by which he secured it to the beams. Guided by the eyelets, the regular bumps along the ends, he checked the knittles, untwisting the thin ropes as needed. The grommets, iron rings holding the knittles, were cool to the touch. When he'd thoroughly checked both the head and foot clues, he fastened the lanyards to the battens, wooden rings nailed into the overhead beams. Finished, Edward threw his weight onto the hammock. The lanyards creaked: his feet dangled free.

He pulled back the blanket and plumped his straw mattress and pillow into a semblance of thickness. Tired and happy to turn in, Edward stripped to shirt and trousers.

"Damn fine spread the gun-room laid out. Good port, too."

"Captain's was better."

Hallard and Fordyce debated the viands, followed by the none-too-steady Mason and Grog.

"Where was the beggar at the table today?"

Hallard never lost an opportunity to needle Edward. What he didn't know was that the warrant officers' mess had sent Edward a plate heaped with goose and stuffing and figgy pudding. A pint of wassail minus the alcohol had also been sent with their compliments, testament to the Captain's ongoing prohibition against liquor for him.

Edward ignored Hallard, but Hallard didn't ignore him. Instructing Mason to see to his hammock, the master's mate leaned on Edward's to prevent him from getting into it.

"Heard you caw today, Scarecrow. Didn't know you could do anything well."

Hallard had been drinking. Not excessively – he was, after all, standing. However, from experience Edward deduced that the more the liquor flowed, the more trouble was likely to happen. He prudently held his tongue.

"Do you know any clown songs?"

Clown references were becoming more frequent as his clothes deteriorated. In the weeks following the incident at St. John's, the lieutenants abused him in the same language to him they reserved for the people. They were trying to goad him into making a mistake.

"I lost five shillings because of you," Hallard persisted. "The gun-room wagered how long you'd last. I said you couldn't go a week without a blunder, and here it is Christmas Day. Talk about miracles!

Lanyards stopped hissing through battens. The mids formed a pack behind Hallard. The master's mate set his shoe on Edward's bare toes. Edward still kept silent.

"Pawned your tongue, Scarecrow? Your wit as well?" Still eliciting no response, Hallard said over his shoulder, "You know, lads, the gun-room reset the wager. Claverall put him down for Twelfth Night, but I say he can't make it past New Year's Day. What say you?"

Mason sneered, "He wouldn't have lasted this long but for the people."

This was true, but his sympathizers had to be careful. An off duty seaman too quick to point out places where Edward's squad had missed slushing the mainmast had paid the price. That same afternoon, Mr. Reynolds accused the sailor of "insolence and disrespect to an officer." His crime? Not to have gotten out of Reynolds way quickly enough. The penalty? A dozen for each infraction at the gangway, an example to those who would help Edward. Still, not everyone was scared off. Traves and Knoles redoubled their efforts. Edward's mess discussed the day's work over meals, making them Edward's tutorials.

Hallard put his whole weight on Edward's toes. Edward jerked a foot back, causing Hallard to off-balance. The others retaliated by knocking Edward to the deck. Cloth ripped; his upper left thigh burned; something warm trickled down his leg. In his fall, his leg had jammed against a sea chest. Edward sat, right leg bent, left leg sprawled in front of him, his right hand palm down on planking. Hallard tried to impale that hand with his foot. Edward snaked it away just in time.

Angered, the master's mate kicked Edward's right knee.

"What's the matter, Scarecrow? Too cowardly to fight? Go on," he said, kicking Edward again. "Give me reason to report you to Cudthumper. We're all anxious to see you seized up at the gangway. Not to mention say good-bye."

A forest of white trousers hemmed Edward. No help forthcoming, he dropped his head between his knees and shielded it in his arms. One particularly vicious kick drove him into a chest, bruising his left side as badly as his right. All this on Christmas Day.

Edward's body, his aristocratic upbringing, screamed to fight back. To hit, to return kick for kick, to shout what he thought of them. His brain forbade it. To do anything other than nothing meant falling into a trap.

His very stoicism spoiled his assailants' game. One by one, the kicks receded. Drafts from swaying hammocks fanned the backs of his hands. His tormentors had settled in for the night.

The marine on duty at the gun-room door translated the order "ship's company, fire and lights out" into "douse glims." In the distance, brisk footfalls announced the master-at-arms making his rounds, checking for hidden lights or men out of their hammocks. Edward pressed himself against the sea chest. The footsteps paused. Edward held his breath. The steps recommenced and moved farther away.

The only sounds were the creaking and groaning of the ship, the mids' regular breathing, and the pounding of Edward's heart. No snores yet, but no more insults or threats either. Edward cautiously moved his right hand until it made contact with his upper left thigh. His fingers assessed a tear of three or four inches. Under the cloth, he felt a stickiness. Blood.

Hands shaking, he checked his sides. His ribs ached but didn't seem broken. His one comfort was that although he'd be sore tomorrow, his clothes would hide any bruises. His fingers traveled down his leg to his knee, the flesh underneath the trouser leg already feeling puffy and warm. Should his knee stiffen, he dare not limp, lest he be asked why.

Edward's ears gained the sharpness of a cornered hare's. Nothing out of the ordinary, thank God. He got his left leg under him, the one least kicked, then did the same with his right and lurched to his feet. He bit his lips to keep from groaning as he struggled into his hammock. As he did, his right arm muscles began jerking uncontrollably. He clamped the arm to his side with his good hand until the spasms subsided. Lying back in the hammock, he thought bitterly how different life would be if his father were captain here.

"Awake, Scarecrow? We could do with some entertainment, you know. Beginning dinner tomorrow, you will sing for us. You don't want to be flogged, do you, Mr. Scarecrow?"

No, he didn't want to be flogged. Or beaten, or insulted, or tormented.

"Can't speak? Shall I send to the officer of the watch and tell him you've been disrespectful of me, a master's mate?"

"I, I'll be there."

"You'll be what, Scarecrow?"

"I'll be there. To sing. Sir."

"That's better. Pleasant dreams, Mr. Scarecrow."

"Good night. Sir." Sleep did not come, much less pleasant dreams. Edward brooded in the darkness. How he longed to tell them all to go to hell. Then a thought made him want to laugh hysterically. He'd no need to tell them. Both they – and he – were already there.

CHAPTER EIGHTEEN

The balance of power.

Horace Walpole, House of Commons,
13 February 1741

Two bronze plates quivered on suspended chains. Edward George Athleigh Evington watched dispassionately. England had regained much of the prestige she'd lost because of the American War. The question was, would she retain it?

Evington abandoned his desk. He'd done his share. The secret delegation to Vienna had gone well. Austria, long discontent with its French alliance, sought allies elsewhere. And where better than England? Count von Kaunitz, Austria's wily Foreign Minister, had initially rebuffed English overtures. That was to be expected; von Kaunitz was a noted Anglophobe. Prussia was his choice. However, Baron Jacobi, Frederick William's ambassador to Vienna, had overplayed his hand by backing a Hungarian revolt. When Evington and Sir Robert Keith, Britain's ambassador to Vienna, confronted von Kaunitz with Prussia's duplicity, the Count had no choice but to thaw. Now Joséph of Austria was in England's corner and neither Prussia nor France was the wiser. Evington had passed on the results of the negotiations to His Grace, the Duke of Leeds, England's indolent Foreign Secretary. It was up to Leeds to make the most of it.

Evington coughed and took out his handkerchief. This cold was such a nuisance. Trim and fit, he was rarely ill. Not many men of fifty odd could make a whirlwind trip to and from Vienna. Still, that unfortunate delay at Phalsburg had cost him. His French was too perfect. The border guards suspected he was an émigré attempting to reenter France. *Monsieur* must wait until they verified his papers. The damp accommodations had left him ill. Damn the French.

He was tired, but he'd have no rest today. This evening he'd dine with Portland. Before that, a visit to his old friend, Sir Colin Lewes. Worst of all, he'd have to deal with Lizzie. He'd traveled so fast, none of his regular mail had reached him. He'd already concocted a tale to explain why he hadn't answered her letters. With any luck, she might not be downstairs yet. But then, he didn't trust to luck.

"Where have you been?"

Contrary to her usual habits, she was up. Evington unhurriedly entered the breakfast room. "Captain Clark's ship came late to Dover." She didn't kiss him, but she'd never been effusive. He noticed she was dressed in black. "Is someone we know dead?" he asked, checking the eggs

"The Captain."

"A pity, I'm sure – for him." The eggs were glutinous.

"Three months, and not a word. Oh, God, he must surely be dead!"

"You'll forgive me, my dear, if I don't follow your meaning."

"Edward! He's gone. Did you read none of my letters?"

"The French post is sadly wanting these days." He bypassed her to get to the tea urn. The way things were going this morning he'd need the entire pot.

"The will! That hateful old man, he stole him from me!"

The tea barely warmed the wafer-thin Anton Grassi cup. Evington put it down. He'd either pacify her or never have another decent meal under his own roof again. "What of it?"

With an excess emotion he found distasteful, she launched into a full explanation, at the end of which she glared at him as if this had somehow been his fault. That, at least, was like her.

"I meet with Sir Colin today and will –"

"You may as well meet with the devil!"

This business about her son was affecting her mind. "I will do what I can," he said guardedly. "If you will pray excuse me, I have an engagement."

"Bring him home. He is everything to me."

She'd moaned the words. If the boy were everything, what did that leave him? Evington made a dismissive gesture and gave a bell rope a sharp tug. Sans emotion, he sent the answering footman running. Hatted, coated, caned, and gloved, he gratefully escaped to his carriage.

Lincoln Fields and Sir Colin's signature russet suit remained reassuringly unchanged. So did the barrel chair by the fire. A jug of spiced cider and a plate of light wigs, his favorite biscuit, had been set out for him. Helping himself, he related amusing anecdotes about the English at Spa, a place he'd been supposedly regaining his health. Sir Colin reciprocated by catching him up on their mutual acquaintances here. Relishing the ease he'd not found at home, Evington stretched his legs to the fire. A man of his word, though, he broached the subject of his grandson.

"What's this I hear about Lizzie's boy?"

"What did her ladyship relate?"

"That his guardianship had been challenged, and that he was presently in the West Indies, on some ship or other."

"True enough, as far as it goes. Did she say anything else?"

Evington shook biscuit crumbs off his silk waistcoat. Lewes had an unnerving habit of making his friends occasionally feel as if they were standing before the bar. "That's the gist of it, I believe."

He should have known better than to give Lewes a free rein. He launched into a full legal version of the affair. Did he expect him to hear this through without breakfast? "Yes, yes," Evington interrupted, "all well and good, but what am I supposed to do?"

Sir Collin rubbed his fingertips. "It goes against us that the boy went willingly with his paternal grandfather, my lord. There is a point, though, which can be made, namely that any child, aged seven or more, has the right to name his own curator, if he does not agree with the one specified by the will. I can, and will, argue the boy did not know he had a choice in the matter. A weak argument, admittedly, based on an obscure clause seldom invoked, but nonetheless something upon which to build." Sir Colin leaned closer. "The crux of the matter is, my lord, that we should get the boy home and put the question to him."

"A simple letter requiring him to quit his ship and come back, I suppose?"

"Highly irregular, I fear. No, what I propose is this: he and his ship return to England."

Had everyone gone mad today? "Do you propose I have a King's ship recalled?"

"Precisely, my lord."

Evington wasn't one to use political favors frivolously, and Lewes knew it. Evington abandoned his chair. A signal he wished to go, Lewes summoned a servant and eased his gouty leg so he could stand next to his friend.

"There is another 'alternative,' my lord. One which I think may have already occurred to you. Left to his own devices, it could be three years or more until the boy returns – if ever."

No wonder they were such long standing friends. Evington smoothed his gloves on finger by finger. "I shall consider your proposals carefully."

Lewes bowed. "My lord."

Evington sheltered the rest of the day at the Tuesdays Club, deliberately lingering there until it was time to dress for dinner. His scheme worked. Lizzie wasn't about when he returned.

As his valet prepared his pomade, he focused on the upcoming meeting with the Duke of Portland, or tried. Sir Colin's comments repeatedly broke into his thoughts. Lewes was indeed a devil. How well he knew Lizzie's boy was a constant reminder of his daughter's former disobedience and disloyalty.

Per his instructions, his valet had one of his new Parisian suits waiting on the clothes stand. Evington submitted to having his grey-powdered hair re-dressed into two finger curls and his queue secured with a fresh satin ribbon. He let the valet envelop him in the sheen of an understated green-and-blue-striped silk suit with a high collar and cut away back, matching breeches, and a waistcoat embroidered with restrained flowers and arches, works of art from Monsieur Saulnier's establishment on the rue St. Honoré. Odd, Saulnier had complained of problems with his child. Things were much the same everywhere.

His entourage was as well turned out as he. The lamplighters would be out soon. Above the usual London din, however, raucous shouts caught his attention. Welcoming a diversion, Evington parted the curtains. Two street arabs fought, to the delight of a growing crowd. Although he strained to see better, the pair were indistinct blurs. He let the curtains fall back. For all he could recall of Lizzie's boy, he might well have been one of the rabble.

At Burlington House, a lackey in livery more bullioned than a comic opera general's uniform announced him. His host, William Henry Cavendish Bentinck, the Duke of Portland, waited in his library. The Duke was a heavy man with a double chin. Six years Evington's junior, he was head of the Whigs, or at least as much head as one could be of so diverse a group. Since July, Portland and his secretary, Mr. William Adam, had worked tirelessly planning, organizing, and raising funds for next year's general elections. He was as determined the Whigs should come to power as an indecisive man could be.

"Splendid to have you back, Evington. I trust my invitation wasn't too precipitous? I left Bulstrode solely to speak with you."

Evington bowed. "Your Grace honors me." Had word leaked out about Vienna?

"Not at all, I assure you. I've invited Mr. Burke to dine with us also."

Edmund Burke had once been a Whig chief, an indispensable aide to the Marquess of Rockingham, the previous Whig leader. Since Rockingham's death, Burke's influence had slipped. Evington had been a Rockinghamite. Was his star also declining? These thoughts in mind, he bowed the requisite, "Your Grace."

Mr. Burke was long in coming. Or perhaps it had been planned that way. Over sherry, Portland discussed detailed plans for Leicester's upcoming elections. His county's politics had undergone a decided shift during Evington's absence. John Macnamara was the Whig member for Leicester, and Lorraine Smith the other. Prior to the King's madness and ensuing Regency debacle in 1788, Whigs and non-Whigs, or Tories as they were now more often called, shared the borough's membership. However, both Macnamara and Smith declined to stand for office. Now the Tories wanted both seats, which meant a contentious and expensive election. Portland concluded with, "We need your help, all such favors as you have to call in."

Evington studied the fireplace. Controlling another seat in the Commons would undoubtedly augment his influence. Of the favors owed him, though, only one was capable of influencing local politics to the extent the Duke hinted. Would his reward equal his services?

Burke's arrival postponed his answer and Portland's response. Dinner immediately followed. Five courses attested the Duke's efforts to please: French dishes swimming in piquant sauces washed down with superb wines. One particularly attracted Evington's attention: a magnificent Margaux. This was no ordinary dinner.

Curiously, nothing much transpired over the meal. Burke ranted about Warren Hastings, the former East India Company governor whose impeachment he'd engineered and whose ruin Burke pursued with a vengeance designed to destroy whatever influence the Whigs had left. Portland merely injected a comment here and there. Evington coughed discretely into a gold lace handkerchief, partly from necessity, partly to hide his annoyance with Burke. More and more Evington doubted his political acumen.

Once the cloth had been taken up and sweetmeats and port served, Portland dismissed the servants. Evington calmly sipped his port. Now they'd get down to it.

"Charles James Fox is warm in his praise of the French reformers. Many are warm in their praise of him, both here and abroad. Some more so than others."

Despite his lack of self-confidence and inclination to be too easily swayed by the last opinion he'd heard, Portland was no fool. The Duke's casual comment had a double meaning. Burke's face wore the keenness he usually saved for the Commons. They wanted his opinion on something – badly. Feeling his way, Evington let Portland continue.

"Take the issue of France. Mr. Burke fears the situation there can only deteriorate. That, for all Count Floridablanca's protestations that Spain will come to Louis' aid, should he require it, Louis will fall. Mr. Fox, however, proclaims only good can come of the Assembly's efforts to reshape France. You were there, Evington, what say you?"

Evington finished his port slowly. The real issue, he sensed, was Fox, not France. Fox, who, for lack of anyone more widely known, was to oppose Mr. Pitt in the upcoming elections. They were friends, true, but the point evidently was the degree of friendship. Fox was well known for his liberal views. Evington, on the other hand... He toyed with the empty crystal wineglass. Glassmakers had a way of incorporating intricate design into small space.

"I am as fond of Mr. Fox as any man, save perhaps the King, but not so fond as Prinny."

Portland asked if he'd like more wine. Burke said he hoped to enjoy his lordship's company at the Tuesdays Club again, now that he was back. The answer evidently had been the right one.

The conversation swung back to France, this time in earnest. Edmund Burke repeated his concern that the French were becoming too violent, with a depth and passion Evington grudgingly admired. How had the royal family been forced to Paris? Was there no courage left among the nobles to defend them? Was there none so chivalrous to shield their fair Queen?

"I fear this thing," Burke concluded. "I fear a France become so torn and divided, that it becomes the prey of a dictator."

Ah, if only Burke would forget about Hastings. In the time Evington had left and re-entered France, he, too, had noted a radical shift. The Phalsburg incident, for instance. When he first crossed the frontier, the French soldiers had been polite and properly uniformed. When he'd returned, they'd been sullen and wearing tricolor cockades. That had been after the October Days. Affairs in France had definitely taken a wrong turning. A dictator, though... War, but that was a different matter. War with France, given England's and France's ambitions, was always a possibility.

Exhausted, physically and mentally, Evington took refuge in his cold. The little talking he'd done had left him hoarse and his throat scratchy. Portland insisted on accompanying him to his carriage. Neither spoke until they were outdoors.

"Remember, my lord, that of which we spoke earlier. My gratitude, nay that of the Whigs, will be profusely forthcoming."

Evington inclined his head. His voice might be dulled but not his wits. "Your Grace may count on me to do that which I deem right and proper."

On the drive back, Evington mulled over the evening's conversation. He obsessed over Burke's forebodings. As things presently stood in Europe, England was assured of a continued peace, one which she still needed to completely overcome the debacle of the American War. Austria now was not only in England's corner but much less so in France's. Joseph of Austria also was pre-occupied with the continuing war with Turkey, as was his ally, Russia. And Catherine of Russia was conducting a war against Sweden. Spain, well, she had a weak king, despite a shrewd foreign minister. But France? True, the government presently was in disarray, but things could change. A constitutional monarchy with a weakened king might benefit England—or it might not. Conditions in France rendered her a wild card in the game of international politics and continued peace, at least for the foreseeable future. But then, Evington, thought, shifting in his seat in his carriage, how much of life could one really ever foresee?

The carriage brake grated. He looked up at the windows of Evington House. Lizzie's room was dark. Let sleeping Lizzies lie. He coughed. He couldn't have a ship recalled and do what the Duke asked also. The climb to his door drained him. His most pressing problem at present, he told himself, was rest. Then, and only then, would he consider that certain favor.

Chapter Nineteen

My first encounter with Death taught me that I, not He,
should be not proud.

Evington Papers, 7752/2

"He's not shamming then?" Lieutenant Claverall demanded of
Amphitrite's surgeon.

"I'll write his sick ticket now, if you like."

Claverall sniffed disapproving agreement. The surgeon waited
until he'd left before whisking out a flask. Sick though he was,
Edward knew the contents weren't water.

"Bloody flux, ague – whatever ails you, 'tis too much trouble
for me. Your health, assuming you regain it." His Adam's apple
worked beneath his neckcloth. Wiping his mouth with the back of
his hand, he swayed out of the hold, likely to his cot and a full
bottle.

The loblolly boy, a black signed on at the island of Domenica to
help with the dirty work in sick bay, sympathized, "They fix you up
good at hospital." Edward leaned on him as he rolled out of the
hammock. He let him help him into his sailcloth trousers. When
asked, though, if he needed help getting to the boat, Edward shook
his head. He had his dignity.

The ladders robbed him of his remaining strength. Topdeck, he
tripped over the coaming, the trim around the hatchway. Edward

shakily straightened. No one would see him cringe. Miraculously, the surgeon met him at the gangway and handed him a sick ticket, the form needed to be admitted to hospital. They parted without further comment. The side ropes burned Edward's hands as he slid into the jolly boat. One of the crew caught his thighs and eased him into the stern sheets. The coxswain ordered the boat to push off.

The January day was hazy with light breezes; the temperature pleasant and mild. An ideal day for this climate. Edward only knew he was hot and cold by turns.

The boat glided over the bay to the West Careenage. "This as far as I goes, sir," the coxswain told him gruffly. But he ordered the crew to help Edward out of the jolly boat and onto the wharf, growling, "Mind him well." His face screwed into an approximate of Edward's pain. "I'm sorry, sir," he said and abruptly made for *Amphitrite*.

Edward held himself erect as they shoved off. Sorry. An understatement of how he felt, sorry and miserable. Like the fortifications atop Shirley Heights, the dockyards were being enlarged in anticipation of the next war. Hammering rang from all sides. Edward's head felt as if it were being hammered, too. He staggered the few paces to the Capstan House and rested on a bollard.

Years ago, Admiral Rodney, after watching the sick and wounded drag themselves from the dockyard to Hospital Hill, ordered a cart kept to carry them there. Unfortunately, his successors were not as compassionate.

Edward drew a deep breath and walked unsteadily onward. A little way at a time, that was how he'd get there. His sense of dignity wobbled, as did his knees. He needn't have worried about ridicule. There was no break in the laughter or lilting work songs. When the spell passed, Edward staggered to his feet again. Only the flies buzzing his face noticed him, and a hen which fled clucking out of his way. Sick sailors were no novelty here.

The area past the Capstan House was level, but to Edward every step was an uphill struggle. He willed himself to the Cordage and Canvass store before allowing himself another rest. Between gasps, he charted his course. Skirt the water's edge, the shortest way to the gate. He moved on to such shade as the two-storey working Mast House and Joiners' Loft afforded. Loud swishing and the pungent freshness of wood, rather than sight, told him he'd gained the sawpit.

He rested there until he felt he could manage the next stage. His right hand scraped brick. Red bricks, English bricks from ballast, formed the walls of the dockyard. He was near the gate. Using the wall as a support, he passed under the bell hanging over the passageway.

Thankfully, the wall continued on. It enclosed the engineers' offices. Odors of pitch, tar, and turpentine followed him. With the sentry watching, he retched.

Beyond the dockyard walls, goats and chickens ranged freely in dry ruts. Workers' huts lined the left side of the road. Mongrel dogs stopped panting to bark at him. A brindled mutt with three legs hopped close and snarled. Edward had neither strength nor will to run. Such action proved unnecessary. The beast recognized him for what he was, another pariah.

Step, pause, step; and so Edward reached a fork in the road. Straight ahead lay the small village of Falmouth. To the right, the road made a sharp uphill turn, leading past the old hospital known as the Captain's House and on up to Hospital Hill, where new facilities were being built to house the sick. It was a long, steep trek up Hospital Hill. He licked his cracked lips. He'd try the aging Captain's House instead.

Even trying was difficult. Shaking from chills, weak from fever, he collapsed into the sandy road. He was past caring if anyone aboard *Amphitrite* saw him. Desperation was what now urged him on. He couldn't stay where he was.

The patched sides of the Captain's House glared in the sun. Edward resurrected his former pattern; step, pause step. By concentrating on this alone, his left foot at last made contact with a rung, his right one with the planks of a porch. His arms extended like a blind man's, Edward groped a door handle and collapsed into a room.

"Get out, you!" shouted a female voice.

The interior was dim in comparison to the outside sunlight. It took Edward's eyes time to adjust. When they did, they saw the source of the scolding, a female dressed in grey. When he didn't answer, she grabbed a broom and shook it at him. "Didn't you hear me? Get out!"

"I'm... ill."

"Where's your sick ticket, then?"

Ticket. The surgeon had given him one. Where was it? He felt his pockets. His fingers trembled, not from fever this time but anxiety he'd lost it. No ticket.

The lady waited with her broom. His stomach cramping, Edward clutched his waistband. It crackled. The sick ticket, he'd stuffed it there. He fumbled it loose and offered it to the woman in grey.

"I can't half make out what it says, the ink's that blurred. And Mr. Young gone to St. John's, too. I've a mind to send you back where you came!"

Women were supposed to be kind. Edward raised his eyes to hers. "Please."

The grey lady sniffed. "Boy! Where are you? You lazy thing, come and help."

The "boy" who answered her call was an adult Negro. Edward gratefully staggered after him to the room the lady indicated–until he saw the soiled straw pallets on the floor.

"I'm – a young gentleman."

"You don't look like no young gen'mun I ever did see."

Did it really matter where he rested so long as he did? Edward glanced a second time at the pallets. Yes, it did.

"I tell Miz Leah you won't listen none."

The loblolly boy decamped. Edward first slumped against, then slid down the door frame. He could go no further. In due course, the assistant returned with the nurse. Edward didn't even try to protest when she accused him of causing trouble. Her ill-humor spent, she ordered the black man to take him where he could keep company with another as crazy as himself.

The loblolly boy had to carry him to a secluded room in another part of the building, where he deposited him on a hard, rough plank floor. As he worked into a less uncomfortable sprawl, Edward spied a man covered by a blanket. The face above the blanket was sallow, the beard matted. Insects crawled untroubled over both face and beard. Was this the fate that awaited him?

Edward spoke but got no acknowledgement. The man just lay there. Edward's uneasiness translated itself into another bout of cramping and shivering. The two remained prone on the floor until the loblolly boy returned. He dosed Edward with a bitter drink, Jesuit's bark, he supposed. The loblolly boy then checked the man, shrugged his shoulders, and left.

Capable of little else, Edward drifted from consciousness. When he awoke some time later, frogs were peeping a mournful chorus to the loss of day. Their litany no lullaby, he stirred fitfully. His new position put his companion in plain relief. Far from resting, the man's arms and legs flailed. When Edward faltered, "Are you alright?" the body twisted toward him. Edward watched helplessly as the man went rigid.

What could he do? He had no medical skills, no experience with such emergencies. Urgency gave Edward the strength to prop up on one elbow. He must get help.

He crawled until he could reach his hand upward to the latch. He pushed, but it resisted his efforts. He pushed harder. Nothing. The loblolly boy had locked them in for the night.

He called loudly and repeatedly for help, but no one came. Despairing, he stared at his fellow sufferer. If he couldn't get help, he'd do what he could. He edged to where the man lay and touched his shoulder. He didn't respond. It was dark. The man was still. Edward swallowed hard. He reached out his hand again, but withdrew it before it made contact. Trembling, he forced himself to lay his hand on the man's breast. There was no rise and fall.

If it had been possible, Edward would have crawled out of there. Sweat, cold and profuse, trickled down his forehead, his back, his body. The man couldn't be dead. Hospital was for getting well, not for – The thought finished itself for him. Dying.

They fix you up good at hospital. The words of hope spoken aboard *Amphitrite* had a mocking ring now. Edward recalled another way to tell if someone were alive. He steeled himself to hold his hand, palm downward, over the man's nose and mouth. Although he held it there for what seemed an eternity, not even the slightest hint of air warmed it.

Edward shrank to the furthest corner of the room. He was alone with a corpse. Would his spirit rise to haunt him? No, no, that was just superstition. But the thing in the room was a body now, not a person. A shivering fit overcame him. Asking the dead man's forgiveness aloud, Edward tugged the blanket free.

Clumsily wrapping himself in it, Edward retreated again to the far end of the room. He should have listened to Lieutenant McAllistair and written to his mother, gone home and forgotten the Service. Now he was left to fend for himself with a corpse. At home he had feather beds and crisp linen, hot chocolate served in bed. Servants who called him "Master Edward" not "Mr. Scarecrow." Friends.

Home. Edward closed his eyes. Draperies swished open, letting in golden sunlight. "Good morning, Master Edward, time to rise and dress. I brought some lavender water for you. All the fashionable young gentlemen splash a bit on."

"Do they? I think I'll wear the blue coat today."

"Her ladyship said you was to wear the green, sir, that she did."

"I said I wanted the blue."

"Her ladyship said –"

"Her ladyship said, her ladyship said! Doesn't what I say matter?"

Edward opened his eyes. The alternatives were no less bleak. The miniature. Before he'd gone to sick bay, he'd tied it on a string and hung it around his neck. In Portsmouth, his Uncle Daniel hinted the portrait might prove his talisman. Clutching his father's relic, he vowed he was not going to die. No one was going to take his body to the Dead House, then bury it in an unmarked, sandy grave to be eaten by land crabs.

Focusing on what he believed his father would want him to do, he blocked out both sight and remembrance of the corpse. He'd written another letter to the Commodore before he'd become ill. Perhaps he'd have the answer he desired when he returned to his ship.

Half dozing, half delirious, he passed the night. Never once, though, did he relinquish the miniature. Light suddenly stabbed his eyes. Daylight.

"My God! Who put this boy in here?"

"Miz Leah tell me, Mist Young. He claim he young gen'mun, so she said to put him in with the other crazy."

The white man bent over the body. "Does she give orders here now?" he asked, as he felt for a pulse in the man's neck. "Well, he's not crazy anymore. Fetch Peter and a stretcher. This needs taking to the Dead House."

The man turned his attention to Edward. Desperate to get his story heard, Edward spoke first. "I'm Edward Deveare, *Amphitrite*, a –"

"We'll worry about that later," the man said and began examining Edward. "Our first business is to make you well."

The surgeon, for he was Mr. Young, questioned Edward. He was wrapping up his examination when Peter returned for the body. After the corpse had been removed, Young summoned his assistant surgeon and gave his orders. Edward was moved from the floor onto fresh bedding. Decent food and drink were given him as well another dose of Jesuit's bark. The assistant even had a second blanket brought when Edward asked for one.

His stomach full, his mouth no longer parched, Edward considered the possibilities. He was still sick and weak. Even with two blankets, he shivered. But the corpse, that grim reminder of mortality, was gone. That alone buoyed his optimism. Edward held the picture of his father where he could see it. He'd survived the night; he'd survive this day. And if the Commodore didn't answer his latest letter, he'd write another.

Chapter Twenty

Now conscience wakes despair
That slumber'd, wakes the bitter memory
Of what he was, what is, and what must be.

John Milton, *Paradise Lost*, IV. 23-25

The dream. It grew more vivid as *Liberty* neared England. Jemmy now knew what waited at the top of the hill: the gallows. He dreaded sleep. Had it been possible, he would have stayed awake forever. Other than the winter-tossed seas, though, the voyage from New York to Bristol proved uneventful. From Bristol, Jemmy used what little money he'd earned for coach fare to London. Fearfully, he sought their old room, only to find someone else living there. Was he already too late? Before panic completely conquered him, Jemmy seized on a plan. He'd question their few acquaintances as to his father's and sister's whereabouts. But no one knew where they'd gone.

Street vendors hawked their goods in the sleet, rubbing their rough, red hands for warmth. Jemmy's weathered face didn't draw attention in a land of raw, soot-smudged cheeks. Dad. He had to find Dad. Finally, he found a clue. A man selling apples said Dad told him he was quitting London forever, going home.

Home to Jemmy meant Albury. Was it possible Dad would be so foolish as to return there? Did Captain Finch have a part to play in the dream?

The roads were coated with frozen mud. The languid warmth of the Caribbean would be welcome now. Misery notwithstanding, Jemmy headed down the London Road toward Leatherhead. The closer he came to a place called Dorking, the more mired his feet became. His legs numb from cold and wet, Jemmy had little choice but to shelter there. It was a bad place to stop, for one of the several Portsmouth roads wound through Dorking. Captain Finch might have heard about his desertion from one of his naval friends. Or from Mr. Deveare. He was one of the quality. He might have written to Finch, telling him about Jemmy's desertion. The quality always stuck with one another. Huddled in an outbuilding, Jemmy had no need to fear either sleep or the dream. It was too cold for either.

A steep hill overlooked Dorking on the northwest, part of the North Downs. The land here was hilly, largely heath and bleak woods. The superfine grass, scented with wild thyme and juniper, the scent Jemmy so loved, was absent this time of year. Home and yet not home; Surrey but not Albury; late winter but not spring.

Wishing to be rid of his thoughts and his coldness, Jemmy tramped the rounds of Dorking's public houses in dismal hope Dad hadn't lost his love of drink. Head down, hat in hand, he asked after a carpenter and a little girl. Time and again, the publicans shook their heads. With each try, Jemmy grew more distraught. There were men here who were plainly sailors. Fighting down concern for himself, Jemmy nerved himself for one last try, the Queen's Head on South Street, near the edge of town. This time a patron, not the publican, spoke up. Aye, he knew of a man with a little girl, foreign folk, as what kept to themselves. Jemmy's voice cracked when asked where. Follow South Street, he was told, till it turned into Coldharbour Lane, on a bit, past Hampstead Lane. There was a track leading into the Holmwood, marked by twin live oaks. Their cottage lay beyond.

Jemmy wasn't sparing with his thanks. Enlivened now, he resolutely ploughed through cold mud halfway to his knees until trees replaced fields. The tangled mass of nude branches must be the beginning of the Holmwood. Jemmy slowed now, anxiously checking for the mentioned path. At length he came upon a rutted trail overrun with last year's dead growth. The path. Jemmy paused. Drink or no drink, Dad had never been one to favor secluded places like this. Nevertheless, Jemmy went forward. Perhaps this was the only place Dad could afford. At the end of the path lay a small, weathered cottage. Not as nice as the home they'd once had, but far superior to the London lodging. Smoke curled from a chimney. At least Dad had wood for fire.

There were no chickens or pigs to herald his arrival. Jimmy waited awhile by the door. Should he knock or go straight in? He drew a breath and decided on the latter approach. It was, after all, his home, too, or so he hoped.

Nan noticed him first. Like a dog wagging its tail, she came to him, holding out her arms. He didn't want her, but she hugged his waist before he had time to protest. He looked over her head at Dad. His father had been bent over the hearth, tending a pot. Alerted by his daughter, he straightened. Jemmy waited for him to speak, but he stood mute.

"I, I be back."

"You gave no word."

"I sent message, afore I sailed."

"Only after you'd gone."

"I be back now. To stay."

"In time for supper."

"I'll help, like I did before."

Dad grunted and went back to the pot. Nan began one of her foolish songs. "Jemmy's home, Jemmy's home!" she crooned. How like her to see only the good. Jimmy laid his bundle on the floor and sat down. Dad sharply ordered her to lay a loaf on the table and a bit of cheese. Nan did as she was bid and sat down. Jemmy waited an invitation to sit also, but none came. Would Dad forgive him?

Dad drew a chair to the table and proceeded to slice the loaf. He cut three pieces of brown bread and then three of cheese. He put one of each on earthenware plates and handed them round. Three, not just two. Relieved, Jemmy sat down.

Father and son ate in silence. There was small beer to drink, another sign of renewed prosperity. Nan filled in the silence. She chattered on and on, about how she and Jemmy would play together now he was home. Of the pretty places she'd show him. Jemmy drank his small beer. Nan, at least, hadn't changed. She probably had found new places to stray.

Before retiring to the loft for the night, Jemmy inventoried the cottage. The space downstairs was large, made even larger by a lack of furniture. Also, there were double doors at the back, large enough to drive a hay wagon through, from the look of them. It made the cottage seem like a storage shed.

Dad was already preparing breakfast when Jemmy woke the next morning. Always a hard one to wake, Jemmy nudged Nan with his foot till she stirred. They dressed quickly in the cold and climbed down from the loft.

His back to them, Dad bustled about the hearth. But it wasn't his father's early rising alone which elated Jemmy, it was his clothes. Leather trousers and hobnailed boots, his working attire. He was carpentering again. No wonder there was food. Dad wrapped a towel around a blackened kettle handle, removed it from its trivet over the fire, and poured steamy water into a pot. Tea. Dad must be carpentering for the gentry.

"Where be your rightful things? You lose them time you was gone?"

"This be what I wear board ship."

"This be no ship. Wear what you got, then, till you get better. There's work to be done."

His father hadn't forgotten how to be critical. Subdued, Jemmy turned his attention to the tea. It was strong and bracing. He'd take the bad with the good.

They left the cottage by the front door. Outside, Dad loaded his tools, together with an ax and crosscut saw, into a wheelbarrow and set off down the path. Nan skipped down the path. Jemmy's shoes sank deep into Surrey soil. For the first time in a long time, Jemmy was almost as lighthearted as Nan.

They came to a farmhouse off Coldharbour Lane. The house was dab and wattle, with an orange-red chimney and red tile roof, a comfortable abode. Its tenant awaited them in the farmyard, a plump man clad in coat, muffler, and hat. The muffler was the color of a stonechat's breast. Jemmy hid a smile. The farmer looked like a red-breasted bird on the lookout for a worm.

"Bright and early, and luck to you. Who's come with you this day?"

"My son."

"I never seed him before."

"He be a good worker."

"Looks one. Reminds me of meself when I was young. Finish today, and there'll be extra. I got some hens ready to be et."

Dad had praised him to the farmer. Jemmy's face flushed under its tan.

"More boards by the granary," the farmer said, pointing to a small outbuilding at the end of the yard. "Make it stout. Don't want nobody breaking in."

The granary was small as granaries went. It stood on steddles and had a steep pantile roof at the base of which, a window, one foot by one foot, let in air. Dad told Nan to play with the farm dog, which had approached her, tail wagging. For once, Jemmy didn't mind her not having to work. He was too happy to be carpentering with Dad.

The granary's exterior had weathered to a dark silver grey with black patches here and there. Dad's work was evident; lighter colored boards showed where he'd replaced rotten ones. From what Jemmy could see, all that remained to repair was the door. He and his father mounted four riserless steps. Dad indicated that the rusted iron bands which served as the hinges be removed. He worked the top one loose while Jemmy struggled with the bottom. Rust stained Jemmy's hands the color of dried blood. Eventually both hinges came free.

They laid the door at the side of the granary, where they had more room. No matter the cold, it was good to be next to Dad again, doing honest work. Jemmy began a chantey he'd learned on the merchantman returning to England. Dad looked up when he came to the ribald verses. Jemmy faltered. But when he father managed a tight smile, Jemmy sang on boldly. Nan wouldn't understand.

After he and Dad had mended the door, they lifted it back onto its pins and set it. Dad swung it open and shut. It didn't even creak. Jemmy glowed. It was a job well done.

Dad told the farmer they'd be back for their pay after they'd had dinner. He called to Nan. She raised her head off the black-and-white flank of the farm dog. Both trotted obediently over to him. When they'd emptied the dinner sack, Dad took the wheelbarrow and headed toward a stand of scrub oak and Scottish pine. Years ago, a terrible storm had blown through Surrey, destroying many good trees. Here and there, a few ancient oaks, those which had survived the storm, remained. Thick trunks, whose limbs reached out like arms and fingers and whose roots sprouted more branches, gloried in their endurance. Nan crawled onto a low, u-shaped branch with the same trustfulness she crawled onto their father's lap. She stayed there while Jemmy and Dad gathered fallen branches and twigs, their firewood.

The farmer wasn't in the yard when they returned. Dad strode to the house and knocked on the door to rouse him.

"Tis done well. Two hens for your trouble, as fine as any five-clawed Dorkings in Surrey."

"And brass?'

"Ah, must wait a bit on that."

"But you said –"

"When the road's passable. Can't do much nor make much till then. *You* know that."

Jemmy wondered why his father didn't pursue the matter more forcefully. Two hens made a good dinner, but weren't enough to pay rents.

"Could tar granary for you tomorrow. Don't be wanting rain to spoil what's inside."

"Nor excisemen neither," said the farmer with a wink.

Jemmy gripped the barrow's handle. Excisemen? They hunted smugglers, or countrymen, as the inland runners were called.

"I'll be tarring it tomorrow. Pay in another month?"

"When the roads be dry. Can't say plainer that that."

Mr. Pitt had done much to reduce smuggling, but hadn't succeeded completely. Jemmy understood the newfound prosperity now. The large room and the double doors, wide enough to let in a wagon, a countryman's wagon. Smuggling. The farmer was part of it, too.

The men haggled over some new work. Jemmy clung to their words, struggling to reassure himself he was wrong. He and Dad were just carpenters.

Nan frolicked ahead, her white breath floating in the crisp air. Dad pushed the barrow down the path to the cottage, oblivious – or pretending to be – of the way Jemmy stared at him. As for Jemmy, all he could do was think of the dream.

The gallows and the hill.

CHAPTER TWENTY-ONE

Malbrook goes off to war,
Mirontin, mironton, mirontaine,
Malbrook goes off to war,
Doesn't know when he'll come back again.

"Malbrook Goes Off to War," Old French song

Louis no longer fretted over missing his lectures. He had more important matters on his mind. For one thing, he'd become an intimate of two "bluebellies," members of the Parisian National Guard. Corporal Lecluselle and Sergeant Beldoque also welcomed the changes in France. Louis tried to win them to his position, but of the many mottos current, they favored *la Nation, la Loi, le Roi:* the nation, the law, the King. They, on the other hand, tried to get him to join them. At first, that meant becoming a soldier. More recently, it meant joining them in a venture in the Indies, a partnership with a friend who'd married the daughter of a cocoa planter from Tobago and now owned land in Spanish Trinidad.

For another, he frequented the meetings of the Assembly almost every day. He often saw Bertrand there, although Bertrand seldom saw him. Albertine's cousin, no longer having Louis to give him money for rent and food, now served as secretary to a lawyer named Danton. Citizen Danton kept his secretary on the run.

157

Of all his reasons for avoiding classes, the last was the most telling. He'd sold all his books. Indeed, he'd sold his watches, shoe buckles, linens, etc. This very day, his father's valet was coming to collect more money.

So sure was the devil of his prey that he didn't ask permission to enter. Outwardly indolent, Louis leaned against the window sill. He had waited, planned, for this moment, and now that it had come, he meant to savor it. "I have nothing for you."

"Come, come, what will your father say?"

"Why don't we find out?"

"But – Monsieur Saulnier – he will be angry."

"Will he?" When Jean-Claude Saulnier found out his valet had been blackmailing his son, his immediate target would be the valet. Later... But Louis had thought about that also.

Louis seized the man by his collar. He grimly relished his every cry, his attempts to free himself. Tightening his hold until the man choked for air, Louis rapped once, twice, on the door to his father's sitting room. Whether his father answered him or not, he didn't care. He opened the door and flung the valet into the center of the room.

"What is the meaning of this?" Jean-Claude said, rising from the desk.

"This one has something to tell you."

The valet merely cowered at his feet. "Louis," Jean-Claude frowned, "is this another of your pranks?"

Beldoque had carefully schooled Louis in the particular move he now executed. Louis deftly side-stepped, blocking the valet's access to his father. He regretted not having a musket in his hands, the way they'd practiced. He would have loved to have smashed the man with it. Adapting to the circumstances, he merely spun Joséph to face his master.

"Prank, my father? If there has been one played, then it has been by him. Tell him what you have been up to. Tell him now!"

"Monsieur, please, have mercy! I only asked for a –"

"Liar!" Louis shouted. "He saw me during the October Days, returning from Versailles with the people. Knowing your loyalty to the King, he demanded I pay him my monthly allowance to insure his silence. Each month he asked for more. I sold books, clothes, all I have. But still he threatens. Will you now show mercy to him?"

"You did this?" Jean-Claude said to the supplicant. "This, to my son, when I pay you well, trust you with my confidences? Why didn't you come to me at once, if you saw such things?"

The valet collapsed in a trembling heap. Fiercely elated, Louis would have elaborated on his crimes, but Jean-Claude stayed him. Calm, detached, totally unlike his normal fussy self, his father now commanded his attention. Louis watched him with new feeling, something not unlike respect.

"I will have no traitors here," Jean-Claude said to the prostrate thing on the floor. "Collect your belongings and leave this house." When the servant whimpered, the older Saulnier raised his voice to a volume Louis had never heard him use. "Go! At once!"

The valet scrambled to his feet. He avoided eye contact with his former master but not Louis. A demon could not have appeared more malevolent.

He and his father were alone. Louis had once accompanied Bertrand to court. The magistrate there had just such a look.

Jean-Claude, the self-important "little big shot," faced his son. His tone, when he spoke, was no different from the one he'd used to the valet. "For years I watched you with pride. You were to fulfill my dreams for our house, my son, a noble of the robe. A thing I could not dare for myself. But you scorned the opportunities I gave you, laughed at me behind my back as if I were too stupid to notice. I told Joséph I tolerate no traitors here. So I now tell you."

Had Jean-Claude spluttered, raved, or moaned, Louis would have produced the suitable defense. But this man voiced ambitions never hinted at previously, and for a life other than one simpering to *les grands*, and voiced them with the dignity of a Junius Brutus.

"My father –"

"I have no son."

"It was the servant's fault, not — "

"Did you not hear what I said? Get out! I will have no more to do with you and your ways!"

"You are unjust!"

Jean-Claude silently pointed to the door. Louis tried to protest anew, but the words died on his lips one by one. His father had become a statue of stone.

Dazed, Louis slowly walked by his father. He turned once, in the doorway, to see if he had softened. The statue remained pointing inexorably to the outside world. They were finished as father and son.

Out of sight of his father, Louis struggled to think. Where would he go; what should he do? Albertine was in Orleans ministering to an ailing aunt. Bertrand? He had little, but his little was better than Louis' nothing. Yes, he'd seek out Bertrand, his mentor and friend. Louis hastened to his room, where he grabbed some clothes and a few personal effects and tied them up in one of his university robes. He'd try the Café du Foy first, one of Bertrand's favorite places.

How he arrived there, he'd never recall. When he got there, though, all he found was the usual round of orators, this time declaiming the inevitability of war between England and Spain over the seizure of English merchantmen trading in Spanish-claimed territory in some far place. One sprang onto a table and shouted, "Citizens, have you heard? The King declares war without the people's consent!"

"To the Assembly," roared others in the crowd.

Louis blindly followed. Bertrand might be there. Column shadows striped the brightly lit pavements underneath the galleries surrounding the gardens. Demoiselles in flowing white gowns with red, white, and blue ribbons adorning curved waists promenaded the gardens and arcades of the Palais-Royal. Good citizenness whores.

Louis's mind recovered another cog. Marie-Rose worked in Belanger's lace shop in one of the wooden arcades of the Camp de Tartares. The shop was nearby. He'd spurned her previous attempts at reconciliation. Perhaps... He stiffened. He'd not go begging.

Liberty trees bloomed on the rue Saint-Honoré. Both the living sort and poles fluttered red, white, and blue streamers on both sides of the street. What must his father think of the travesty? The Monastery of the Jacobins, the meeting place of the Society of the Friends of the Constitution, the new club to which Bertrand belonged, was on the right. The Tuilleries gardens where the Assembly met lay just ahead.

A month after the people forced the royal family from Versailles, the Assembly moved to Paris. The riding ring in the gardens had been converted into a political ring with wooden risers erected for spectators. Louis scanned the area. Many of the Assemblymen still wore colorful, stylish clothes made by men like his father. Others wore the more virtuous, but still fashionable, black. Louis searched for Bertrand.

The ongoing debate was amusing, as well as enlightening. Assemblymen, some pompous *aristos* turned would-be citizens, hired actors to instruct them in declamation. Such a one now argued that the Family Compact, the alliance of a Bourbon of France with a Bourbon of Spain, had no meaning for the new France.

At last, Louis spotted Bertrand. He sat above and to the right of the President's chair, where he had a good view of the proceedings. Louis gained his side as another speaker shouted, "Fourteen ships-of-the-line readied? And who will pay for them? The people!"

"Bertrand –"

Albertine's cousin pinched his arm. "Shh. De Lameth speaks next."

Bertrand, preferring the words of an *aristo* to his? Louis deliberately raised his voice. "Bertrand, I have –"

"Enough! Can you not see the fate of France, of the people, hangs in the balance?"

"I hear only the filth of *ci-devants,* of a count, a duke, and a baron, who –"

Jean-Louis Reubell spoke. "Let France be above deceits and avarice. We press onward to the golden age! What is another Bourbon king to us? In the future, let us recognize as allies only those peoples who are just. We no longer wish to have anything to do with dynasties or ministerial wars, conducted without the nation's consent but at the cost of the nation's blood and the nation's gold. Let all men embrace each other as brothers!"

Bertrand was on his feet with the rest, cheering. Louis agreed in principle with what had been said. But it had been said by an *aristo,* and Bertrand extolled him.

"He is a fool – and so are you!"

"But why?"

"No true Frenchman wishes for peace with England."

"Do you think you are the only 'true Frenchman?'"

"Yes!" Louis shouted, to the annoyance of those near. Braving a mountain of knees, he abandoned Bertrand to his folly.

Louis had done what he once claimed was impossible, quarreled with his idol. The Tuilleries' gardens possessed form but not beauty. Couples strolled apart. Life had come to have the taste of sour wine.

Louis damned his father's stubborn adherence to the King and Bertrand for abandoning their commonly held ideals. His father. Had he shown such sensibilities before they might have been friends, despite their opposing political views. The rue de Bac ended at the rue de Grenelle. Louis turned right. The Hôtel des Invalides loomed ahead, the establishment for wounded and disabled soldiers. An old man, crutches thrust under both armpits, swung along. His clothes befitted a decayed corpse, as did his body.

An open space, the fields of the Champ de Mars, beckoned. The École Militaire, the military academy, where aristocrats trained to be officers, lay at the far end. Cadets drilled and paraded on the field, a younger version of the National Guard. Doting mothers and fathers watched them; smaller brothers and sisters marched alongside. The cripple cried, "These are the glory of France!"

The "glory of France" included many whose fathers were *aristos*, like La Fayette. Self-assured in fine uniforms, Louis had little trouble picking them out. The National Guard, young and old, was just a club for *aristos* and propertied men. Citizen soldiers, that's what France needed, brave, sensible men, like, like...

Beldoque and Lecluselle. They stood at the far end of the field. A Guards officer in uniform accosted them. The pantomime being played out at a distance did not favor the *aristo*, though. The officer put his hand on his sword. People nearby assumed threatening postures. The officer backed off.

It was the tonic Louis needed after the day's disasters. He eagerly sought his friends. Lecluselle embraced him. He'd been frequenting the *guinguettes* of Belleville from the smell of his breath.

Beldoque, too, smelled of cheap wine. "Today we celebrate; tomorrow we depart; afterwards, we become rich men. Come, partake of our good fortune."

"Before you are taken and shot?"

"One must first be a soldier to be court martialled. We are simple citizens."

"You deserted, then, Beldoque?"

"No," Lecluselle said. "Resigned"

"Fortune awaits us!" Beldoque shouted.

"Where is this 'Fortune' of which you speak? Belleville?" He found himself marching with them.

"Hear him! He deserves to be made a general," Lecluselle said.

"A marshall, at the very least." Beldoque began to sing, "Malbrook goes off to war."

Lecluselle provided the chorus. "Mirontin, mironton, mirontaine."

"Where do we go?" Louis had to shout to be heard above their off-tune, in-step melody.

"Malbrook goes off to war." Beldoque kept to the lyrics.

"I want to know where!"

"Trinidad. I told you last week. You are out of step."

"What!"

"Malbrook goes off to war." Beldoque began anew.

"You can't mean that!"

"Mirontin, mironton, mirontaine." Lecluselle picked up where he'd left off.

"But it is so far —"

"Malbrook goes off to war."

"Doesn't know when he'll come back again," finished Lecluselle.

"The money for the passage?" Louis no longer marched out of step.

"A loan from a comrade. We will ask more for you."

The song was a good one. Louis began the verse. "Malbrook goes off to war."

"Mirontin, mironton, mirontaine," chanted Beldoque and Lecluselle.

"Malbrook goes off to war."

"Doesn't know when he'll come back again!"

"Doesn't know when he'll come back again," Louis echoed. But then, did it matter? He'd cut all his ties. If he could not support the revolution here, he'd spread its precepts abroad. And who knew, perhaps there really would be war, against the English, which suited him well. As for Bertrand and his peace? Bah! What was peace, if not prelude to war?

CHAPTER TWENTY-TWO

I am tied to th' stake, and I must stand the course.

William Shakespeare, *King Lear,* III.vii

The February day was cloudy with gales. *Amphitrite* had weighed anchor and sailed around noon. Working her way under double-reefed topsails and courses to Nevis, she reached Charleston Bay around half past one PM and came to anchor with her small bower in five fathoms. At present, she stood off from Nevis, close hauled on a starboard tack.

Edward speculated on which was worst: being sick in hospital or being semi-well and aboard ship. He'd languished in the Captain's House at English Harbor for nearly a month. Even though the surgeon, Mr. Young, had transferring him to better quarters on top Hospital Hill, Edward's recovery hadn't satisfied either of them. Two weeks ago, Captain Neville insisted Edward be returned to duty, and Young had to comply.

Off duty and about to go below, Edward heard the lookout cry, "Sail ho!"

"Where away?" hailed the officer of the watch.

"Fine on the starboard bow, sir."

"How do you make her?"

"Half hour distant, at most."

Edward studied the ship. From her outline, she looked to be a frigate. Neither *Maidstone* nor *Sybil* presently cruised this far north, and if Commodore Parker had any messages to send, he'd do so via a tender. Could she be a Spaniard?

"Clear out, Scarecrow. I want my view unimpeded – by boobies."

Hallard was trying to goad him into a fight in front of the officers. Edward disappointed him, and them, by going below.

Mason and Grog were the only ones in steerage. Mason slumped in a chair doing nothing; Grog mended a shirt. Propped against the berth's canvass side were the single sticks used in fencing practice, ready for small arms practice later. Edward skirted wet cable. He could take refuge here only for a little while. He had the next watch.

"Jeff, don't you think the Scarecrow looks a little pale? Like he needs some exercise to get his color back?"

Edward looked up to see Hallard, with Fordyce behind him. They had followed him below. The master's mate shoved him into Fordyce, who shoved him back again. Edward banged against the berth's doorway, only to be knocked back into play by Grog. Mason joined him.

Edward fell sideways onto the cable. In his attempt to rise, the miniature fell out of his coat. All these months, he'd kept it hidden. He desperately wanted to keep it so, but Mason grabbed it.

"Give it back."

Mason showed it to Hallard. He smiled, "Your 'Captain' father, Scarecrow?"

Edward breathed hard. He was weak. They knew it; he knew it. Even if he fought to regain the miniature, what good would it do? He'd be finished.

"How much do you think we'd get if we pawned it?" Fordyce asked.

"Why don't we just smash it?"

"Good one, Mason," said Hallard. "Care to watch, Scarecrow?"

It was the only thing Edward had of his father. But if he fought –

Mason laid the miniature on the deck. Edward hurled himself against him, knocking the bulky mid off balance. Edward lashed out with his fist. Mason's head swiveled. Edward hit him again.

"Give it to him!"

Mason rallied at Hallard's cry. Edward danced out of reach. Who had the miniature now? He tried to grapple Mason, but a terrific force smashed his nose.

"Get him! Get him!"

A second blow caught Edward on the side of his face. He fell over the cable. It was only a matter of time, but he'd fight to the last. Then Mason did something unfair, ungentlemanly – and inexplicable. He grabbed one of the single sticks.

The possibilities. Edward had a chance, now, if only a slim one. The husky reefer swung viciously. Thinking quickly, Edward circled, dodged – and snatched a single stick.

Whatever he did, it had to be done quickly, for even with single sticks the odds favored his stronger and healthier opponent. Intent on lulling Mason into a false sense of confidence, Edward thrusted, parried, then fell back. Overconfident, Mason moved in too fast and too carelessly. With all the force he could muster, Edward rammed his stick into Mason's middle. Wood clattered onto wood. Mason's single stick fell to the deck, Mason after it. Edward threw himself on top him, searching for the miniature.

"Looking for this, Scarecrow?"

Hallard must have retrieved the miniature during the scuffle. Edward rolled off Mason.

"Mr. Fordyce, Mr. Hallard! Return to your stations immediately, sirs!"

Fordyce and Hallard lost no time obeying Mr. Reynolds' order. Four rungs up the ladder, though, Hallard turned around. "Here. Take it. It will look good at your flogging."

Edward caught the precious miniature. His possibilities run out, he now was free to say what he felt.

"Go to hell!"

CHAPTER TWENTY-THREE

He's the damnedest thing I've ever clapped eyes on.

Private letters, by permission of Sir Reginald Pearse, Bart

Left hand on hip, legs wide, Captain Richard Pearse surveyed the progress from his quarterdeck. The foretopmen had furled the royals and topgallants on all masts, clewed up the fore, main, and mizzen courses, and shortened other necessary sail. In compliance with his signal, the vessel to larboard backed her topsail. Pearse approved *Amphitrite's* smart handling.

Blanche coming up fast on *Amphitrite's* weather bow, he turned to his first lieutenant. "Brace up the main and mizzen topsails, Mr. Stark, and see to it the lee fore yardarm is hauled aft. When the people have completed this, hoist out the large pinnace by the boom." Pearse disliked having to spell things out, but he had little choice with Stark.

Mr. Stark touched his hat and bawled, "Make ready to brace aback! Weather main, lee cro'jack braces!" Manning the braces, the ropes two per yard rove through blocks stropped to the yards which controlled the movement of the yardarms, the people hauled hand-over-hand, bringing the main and mizzen yards almost square with the mast. With a thunderous crack, the topsails flattened against the masts, and *Blanche* lost way.

Pearse preferred bracing the mizzen with the main, although man-o'-war fashion bracing the main was considered sufficient–

and elegant–enough. He'd found doing the two together lessened the ship's lurch to leeward, and *Blanche*, needing an overhauling of her stern caulking, required all the assistance he could give her.

Satisfied he'd done all he could to match the handling of the smaller frigate, Pearse waited until the orders "Away aloft!" and "Lay out!" had been given and executed, meaning the men were spaced at regular internals on the yards, ready to rig the tackles and hoist out the ship's boat. Pearse didn't stay to see it through. Instead, he used the time to visit his cabin.

He tossed his new bicorn, the one upgrade to his existing uniforms, onto the desk in the fore cabin and sat down. Before him lay packets of letters and news sheets. Separate from these were two individual letters. One was from the Admiralty, addressed to Captain Hidcote Neville; the other, from Commodore Parker. The top drawer contained the Admiralty orders he'd received after obtaining his commission, namely Orders 20, 34, 48, 53, and 54. The first two required he carry Mr. Venour of the Royal Academy and Captain Collins, who was to assume command of *Jupiter*, Commodore Parker's flagship, to the Leeward Islands. Order 48 authorized him to receive fourteen days' spirits in addition to his other stores. Orders 53 and 54 respectively dealt with his proceeding to the Leeward Station and placing himself under the command of Commodore Parker, the commander-in-chief there. All done in neat clerical script, all duly signed Chatham, Hopkins, and Hood: the First Lord of the Admiralty and two Admiralty lords. All addressed to Richard Pearse, Esq., Capt., *Blanche*, Spithead. Routine stuff, but none of it explaining why he'd been sent out to replace a ship lately come on station.

Not that he wasn't glad to have a commission again after three years and seven months on half-pay. Life had gone from meager to pinched. He balked at touching the little money he'd invested, refusing to spend what he'd set aside to buy a property. The day would come, and none too soon, when he and his cousin, Peggy, would marry.

The events surrounding his new command had been strange. Admiral Hood, recently appointed to the Admiralty board, had offered *Blanche* to his friend, Samuel Pearse. Samuel Pearse had declined the commission but indicated his nephew, Richard, was in need of employment. That much had been straightforward enough. As had Richard Pearse's command, which lay at Portsmouth. A new ship, *Blanche* was one of the projects of the

Comptroller of the Navy, Sir Charles Middleton, built in '86 at Burleson but rotting in ordinary ever since, like so many other King's ships. Her fitting out, however, had been rushed. Poor *Blanche* had been sent off quicker in peace than Pearse had seen ships go out in war, and her seams were inadequately caulked.

Rear Admiral Sir John Laforey had been in Portsmouth in December. Laforey had recently been knighted and made rear admiral of the blue. He'd received orders to hoist his flag aboard HMS *Trusty*, ready his ship and squadron, and then proceed to the Leewards to relieve Commodore Parker. Pearse and Sir John had dined together on several occasions. At first Sir John, trying to get over a sore throat and grumbling about having to repeatedly petition the Admiralty to stay ashore long enough to recover, had also grumbled about Pearse's preceding him and the squadron on station. Pearse had some hard wooing of his admiral-to-be. Luckily, Sir John regained his health and temper before Pearse sailed. This, together with some excellent dinners at Pearse's expense, had helped convince Laforey *Blanche's* captain knew as little of the reason for his ship's hasty departure as did Sir John.

Yet what was the reason? Via Portsmouth gossip, Pearse heard Neville had made many enemies, from the dockyard contractors he'd accused of thievery to the new port admiral, Vice Admiral Robert Roddam, whom he'd harassed with complaints. Given Neville's quick recall, probably someone high up in the Admiralty as well. Having had his own skirmishes with contractors, Pearse sympathized with Neville.

Whatever the reason, here he was, ready to deliver the letter ordering Neville home, per Commodore Parker's order. Arrived at English Harbor 24th February, Pearse found Parker and *Jupiter* anchored there. He'd manned the yards and saluted the Commodore with thirteen guns, being returned eleven. Aboard *Jupiter*, Parker also had done his share of wondering. Despite his protestations, the Commodore ordered him to intercept *Amphitrite. If your pumps worked to such good effect sailing in winter, you may make these last leagues as well.* Pearse could hardly wait for Laforey to replace Parker.

Pearse took out his watch. The pinnace should be ready by now. He gathered up his hat and the Admiralty order. He was almost to his door, when he remembered that other letter. He doubted he'd need it, but he fetched it anyway.

"Mr. Stark."

"Sir."

"Directly I board *Amphitrite,* head round and get on her lee quarter. I do not desire the men row back in this wind."

"Aye, aye, sir."

Pearse paused just long enough to acknowledge being piped over the side. As soon as his coxswain saw him in place, he shouted, "Cut the painter!"

The ropes securing the boat fore and aft to the ship were thrown down; a man forward caught them, coiled them, and stored them. Facing forward, Pearse was all affability. His boat crew were rigged in their best. White hats announced the ship's name in large gold letters on a red band. Their blue jackets were waist length, duck, double-breasted with brass buttons, under which they wore white waistcoats with open neck white shirts. Red silk scarves, white duck trousers, white stockings, and black canvass shoes completed their outfits. The hats, shirts, and scarves he'd provided; the rest were slops' make-overs. Not as good as he'd have had them with a little prize money under his belt, but respectable enough.

Pearse spread the mantle of his satisfaction over his aide, Mr. Trewethey. "While I meet with *Amphitrite's* captain, you may palaver with the reefers. Just stand ready, as our stay will likely be a short one." Given the news he brought, it couldn't be anything else.

Pearse was more than satisfied with his choice of mids. Trewethey was his best friend's son. Serious, dedicated, and a damned fine hand. At the other end of the spectrum lay Barnes and Farnsworth, graduates of the Naval Academy at Portsmouth, Admiralty appointees. Not his choice, but he'd had to take them, chock a block with reefers though he already was. Their many pranks were worthy to earn them engraved seats at the crosstrees, were such a thing possible. No Honorables or Right Honorables, though, thank God. The only fault he found with his admiral-to-be was Sir John's tendency to ship too many of those. Since the King had sent one of his younger sons to sea, the Service had become an acceptable dumping ground for the jetsam of the gentry and aristocracy. Let the Guards or some other regiment take them, and good luck to them.

Mr. Trewethey struggled with his hat. His friend had a son of whom he was justly proud. A son. Pearse looked seaward. One day, he'd have a son in the stern sheets with him.

After the hail, "Boat ahoy," and his coxswain's two fingers held high and answering, "Aye, aye, *Blanche*" the side boys threw down ropes covered in green cloth, a captain's prerogative.

He timed his ascent with the cresting of a wave, thereby gaining the highest possible rung and a shorter climb. At the break of the bulwarks, he was greeted as he should be: the steady-rise-steady of the bo'sun's mate's call; the marines in red stiffly at attention; the side boys in everyday dress not so stiffly at attention; and a trim midshipman of the watch hat in hand.

Fifteen years at sea, man and boy, had taught Pearse to notice much in little time. The sanded white decks underneath the awnings were commendable. Brass fittings and iron cannon fittings gleamed. Ropes neatly stowed. The people went about their work in an orderly way, no shouting and re-shouting of orders by bo'sun's mates or midshipmen. Everything on board *Amphitrite* was as it should be. Odd someone had requested a transfer from such a smart ship.

Pearse was about to proceed to the quarterdeck when he caught the one anomaly in the otherwise perfect turnout. A ship's boy by the look of his checked shirt and trousers, held something protectively with one hand; the other hand was cupped to his nose. The boy, suddenly aware of his scrutiny, grabbed his hat with his right hand, the one sheltering his nose. In that second, Pearse noted two things he'd missed: the hat the boy respectfully removed was a midshipman's cocked hat and the nose from which he'd removed his hand bled.

"Welcome aboard, sir. I'm John Claverall, senior lieutenant, and this is Mr. Reynolds, our junior. This way, sir, if you please. Captain Neville awaits you."

Pearse turned his attention to a top-hampered officer wearing Frenchified epaulettes. So this was the captain he was replacing. He vastly preferred the scruffy mid.

"Who are you, sir, and where are you bound?"

"Richard Pearse, *Blanche*. Leeward station."

"This station? How so? The new squadron isn't due yet."

"I'm here because their Lordships saw fit to send me."

Neville frowned. "A fifth rate. Just."

"I find thirty-two guns sufficient," Pearse said coldly. "If you please, sir, I have something for you from their Lordships."

Captain Neville accepted the offered letter. Checking the wax seal, he said, "Join me over a glass. You can enlighten me on happenings in England."

"I'm a poor speaker."

"Do you disdain my hospitality, sir?"

Not wanting to make a scene in front of *Amphitrite's* officers, Pearse stiff-kneed it down the ladder. Neville's day cabin was similar to his, only smaller. It had cannon on either side, stained paneling which could be quickly removed, salt-encrusted stern windows. Office and day cabin ran together. The resemblance ended there. The deck was covered by sailcloth painted checkerboard fashion. A thick, patterned carpet lay over it, the kind imported from the East, and the stern cushions had leather covers. While Pearse sat down, Neville removed a weighted brandy decanter from a silver tray and poured two glasses.

"Your health, sir."

Pearse raised his glass and sampled the brandy. Neville knew his spirits. Savoring it and a second glass of brandy, Pearse thawed. "Much the same about the upcoming elections and France. As for the dons, some say it might mean war."

"The Government anticipates war with Spain?"

War meant prize money and promotions, but Pearse had another reason for wanting it. Assigned to the home fleet in '79, he well remembered how a Franco-Spanish armada had sailed the English Channel unopposed that summer. Out here, the French had picked off British possessions one by one until Rodney, with Hood and Sam Pearse under him, had stopped them at the Saints in '82, preventing the fall of Jamaica. Pearse ached to settle old scores.

"Possibly." Pearse relished the brandy's silky fire. Damned fine stuff, he'd ask its source. Then Neville opened the Admiralty letter. Pearse had seen hanged men with less purpled faces.

"By the God of War! You laid your plans well – a larger ship and my place!"

"I was offered a commission, and I took it. Nothing more."

"I would I could wish you well, but from what I can see, such a thing is impossible. You handle your ship poorly."

Men called each other out for less. *Blanche* didn't answer the helm as readily as she might because of her taking in water, but she wasn't crank nor was he inept. Pearse groped for a suitable insult. There wasn't much he'd seen to *Amphitrite's* detriment, except –

"I suppose all your young gentlemen go about poorly clad and brawling?"

"What? Poorly clad, fighting, you say? By God, I have him!" *Amphitrite's* captain hurried to his cabin door and flung it open. "Pass the word for Mr. Deveare," he shouted at the marine on duty. "And be quick about it!"

Pearse rued his pettiness. The youngster in question had probably been in a normal below deck scuffle. His bloody nose might or might not be noticed by the lieutenants. He might or might not otherwise have been punished for fighting. Now there'd be no question of it.

"Despite your scheming to supplant me, Captain, you've done me a good turn."

Pearse doubted he'd ever loathed himself as much as he did this moment. "I'll be going, if –"

"You pity him? Ah, but you don't know the whole of the matter. This creature was thrust upon me at the last minute. I injudiciously owed his wine merchant father money for spirits I purchased for this voyage and one other. He and another of the tribe accosted me at Portsmouth, threatening me with debtor's prison if I didn't take the boy. Ashore, this scoundrel was a troublemaker unwanted by his family. He joined my ship in rags, his face bruised from fighting. Afloat, he has proven himself incompetent at every turn. His own mess turned him out. Oh, how I've waited, but now I have him!"

If the boy were as bad as he were presented, why had Neville waited so long to punish him? It didn't make sense. But before Pearse could do or say anything else, *Amphitrite's* captain roared, "Come!"

Light outlined the slight figure who now wore a shabby facsimile of a uniform, "You wished to see me, sir?"

He spoke as respectfully as any officer could wish. Close up, Pearse saw he wasn't just thin, he was gaunt, his cheeks hollow. The lighting wasn't the best, but even a skylight couldn't yellow a tan that way. He was or had been ill. This Mr. Deveare had an unusual dignity, though, rare in one so young, for Pearse put his age at thirteen or thereabouts. He studied him carefully for signs of sullenness or aggression, the trademarks of a brawler but found none. Nor did the boy cringe or fawn. Pearse would wager a year's pay Mr. Deveare hadn't started the fight.

"Get over there, by the windows, where I can see you better!"

Neville herded the youngster to the stern windows, where he twisted his face to the light. Mr. Deveare stoically endured the manhandling.

"Bruises! Here," Neville indicated the boy's cheekbone, "and here, around your eye! You've been fighting, haven't you?" He yanked the boy's chin free.

Strands of dark hair straggled over the thin face. The boy tried to smooth them with his right hand, but it convulsed. Mr. Deveare clamped it to his side. "I don't deny it, sir."

"D'you remember what I told you? What I'd do, if you gave me cause, damn you?"

Had he been dealing with a drunken, mutinous fo'c'slman, such actions and language might have been appropriate, but not with a sick child. Pearse tensed as Mr. Deveare let go his afflicted arm. The boy squared his shoulders and raised his head. Pearse recognized the gesture for what it was. He'd nailed his flag to the mast, determined to go down with all colors flying, God help him for it.

"You told me you'd flog me, sir."

Poor youngster. His bottom bared and whipped, publically humiliated for all to see.

"Having you seized to a grating wasn't all of it. Say it! Now!"

"Flogged and dismissed the ship. That's what you said, sir."

It took several moments for Pearse to comprehend what he'd heard. Flogged, like a common sailor? Even a boy's cat, hurled with the force of a mate's arm, would stave in those frail ribs, the child then left to fend for himself out here as best he could. The man was mad! And it was his fault. He'd brought the matter to Neville's attention. Impossible to undo what he'd done; the boy was *ultra vires*, beyond his power or right to interfere. Bringing charges against Neville for cruelty wouldn't save the boy either. In despair, Pearse looked away. On the table lay the Admiralty letter. Letters! It must have been Mr. Deveare who'd petitioned Parker to leave this ship. Pearse pushed between him and Neville.

"By the God of –"

B. N. Peacock

Wishing each word had been the stroke of a cat, Pearse snapped, "The God of War be damned! The youngster requested a transfer, and Commodore Parker approved it. Mr. Deveare, fetch your chest. You're coming with me, sir, aboard *Blanche*."

177

CHAPTER TWENTY-FOUR

...the Captain is not most; he is <u>ALL.</u>

Evington Papers, 7755/2

There was no doubt whom Edward wanted to obey. But his fate wasn't settled yet.

The two officers squared off. Neville stepped forward, but a sharp quarter turn of the stranger's head checked him. Edward fully expected him to strike the stranger. All he did, though, was bluster and demand to see the order.

The other captain didn't reply. Was there really a transfer, Edward worried? Slowly, the visitor reached into his coat and produced a sealed sheet of paper. He extended it to Neville – who let it drop to the deck.

"Pick it up, Mr. Scarecrow."

Five months of man-o'-war discipline had conditioned Edward to obey. Yet picking up the paper meant more than following a simple directive. Obey and he yielded to Neville's authority in every point, down to flogging and dismissal. Refuse and – He searched the stranger's eyes.

"Get your chest, youngster."

Quiet words of command and corroboration, Edward needed nothing more. Before either captain could change his mind, he rushed out of the captain's cabin before he could wake up. Going down the main ladder, he blundered into Knoles.

"My chest," Edward said. "Help me get it."

Whether he was on duty or not, the topman followed him down two ladders. He hurried forward, however, when they reached steerage. Left alone, Edward faced his berth's occupants. Mason sulked in the farthest corner of the hatchway berth. Grog sat mute at the table. For once, they let him be. Edward threw his odds and ends into his chest. The banging lid prefaced his parting remarks.

"You're nothing but a set of mean-spirited cowards. I hate you all!"

He trusted Knoles to get his chest. No shivering or spasms assailed him as he sped up the ladders. Above decks, he hurried just short of running to where the visiting ship's people congregated. Hallard, Fordyce, and a midshipman who'd come over from the other ship chatted at the break of the quarterdeck, aft the entry ladder. Hallard broke off at the sight of him.

"Here he is in the flesh. All set to get a checked shirt at –"

"Get about your business!"

It was Edward's new captain. Edward had never seen Hallard remove his hat so fast, not even for Neville, or get out of the way so quickly either. Hallard, however, wasn't the only one who moved fast. Knoles swayed up with Edward's chest and set it down near the gangway.

"I – here," he said, whipping off his cap. "This is for you, Mr. Deveare."

Knoles thrust a small, canvas package at him. Edward stared stupidly at what had been placed in his hands. Before he could either refuse or thank Knoles, the foretopman ducked out of the way of the visiting captain and Edward's life.

"Mr. Trethewey, into the boat. You, too, youngster."

Everything happened quickly. The captain ordered his boat crew to hand down Edward's chest. Package in hand, Edward went in next, then the other midshipman. Edward regretted not being able to say good-bye to his messmates, but that was his only regret. The boat barely rocked when his new commander took his place in the stern sheets. The painters collected, the men nearest *Amphitrite's* lee side pushed off. Then it was "Down oars!" and pulling hard.

B. N. Peacock

Never would he look back. Edward focused on his new companions. The mid who'd conversed with Hallard sat thwart-ships; Trewethey, that's what the Captain had called him. In all that had happened, Edward realized he hadn't caught his new captain's name. The officer was giving him a quizzical sidelong glance. Edward hoped he didn't regret taking him.

They gained *Blanche* without further incident. Before disembarking, Edward fumbled the package in his hand. He recognized the shape at once: Knoles's razor.

"Mr. Trethewey, take Mr. Deveare to the larboard berth and get him settled. Then bring him to my cabin."

"Aye, aye, sir."

Trewethey dropped into the waist and summoned a seaman to carry Edward's chest. Edward looked around as he followed the mid. By her waist alone, *Blanche* was the larger ship: three hatches, one large and two small, between her main and foremasts to *Amphitrite's* one. Aloft, the coxswain and part of the boat crew manned the tackles on the main yardarm. The rest of the boat crew stayed in the pinnace and secured the falls. *Blanche's* crew hauled in the ship's boat in no time. His new ship didn't equal *Amphitrite* for smartness, Edward exulted, she surpassed her.

He and Trewethey descended the largest hatchway to steerage. Below, twin berths decorated with painted canvass flanked either side of the ladder, the larboard one gaudy with the ship's name and crossed swords. The seaman dropped his chest while the available members of both berths watched. Not wanting to admit his poverty, Edward resorted to a half truth. "I'll give you your shilling when I get my next draft." God only knew when that would be, but it saved face. The sailor gone, Edward cracked the lid and stuffed the razor inside.

Four youths, two from each berth, met them. Trewethey did the introductions. "This is Mr. Deveare. He's joining us from *Amphitrite*. Deveare, that's Thad Cowdrey, junior master's mate, and Gustavus Willoughby, gunner's mate. They're in the starboard berth." Stripped to a reasonably clean shirt and trousers, Cowdrey had a well-proportioned body and a handsome, ruddy face. He gave Edward the once-over, shook hands, and returned to his berth. Willoughby came next, a round head on a rounder body encased in a dingy shirt and jean trousers. His outfit was almost, but not quite, as bad as Edward's. Edward mentally sketched him

181

as a cannonball with arms and legs. The Cannonball pumped his hand.

"Hard up? A true reefer! I'd help you if I could, but I blew what I had left at Barbados. Won't get more from Pater, not for ages."

Trewethey motioned toward a boy with an irrepressible light in his eyes, "That's Barnes," he said, "and Farnsworth," indicating a tall boy with a broad face and a streaky blond nest. The omission of first names, together with hairless chins, marked them as youngsters.

Farnsworth stared at Edward's chest. "Anything to eat in there?"

"He's a pig!" Barnes said. "See those rules stuck to the door? All the ones about eating out are because of him."

"Pity they put you in with the young crowd," the Cannonball interposed, "though from the looks of it, you're younger still. Do you mind if I call you Ned? I've a cousin in the artillery by that name. You remind me of him."

"No," Edward said, relishing being called something other than Scarecrow. "Not at all."

"Come along, Deveare," Trewethey said. "The pu'sser's cabin is just here. He'll issue you hammocks and bedding as well, since you don't seem to have brought any with you."

Edward's new messmates returned to their table and its stack of books and papers. Instead of getting down to work, however, they began a game of able whackets, a card game where the loser was penalized by being whacked with a sock filled with sand on the backs of his hands. Yes, he was going to like it here.

The pu'sser's cabin was forward the reefers' berths. Trewethey's knock on the wooden frame went unanswered. Privacy a scarce commodity aboard ship, Trewethey maneuvered Edward into a recess the other side of the canvass wall.

"I heard about you, Mr. Scarecrow," he said, so low only Edward could hear. "But since I value the Captain's opinion, I'll say nothing to the others. I'm warning you, though, don't try any of your tricks here, or I'll be the first to inform Mr. Stark."

He should have expected as much. "I judge others by their own words and actions," Edward said, "not by another's slander."

Trewethey sniffed. In silent disapproval, he herded Edward to the Captain's door.

For the second time that day Edward found himself in the unfamiliar territory of a captain's cabin. On entering, he moved to what appeared to be an office. Two curved swords and a musket hung on the raised wood panels above the door to a larger space. Edward glimpsed part of a dining table, stern windows, and cannon beyond it. In the office itself, a gun was lashed sideways to its port. The foot of the mizzen mast lay across from it, in front of which a drop-front desk hosted two Windsor chairs. His new captain sat in one of them, directly underneath the skylight.

"Welcome aboard, Mr. Deveare." He pointed to the other chair. "All settled in?"

"Yes, sir." Edward sat next him. No need to trouble the Captain about his bedding.

"Good. I'll not keep you long as you're no doubt anxious to give us a look over. I generally like to know a bit about my young gentlemen before taking them on. In your case, I've taken you on, and now must find out about you."

Edward wanted the truth known – but not all. No one had asked him about himself aboard *Amphitrite*. Old Ramillies Wig probably had supplied Neville with whatever he required, exaggerating or distorting the facts as he saw fit. Edward studied the man opposite him. His features were resolute rather than handsome. His thick curls required a bag to secure them into a queue. Black eyebrows noteworthy for their evenness shaded dark brown eyes. A shadow beard outlined the lower half of his face. His shadow far exceeded Edward's substance.

"Your name is Edward Deveare?"

"Yes, sir."

"Nothing else?"

"No, sir."

"Your chest had the initials EED inscribed."

The Captain was an astute man. Did he also read the London papers? The name Evington frequently appeared there. "Ahh, middle name, ye-es. Edmond. My middle name is Edmond, sir." His great-uncle wasn't here to mind borrowing his Christian name or to contradict him.

"Indeed. How old are you, Mr. Deveare?"

"Fifteen, sir."

"Fifteen?" The officer stroked his chin. "When were you born?"

"1774, sir, 29th June."

"The year I first went to sea. Where were you born and raised?"

Edward visualized his mother. "Surrey, sir."

"Surrey? Not Hampshire, not Portsmouth?"

"Surrey. That's what I've always been told, sir."

"What town in Surrey?"

"It was in the country, I believe, sir."

"Near what town? Guildford, Richmond?"

"Dorking. It was closest to Dorking, sir." Things were getting a little too close to home. "That's what I was told, sir."

"You yourself don't recall it?"

Was he mocking him, teasing him – or baiting a trap? Whatever the intent, Edward decided the truth was the safest thing, about remembering, that is. "No, sir, I'm afraid I don't."

The older man left his chair and walked over to the stern windows where he stood with his back to Edward, left hand on hip, head cocked to one side. "Where were you educated?"

Who would believe he'd been at Eton? And if the Captain did, what else would he ask? "I – attended a school – near where I was born. Though not so near as some."

"Where?"

"Near Surrey, sir, as I –"

The officer spun on his heel, his face as grim as it had been when he'd faced Neville.

"Damn me, sir, I took you from a situation which could have only resulted in your ruin, gave you the benefit of the doubt, despite your captain's black assessment! Will you at least do me the courtesy of telling the truth?"

The Captain had brought him up with a round turn. No longer able to evade or equivocate, Edward found he was actually relieved. He'd be able to share the burden he'd carried for months. "I was born at East Dene Park, sir," Edward said, rising from the chair, "one of my maternal grandfather's properties, in Surrey. My mother is Lady Elizabeth Deveare; her father, Lord Evington. My father was Captain William Deveare of Portsmouth. I never knew him. My mother left him just before I was born. I was educated first by tutors, then at Eton. After my father's death last year, his father, Benjamin Deveare, became my guardian. It was he who arranged for me to ship aboard *Amphitrite*."

"Why all that nonsense, then?"

"I – was afraid – that you'd send me back to England, sir."

"Why?"

"I, I've wanted to go to sea ever since I first learnt about my father. My mother forbade it. She swore she'd have my guardianship overturned. She may have already done so."

"And you didn't wish to go home, even though you were having a hard time of it?"

"No, sir." Edward's arm tensed. "I know I didn't tell the truth at first, sir, but please believe I'm telling it now. Going to sea is what I've always wanted most in life." A half truth, actually. There had been something he'd wanted more. It was a risk to be that candid, but this man had intervened for him. Edward took a deep breath. "Save one."

"And that is?"

Telling the whole truth was like being asked to strip naked. Edward opened and closed his lips twice before he could bring himself to whisper, "To be with my father, sir."

The Captain regarded him several long seconds. He slowly retraced his steps, opened his desk, and took out some sheets of paper. "Sit down," he said, laying them on a blotter. "You're going to write some letters. First, to your guardian, then, to your mother, informing them of your whereabouts."

Uneasy under the Captain's stare, Edward sat down, dropped his hat, grasped the pen.

"How are you situated with respect to clothes and money?"

"I... have no money, sir. My clothes, well, this, another uniform, and some slops."

"In what state?"

"Worn, sir, like these."

"Supplies?"

"I have a journal, a text on spherical trigonometry, a pencil, pen and ink, a quadrant, and a sword, sir."

"Anything else?"

"No. Wait – yes, a razor."

"Which of your grandfathers is financially responsible for you?"

"I suppose the one who's now my guardian. But I refuse to ask anything of him!"

"Hmm. We'll try the other, then. Begin. My Lord, I wish to inform you I am at present aboard His Majesty's ship *Blanche*, Richard Pearse commanding, on the Leeward station. As I was sent on foreign station without proper outfitting, I shall require, ah, let us say, a draft of one hundred pounds to purchase necessary clothes and supplies. Moreover, I request an additional sum of forty pounds to cover one year's mess fees, and another thirty for my schooling aboard said ship. These are to be deposited with Mssrs. Black and Dingle, Plymouth, agents and prize masters for Captain Richard Pearse. I am, Sir, Your grandson, Edward Edmond Deveare."

"Sir?"

"Yes?"

"My middle name – it's Evington, after my mother's family."

"Indeed. Have you any other revelations to make, Mr. Edward *Evington* Deveare?"

"No, sir."

"Then if you've finished, we'll begin the next letter. My dear Mother –"

Edward squirmed. Captain Pearse's hand returned to his hip.

"She won't believe I wrote that, much less the rest of the letter."

"No? All right then, how do you begin? Your ladyship?"

"Madam."

"Madam?"

"I always address her as such, sir."

"Hmm. Madam. I am presently in good health. No, damn me, don't write that! You look to be in anything but good health. Seek out the surgeon after I've done with you. After which, visit the ship's barber and have him do something about your hair. It's disgraceful. Now where were we? Oh, yes. What, another sheet? There, in that drawer. Ready? Madam, I am presently aboard HM ship *Blanche* on the Leeward Station and am in dire need of funds. Please encourage – how do you style your grandfather?"

"His lordship."

"– his lordship to forward a draft for one hundred and seventy pounds to Messrs. Black and Dingle, Plymouth, agents for Captain Richard Pearse posthaste. Close it as you normally would."

The quill scratched the paper and splattered ink. Drops splotched a folded paper on the desk.

Edward used his ruined sheet to blot his work. One good had come of this, he now knew the Captain's name. Richard Pearse, HMS *Blanche*. Pen in air, Edward fantasized. Some day... Edward Deveare, HM ship, Captain.

"Finished?"

Edward brought the pen back in touch with the paper and signed his name. "Yes, sir."

"Good." Captain Pearse leaned over him and reached into a drawer at the base of the desk's compartments and retrieved a stick of sealing wax. "Fold those and address them. I'll forward them by the first ship bound for England."

"Yes, sir." Edward retrieved his hat. His lower arm was cramping again. Although the things he'd written boded well, he wanted verification of an important point. "Then I can stay, sir?"

"You may stay until we hear otherwise – or you prove unequal to your duties. For now, present yourself to Mr. Jameson and have him assess the state of your health and require he report the same to me. Then inquire for the ship's barber directly you leave my cabin. Tell him I desire your hair be cut the way the other youngsters wear theirs. Questions?"

"No, sir. Thank you, sir."

"Wait."

"Sir?"

Crinkles radiated from the skin around Captain Pearse's eyes. "Who won?"

Edward immediately caught the inference. No lecture, no warning not to "behave in such a manner here." Head high, chin proud, Edward said, "I did, sir."

"Indeed." The crinkles disappeared. "Mr. Deveare."

"Sir?" Edward asked, his head not quite so high. There was to be something else.

"If ever you decide to take up lying, there's one person to whom you must never do so."

"You, sir?"

"I trust you will not attempt it again. No, Mr. Deveare. Yourself."

The passageway to the half-deck, the area directly outside the cabin shaded by the quarterdeck overhang, seemed brighter. Edward paused briefly abreast the clerk's office. Even now, the clerk might be adding his name to *Blanche's* muster.

He lingered on the quarterdeck before fulfilling the Captain's orders. His situation had improved but was not yet resolved. Trewethey disliked him and might try to turn others against him. He was destitute. His career in the Service could be ended by a word from his mother or current guardian.

Aloft, the sails were set and filled. But his new captain was fair, and the other mids he'd met decent. Most important of all, he was alive. *Blanche* made fresh way. Edward drank deep of the wind. Life was once more full of possibilities.

CHAPTER TWENTY-FIVE

Changes never answer the end.

Roger North, *Examen*, 1740

The only good thing about Portsmouth, Evington concluded, was its Whig bias. The town was another Wapping, a notorious London dockside slum. It amazed him Lizzie had lasted here six years.

It was a fool's errand, coming here. Even more foolish had been the waste of a valuable political favor, but it was too late to remedy either.

Admiral Roddam's aide ushered them into a room Evington considered not too badly furnished for a sailor. He glanced sideways at Lizzie. He'd warned her he'd handle things. Hearing and obeying, though, weren't quite the same thing for her.

"My lady. My lord," Roddam said, with a gentleman's courtesy, "I trust both of you had a pleasant journey from London?"

Evington murmured a polite nothing. Privately, he thanked a God he rarely consulted as Lizzie merely inclined her head. Their errand required the Admiral's good graces.

"My apologies for the inconvenience, my lord. Captain Neville will be here shortly with your grandson." Their silence frosty, Roddam attempted humor. "Boys that age can be a long time saying their farewells."

Evington held the Admiral responsible for the delay, for a superior officer was ultimately responsible for the behavior of his men. Meanwhile, he uncharitably attributed the port admiral's florid color to indulgence in something stronger than port.

"Ah, here they are."

A man who was young by Evington's standards, in his late twenties perhaps, entered. Hair a middling blond: moonlight rather than sunlight. Presentable, in a middling way. Middling height, middling build. Middling.

Captain Neville stopped the instant he saw them. No, not stopped, Evington mused, hung suspended. Neville darted a look at Lizzie's full mourning and another at him. His rapid eye movements were reminiscent of a snake's flicking tongue.

The Captain was alone. Edward Evington waited for Edward Deveare to follow. Lizzie didn't wait at all.

"Where is my son?"

Neville fingered his sword hilt and looked uncertainly at Roddam. Evington intervened, not out of sympathy for the officer, but to cut off his daughter. "Admiral?"

With considerably less ease than he'd made light of the Captain's tardiness, Roddam said, "Lady Elizabeth, Lord Evington, permit me to introduce you to Captain Hidcote Neville. Captain Neville, Lady Elizabeth Deveare and the Right Honorable Edward, Earl Evington." Lips tight, he added, "Captain, where is the young gentleman?"

His right hand clasping and unclasping his sword hilt, Neville bowed. "My lady. My lord." To the Admiral, Neville whined, "I cannot produce that which was taken from me, sir."

"Explain yourself, Captain."

Evington noted Neville's lack of eye contact and the sullen droop to his mouth. He recognized the type. Cowards when forced to own up to their actions – but only to a superior, and then only lacking no other alternative.

"The boy left my ship off Charleston Roads, preferring to go off with my replacement, Captain Pearse, who enticed him with prospects of serving on a larger ship." Neville swiveled in Lizzie's direction. "Of course, it was his decision, but Mr. Deveare's behavior cut me to the quick. I'd taken him on as a favor at the last minute, and do not think I was wrong in expecting a certain amount of loyalty in return."

Neville's words had the effect Evington feared. But before he could act, Lizzie tossed her head and charged.

"My son honors his obligations."

"My daughter is understandably upset by the absence of her son," Evington said equitably. "Captain, if you'd enlarge upon your claims, perhaps we might gain insight into his actions."

"I perceive, my lord," Neville said, almost meeting Evington's eyes, "you are a stranger to the ways of the Service and of such men. Captain Pearse came on station in a fifth rate. He was to stay, and I was to leave. He made much of that."

"Edward would never stoop to such pettiness! I'm his mother. I know he would tell a different story were he here!"

Evington caught the quick look Roddam gave the Captain. The balance had shifted. Hand now firmly in command of his sword hilt, Neville said, "My lady, I, too, have little doubt Mr. Deveare would tell a different tale, for such is the opinion I've come to have of him."

"Are you calling my son a liar? If anyone is lying –"

"Elizabeth!"

Neville gave Lizzie a pitying smile. True, Lizzie had acted foolishly, but Evington would not allow her to be disrespected by a nobody.

"Captain, whatever the reasons, it is obvious you were bested both by the boy and his new commander. Admiral, it is equally obvious matters appear to have bested you. Sirs, I shall commend you both to Lord Chatham."

The stunned silence which followed amused Evington. Admiral and Captain were slowly digesting his threat to inform the First Lord of the Admiralty about their lack of cooperation. Lizzie on his arm, he leisurely exited. Equally enjoyable was the way his daughter's coldness paralyzed the subordinates. He only regretted she didn't stay that way with him.

"Protest to Chatham, have them dismissed their posts!" she said as they drove off. "Do something! Do anything, but for God's sake, bring Edward home!"

"I believe I already have attempted the latter."

She had badgered him night and day until he'd maneuvered to get her son back. It was sour comfort the boy was not here. Lizzie, recognizing his cold anger, now backed off. The son began where the father had left off, spoiling things between them. Sir Colin had been right; he should have done nothing.

They crossed the bridge connecting the island town to the rest of Hampshire. The tide low, numerous boats and small craft lay stranded on the gray-green mud flats, encrusted bottoms exposed. Random refuse littered the mud. Good-bye and good riddance to Portsmouth.

Evington weathered a jolt. The boy couldn't have known why his ship had been recalled. Was he an opportunist, as his former captain implied, and a liar? His inability to find the precise box in which to fit Lizzie's child irritated Evington more than anything that had happened today. His orderly universe had been disturbed.

Butser Hill loomed ahead. His daughter gripped the seat. Even after all these years, she remembered her childhood carriage accident and feared steep inclines. Poor Lizzie. With the Spanish crisis escalating, the odds for the boy's return weren't good. No, not good at all.

The Spanish crisis. Evington frowned. England should not, *must* not go to war. And he would do his utmost to insure it.

Chapter Twenty-Six

Suspicion may be no fault, but showing it may be a great one.

Thomas Fuller, *Gnomologia*

The worst of the spring rains past, men traveled the Surrey roads with increasing ease. So also did the countrymen. They paid Dad well for doing little, just letting them keep their wagon at the cottage for a time. It was so simple, Jemmy questioned his nagging fears. Dad was more content than he'd been in months and no longer drinking.

Jemmy indulgently watched Nan dancing along. The sun shone, and the clouds bid fair weather. They were en route to Dorking, for today was Thursday, market day, and Dad had promised each of them a special gift. Jemmy had spied a red-handled hunting knife on an earlier visit to town. A frivolity, no doubt, but he thought about it now and again. Nan leaped and twirled. She was so simple, so easy to please. What she wanted he didn't know.

Simple, but exasperating. Just last week, she and Jemmy had stayed behind while Dad finished some work for the farmer. Jemmy had gone to gather firewood and left her to put away the breakfast things. He'd warned her not to stray, but when he returned, the cottage was empty. Trying to stay calm, Jemmy called her name. When there was no answer, he hastily climbed the ladder to the loft and checked there. No sign of Nan, he ran

193

down the path to the place he'd last tracked her, a gentleman's estate. He knew the way she'd take, through the breach in the wall enclosing the park. His heart thudding, he inched forward. She was exactly where she'd been before, beside the lake. A small figure in a stained smock on turf mown and rolled so fine it rivaled the gentry's velvets, she was dipping her hands in the water and singing a non-song.

The song had ended abruptly when she'd sensed, not seen, him. When she spoke, it seemed she'd begun another refrain. "Jemmy come."

Jemmy responded by pulling her to her feet. Nan hadn't just resisted him; she'd sprouted roots. "Can't you see?" he'd asked, his brown eyes darkening. "We get no welcome here. Come, before the groundskeepers catch us."

"Jemmy don't like?"

Jemmy remembered the last time he'd tracked her here. Like today, trees grew a second time in their reflection at the lake's edge, and white buildings on a small island made a gently rippled impression. Ducks pecked at the banks while swans with arched necks approved their beauty in the water mirror. A gravel drive made a white ribbon through the green lawn. Who wouldn't like this place? But it belonged to a lord, Evington, their farmer friend claimed.

The place where Nan had lain was a circle of dead grass with mushrooms, a fairy ring. No good would come of that, the old sayings ran. To Jemmy's mind, no good had ever come of Nan.

"I'm mindful to leave and let them sell you to gypsies."

She slipped through his grasp and danced to the sound of her own laughter. "Gypsies play, Jemmy play." He unsuccessfully tried to grasp her will-o'-the-wisp body. Nan rarely made sense to those who didn't know her and sometimes not even to those who did, but Jemmy understood. She wanted him to play the fiddle. Dreading the punishment he knew would fall on him if Dad found out, he'd hurried her through a plantation of beeches, every tree a potential hiding place for pursuers. Scrambling through a moss-covered break in the wall enclosing the manor's park, humus flaked onto them, the smell of damp earth heavy. With the turning to the estate just ahead, Jemmy's mood darkened. Who knew when Nan would stray there again, and who might find her?

Weaving a crooked path, Jemmy guided her onward. Not until they reached the muddy track of Coldharbor Lane did he relax. They were near the outskirts of Dorking, an old town with old streets, old buildings, and poor lighting. Its market house needed much work, but since the grain trade had shifted to Horsham, the town wouldn't mend it. Still, people came to buy and sell what they had.

The lane dipped through the Hollows and wound into South Street, where it passed the Queen's Head public house and the grim work house. A place, Jemmy worried, that one day might yet claim them. Then on to East Street, Dorking's main shopping street and thoroughfare. Although they knew few people, Jemmy's eyes were drawn to a man lingering by the Post Office who seemed to be watching them. Ill at ease, Jemmy kept walking. It was nothing. The stranger was likely waiting for a letter or for someone in the Wheatsheaf Inn opposite.

Anyway, he had more important things to consider. Jemmy stopped at the cutler's shop. "See that one, Dad? It be fit for a lord."

"You like that knife, Jemmy?"

Eyes riveted on the ornate handle, Jemmy breathed, "Yes, sir, I do."

Dad went in; Jemmy followed. The cutler pushed his spectacles to the end of his nose and asked what they wanted. The red-handled knife in the window, Dad told him. Somewhat skeptical, the cutler removed it the display and offered it handle first to Dad. Dad waved toward Jemmy. "It's for the boy."

Jemmy lovingly slipped the knife out of its supple leather sheath and examined it. The handle bore intricate carvings of a stag hunt. No poacher, he'd use it to cut his vegetables and meat. He touched his fingertip to the blade. Its keenness gave him a pleasurable thrill.

"How much?" asked Dad.

"It's a fine 'un. I'll not take less than one pound ten."

"Make it a pound, and I'll take it."

"I could sell it easy for what I ask."

"Then why be it in the window?"

"Times are hard, but that don't mean –"

"Times be hard for me as well. One pound. I've it with me."

Would the cutler agree to the price? Jemmy clutched the knife as if for the last time.

"One pound five."

"A pound, take it or no."

The shopkeeper pushed his spectacles down his nose. "Have it, then, though I can't see it going to good use."

It was his. Something he'd longed for actually his. In an agony of pleasure, Jemmy barely got out the words, "Thank you, sir."

"Don't thank me, thank your father. Shall I wrap it?"

"No, sir. I'll take it as is."

Dad took out a leather drawstring pouch and counted out the coins. The cutler scooped them into a drawer. "I sharpen knives, too," he said. "Not that it needs it."

"I've whetstone of my own. Good day to you."

Thwarted in his bid for future custom, the cutler wished them a cold good day. Despite their less than cheery send-off, Jemmy pranced out the door. "Thank you, Dad. I'll not complain no more over work."

"Nor tending Nan?" Dad's eyes flashed as bright as the cutler's spectacles.

"Nan see?" His sister, who'd been docile till now, squirmed to get at the knife.

"Little maid, knives not for you. What of a pretty dolly? There's a shop as sells such."

Any other day, Jemmy would have fretted while his father did his business. Not today. He waited patiently outside while Dad and Nan entered a small shop, sheathing and unsheathing his knife. How could it belong to him, something so fine?

When his family emerged, Jemmy dogged them up East Street. Nan held a doll by its arm, its patterned skirts dangling loose at her side. A porcelain doll, an expensive gift, like his knife. She didn't seem to value it, though.

Inside the Black Horse Inn, grain stuck in the cracks between the floorboards. The harvest months past, no farmers cast down handfuls of wheat to verify the quality to potential buyers. Nevertheless, it was market day, and the tables were filled.

Dad cast about for a place. Jemmy would have liked one of the high back booths, but a serving girl in a brown print dress with starched white apron cleared a small, round table by the fireplace. Hunting horns and farm implements glinted over the mantle.

"Take care," Dad said to Nan after she dropped her doll on the floor. "T'will be a while fore you get another."

Nan patted Dad's arm. "Like Dolly better."

Dolly was a wooden toy Dad had fashioned, its blue-black eyes owing their color to hurtberry juice, blueberries some called them. Its tresses were dried blades of wavy-haired grass. No match for the porcelain doll, but Nan obviously preferred the homemade one.

Dad gently placed the doll on the table. The girl brought two mugs of small beer, a pint of ale, and a basket of brown bread. Jemmy helped himself to a thick slice. Dining here, like their gifts, was a special treat. He couldn't see how the day could be any better.

Jemmy stretched his legs long underneath the table. The crowd seemed a good lot, farmers mostly. He didn't see their friend, though. As Jemmy reached for a second slice, a bright shaft of light illuminated the room. Two men entered, one of them the man Jemmy noticed at the Post Office. Jemmy felt the room had darkened.

The man from the Post Office looked around, this way and that. When the serving girl came to show them to a table, he refused it. Instead, he came to theirs.

"A knife and a doll. Cost a bit, I should say."

It was no innocent chance remark. Jemmy glanced apprehensively at his father.

"What business be that of yours?" he asked.

"Just wondered how a man new to the Holmwood and not seeming to do much of anything came by the brass to buy these."

"I earnt it, that's how."

"Not by carpentering, I'll be bound."

"My children need their meal."

"Ah, yes, the children. Hobbs, do they look familiar? Like the ones his honor, Lord Onslow, said to keep a lookout for? The ones you saw trespassing only last week?" The man quizzed the stranger who'd accompanied him.

Dad clinched his fists. "You leave my children be!"

The pleasant hum of conversation faded. Jemmy wished the two men would go away. They could have his knife, anything, just leave them alone.

"Well, Hobbs?"

The second man sized up Nan and Jemmy. "I never could get close enough to see them proper. But they're right size and all; boy and girl, too."

"I don't know what you be talking about," Dad said.

"Don't you?" the first man asked. "Two children trespassed East Dene manor, boy and girl. The lady there, being alone, sent to Earl Onslow. His lordship opined they were putters up, sent to spy out what they could for robbing. I say, they were sent to put him off. Smugglers freer to do their dirty business then."

The world stared at them. Jemmy prayed Dad would find the right words – and only words.

The veins in Dad's temples pulsed. "My children be no putters up nor I robber."

"Nor countryman?"

Hobbs backed off as Dad erupted from his chair, but not the other man. Jemmy feared Dad would strike the stranger, the way he had Finch's agent. Seconds passed, but Dad neither spoke nor moved. He didn't have to; his anger spoke for him.

The first man finally retreated a step or two. "Don't think you and your smuggling friends so easy be rid of me. I'll bring you to justice yet!"

Without ordering their meal, Dad flung down some coins on the table and helped Nan gather up her doll. The red-handled knife lay on the table like an accusing finger. He'd been wrong to want something so fine. Look at the trouble it had brought them. Considering it now a rebuke of his selfishness, Jemmy left the knife for whoever wanted it.

A buzz like the drone of a disturbed hive followed them out of the inn. Smugglers. Everyone knew they were smugglers now. And trespassers. They'd be driven out, just as they'd been at Albury, or worse.

The doll flopped at Nan's side. They were well down Coldharbor Lane and the turning which led to the lake. With every step, the lump in Jemmy's throat constricted. The longer Dad went without speaking, the worse it would be for him. Then the tempest burst.

"You shamed me! I trusted you to look after her, not go running to great houses."

Jemmy could have borne the outburst had Nan not been the cause. "Why don't you never blame her 'stead of me! She runned there. Always straying, and I be the one you thrash."

"I set you to watch over her. You be responsible, not she!"

Jemmy kicked a stone. If he hadn't been so upset, it would have landed near his sister. Dad always excused Nan because she was simple – and blamed him. He'd get a whipping when they reached the cottage; he was certain of it. Nan dragged her doll in the dirt. Dad paid a pound for his knife but probably more, much more, for the doll. Jemmy regretted leaving his gift. It would be useful now, to slash her toy.

Distance and failing light enshrouded man and girl. Jemmy reluctantly trailed after them. Nan, always Nan, but never him.

Chapter Twenty-Seven

The event corresponds less to expectations...

Livy, *History of Rome* XXX

The best part of the journey, from Louis' perspective, had ended at Bordeaux. He, Beldoque, and Lecluselle had talked, sang, and walked and rode the miles from Paris. After that, a long, cold, damp, cramped voyage across the sea to a chaotic stay at Saint-Domingue, and then, embarkment on a plodding coastal trader to Trinidad. To Louis, only madmen liked the sea. Or the many Englishmen they'd sighted, but then, he counted them one and the same.

In Paris, war between England and Spain had been a discussion; here in Trinidad it was a near reality. English ships redoubled their cruising. On the island, militia groups were forming to fend off a possible invasion. Louis and his friends talked of their eventual enlistment.

War aside, there was much to see and learn. For all its Spanish governor and allegiance to Spain, Trinidad was rapidly becoming more French than Spanish. The 1783 *Cédula* of Population opened the island to settlers from other nations, particularly French planters displaced by France's shameful ceding of its islands to Britain at the end of the Twenty Years' War, and to a lesser extent, the American War. Louis fingered an imaginary musket. He would gladly avenge French wrongs.

He assumed most Frenchmen here would as well. Hadn't the master of their first ship cursed every English vessel they'd sighted? Louis hadn't reckoned on the devilry of the English, though. They'd encouraged trade between Trinidad and the nearest British possessions, so that French planters actually complained about potential hostilities.

"Monsieur, do you repay my generosity by inactivity?"

Alphonse Caron sat his horse poorly as befitted a parvenu. Co-owner of La Belle Aurore plantation, he sought to make good the loan for their passage by having the three work off their debt. Instead of getting rich, they were indentured servants. Beldoque's former comrade was their lord and master and never lost an opportunity to remind them of it, particularly Louis. For his part, Louis never lost an opportunity to preach the gospel of the new French politics to the workers he oversaw. Caron found this especially galling, as those workers were slaves.

The blacks' naked torsos shone with sweat, their reward for clearing a new field. At present, a massive stump challenged them. Had Caron been absent, Louis would have rested the slaves, for rested men worked better. Instead, the plantation owner shouted for them to work faster.

"Citizen –"

"Citizen! What treason is this?" Caron kicked his horse close. Leaning down, he spoke so only Louis could hear. "I care nothing if you get your throat cut. I, however, have no wish to be murdered, less still, my wife and child. These beasts have ears."

The incessant lift and thrust of picks hadn't slacked. Caron, Louis fumed mentally, was an *aristo*, pure filth. His sort not only called workers beasts but considered them such.

"Citizen Caron, I ask you – "

"Monsieur Gleason awaits you at the house."

How long Beldoque had been there or how much he'd heard, Louis couldn't say. His insouciance hinted he'd only just come. That meant nothing, though. Beldoque wasn't above pretending ignorance to further his ends.

The planter grimaced. Gleason was a neighbor, an Irish planter, acceptable to the Governor and his Spanish king because of his Catholicism. Caron had no wish to offend a neighbor. Reining his horse around, he told Beldoque, "Look to your friend while I am gone. If he and his slaves do not finish, I will hold you responsible."

As Louis thanked Beldoque for what he supposed was his sympathy, the soldier cut him short. "Mark well what you do – for all our sakes. This isn't France."

Once Beldoque returned to his own field, Louis did what he'd intended all along: he rested his slaves and pondered the situation. Caron was another little big shot. La Belle Aurore sugar plantation was named after his wife, the true source of his wealth. Aurore's father had emigrated from Grenada soon after the *Cédula* had been published. Chevalier de Montcourt brought his family and twenty slaves. In accordance with the *Cédula's* stipulations, he received four and two-sevenths fanegas of land – approximately thirty acres – for each white person and half as much for each slave. Thus, his family brought him 150 acres of land; his slaves, 300. Before his death, de Montcourt's holdings had increased to 1500 acres. He chiefly owed this increase to his daughter's marriage to a slaver, one Alphonse Caron.

Caron had drifted to the islands at the end of the American War. A clever man, he became the employee and then partner of a slave agent in quick succession. An astute man, he wooed Aurore de Montcourt. When Louis had praised her for making an egalitarian match, Beldoque, the source of his information, noted dryly the "Chevalier" had ennobled himself.

When the sweat on their backs lessened, Louis ordered his crew back to work. They attacked the stubborn stump with renewed vigor, singing as they did. Louis called each by name and praised them. They were no "beasts" to him.

He and his crew cleared almost double the area Caron had set them. As he headed towards the hut he shared with his two friends, Louis looked up at the comfortable white frame building situated on the rise of hill, the manor house of La Belle Aurore. Timothy Gleason lounged on the veranda beside Caron. Gleason was an Irishman who'd emigrated from Grenada, also drawn by the *Cédula*. Louis had heard him boast he preferred the freedom offered by Spain to the tyranny of the English. For that, Louis esteemed him. However, Gleason, too, owned slaves.

Beldoque had said Gleason considered changing from cotton to the more profitable crop, sugar. He'd recently bought some land for that purpose, adjacent to La Belle Aurore. Louis also approved that Gleason used an American agent at Port of Spain, rather than as English one, like Caron. Yet to his dismay, both planters exported their crops to the free trade port of St. George's, Grenada, and the firm which ultimately paid them was English. Money outweighed ancient animosities here.

The next day brought a welcome change of duties. Aware Louis had attended University, Caron ordered him to give his agent at Port of Spain the account of his recent expenditures. Louis could ride one of the donkeys there and back, but was enjoined to take good care of it. Caron notably mentioned nothing about Louis' welfare. As he set out, Louis muttered that the real donkey was Caron.

It was good, however, to be on his own, away from Monsieur and Madame's disapproving eyes. Caron's holdings lay in a rich valley near the coast, southeast of the new capital of Trinidad, Port of Spain. The surrounding vegetation was lush, worthy of Eden. Eden only for whites, though. Slaves toiled under the tropic sun cultivating Otaheite cane, the new variety brought from the Pacific. But if their servitude offended him, what Louis found even more repugnant were the artisans swarming over a sugar mill. Free blacks, French creoles from their patois, and they also owned and worked slaves, their fellow citizens. Someone must convince them what they did was against nature.

The outskirts of Port of Spain appeared long before he resolved the question. Under the rule of Governor Señor Don José María Chacón, the new capital flourished. The main street led past opulent – for this part of the world – new townhomes, wooden like their country counterparts. The houses mostly belonged to French planters, barring some anomalies like Gleason and a scattering of English and Prussians. The *Cédula* aside, the surge of settlers here owed itself in no small part to a Frenchman, Roume de St. Laurent. The original Spanish settlers had done little to develop the island. Frenchmen like St. Laurent, though, were quick to see the opportunities offered by rich, virgin lands. If the present rate of French emigration continued, Louis mused, and it appeared it would, Trinidad might well become a French colony.

He'd no trouble finding the street leading to the agent's office. The only trouble he had was discharging his obligations. The sooner he did, the sooner he'd have to return. Who was to tell if he indulged his curiosity and looked around? If questioned about the time he took to make the trip, he'd blame the donkey's slowness.

There were no walkways in Port of Spain, nor paved streets. The drains, though, were better served. Laventille limestone served as their beds, along which flowed whatever had been thrown into them. His destination the center of town, Louis hopped one such ditch. His vigorous leap landed him directly in the path of a white-wigged stranger dressed *à l'anglais*. Louis' initial reaction was to apologize. But the cold, chiseled features marked an *aristo* by birth and despite the cut of his coat, a Frenchman from France.

"Out of the way, oaf!"

The man's attendant shouted this in poor French. Swarthy, dressed in a green and white uniform, Lewis recognized him as a Spanish officer. When Louis didn't budge, the attendant drew his sword. A believer in fraternity, Louis addressed him as "Citizen." A believer in life – his own – Louis backed off.

Louis had some difficulty convincing himself what he'd done was wise, not cowardly. Was he not needed to spread the seeds sown in France? He hadn't gone far before he came upon an undistinguished building enlivened by the sign *Gazetta* over the door. A printer plied his trade there. Louis wistfully recalled the broadsheets and articles he'd helped Bertrand write. He'd left him no note, no word of his destination, nor Marie-Rose either. His sole missive had been a quick letter to Mother Albertine. Louis hoped his father hadn't destroyed it.

The print shop was further proof the Spanish governor was an enlightened man. Was it possible he allowed news of the outside world to be published, of events in France? Louis smiled. If so, he'd just found the means for spreading his ideas.

Two men toiled over a printing press, one white, the other dark. The white greeting him in French, Louis responded in kind.

The printer wiped his hands on a leather apron. "Monsieur is from France?"

"The Citizen has a discerning ear."

"Citizen? What address is this?"

Despite his rough linen and ink-stained apron, the printer reminded Louis of Bertrand. The memory of their last meeting lent asperity to his tone. "I was at the taking of the Bastille, one of an army of citizens."

The printer brightened. "Monsieur – Citizen – I long to hear. Anything, everything!"

"Everything? That will take some time."

"No matter. I have wine. And food, if you are hungry. But, pardon, I am Jean Villoux, proprietor of the *Gazetta*."

"Louis Saulnier, patriot. I will tell you what I know, on one condition."

"Yes?"

"That you print what I say, that all may know what patriots are accomplishing in Paris."

Chapter Twenty-Eight

If a man will begin with certainties, he shall end in doubts; but if he will be content to begin with doubts, he shall end in certainties.

Francis Bacon, *Advancement of Learning* I

"Mr. Pitt tries to quiet the people, but the clamor against Spanish arrogance grows daily. If Floridablanca's insolence that Spain owned all territories to the 60 degree North boundary hadn't proved inflammatory enough, word of how four English ships were searched, three of them and their cargo seized and the *Argonaut* and her crew cruelly imprisoned and manhandled have raised it to fever pitch."

"But Sir John," Richard Pearse said, well pleased to have an audience with the newly arrived commander-in-chief, "trade with Trinidad continues undisturbed."

"And so it should, Captain. The King does not wish for war, and because of him, neither does Pitt, largely because of our commercial interests. Need I remind you that England has trebled her shipping since the end of the American War? I've heard it said that even now, we treat with Spain to access more ports in Spanish America."

"And for these, forego trade with the entire Pacific, Sir John?"

207

A Tainted Dawn

"Never! Spain may threaten, but since Captain Meares arrived and gave his first-hand account of what transpired at Nootka, Mr. Pitt has become emboldened. To counter the dons' show of force, he's ordered twenty-nine ships of war readied. We'll match them ship for ship!"

"Then – it is war, after all?"

"A *show* of force only. Their lordships at the Admiralty made that abundantly clear. We are to do nothing, absolutely nothing, which could be interpreted as an act of war."

No hostilities; that was the final word. So be it. Pearse, like Sir John, wished the conversation to move elsewhere.

"I exercise my people at the great guns, frequently – more than the Commodore requires."

"I hear you don't get on very well with Parker," Laforey said, tipping the port decanter.

Seated in the great cabin of HMS *Trusty*, Pearse had hoped Sir John would bite on the bait. Admiral Laforey had arrived in English Harbor on 2 June and Pearse knew he'd already met with Commodore Parker. Pearse wanted his position about a certain matter clarified.

"We had a difference of opinion over my transferring a youngster from *Amphitrite* to my command. The Commodore himself had given me the order."

"Parker said Neville complained you exceeded your authority aboard his ship."

"That was Captain Neville's account. Mine is somewhat different, Sir John."

Although it was late in the afternoon watch, nearly time for supper, admirals enjoyed the privilege of dining late. Laforey, rear admiral and owner of the Belmont, Thomas's, and Tuck & Farley's Gardens, plantations on Antigua, liked a leisurely dinner. "Go on."

Pearse had prepared his case beforehand. "I overtook *Amphitrite* and delivered the order requiring her return to England. Captain Neville opened it in my presence and took offense."

"You had words and exchanged insults; that's what I made of it."

After one insult too many, Pearse had suggested his second wait on Captain Neville's. Like the bully he was, Neville declined

208

the challenge. Things hadn't ended there either. Neville timed his backstabbing perfectly. When he'd been absent, *Amphitrite's* captain whined to the Commodore that Pearse had threatened him. That had been just prior to his sailing for England. When Pearse returned to English Harbor from a cruise round St. Kitts and Nevis, he faced a verbal reprimand from Commodore Parker. Relations between them had been frosty ever since.

"We disagreed over the timing of Mr. Deveare's transfer."

"You interfered in a routine disciplining of an obstreperous youngster, siding with him against his captain and insinuating the boy would do better with you."

"I intervened before a sick child could be flogged and dismissed his ship for having defended himself! And, by God, I'd do it again, even if it meant a court martial!"

"Calm yourself, Captain, please." Sir John's next words did the actual soothing. "If I hadn't already been inclined to your side, your passion alone would sway me. Why didn't you tell Parker this? Such charges deserve investigation."

"Despite what I urged, Mr. Deveare declined bringing charges against his former captain." Pearse fretted over the boy's recurring spasms. Sickness was understandable out here, but both he and Jameson were at a loss about his arm. *Blanche's* surgeon had tersely commented that no matter the initial cause, continued use had exacerbated the problem. Pearse agreed.

"Ah, yes, the boy. Do you recall our wondering why you'd been sent here before the rest of the squadron?"

"I thought it had something to do with Captain Neville."

"He certainly has his detractors. Actually, he was meant to bring home the very youngster you took off. Not, mind you," Laforey said, forestalling another outburst, "that the boy didn't need saving, but his family chose this method to get him back. Brandy, Captain?"

In his darker moods, Pearse often speculated about the boy's aristocratic connections and what that meant for him. Aloud, he asked, "Which family, Sir John?" and accepted the brandy.

"His mother's, of course. Lord Evington is a Whig grandee, one of the few whom His Majesty respects. It was through his interest your ship was commissioned and ordered on Station. His lordship came in person to fetch his grandson at Portsmouth. Let me tell you, he was not amused when there was no grandson to fetch. I had that straight from Roddam."

"The boy's to go home, then? With Parker and his squadron?"

Laforey twisted the lace frill underneath his stock. "Now we come to one of the most peculiar threads in this Byzantine web. He stays. All I have is a letter for him from his mother, Lady Elizabeth Deveare. Be thankful, Captain, you've not had the 'honor' of meeting the lady. If even half what Roddam says is true, she's a virago par excellence, by Gad! Poor Deveare, no wonder his marriage foundered."

"You knew the boy's father, Sir John?"

"Slightly. A good enough officer in his way. Fond of the ladies, and they of him. Fond of his bottle, too, but that was later, I heard, toward the end."

"Mr. Deveare has no inclination for either."

"Ah, but he's young, a child, you say. You know," Laforey said, sipping his liquor, "after all this bother about him, I confess to wanting to meet this Mr. Deveare."

"Had I known, Sir John, I would have brought him along. If you like –"

"Not now. But do bring him to Government House tomorrow evening. Tell me, Captain, does that cook of yours still conjure up those delicious meat pies?"

Those dinners at Portsmouth had served Pearse well. He now had the ear – and support – of his admiral. "When may I have the pleasure of entertaining you, Sir John?"

"After the King's birthday ball. I'm anxious to hear your view of things here. Before you go, don't forget to collect your letters. My secretary will give you the usual lot. These," he said producing a thick packet of letters, "are for you alone. This, from Lady Elizabeth, to her son." Laforey held the latter between his thumb and forefinger. "Don't let it bite you."

A joke, of course. Nevertheless, Pearse separated her ladyship's missive from the rest. The Admiral's secretary waited outside the great cabin with the other letters. That accomplished, Pearse made his way to his ship, an easy thing, since *Blanche* was moored with a stern cable to the Commodore's Wharf, next to *Trusty*. Pearse had barely been piped off one ship before being piped aboard his own.

Some of *Blanche's* people ferried bales and cases of slops from the dockyard: kersey jackets, waistcoats, and breeches, linsey waistcoats and drawers, shirts, frocks, trousers, stockings and caps, Dutch caps, shoes, beds, and hammocks. Pearse saw to it his people were well-clothed. He studied the slight figure in charge of the boat. If he did that much for his people, how could he do less for Mr. Deveare?

He called the boy to him. Mr. Deveare ordered the coxswain to oversee the rest, with firmness, not harshness. The people obeyed him willingly, Pearse noted.

"Sir?" Mr. Deveare stood in front of him. Pearse didn't recall that hook beginning just below the bridge of the boy's nose. An aristocratic hook. "From your mother," he said, somewhat tersely. "Perhaps she's sent you something."

Mr. Deveare scanned the sheets. "I don't think she'd received my letter, sir. She says nothing about money."

"Hmm. Well, perhaps she'll have gotten it by now, and we'll have something from her or your grandfather when the next mail packet arrives. To your duties, youngster."

"Aye, aye, Captain."

"Mr. England." England was his second lieutenant, a competent officer.

"Captain?"

"Kindly distribute these. Perhaps one bears news of your brother's promotion." England's brother was to have stood for his lieutenant's examination.

"I hope so, sir."

Pearse waited until he was in his cabin to open the last packet. He'd save Peggy's letters for last, to read and re-read at his leisure. At his desk, he broke the seal of his uncle's letter. Words written in a familiar large hand crawled across the page; he couldn't make any sense of them. Pearse yielded to what was uppermost in his mind. He hadn't spent that much on the lad, if it came to making good the credit, nothing near the almost two hundred pounds he'd had the boy request. On the other hand, if the debts were called in, they wouldn't help Deveare's finances. Had the mother in fact received her son's request for money and chosen to ignore it? The captain got up and looked out his stern windows. The water, normally a clear turquoise sans a full complement of ships at anchor, was a murky brown. Slaves were cleaning and deepening the harbor. Parker, for all Pearse's dislike of him, was right to urge more fortifications and improvements. Governor Shirley also aggressively pressed for more monies and more forts around English Harbor. The Antigua legislature had voted over eight thousand pounds sterling to be used for fortifying Dow's Hill, the heights above Freeman's Bay. The French island of Guadeloupe was more than just an outline on the horizon. And despite what Sir John had said about peace, the French were always ready, willing, and able to cause trouble.

From where he stood, Pearse couldn't see the waters beyond Freeman's Bay; he could visualize them, though. Deep blue, the exact color of the boy's eyes. No wonder Mr. Deveare so desperately wanted to stay in the service; he was made of the same stuff as the sea.

The Service. It ran in the boy's blood as it did his. Pearse's uncle was a post captain, likely to become an admiral should another war occur. Mr. Deveare had a captain for a father and an admiral for a grandfather. The father, though, had been a womanizer with a taste for drink, and the grandfather had never hoisted his flag at sea.

Pearse thought back to Mr. Deveare's first days aboard *Blanche*. He'd visited the boy regularly in that tent-like affair Mr. Jameson had rigged in the forecastle, to take advantage of the breeze, the surgeon explained. He recollected the sleeping innocence of the boy's haggard face. What hell had he endured, what purgatory, to stay afloat?

Pearse already missed those days. The boy had anticipated his visits. He'd be sitting up in his cot, waiting. Pearse had talked about his own scrapes as a reefer, but try as he would, he couldn't get Mr. Deveare to reveal what had happened to him.

Pearse smiled wryly. He was a fighter, that boy. Someone who wouldn't quit, no matter the odds. And as for that precipitous fight, Pearse believe Mr. Deveare had indeed been the victor.

He stopped smiling as he recalled the boy's father. What sort of man would walk away from his only son? Pearse would have emigrated before he'd let anyone take such a son from him, no matter how wealthy or influential the mother's family. And yet, the youngster was loyal to his father, despite his deserting him. Pearse struck an overhead beam with the flat of his palm. Such a man didn't deserve a son.

B. N. Peacock

A page fluttered on his desk. It had begun with a letter requesting Mr. Deveare's transfer. Would it end with another demanding his return to England?

CHAPTER TWENTY-NINE

There are two things wrong with youth and love –
youth and love. Time cures both.

Evington Papers, 7768/3

Edward's morning trip ashore to St. John's had been in vain.
The marketplace had been crowded with planters and their
families, but not the young lady he'd glimpsed months earlier. He
prayed she'd be at Government House tonight, as would he.

It was a rare treat to be given a day's grace from his duties, and
not because of ill health. He looked down from the quarterdeck
into the waist, where Barnes and Farnsworth protested as they
were hosed down. The two pranksters had gone ashore with him.
They'd returned with a suspicious pot of ointment, which, they
claimed, would grow hair. Aboard, they'd rubbed the stuff all over
their chests and faces. The resulting stench defied belief. Mr. Stark
ordered them to strip and scrub until they smelled human again.

They were naive, of course. Nothing could make whiskers or
chest hair miraculously appear. Nonetheless, Edward rubbed his
chin. Had he even a little stubble on his cheeks, he'd look older –
and be taken more seriously as a result. Sighing deeply enough to
fill *Blanche's* mainsail, he considered the possibilities of dancing
with Miss Jane Vaughan. She was a goddess, an angel, a more than
Helen. Based on past experience, none.

"How are those sketches of the harbor coming along?" Mr. England asked.

"Sketches? Oh, I redid them, the way you suggested. Would you like to see them, sir?" The second lieutenant taught drawing, the detailed kind including coastlines and harbors, preparing them for such a time as they might need to sketch an undiscovered island or enemy positions as a lieutenant or a captain. Mr. England had asked Edward to do his over, not because he'd done a poor job, but because he was giving him advanced instruction. Although they shared a love of art, England had never heard of Velásquez, much less seen any of his paintings.

"If you please. Then you'd better get yourself rigged for the ball. It's getting late."

The drawings were in his chest. Edward hurried below.

"Another 'beardless youth.' Do you stink, too?"

Trewethey sat polishing his pumps to a high sheen. Others out of earshot, he indulged his contempt for Edward. With no one around, Edward reciprocated.

"No more than you."

Trewethey reddened. "You think you're something, don't you, Scarecrow? Fawning over the lieutenants and playing the Captain for all your miserable worth. Well, I'm not taken in. The other day, at single sticks, pure luck."

Edward bridled at the name "Scarecrow," something he hadn't heard for ages. He'd scored a touché over their fencing instructor, Marine Lieutenant Radley, something Trewethey, the mid's champion fencer, had never done. Savoring that double triumph, Edward let the older mid stew.

"Why don't you take your filthy self and –"

"Is there something wrong here?"

Avoiding eye contact with both Lieutenant England and each other, the two mids quickly made the requisite denials. Edward hastily retrieved the drawings and handed them to the second lieutenant. He accepted them with a stern glance and said, "That will be all. Understand?"

"Aye, sir," Trewethey and Edward sang in unison.

"Has that putrid rot cleared out yet? Oh, sorry, Mr. England, didn't mean you."

Thank God for the Cannonball. Willoughy galumphed into the berth. "'Lo, Tre, 'Lo, Ned. Damn that boy! He hasn't brushed my kit."

Edward removed a dark blue wool coat and white kersey waistcoat and breeches from his chest. He owed Captain Pearse much. No, there would be no fighting. Trewethey wasn't worth ruining what he had here. He'd be more careful in the future.

When he scrabbled for his silk stockings, Edward discovered his sole pair had runs. "Any spares?" he asked Willoughby, holding them up.

"Mine all have holes," he said cheerfully. He pulled off his shirt and exposed a chest with hair enough to make a goat envious. "Just sit with your legs together."

"What if I get up to dance?"

"Dance?" Willoughby looked as if one of his beloved cannons had come loose from its trunnions. "Ladies don't dance with reefers, not while they have lieutenants and captains and majors handy. See these white patches?" Willoughby held out the ends of his coat collar with their white turnbacks or "weekly accounts." "They're the mark of the beast. Have a good feed. Drink to your heart's content – or somewhat less. Old lady Stark'll be on the prowl."

Edward's collar lacked white patches, the insignia of a rated midshipman. He was tempted to shave again, but the razor recalled Knoles and *Amphitrite,* moreover, the fiddler boy who'd deserted with Jake. Wishing to rid himself of such memories, Edward attacked his shortened hair with a brush, hating it for emphasizing his boyishness. Still not long enough to club into a queue, he hid the mess under a wig borrowed from a marine.

The stay-behinds drifted back for supper. They mixed orders with insults to the berths' servants as they readied the tables for supper while the others finished dressing. Dressed, Edward accompanied Willoughby topside, where they waited to be taken ashore. He mumbled half-hearted rejoinders to the Cannonball's comments about a Dutch brigantine in St. John's Roads. A quick pull and a short walk later, and slaves relieved them of their hats at Government House. Another took their names and announced them. Edward and his friend sought the sounds of music, talk, and laughter.

A TAINTED DAWN

The windows in the assembly rooms were open, not that it did any good. The crush of people blocked any relief a breeze might bring. Willoughby hailed an ensign from the King's Royal Rifle Corps. Edward began searching for Miss Vaughan.

In the first room, Commodore Parker spoke to a gentleman whose gold braid marked him as the new commander-in-chief. Two captains stood in respectful attendance, neither of them Pearse. Edward wandered to an adjoining room where hidden musicians played unseen instruments producing unheard sounds. She was there, dressed in airy white silk and pink satin, admirers in tow. A piece of debris in the comet's tail, Edward followed. When he finally came out of his trance, the crowd had erased all trace of her.

Upset but still determined to find her, he trudged from room to room. Wherever he turned, she eluded him. Without being asked, a Negro in puce satin filled his hands with a cup of rum punch. Miss Vaughan's face filled his mind.

"The heat troubling you, youngster?"

"What – Oh, Captain Pearse. I – what did you say, sir?"

"I said," the crinkles marshaled around Pearse's eyes, "are you hot?"

"Hot? No, not – well, perhaps. A little, that is."

"Then I suggest you drink your arrack – before you douse yourself with it."

Edward's mind worked backwards. His hand must have flown to his head to remove the hat he'd already left at the door. "I'm sorry, sir," he said, wiping punch off his coat.

"Why? It wasn't me you nearly drowned. If you're not engaged at the moment, I wish to introduce you to Sir John. But put that glass of punch down first. It won't do to dump it on him."

It was an honor to be introduced to the new admiral. They found Sir John in the same room where Edward had first seen him, minus Commodore Parker. Laforey nodded recognition.

"Quite a press, Captain."

"Indeed, Sir John, the whole of Antigua appears to have turned out."

Edward gathered his wits from the four winds while the officers exchanged pleasantries. Waiting his introduction, he positioned himself at Pearse's elbow.

"And this is Mr. Deveare? How do you do, sir?"

Edward bowed. "Quite well, Sir John."

"Adjusting to life in the tropics? I understand you've been ill."

"Yes, sir, I was. But I'm completely recovered now and able to attend my duties."

"Not missing home? Or wishing you'd pursued some other career instead?"

The questions appeared calculated. Had someone suggested he'd had other plans, his mother perhaps? "The Service is the only career, sir, I have ever wished to pursue. I intend that neither my King nor country need ever regret employing me."

"Indeed." Sir John took out his snuff box. "Captain, what do you think of the sugar crop this year?"

He'd been introduced and dismissed – like a child. Adrift in the crowd once more, people had regained their faces, the florid ones belonging to planters, the pale ones to ladies. Sounds transformed themselves into words. *The drought. Sugar crop sparse a second year. The Spaniards. Convoys needed to get our crops safely to England. I hear the Spaniards are everywhere arming. The Spaniards... The French... The slaves...*

Edward returned to where he'd last seen Miss Vaughan. Musicians played a contradance. He scanned the lines of dancers. Miss Vaughan made one of the pairs; her partner, a fat major of the 60th Royal Americans. Edward crashed on a rocky shoal.

The set went on endlessly. At last, the dancers dispersed. A brunette in a pearl grey gown with a plunging décolleté and a dashing colonel in red were the first to promenade by. Edward got behind them. This time would be different.

The major flatteringly took his leave of Miss Vaughan. Too shy to approach, too besotted to leave, Edward stayed where he was. Another officer took his place. Mr. England and Captain Pearse entered. They saw him. Edward couldn't pretend not to see them.

"Enjoying yourself, Mr. Deveare?"

Miss Vaughan had a new partner. "Immensely, Mr. England."

The men of the *Blanche* hadn't opportunity to say anything else before an old lady dressed in a hooped gown fashionable a decade ago and now only worn at court, bore down on them like a three-decker in a gale. Edward had first seen her at Nevis. She was

Rachel Jarvis, the widow of Thomas Jarvis of Nevis and Antigua, a formidable old lady, as outspoken as his mother.

Captain Pearse and Mr. England dropped their heads. It did no good. Mrs. Jarvis stopped directly in front of them, fanning herself hard enough to make even Edward feel it.

"None of our ladies capture your fancy, Captain? No matter. I'll dance with you."

The elderly had certain liberties allowed them, but in asking rather than being asked, Mrs. Jarvis exceeded the bounds. Captain Pearse cleared his throat.

"As it happens – "

"Come now, Captain. I've no husband for you to worry about."

"Well, I'm, hmm, honored, ma'am, but I – hurt my leg. Yes, earlier, disembarking my ship." Pearse shifted his weight onto his left leg and lifted his right foot just off the floor.

"You haven't limped once all night that I've noticed, Captain."

"The pain came upon me suddenly."

Edward watched Miss Vaughan and a naval lieutenant form a new set. A second couple joined them, and a third. From their positions, Edward guessed they must be forming a cotillion, a dance in which four couples formed a square, changing partners.

"How sad. And you, Lieutenant? You look sprightly enough."

"I've danced so much, I fear I'm fatigued. Not that I don't appreciate your asking."

Edward re-checked the square. No fourth couple showed signs of joining. Ladies don't dance with reefers, not while they have lieutenants and captains and majors handy. He stepped in front of his officers and offered his arm. "Madam?"

Rachel Jarvis stopped fanning. "Youth and age, won't we make a nice pair. Well, why not? Come along then, young man, before you change your mind. Captain. Lieutenant. I hope you recover from your indispositions as rapidly as you came by them."

They joined that all important square just as the musicians began playing. Edward would have partnered a hyena for the chance to be near Miss Vaughan.

"May I flatter myself you felt sorry for me, or is there something more?"

"I am *most* happy to dance with you, madam."

"As I thought. Something more."

The cotillion was the "La Royale," an old stand-by, but then, these were the colonies. The couples joined hands and began the "grand rond." Edward and Mrs. Jarvis stood to the left of the first couple and the right of the third. Mrs. Jarvis took the hand of the gentleman partnering Miss Vaughan; Edward glided clockwise with the brunette in iridescent grey.

"The English are so serious when they dance, even the young."

The remark had been addressed in English with a French accent. "Madame?" he said. He assumed she was a "madame" and not a "mademoiselle," for she looked old, past twenty. The lady arched her eyebrows, commenting in French how tiresome balls could be. Edward answered in French it depended on who was present.

"The accent... You surely did not come by it here."

They'd reached the position the first couple had originally taken. "No, I did not." Back at their starting positions, he let go her hand.

The two head gentlemen, those from the first and third couples, took the hands of the ladies on the side and chassed – glided sideways – to the opposite side, then turned halfway; the ladies ended at the sides and the men at the head positions. She was so close; he was so far. The side men had their turn. As required, Edward walked the Frenchwoman to the opposite side.

"Where, then, did you learn?" she asked, as if they'd never parted.

"In England from tutors, in Paris from Frenchmen, then England again."

"Ah, yes. France."

She graced the circle with the other ladies. Edward envied Mrs. Jarvis her hold on Miss Vaughan's hand. The ladies circled and returned; the men followed. During the second change, Edward paired with the old lady.

"I'd watch that female if I were you, young man."

Rachel Jarvis said it so everyone could hear. The French lady inclined her head as he stepped to his left and turned another lady by her left hand. Edward blushed for the old woman.

The dancing returned to the figure. Edward completed the turn with the Frenchwoman. She seemed amused. Then, ah then, came the time for which he'd longed: the Grand Chain. Edward gave Mrs. Jarvis his right hand and walked past her. With the awkward gallantry of adolescence, he gave his left hand – and heart – to Miss Vaughan.

"You stupid boy! You've made us out of step with the music."

Edward groped for the next hand, the Frenchwoman's. She murmured something he didn't catch. Back with Mrs. Jarvis again, the old lady sensibly kept quiet. The dancers did the figure a last time and bowed to their partners. The cotillion had ended.

Edward tried to out-walk the old lady, but she kept abreast. To make matters worse, Pearse came to meet them.

"Not many would humor an old woman, Captain. The hunting begins in September, while your ships are still laid up for the hurricane season. My sons say the shooting looks to be prime."

"I thank you for the invitation, ma'am."

"You needn't wait just for the hunting. The two of you are welcome anytime."

They were trying hard to make him feel better but only succeeding in making things worse. Edward determined he'd get away, make some excuse to Captain Pearse and leave, go somewhere were he could be alone. A graveyard, perhaps.

"I don't believe you ever finished that glass of punch, Mr. Deveare."

Edward half-listened. In the end, it was Pearse's solid presence, the familiar aroma of brandy and sweat that brought him round. The same Negro served them punch. Pearse raised his glass. "To you, for saving Mr. England and me from that old bat."

The *Captain* calling Mrs. Jarvis an "old bat"? Edward pictured a fuzzy white mammal with the old lady's head. The corners of his mouth widened into a mischievous grin.

"First time I've seen you smile, youngster. You should do it more often. You know," he added after downing his cup, "you impressed the Admiral. Made your ship look good."

He'd worked hard to gain the Captain's good opinion. As far as he knew, Pearse hadn't noticed his triumph over Lieutenant Radley. Edward reverted to his old habit of imagining his father standing there, praising him. Instead, all he saw was Pearse. Then a stranger approached.

"Captain Pearse, do you think war with Spain imminent?"

"You've the advantage of me, sir," Pearse said to the newcomer. "You know my name, but I don't yours."

"Forgive my poor manners. I've heard you mentioned and your person pointed out so frequently tonight, I'd forgotten we hadn't been introduced. I'm Josiah Wilkins, post, but half pay. And this, no doubt," the stranger said, with a too familiar smile, "is your son?"

Captain Wilkins wore a plain green frock coat, striped waistcoat, and fawn breeches. That much about him was proper. His presumption, though, alienated Edward as much as it did Pearse. From anyone else, being mistaken for Pearse's son would have been a compliment of the highest order. Coming from this man, it almost seemed a slur.

Pearse maintaining a forbidding silence, Edward replied for him. "I've not that honor, sir."

"Brother, then, or cousin or nephew. There's no denying the bond between you."

"He's merely one of my young gentlemen."

"Only that?"

"You'd do well to return to England, if you're without a commission."

"Home? I haunted the Admiralty chambers more faithfully than a ghost its grave since the end of the American War. I finally gave it up, came out here to see if I could master a schooner, or should war come, a privateer."

"I find little difference between privateers – and pirates."

"And I find little difference between prigs – and certain captains."

Edward waited for Pearse to issue the inevitable challenge, but it never came. Commodore Parker had entered with the Admiral. Wilkins lost no time greeting Parker, who clapped him on the back. Pearse bowed to his superiors and sought other company. Edward had no desire to remain either. Off the punch room was a drawing room. The French lady claimed the sofa, presiding over a court far more extensive than Miss Vaughan's. Protestations for her not to leave were coming from all sides; offers to escort her even more. The fat major begged the loudest. Edward damned him for his fickleness.

"Will Monsieur see me to the ship?"

She smiled languidly at him. Edward wasn't about to be made sport of by another woman. "Madame would do well to ask one of her other cavaliers," he said, also in French.

Her glance round the crowd of men was a statement of sorts, what he didn't know.

"I prefer Monsieur."

The humphing of the fat major decided Edward. She linked her soft arm in his. Without saying good-bye to Antigua's officialdom, they promenaded toward the entrance doors: "French leave." In the antechamber Edward clapped on his hat athwartships while a female slave produced Madame's gauzy wrap. Leaving the hum of Government House behind, he escorted her to a pier where ships' lights danced on the water. Light breezes played with her wrap. He'd never been so aware of a woman before, not even Miss Vaughan. To break the growing spell, Edward resorted to the mundane.

"Where is Madame bound?"

"To France."

"Matters are unsettled there. Have you no fear?"

"What I fear is what must inevitably happen here, retribution far worse than what Frenchmen may exact from other."

She'd openly voiced what so many silently dreaded: a slave revolt. A constant fear among the planters, made worse by cries of freedom raised by the Americans and now, the French. Edward was impressed by her insight. She was different from other ladies he'd met. Around them, ships lay peacefully at anchor. Moonlight made even the most weathered ones smart. The breeze wafted the lady's scent his way. It was a mixture of many things, a fragrance as elusive as its wearer. Edward inhaled deeply.

A ship's boat waited; hers, for the coxswain jumped out when he saw them. Edward helped her in. Her hand sent strange sensations through his. Without being asked, he joined her. They rowed in silence to the Dutch brigantine Willoughby had pointed out. A bo'sun's chair was lowered as soon they came alongside. Edward caught and steadied it. Madame sat down, brushing against him as she did. He quickly climbed the side.

Her cabin was small; two bunks, a table, two chairs, and two trunks. Madame was traveling with someone. Husband, lover, or child? Edward wondered if he should go.

"Chloe, some wine."

B. N. Peacock

"*Oui*, madame." The slave fetched a bottle. She worked a cork until it came open with a loud pop and poured golden bubbles into long stemmed glasses, curtseyed, and left them alone.

Madame rested her arms on those of the chair, "Tell me, where in France did you travel?"

Edward tried the wine. Champagne. He'd tasted it long ago in France. "To Paris. I stayed there some months with my mother."

"And then?"

"The usual route, Calais to Dover." Edward had no desire to talk about his schoolboy days. "Madame has not yet told me the reason she brought me here."

"I hope you will not think badly of me for hearing it."

"Badly, Madame?"

"Monsieur, after that cotillion, I conceived a dislike of a certain young lady. I determined to humble her."

"I'm afraid I don't –"

"To show my favor publicly. Some will envy; some will talk. None will know."

Her eyes had golden depths in them. Scenes aboard *Amphitrite* and elsewhere flooded back, remembrances Edward tried hard to suppress in the company of ladies. His breath quickened. He shouldn't have come.

Madame leaned forward. "One day Monsieur will be something more than handsome."

One day. He'd had enough of being treated like a child. Edward kicked aside his chair and pulled her to him, so that every part of him felt every part of her, kissing her the way a man kisses a woman. It was the shock of what was happening to his body that made him draw back.

"One day, Monsieur, one day."

Calibrating the exact depth of his bow, Edward bade her adieu. Topside, he shouted for the boat crew to take him to St. John's, whether they understood English or not. Seasoned sailors, they guessed correctly.

At Government House, he thrust his hat into a slave's face. The receiving room empty, the musicians not playing, Edward supposed everyone had gone in to supper. He stood before a pier glass and tilted his chin, examining one cheek and then the other, running his fingers over every pore. When he'd finished, he noticed another head above his in the mirror. Edward slowly faced it. Hands on hips, Pearse confronted him.

Some will envy; some will talk. None will know.

CHAPTER THIRTY

For murder though it have no tongue, will speak,
with miraculous organ.

William Shakespeare, *Hamlet* II, ii

Last night, the dream had been more vivid than ever. Jemmy could now identify the hill as the one above Dorking. Tonight, a horse snorted; a tawny owl called. Something was wrong.

Emerging out of the night, the countrymen looked over their shoulders as they backed the wagon through the double doors. Dad shone a dark lantern while the men unbuckled the traces. Double the usual run of brandy. Jemmy noted they were short three men, one being their leader.

His voice edged with their tension, Dad asked, "How long?"

"Two nights, maybe three. Exciseman's dogging us."

The countrymen had never left contraband more than one night and then, not with the wagon. Jemmy looked at Dad, but the dark lantern his father held illuminated the horses, not his face.

The smugglers finished and faded back into the night. Jemmy bit his knuckles. What they did was wrong. What he and Dad were doing was wrong. Did the dream show the inevitable result?

The wagon safely stowed, Jemmy climbed back into the loft. Afraid of dreaming, he fought sleep. Morning brought blessed relief. Jemmy held his breath when he climbed down the ladder. Maybe, just maybe... The wagon was still there.

Dad kept working when he came down. Jemmy also did his chores in silence. The wagon and its contraband cast a pall over the cottage.

Only Nan found nothing unusual. Over breakfast, she babbled about the pretty bird on the rowan limb. On their way to Dorking, she picked bluebells. Today was market day.

When they passed the farmer's house where they'd rebuilt the granary, Nan ran through the gate and hugged the farmer's wife. The woman laughed and kissed her. People always warmed to silly Nan.

All went well until they came to the fork in the road leading to Bury Hill.

"Jemmy, lake."

Jemmy grasped Nan and hurried her down Coldharbor Lane. He was thankful Dad hadn't heard. Green tiger beetles raced along a sandy patch, launched into short flight, and dropped to earth again. They and the green woodpecker flying overhead had likely found a cache of ants. Nature's normalcy temporarily allayed his forebodings.

The crazy Frenchman's house, Hole in the Wall, lay behind the houses on the right. Jemmy lifted his hat, and ran his arm over his forehead. From what he'd heard, the Frogs had gone mad. Not only that, there was talk of France siding with the dons against England. Jemmy clenched his fists. The Navy would teach them not to harm British sailors. His flash of patriotism flickered. As a deserter and a smuggler, the Navy was now something to be feared.

On Butter Hill, women haggled over the price of eggs. A farm girl told a town woman she'd no more cheese to sell. Moving on, to the corner where West Street, South Street, and East Street converged, the Sweetmans turned into East Street. Jemmy slowed going past the cutler's shop. None of the knives there equaled the one he'd owned for less than an hour.

The spires of St. Martin's Church dominated the town. Near the church, men with walking sticks and women with market baskets pointed to a tired horse and talked excitedly. Wondering what it meant, Jemmy drew closer.

"Murder, that's what I say! As bad as the old Hawkhurst Gang!"

"My Kate does for the family. She said his missus were beside herself this morn. Couldn't eat nor drink, she were that worried."

Jemmy stiffened. The Hawkhurst Gang had been desperate smugglers, their exploits so wicked local folk still recounted them in whispers these many years later. They'd brutally murdered two men: one an old man, a tide-waiter in the Customs office; the other, a witness who was going to testify against them. Last night, the bother about the exciseman. Dear God, no, Jemmy anguished, they can't mean him.

"Jemmy, take Nan and go home. I've business to tend, something I hadn't thought on afore." Dad, too, had heard. He, too, anticipated trouble. Jemmy longed to stay with Dad but judged it wiser to obey. But when he looked for his sister, his uneasiness turned to panic. She was gone.

A man with a wicker hamper full of chicks scolded as Jemmy ploughed clear. Nan liked Atlee's pond. Jemmy reasoned she'd go there to watch the mill wheel, like she sometimes did. The back of his mind doubted it. Still, he raced upstream, to where the mill wheel churned water into shafts of vari-colored light, which in turn, collected into sparkling ripples. Up one side of the Pippbrook and down the other, children played but not Nan.

Water. The lake. She'd stopped at the lane to the estate. Jemmy ran down Mill Lane, then East Street. Panic drove his legs. The exciseman had connected them to the estate, and Dad to the countrymen, and now the exciseman was missing.

He came to the fork where three streets met. West Street, he'd go by West Street rather than South Street. If, by some chance, Dad was making his way home, Jemmy would be less likely to meet him. Fewer people ranged this part of town. He ran full out, past Clarendon House, to where West Street became the Westcott-Guildford Road. Where South Street ended and Coldharbor Lane began, a side track veered to the right. Jemmy raced down it.

Farmers and their wives drifted down the lane. A cart piled with empty baskets rattled down South Street. Jemmy ran into a field to avoid it. Not wanting to be recognized, he kept to the field and ran west. A better route, he'd reach Hampstead Lane sooner.

When he got there, he had to rest. His lungs burned from running, and his side ached. He only stayed long enough to get his wind. Nan, crazy, straying Nan. She'd bring ruin to them all.

Mad to find her, Jemmy groped for the tumbledown section of wall. Rubble had been cleared, and fresh brickwork begun. Begun, but fortunately not finished. Jemmy anxiously grasped either edge of the wall and hoisted himself over. Sunlight made delicate patterns on beech leaves. Bracken sent new fronds curling upward. The place was as serene as ever, the opposite of what he was. There, by the lake, sat Nan. He started toward her.

"We've bagged the beggars, by God!"

The hand grabbing his shoulder tightened to a vise-like hold. Struggling helplessly, Jemmy watched his captor's companion seize his sister. Jemmy's captor marched him down a graveled walkway. Nan held the other groundskeeper's hand and trotted meekly after him. Nothing could save them now.

The manor house proved less grand than he'd previously imagined. A simple brick building with multiple chimneys nestled in a hollow or dene. The party skirted the house to a neat cottage nestled among oaks.

"Mr. Lawry! We caught them young rascals as what's been trespassing."

A man in a brown suit exited the cottage. The look he gave Jemmy made him feel like a worm. "Hobbs," he said, "send for the steward. He must know of this as well."

The groundskeeper holding Nan handed her over to Jemmy's captor and ran to the manor. As if Jemmy weren't apprehensive enough, the name jarred. Hobbs, hadn't he been the one the exciseman brought that day to identify them?

"Please, sir," Jemmy said. "We don't mean no harm. My sister, she's simple. If you just let us go, I'll see to it she don't never come back."

"What's your name, boy?"

"I – Jemmy, sir."

"Jemmy who?"

"Just Jemmy." He refused to link Dad to them. "Please, your honor, let us go. We won't come back. I promise. Not ever again."

"Nan come back," Nan said, contradicting him.

Had he been able, Jemmy would have smacked her. His indignation was damped by the arrival of Hobbs with a tall, genteel man.

"This calls for the bailiff, Lawry," the newcomer said.

"It's market day, Murdoch," Lawry said. "Easier to send them to him."

Jemmy watched the debate between the steward and gardener with growing dread. Dad mustn't be brought into this, not with the exciseman missing. Yet the arrangement contrived dashed his hopes of escape. Three groundskeeprs would take them to Dorking and hand them over to the bailiff, Hobbs commanding.

The servants herded the children to town as if they were errant cattle. Jemmy grew rebellious as the men bragged of the reward they'd get for bagging the smuggler's brats. One of them cuffed him for calling them names.

In Dorking, Hobbs importantly inquired for the bailiff. Try the Red Lion, they were told. Before they came to the inn, however, they met an excited crowd. Their group temporarily forgot their purpose and moved closer. Jemmy strained to catch the interchange between two men in the center of the mob.

"When did you see Tim Vining last?" an official sounding voice asked.

"I never seed any such one."

"Come now, my man. Vining accused you of being a smuggler and thief, before witnesses."

"If he be the exciseman, the first I saw him 'twere the last, and that be the God's truth."

"His horse came home without him, the saddle bloodied. I say you saw him again."

"I didn't see nor hear nothing last night. I be home, with my children."

Jemmy's frantic attempt to wrench free and go to his father only recalled Hobbs to his errand. He approached the bailiff, Dad's accuser.

"We caught these two East Dene way, by the lake," Hobbs said, puffing out his chest. "Could be the two crimes is one."

"Don't you be dirtying my children with your lies!"

"If they're so good," Hobbs said, "why was they at the manor?"

The veins in Dad's temple swelled. Jemmy took action before his father did anything rash. "Nan strays. She don't know half o' what she does. Ask anyone hereabouts. I'm always having to chase after her!" Jemmy checked the crowd for the farmer, for anyone to verify his words, but no one stepped forward.

"You got horse but not man," Dad said. "Might be Vining come back. Let us be."

The bailiff looked uncertainly from the father to the children. It seemed he might let them go until Hobbs stuck his nose in again.

"The young ones trespassed on Lord Evington's lands. Lord Onslow hisself taking her ladyship's concern, seems to me you should do your duty by them."

Dad took out some coins. "If my children did harm there, I'll pay."

"Wasn't a matter of harm," Hobbs blustered, "just their being there."

"If I give you this and my word they won't stray there no more, will you let them go?"

Hobbs licked his lips. He badly wanted the money. The question was, Jemmy wondered, would his fear of his master's retribution outweigh his greed?

"This will save having to send for the Justice," the bailiff said, more like a man more eager for his dinner than for weighty justice to be done. "As for you, Sweetman, go, but not too far. Should you try to flee, we'll come after you!"

Dad handed his purse to Hobbs. Jemmy might be free from his captors but not his foreboding. What if someone followed them and found the wagon and the contraband?

Dad beckoned them to him. Nan sheltered beside her father; Jemmy slunk behind. Muttering ugly things, the crowd let them pass.

It was a long, dreary walk home. Jemmy trembled when Dad opened the door. The interior was dim, but not so dim Jemmy couldn't see. Or rather, it was what he couldn't see that made him gasp. The wagon was gone.

CHAPTER THIRTY-ONE

... every citizen ought to be a soldier and every soldier a citizen.

Jean-Jacques Rosseau, *The Social Contract*

"*Mon dieu*, you couldn't kill a chicken, let alone a man."

Beldoque was unmerciful. He'd ordered Louis to attack him with his "bayonet." Yet when Louis charged with his wooden musket, Beldoque not only parried his thrust, he knocked the pretend weapon out of his hands. Louis didn't know which hurt most, his wrists or his pride.

He'd show Beldoque. Louis rushed his friend. Although Beldoque looked like he was lounging, he deftly sidestepped and whacked Louis with his "musket" as he shot past.

"Citizen Fool, do you think I survived '*la fête*' by falling for such tricks?"

Louis shook his head in an attempt to clear it. This had become a matter of honor. Clutching his make-believe weapon, he drove headlong into Beldoque – and ended facedown on the ground.

Beldoque planted his wooden musket at the base of Louis' neck. "Three times I could have killed you. That is enough for one day, I think, Private Saulnier."

Beldoque lifted the stick. The wind knocked out of him, Louis lay there a while. When he did struggle to his feet, it was to the tune of Lecluselles' merry, "The English have nothing to fear from you."

The English, the ultimate insult. Louis called Lecluselle an ass and stumbled toward the hut. It was because of the English they'd joined a militia unit, one of many forming to defend Trinidad from an English attack. Rumors had it Spain was sending troops and ships to the region to protect its interests. In the meantime, her colonies had to protect themselves as best they could. Angry, frustrated, and hurting, Louis vowed he'd fight to the death. Halfway there, chagrined, somewhat more realistic, but no less hurting, he had an unpleasant thought. Would death happen as quickly as defeat had at Beldoque's hands?

"Eh, my friend, do not take this morning's exercise too seriously. I, too, did poorly when I first joined."

Lecluselle attempting humor again. He was funny only to himself, or rather to Beldoque as well, for his two friends sported wide grins. Nor did they offer apologies. Louis scowled so deeply the lines threatened to permanently etch themselves into his skin. He slammed the door behind him.

Safe inside, he collapsed groaning into a chair. Soon, he must again see to the never-ending removal of trees and stumps. The Spanish had owned this island many years; thanks to their indolence, the land remained much as they'd found it. Louis cursed them for their laziness for it made more work for him.

His latest contribution to the *Gazetta* consoled him. Jean Villoux's commentaries about the Constituent Assembly had not been well received. Under Louis' tutelage, he extolled the role of the citizen and decried that of the King. Not that the Fat Veto counted much, after the October Days. Out here, though, monarchs still commanded reverence, or at least to the many. But there were the few. During his last visit to Port of Spain, Villoux had introduced Louis to a "friend of liberty," one Juan de Mendoza. Some colonists longed to emulate the Americans and rid themselves of Spanish rule. Mendoza said little of his own activities, but eagerly drank in all Louis had to tell of events in France.

His musings were interrupted as the door opened and a more serious Beldoque pulled up a chair beside him. Wood grated on wood, clean wood, for slaves tended them. Slaves everywhere. And yet, in Paris, orators argued all men were free.

"Are you recovered yet?"

"Do you really wish to know?"

"Your tongue is sharp; you must be well. Listen, my friend, what I did was for your own good. From now on, we must drill in earnest, else –"

"In earnest? What do you call what we did this day? Play?"

"I tested you, to see of what you were made."

"You said you could have killed me three times."

"And so I could, so anyone could. You are hot to fight, but the problem is, you do not yet know how. We must use every free moment to drill, to teach you to control your impulses, to assess your opponent's weaknesses. Then, who knows, you may try to take me. Try, I say."

"And succeed, Citizen."

"I would not use that term here. Caron and the others are royalists, as is Governor Chacón. Me, I do not care, nor does Lecluselle. No real equality can ever exist between man and man."

"If all insist on accepting the way things are, rather than struggle to make them the way they ought to be, then there is nothing. All are enslaved, save only the King."

"The printer of the *Gazetta* has not been to Paris. Yet from what he writes, someone has. Was that someone you, my friend?"

"You know I owe Citizen Caron my passage money," Louis said sullenly.

"Forbear that word!"

"I thought once you believed as I do."

"I believe what I believe," Beldoque said, "and keep my beliefs to myself. I advise you do likewise. Trinidad is not Paris."

Beldoque had progressed from martinet to philosopher. To escape the scourge of his words – and of his conscience – Louis collected his field attire. The large straw hat, so like that of the planters, repelled him. Sunstroke or no sunstroke, he rejected it.

Beldoque wasn't finished with him, though. "The grandee from France is everywhere feted. Alphonse attends a party in his honor at the Leyperouse plantation. That ought to put him in good humor. Let us do nothing which might reverse it on his return."

Louis couldn't believe what he heard. Caron had made his former comrades in arms into indentured servants, years of work to be exacted for their passage. How could Beldoque urge him to keep silent? Louis showed what he thought of Caron and his kind by stomping on the straw hat. *À bas* Beldoque and his caution! Villoux thought as he thought. He'd see to it he learned more, and printed every word. And with Caron absent, a surreptitious trip to Port of Spain would be easier to arrange.

Not yet midday and the day already was steamy. Louis thought the heat raised the scent of flagrantly bright flowers to overpowering cheapness, like that of the Palais-Royal demoiselles' perfumes. Oh, to be anywhere but here. Despite Beldoque's not so subtle warning, he'd tell Villoux more of the Palais-Royal and its cafes and speakers the next time he saw him. And something else besides, that song he'd heard before he'd left Paris. He'd previously judged it too taunting to repeat here. Not any more.

> Ah, it goes well, it goes well, it goes well,
> The people of today sing without ending.
> Ah, it goes well, it goes well, it goes well,
> Despite traitors, success is all impending.
>
> Let us rejoice for the good times are coming,
> The French people once were nobodies
> But now the aristocrats say, "We are guilty."
> Ah, it goes well, it goes well, it goes well.

The slaves waited at a new clearing, guarded by a mulatto freedman. Had they heard him? The mulatto complained Louis was late coming. Louis pointed to the path. This time of day, the slaves were usually in the middle of some rhythmic chant. Today, however, they didn't sing. It was as if they were expecting someone to lead them. Louis shrugged. So be it. He took up where he'd left off.

> And we will no longer have nobles or priests.
> Ah, it goes well, it goes well, it goes well,
> Equality will reign throughout the world
> And the Austrian slave will follow it.

236

B. N. Peacock

The slaves stopped work. Perhaps he'd gone too far. Perhaps he should have paid heed to Beldoque. Perhaps –

Then he saw their rags, their ribs showing through their skin, their unkempt wooly hair. Why shouldn't he sing the song? Louis threw back his head. In a voice lusty enough for the world to hear, he sang,

Hang the aristocrats from the lamp posts!

Let tyrants hear and tremble. As soon as he finished, he'd slip into Port of Spain and give Villoux not only what he'd written, but the lyrics of "Ça Ira" in their entirety as well.

CHAPTER THIRTY-TWO

Cry "Havoc!"and let slip the dogs of war.

William Shakespeare, *Julius Caesar*, III.i

The last of eighteen men pressed from merchant ships off Sandy Point, St Kitts had been gotten aboard. The Admiralty had sent orders that all ships on station be brought up to fighting complement. Laforey had sent word via the schooner *Berbice* for *Blanche* to add twenty men to her official complement of two hundred.

Pearse watched Lieutenant Stark muster the new men, only eighteen, but prime hands from the looks of them. Two reefers, pistols in hand, acted as sheep dogs to the fold, Mr. Deveare one. He'd instructed Mr. England to take the boy along. He had to be broken in to the dirty side of the Service sooner or later.

The Captain addressed them from the break of the quarterdeck. "I'm Richard Pearse of His Majesty's ship, *Blanche*. No doubt most of you have served in King's ships before, so I'll be brief. I'm a fair man and look to the welfare of my people. Do your duty, and all will go well. Do less, and you'll find I'm no soft captain. You've already made the acquaintance of Lieutenant England, our second. He'll see to it our purser outfits you with such slops and bedding as you require. Lieutenant Stark, our first, will take your papers and assign you your stations." Carefully forbearing to roll his eyes, Pearse left the rest to Stark. It was a bad thing to undermine the authority of your officers in front of the ratings, no matter how dense they might be.

Laforey had sent word for *Blanche* to proceed north and rendezvous with *Trusty.* Pearse speculated there might be problems with his seizure of the *William* brig his last cruise round Grenada. She purportedly hailed from St. John's, Newfoundland, but her master and several seamen were undeniably American, in contradiction to the Navigation Acts. The judge of the Court of Admiralty in Grenada, who also happened to be the Chief Justice in the Common Pleas there and a plantation owner, had refused Pearse a certificate of probable cause for taking the vessel.

It was a short sail from St. Kitts to Tortola. Sir John wasted no time getting down to business.

"Your ship full complement?"

"Nearly. We'll bag the others soon, Sir John."

"Good. You'll have need of them. The dons are arming. The governor of Porto Rico contracts for timber to build barracks for the two regiments he daily expects from Spain. The French may yet stick their noses in. Remember, they've a seventy-four for their flagship and more ships than we. Parker and his ships have left, and I must send *Sybil* home soon. Then there's *Bonetta,* set to convoy our merchantmen to England, leaving us scarcely enough ships to defend Antigua, let alone the other islands. Spanish ships harass our fishing boats, and Sir John Orde complains I must do more to protect his precious Domenica. And now this!"

All attention, Pearse waited for him to proceed.

"The governor of Trinidad alleges an English privateer plunders Spanish ships."

"An English privateer? But that's preposterous, Sir John!"

"So say I."

"Do you think the Spanish want to create an incident, then, and force us into war?"

"Had this come from anyone save Governor Chacón, I'd say yes. That is what's so puzzling. He is eminently reasonable, no firebrand, and profits much from trade with Grenada. Still, it could be a trick. You're to deliver my official denial to His Excellency. Verbally, you are to reiterate that insofar as I know, we are not at war, and I have not issued any letters of marque. Along the way, notify whatever merchant ships and HM cruisers you bespeak that the sugar fleet gathers at Antigua, thence to be convoyed home by Ricketts and *Bonetta*. I also charge you to gather as much information as you can on the deployment of Spanish men-o'-war and merchantmen as well."

"When do I make sail?"

"The instant you finish taking on necessary stores. Remember, the hurricane season will soon be upon us. Hostilities apart, you must try to return by the end of July. Do you speak Spanish?"

"No, but my second lieutenant was the dons' 'guest' during the last war."

"Anyone else?"

Pearse considered *Blanche's* officers. Stark was fortunate to speak English, let alone Spanish. The Master, Mr. Duncan, doubtful. Jameson, the surgeon, definitely not, although he spoke some French. As for the midshipmen, nothing there. Except –

"Mr. Deveare claims he speaks three languages, one of which is Spanish."

"Deveare? Well, it's to be expected, I suppose. The mother's a bluestocking as well as a shrew. Be careful of him, though. I've a feeling the First Lord himself will yet send for the boy."

"I'll do what I can, Sir John, but he must take his chances like the rest of us."

"So he must. My letter to His Excellency, Captain. And your orders."

Pearse pondered the Admiral's commands. Two more impressed men and victuals were easy enough to come by. A competent translator, though, was another matter. Could he rely on Mr. Deveare, should England fail him? Be careful of him, Sir John had warned.

One month to do all he'd been ordered and return to English Harbor. His errand to Trinidad and back wouldn't take that long, if all went well. Pearse looked up at *Blanche's* side. He'd do his best to see things went well, by God, translator or no translator. Or Mr. Deveare.

Chapter Thirty-Three

In the prospect of poverty there is nothing but gloom
and melancholy.

Samuel Johnson, *The Rambler*, No. 53

Jemmy dumped the basin of washing-up water in the yard. He
hadn't had much cleaning up to do after supper. There hadn't been
much supper.

Ever since the exciseman's horse had been discovered,
speculation buzzed about what had happened to him. They no
longer went to Dorking since Jemmy and Nan had been caught at
the lake. With suspicions running high, it wasn't safe.

Jemmy went back inside and set the basin on the table, leaving
Nan twisting blades of grass outside. Dad would be home soon.
Jemmy guessed he'd been to the Queen's Head, the nearest public
house their side of Dorking. Jemmy carefully stored the basin on a
dry sink, tidied the shelves a last time, and checked the pantry. He
didn't want to give Dad reason to be angry.

"Can't a man come home without shouting for his own?"

Jemmy stuck his head out the door. His father's gait was
unsteady. "I be clearing up, inside, like you said," he said warily.

The older Sweetman hung onto the door. "Why can't you be
there to greet me like Nan?"

Jemmy kept to the farther end of the table. Oblivious to reality as always, Nan hugged her father's legs. Twisted blades of grass fell onto the freshly swept floor.

"Might come tonight."

Dad said that every time he came back like this. The countrymen hadn't come since that last night. No one came.

"Put up the table. Can't see to do it in dark."

They'd upended the table whenever there had been word of a run. Without the table to divide them, Dad would have a clear field at him. Jemmy grasped an end. The table edge left a mark on his hands. Jemmy jerked sideways. His right hand lost its grip, and his arm flew back. The pain in his elbow told him he'd hit something.

"They be coming! Quick, Jemmy, take Nan and hide!"

Dad had schooled them in what to do if they came to arrest him. Jemmy and Nan were to hide in the space their father had fashioned at the side of the chimney. Dad was to scurry up the loft and escape out the back.

"Daddy go now?"

Her words had a sobering effect on their father. He laughed awkwardly. "Nay, little maid, 'twere just foolishness."

Dad more in his right senses, Jemmy worried he looked so worn. He brought out the little bread he'd saved and laid it before him.

Their father gazed at the plate. "You be a good boy, Jemmy," he said but didn't touch the food. Instead, he stroked Nan's hair. "My little maid. Don't you never forget your Dad." He rested both hands on top her head, like a priest Jemmy had once seen blessing a baby. Dad's eyes moistened. "Never let them part you and Nan."

Part them. Jimmy decided it was time to broach a subject he long been considering. "We could go away, far from here. I was in a place called New York. It –"

"We be Englishmen! I don't be going to no place what rejects its King."

"Daddy see them?"

Jemmy and Dad stared. Through the open door, five men could be seen hurrying down the path. What they had long feared was happening.

"Quick, Jemmy!"

Jemmy grabbed Nan and pushed a wooden frame that appeared to be nailed to the hearth bricks. He crammed his larger body in after his sister's and pulled hard. The frame wouldn't swing shut. Jemmy grasped it with both hands and pulled with all he had. When it yielded, he fell backwards against Nan.

"There he be, the murderer! Bold as brass!"

That's why the frame had swung shut so easily, Jemmy realized with horror. Dad had stayed behind to close it. Jemmy heard every word clearly. The men must be in the room. Not trusting himself, let alone Nan, he clamped a shaky hand over her mouth.

"Thought no one would find where you buried him, Sweetman?"

Jemmy recognized the voice. It belonged to the bailiff.

"I be bloodguiltless."

"Bloodguiltless? We found this stuck in Vining's ribs. It's plain whose it is."

Jemmy pressed his head against the bricks. *None of this is really happening. I'll wake and find it naught but a dream.* The dream. So this was how it would come to pass.

Mettle rattled and clanked. They must be putting manacles on Dad's hands and ankles. Jemmy wanted to scream, "The others did it, not him!" but no sound came. *Think on you and your sister, Jemmy. And me.* That's what Dad had told him that when they'd first practiced hiding. He was to keep quiet no matter what happened, before and after. Smugglers were dangerous men. Were Jemmy to talk and Dad go free, they might hunt them all down and kill them. Desperate to the point of almost opening the frame, Jemmy raged there had to be a way to save Dad.

"What about the children?"

Recalling his sister, Jemmy mashed his hand against Nan's mouth until her teeth pressed his palm. She wriggled but did nothing else. Dad had made her promise to keep silent, too.

"You leave my children be! They done nothing, no more than me!"

"Find them," said the bailiff. "They can't be far. The cutler swore t'were the boy's knife."

The hunting knife? Someone must have found it. And used it to –

"Let's get the murderous dog away. Don't want to be caught out at night with the rest of the gang loose."

Nan whimpered. Jemmy repositioned both hands until they covered her face, her nose and eyes as well as mouth. He'd choke her if she so much as swallowed.

The tromp-tramp began anew, together with crashing and banging. They were looking for him and Nan. They stayed in the hiding hole until the the tread of heavy footsteps had left and their cramped young bodies could stand no more. Jemmy cracked open the frame. He pushed harder, pausing to make sure no one there was before exiting the space. Nan scrambled past him.

"Daddy, Daddy! Nan want you!"

When their father didn't answer, Nan flailed the air with her hands. Afraid someone had stayed behind, Jemmy crushed her to him. Her small body twisted and writhed. For the first time in her life, she sobbed. For the first time in his life, Jemmy hugged her tenderly to him.

He waited until she'd quieted before he let her go. When he moved, his shoes crunched broken crockery. Treading carefully, Jemmy salvaged what he could from the wreck. It wasn't much, a shirt, a smock, some tools. Remarkably, his fiddle was undamaged. Perhaps it was the only part of their lives that still was.

Nan stroked the instrument. Jemmy struggled to find something to say that would reassure them both.

"Don't fret," he said at last. "We'll find Dad."

CHAPTER THIRTY-FOUR

Who truly are active citizens? Those who have taken the Bastille...

Camille Desmoulins,
Les Revolutions de France et de Brabant.

Albertine Saulinier wrapped her cloak tightly about her. The weather was wet and cool for summer in Paris. She hadn't stopped by her husband's room to tell him she was leaving. There was no need. She attended her charities, just as she had for all the years of their marriage. Besides, she'd little to say to Jean-Claude once she'd learned about Louis, or he to her. Father and son, they were both stubborn fools, according to their ways. Her trouble was that she loved them both, foolishly, each according to her own way.

A hamper with provisions waited on the stand by the door. Despite all the upheavals designed to help them, the poor needed food and drink more than ever. She resolutely grasped the handles of the basket. Let it be so. She would again succor the needy. Others needed her care, others who might know something about Louis.

The fiacre that usually waited at the corner wasn't there. She peered down the street in hopes the cabby had moved to a more advantageous spot, the better to attract the throngs daily arriving for the Fête de la Fédération, but no cab was in sight. The cabby probably had already found a fare.

She tugged her hood impatiently as she angled her head to avert the drizzle. Riverlets coursing down the paving stones damped her feet. Come what may, she'd fulfill her mission.

"Madame?"

The query was twice repeated before Albertine realized she was being addressed. In a world increasingly styled "Citizen" and "Citizeness," the old form was reassuring.

"Madame, if you would be so good –"

A young woman addressed her shyly. Beneath her woolen shawl a blue muslin gown hung limply, and her mobcap was as soggy as the red, white, and blue ribbons pasted to it. The tricolor. If the girl was a beggar, she had chosen the wrong benefactress.

The stranger tried again. "Your son, I – have not heard from him."

"Mademoiselle, do I know you?"

"Pardon, Madame. I am Marie-Rose Barré, a friend of Louis."

"His mistress, you mean."

The girl hung her head. Albertine was gratified she had the grace to be ashamed. Shame and something else. Tears, not raindrops, trickled down her face. She must be in love with him.

"He has left France, to seek his fortune in the Indies. More than that, I cannot say. I seek one who may know more. If you like, you may attend me."

Liberty trees bloomed on the streets leading to the Champ de Mars. Some were real trees bedecked with the red, white, and blue streamers, others just poles crowned with red hats, liberty caps, they were called. Albertine had as little success in shielding her thoughts as she had her face from the rain. In the space of a year, Paris was much changed.

With less than a month until the celebration of the fall of the Bastille, National Guard units, or federations as they were called, gathered from every part of France. Citizens shoveled the dirt of the Champ de Mars into a swamp, alongside their fellow Guardsmen from Paris, alongside the famous and the great. None were too good to ready the field for the Fête de la Fédération, not even the King.

In a crowd of soggy strangers, Albertine searched for a figure dear to her since childhood. Bertrand must surely be here. He *had* to be here.

B. N. Peacock

Half-built structures erupted like boils from the earth. Central to the celebration, the Altar of the Fatherland looked more like a chewed honeycomb than a pyramid. Workers stopped as she passed. She listlessly let them rifle the contents of her basket. Adhering to the current custom, they rummaged more than they took. No one wished to appear a greedy *aristo*.

Bertrand saw her before she saw him. Bertrand Meslier, erstwhile advocate, pamphleteer, friend of Danton, hailed her.

"Albertine! *Mon dieu*, what do you here? You will catch your death in this deluge."

"If I catch my death, it will be because of other things."

"Your husband, no doubt," Bertrand said, leaning on his spade. He wore the black of the people, his hat adorned with the slogan, "*Fraternité*." "Has his intransigence driven you here?"

"I am no popularist. I came – we came – to learn news of Louis."

Bertrand, never the gallant, hastily tipped his hat to Marie-Rose, who nearly slipped in the mud delivering a curtsey. She was sweet, this little one, Albertine mused. A demoiselle would have been much more brazen.

"That scapegrace?"

"You have no letters from him?"

"Me? Assuredly not. Go home, my cousin, and dry yourself by the fire. When I do hear from him, I will not hesitate to tell him what I think of him!"

Bertrand's attempted comfort was as soothing as a lamppost's embrace, but hadn't he always been awkward around women, even her? Anxious to leave activities she disapproved, she thanked him for his time. With a clumsy pat on the arm, he bade her good-bye.

The soil where she walked hadn't been touched, but Albertine's progress was labored. There was so much to think about, and to worry about, even more. Finally, even she had to notice how her muddy skirt weighed her down and her legs made hardly any forward progress. The little one, the shy one, came boldly to her aid.

"Madame," Marie-Rose said, taking the hamper from her, "allow me."

Albertine murmured a heartfelt thanks. Both hands now free to lift her skirts above the ooze, she started slowly onward. "It is as

249

the Citizen says," she resignedly told her helper. "We have no choice but to wait until Louis writes."

CHAPTER THIRTY-FIVE

The miserable have no other medicine
But only hope.

William Shakespeare, *Measure for Measure*, III. 1

Having no one else to turn to, Jemmy stealthily made his way to the farmer's home after Dad's arrest. After much pleading, he, or rather his wife, agreed to shelter Nan. As for Jemmy, they were adamant. He had to take refuge elsewhere.

Despite their refusal, the farmer's wife provided him with food and drink and directed him to a cave where he could hide. The area around Dorking abounded with caves. Jemmy had heard of them before; the large one in town was used as a wine cellar. There were tales of how the caves extended all the way to Guildford, and how the countrymen used them for their trade. Jemmy knew the countrymen's route well enough to scoff at such tales. But caves there were, and such as they were, offered him sanctuary, if only for a night.

Actually, the farmer's wife had no need to give him directions. Jemmy already knew about this certain cave. In happier times, Nan had led him there, prattling of the flowers she'd found. The cave's location was pleasant enough in daylight, sheltered at the bottom of the hill behind their cottage. But this was night, with smugglers and officials eager to find him.

It was so dark. If only they could have let him stay. His nerves stretched tauter than his fiddle strings, Jemmy crept down the path leading from the farmer's house. As soon as he could, he left the path for the shelter of such trees as he could find. He heard a noise and started. A fox ran across the field. Jemmy berated himself for his foolishness and moved on.

When at last he came to the cave, he eased his body cautiously into it. As caves went, it wasn't large, but it would do. He pushed in until he was satisfied he could not be seen. He tried to sleep but his conscience attacked him. The red knife, if only he hadn't asked Dad to buy it. An even worse thought surfaced. He'd returned to England meaning to protect Dad, but instead become the instrument of his doom.

"Be you there?"

Sounds had built themselves into words many times over before Jemmy stirred. He must have dozed.

"He's been taken away. You have to go. Now. Before someone's catches on."

The world the other side of the cave was dark, but not as dark as his. Jemmy worried someone might see them. "Where they be taking him?"

"Hsst!" The farmer doused his light.

Like a startled turtle, Jemmy withdrew into his shelter. He prepared himself for the worst, but this time, the worst didn't come. After interminable minutes, the farmer's hoarse whisper penetrated the cave.

"I brought these for you. Can't have them, lest they be found."

A sack clanked at the mouth of the cave. From the sounds, Jemmy supposed they were the remnants of Dad's carpenter tools, the ones he'd salvaged from their cottage. He started to untie the rope fastening the sack, but the farmer, in his anxiety to be rid of the threat Jemmy posed, urged him to take them and go.

"Where they be taking Dad?" Jemmy asked, risking normal tones to force the man to answer.

"To Kingston, to the Assizes," the farmer said, fleeing, "God help him!"

Chapter Thirty-Six

Vive la nation, au diable les aristocrats!

Citizen soldiers of Champagne, 1790

"Face to the right.

"Face to the right about.

"Face to the right about.

"Face to the right about.

"Poise your arms."

Louis unerringly executed every one of Beldoque's commands. He stood at attention, proudly gripping the '66 Charleville with which he now practiced. Beldoque sniffed it was one of the relics sold to the Americans during their war against the English. The 60-inch musket weighed 10 pounds, and its walnut stock felt bulky to the hand, but to Louis, it far surpassed drilling with wooden sticks. He'd memorized its every feature: a button rod to ram powder and a .69 calibre ball down the 44 ¾ inch smooth bore barrel, a banded barrel, i.e., one attached by steel bands to the stock, making it more reliable in hand-to-hand fighting. Moreover, it had a double-throated cock and a friction held bayonet, making it superior to the Spanish *escopetas*, and the much overrated English Brown Bess. His one regret was that this particular Charleville had a touch of rust on the priming pan, a casualty of the climate.

When Beldoque was satisfied, he barked, "Dismissed." Louis returned the Charleville to a waiting stand. It, like the musket, had been provided by the Marquis. Where he'd gotten the cache, no one knew. Louis begrudged the source but valued the arms. Militias were forming to combat the growing English threat.

Caron commanded their unit and charged Beldoque with training the raw recruits. Lecluselle grumbled about the injustice, as he put it. Lecluselle had told Louis much about Beldoque, the latter being laconic about his past. Beldoque hadn't been just a sergeant but an *officier de fortune*, a rank something more than a sergeant but less than an officer. The Segur law sealed his fate in the French army, making it virtually impossible for him to become an officer before middle age and even then, able to progress no further than captain. Yet because Caron had successfully forged his four quarterings of nobility, with the help of Madame, his wife, he named himself colonel of their unit. Beldoque said nothing, but Louis agreed with Lecluselle. It was more than an outrage.

"Good, but not good enough. Still, it must do for now."

"What do you mean? I made no mistakes."

"None that matter for a militia. On the parade ground, in a real army, ah, that would be a different matter."

"But –"

"Enough. Let us enjoy our dinner while we may. We drill with the entire company, such as it is, later."

"Such as it is" was a swipe at the motley group of *grands blancs* and worse still, *petits blancs* drawn from the surrounding plantations. Of the *grands blancs*, Gleason opted out, claiming his French wasn't good enough to understand complicated orders. The other planters came, bringing their hunting rifles with them, as if they would do any good. A well-handled Charleville could get off three rounds per minute; a rifle took two to three minutes just to load. The rifles had value as skirmishers, or *tirailleurs*, but the *grands blancs* considered such employment unworthy. Of the *petits blancs*, the poor whites, only Beldoque, Lecluselle, and Louis transcended uselessness.

Louis and Beldoque dined together, minus Lecluselle, who did his turn overseeing the work at the clearing. The slave who served as their cook had the table laid and the dinner ready to serve.

The smell of lentils and yams didn't stir Louis' appetite. He ate out of need alone, longing for chicken stewed in herbs and a glass of good Bordeaux: French food, not Creole. France, what was happening in the Assembly, at the Palais-Royal? Were his friends at University still studying ancient trivia when they could be making history in the streets? Did they think of him? Mother Albertine would regret his absence. And Marie-Rose, did she regret her temper? Did Bertrand?

"Saulnier, Caron has his ear stuck to the Marquis' mouth. He demands stricter discipline, to improve the militia's performance."

"I am superior to most, save you and Lecluselle. I have nothing to fear."

"From me, no. I have heard rumours, though, the *Gazetta* intends to publish the *Declaration of the Rights of Man and Citizen*. The Marquis will not be happy to see it again. It is said citizens sacked his chateau after they heard its provisions."

"What has this to do with me?"

"Monsieur Gleason claims he saw you with the *Gazetta's* printer."

"I am free to speak to whomever I choose."

"Are you? The Marquis worships Prussian discipline. Caron has become his fool."

"The truth cannot be silenced."

"The truth, perhaps, but you?"

Beldoque was a fool if he thought he could frighten him. For once, Louis hastened to his drudgeries. He found the foreman waiting at the foot of a banyan tree, the slaves with him. The day's goals outlined, Louis urged the workers down the path. Their rhythmic chants formed the perfect backdrop for his thoughts.

What should he do next? He'd not yet handed over his copy of the *Declaration of the Rights of Man and the Citizen* to Villoux. And if he did? Louis stared beyond the slaves, toward the plantation house. So Caron was after him, egged on by the Marquis. Caron was a spineless ninny, like his father. Louis stopped midstride. Yet in the end, his father had stood firm.

One of the slaves shifted to a different tune. Sans words, it took Louis time to recognize it: "*Ça Ira*." He walked boldly onward. No *aristo* would intimidate him, nor any faux *aristo* either.

By the time the slaves had finished for the day, some fifty whites milled about the "parade field," Caron cavorting in front of them. The *grands blancs* chose their muskets first. Ever the revolutionary, Louis didn't wait his turn. He removed a Charleville from the rack alongside them. Angry murmuring rippled through both the planters and poor whites, but nothing else.

At a command from Caron, the ranks formed. Louis took up his position in the last line. He had the same musket he'd had this morning, the one with the rusty priming pan. But then, one or two of the others were just as bad.

The Marquis idled nearby. He beckoned Caron to him. As a result of their discussion, Caron ordered a general inspection. Louis suppressed his contempt. What was there to inspect? No one had a uniform. What was meant, however, was their muskets. Caron walked the lines, randomly ordering men to show him their Charlevilles. Naturally, he bypassed his fellow planters. The poor whites were a different story. After three stops, he indicated Louis hand over his musket. The rusty pan. A little less contemptuous, Louis handed it to him.

Caron carefully studied the different parts in turn; the frizzen, the spring, the cock, the priming pan. The priming pan, the rust. A smug Caron thrust the gun back at Louis.

A series of orders flew thick and fast, all of which Louis only half comprehended. Notably, none included Beldoque or Lecluselle. One of the planters, designated a lieutenant by Caron, ordered Louis out of line. Escorted by two *petits blancs* either side, Louis was marched to the center of the field. At an order from the lieutenant, one took his musket from him. The lieutenant barked another order. Louis did nothing. The lieutenant repeated it a third time, to muffled laughter. Louis stood there dumbly. Finally, the officer shouted at two poor whites. They loosed the flaps to his breeches and bared his buttocks. Too late, Louis understood. He struggled to retrieve his garment but was shoved over, his naked behind facing the ranks. The sting of cold metal struck his exposed flesh. Physically, the experience did him little harm. Emotionally, it seared him. He was a Frenchman, a citizen. This could not, should not, be happening.

The lieutenant, his chief accomplishment the many black women he'd bedded, smirked and ordered him to pull up his breeches and return to line. Anxious to hide his nakedness, he fumbled with the buttons. Done, the rusty Charleville, his nemesis, was slammed back into his hands.

Sword held casually by his thigh, Caron stepped back. Louis dimly connected that it had been he who had administered punishment. On command, Louis marched forward, left, and right. On command, he fixed his bayonet and stabbed air. In his mind, he stabbed the Marquis – and Caron. Permission or no, he'd see Villoux. *The Declaration of the Rights of Man and the Citizen* would be published as planned.

CHAPTER THIRTY-SEVEN

I count it the mark of a gentleman that he possess a
good intelligence.

Evington Papers, 7754/3

"What did he say, Mr. England?"

The second lieutenant lowered the speaking trumpet. Edward,
like Captain Pearse, waited for Mr. England's translation. *Blanche*
was hove to off St. Vincent, her main topsail backed, a little
headway on. A large three-masted Dutch pink, foretopsail backed,
rocked to leeward with just her jib set. No one on the Dutchman
spoke English, and no one on *Blanche* spoke Dutch. The master of
the pink hauled out a Spaniard, perversely reasoning he would be
understood where others had failed. Pearse ordered Mr. England
to parley him. The second lieutenant haltingly conveyed to his
captain that the ship had recently sailed from Guyana.

"Tell them I wish to see the ship's papers." Pearse's hand rode
his hip.

This exchange went even more haltingly. Sniggers came from
some midshipmen. The Captain's upraised hand forestalled more
efforts at parlaying. Pearse rounded on the mids.

"Mr. Deveare."

Vowing to square matters later with Barnes and Farnsworth,
the source of the mirth, Edward stepped forward.

"Do you understand Spanish?"

Edward liked Mr. England. He didn't want to show him up. On the other hand, in one of their conversations, he had mentioned to the Captain he spoke Spanish.

"A little, sir."

"Inquire the name of the ship and its business here."

Edward obeyed. "She's the *Gertrude*, sir, bound for St. Eustatia with a hold full of cacao."

Pearse had him ask a few more questions, which the don conveyed to the Dutchman in turn. Satisfied with their answers, Pearse had Edward pay his respects and gave orders for *Blanche* to drop astern the pink, a small ship with a narrow stern. From his sessions with *Amphitrite's* topmen, Edward understood this maneuver prevented the frigate from taking the wind out of the pink's sails, thus allowing the smaller ship to shoot ahead. Edward assessed the merchantman's sluggish efforts to fall off through a man-o'-war's man's eyes. The pink's afteryards had been braced up too sharp. With such lubberly handling, Edward concluded the ship would be a long time making the Dutch colony north of St. Kitts.

Since leaving Tortola, *Blanche* had followed her normal southerly cruise: past Antigua, past Guadeloupe, Domenica, Martinique, Saint Lucia, and All Saints. The Leewards left behind, she followed the curve of the Windward Islands, sailing on to their present position just south of Kingston Bay, St. Vincent. Curiously, she hadn't made any of her usual ports of call.

All the way out, the midshipmen's berths hummed with speculation. Oldsters and youngsters alike concluded war had been, or was about to be, declared. Over meals, prizes were captured and prize money shared. Edward prayed it would be so, for he owed Captain Pearse much and had no means of repaying him.

Soon, Grenada was left behind, the last British possession. The Spanish island of Trinidad loomed ahead. *Blanche* worked her way through the Dragon's Mouth, the tricky strait separating Trinidad from the long arm of land jutting out from Venezuela. With Port of Spain, Trinidad's capital city on the horizon, Pearse summoned Edward to his cabin. The Captain's best uniform lay on a chair. Something momentous was in the wind.

"Sir."

B. N. Peacock

Pearse stood under the skylight, watching him enter. Edward had gotten used to his moods. Even so, when he continued silent, Edward became uneasy. Had he done something wrong?

"Mr. Deveare," Pearse said at last. "You are to embark under a flag of truce to Port of Spain. My barge and its crew are at your disposal. If you are so fortunate as to make the quay unchallenged, communicate to the commandant of Fort St. Andres I seek an audience with His Excellency, Governor Chacón. You will await the reply. Under no circumstances is anyone but you to set foot ashore. Under no circumstances are you or anyone else to do anything provocative. Do I make myself clear, sir?"

It was a great honor to be charged with such an important mission. A great honor and a great responsibility. Edward hesitated, but only for a moment.

"Yes, sir. Perfectly clear, sir. When do I leave?"

"As soon as we are in rowing distance of the harbor."

CHAPTER THIRTY-EIGHT

Be my brother, or I kill you.

Nicolas-Sébastien Chamfort, *Oeuvres*, I

As many times as he'd been there, Louis had no problems making his way to the *Gazetta's* offices. Inside, he found Villoux and his assistant at work as usual. De Mendoza, too, was there, commenting on some uprising on the mainland, an uprising which he said had been brutally putdown. He said something else in a low voice, about an Englishman who promised to help the patriots. Louis could have misunderstood him, for de Mendoza spoke with a broad Spanish accent. At any rate, Louis judged it time he make himself known.

"Citizens, I salute your excellent work!"

Villoux turned. He seemed startled but recovered quickly enough. "Welcome, Citizen Saulnier," he said affably. "Have you brought what you promised? I have left room — "

A rock smashed through the window. De Mendoza acted instantaneously.

"Get down! Now!"

De Mendoza hit the floor as Jean Villoux's helper pushed Louis and the printer behind the press. More rocks sailed into the *Gazetta's* front office, more glass shattered. French voices screamed "Traitor!" Their reaction to the copies of *The Declaration of the Rights of Man and the Citizen.*

Ironically, Louis had not been the one to give Villoux the text. Aware Louis was being watched, Beldoque had made the journey to Port of Spain in his place. Caron's unjust usage of Prussian discipline had solidified Beldoque's opinions, and Lecluselle's. They were with him now, all the way.

Regardless of the danger, Louis slipped away to get a copy of the *Gazetta*. The attack hardened his resolve to see more printed. A free people needed a free press.

"I will go and reason with them," Villoux said. "They do not understand."

"No, Jean," Louis said, restraining his friend, "the honor is mine."

Rocks littered the floor but no longer the air. Window panes no longer existed; jagged slivers clinging to raw pieces of wood remained. The shards were unnerving, but Louis firmed his resolve. He would confront their assailants.

Howls of rage greeted him. Several men stooped for more stones. "Citizens," he shouted, holding up his hands, "there are none within who wish you harm." He ducked a stone.

"Frenchmen, I appeal to reason. In Paris, men are coming together as brothers in a new order. The old order has –" A fusillade let loose. Louis sought refuge inside the *Gazetta's* office.

With the door bulging from the assault without, Louis, Villoux, and the assistant threw their weight against one side of the door while the enraged crowd pushed with their combined might on the other. The door cracked open. Shouting *Vive le liberté,* the *Gazetta's* defenders hurled themselves against wood. No daylight appeared between door and frame.

"What do we do when they use their heads and attack through the window?"

De Mendoza's sagacity stunned the other three, who stared dumbly at the broken panes. But the threatened double assault never materialized. Instead, the push and shove from the other side lessened. Louis felt a sick churning in the pit of his stomach. Their weak point had been discovered. Before they had either the wit to think of a plan or the speed to enact it, a dull boom resounded.

"Mon dieu," Louis said, "cannon!"

"The English!" Villoux cried. "We are being attacked!"

Drawing on his experience in Paris and from Beldoque's lectures, Louis listened for answering fire. There was none.

"The fort's guns. Something is amiss," growled de Mendoza.

"M'ssieurs," said Villoux's assistant, "the voices. They are leaving."

Louis first, they edged to the window. The street outside was emptying of angry Frenchmen. Again, Louis first, they cracked the door. A general exodus was heading toward the harbor. The mob an almost distant memory, Louis broke into a run. If English ships were in the harbor, he wanted to be at the battle's front. They were all Frenchmen now.

The closer he came to the quay, the more difficult the going became. Finally gaining the jetty, Louis saw what the crowd had spied: a large ship standing out to sea. From the excited talk going on around him, Louis learned a boat from that ship had landed.

His companions left behind, Louis wedged through the crowd until he was able to see a boat bearing an oversized white flag made fast to the quay. But the boat's crew lacked an officer. Craning his neck and jostling harder, Louis followed fixed stares to their focus. Louis cursed English impudence aloud. The officer was a mere boy. He held his white-wigged head high, as though oblivious of the furor he caused. Proud, arrogant, like an *aristo*, like – the Marquis.

The same frustration he'd felt when La Fayette treacherously knelt before the Austrian women overcame him. Louis shouted, "*À bas les Anglais!*"

He waited impatiently for others to take up the cry. Frenchmen, who stupidly opposed their own best interests as represented by the Rights of Man, still could rally against their ancient enemy, could remember the heroism of du Couëdic, the French captain who conquered the English ship, *Quebec*. One Frenchman was worth ten Englishmen.

The English boy officer coolly returned his gaze.

It could not be, and yet it was. The brat from his uncle's shop in London.

CHAPTER THIRTY-NINE

I do not dislike the French from the vulgar antipathy between neighboring nations, but for their insolent and unfounded airs of superiority.

Horace Walpole, *Letters*
To Hannah Moore, 14 October 1787

In many ways, Port of Spain was typical of other Caribbean ports Edward had seen. Ridges rose protectively out of the curving harbor, like fingers combing lush green hills. Mangroves and other great trees lined the banks of a river which fed into the bay, insufficiently large for the amount of mud in the water. That took a much larger source, namely the Orinoco and its many mouths, which dumped Venezuelan dirt into the Gulf of Paria. An idyllic place, but for the warning shot fired as the Captain's barge made for shore, with Edward commanding, but for the mob running to meet him before he'd even disembarked.

His mission presented an excellent opportunity to justify the Captain's trust in him, should he succeed, which he was confident he would. As the boat neared the shore, Edward made mental notes of the long mole and wooden quay projecting out from the waterfront, and the half-moon battery known as Fort San Andrés protecting it. They'd heard the Spanish governor had been building up the island's defenses. The harbor was filled with ships also, for all the tension between Spain and England. Edward strove to take in more details, but his boat hadn't even touched land before a mounted officer in green and white, followed by soldiers in green and white bearing muskets, positioned themselves between him and the land. The Spaniard heard Edward's request for an audience with the Governor impassively. Ordering his men to remain at the quay, he galloped back to his immediate superior to inform him an English captain wished to meet with His Excellency the Governor, Don José Chacón.

It was impossible to use the dead time profitably. The Spanish officer and his men watched Edward closely, not to mention the burgeoning crowd. Among the groundswell, Edward found French the predominant language. He'd heard the Frogs had flocked to Trinidad, but never had he expected such numbers.

When "Down with the English!" had rung out, Edward clutched the hilt of the ceremonial sword he'd borrowed from the Marine lieutenant. Before he'd sailed from England, Edward had read what French crowds had done in Paris, of poor de Launay, beheaded and his heart cut out after he'd surrendered the Bastille. A jeweled sword wasn't much use, but he'd defend himself as best he could, if it came to it. No one else shouted anything, though, and no one made any effort to attack him, no doubt because of the soldiers. His breathing more measured, Edward searched the crowd for the rabble rouser.

Eyes lit with the slow match of centuries-old animosity challenged his. They belonged to a tall, disheveled figure with a cut face. Whoever he was, he plainly hated him and was determined to let him know it. Edward tilted his head back more to let him know he didn't fear him.

The figure pushed its way forward, until the man stood at the very limit of accessibility to Edward and shouted again, "Down with the English." Tall and blonde, with skin tanned by the equatorial sun, he challenged Edward. Not breaking eye contact, Edward began to move forward when Pearse's injunction came home. No incidents. Edward grit his teeth but stayed where he was. He had his orders. He'd obey them, too, even if it meant allowing Monsieur Saulnier's arrogant nephew to insult him and his country.

CHAPTER FORTY

A man may be an enemy and still be a gentleman and a
man of honor.

Evington Papers, 7759/7

The crowd parted like the waters of the Red Sea before a
mounted aide-de-camp, who delivered Governor Chacón's reply.
*His Excellency will meet with your Captain at the Governor's
residence this afternoon, at 3 P.M., a carriage and escort will
convey him there.*

The answer carried to Pearse, *Blanche* entered the harbor and
came to anchor, ceremoniously delivering a seventeen-gun salute
to the governor and being returned the same by the Fort. In the
carriage on the way to the Governor's residence, Edward glimpsed
Trinidad's capital as he sat opposite Pearse. Many of the houses
had brightly painted timber siding, decorated with graceful iron
balustrades. New buildings, for their paint hadn't yet been faded
by the tropical sun.

Port of Spain wasn't large, despite its growing population.
They and their escort shortly arrived at the Governor's residence.
The honor guard, with its three pennants, one imperial, one
regimental, one the Governor's own, wheeled aside to let the
carriage pull up at the entrance.

The building's interior gave the illusion of coolness. Crucifixes
with agonized Christs hung from the wall or expired in alcoves.

269

Not all the decorations were papist, though. Edward touched the bust of a Roman of the early empire, its marble surface alternately indented and raised to simulate individual locks of hair.

An equerry led them to an antechamber. Pearse gave Edward a quizzical look. Edward hadn't the opportunity to decipher its meaning before an official inquired their names. Carved doors opened to admit them.

As they advanced into His Excellency's reception rooms, Edward perversely inventoried the paintings. One in particular struck him, the portrait of a gentleman with a pointed beard. The interplay of light and darkness reminded him of something familiar.

The same lackey who'd announced them recited the Governor's many honors in Spanish, from Captain of the *Marina Real* to Knight of the Order of Calatrava. The Knight was a thin man with long legs dressed in a trim blue uniform with wide red facings. A blue enamel badge set in gold hung from his breast, an order of some sort, perhaps that of Calatrava. He wasn't too old, about Pearse's age, Edward judged. The Governor of Trinidad didn't strike Edward as cruel, as Spaniards were said to be, nor stupid either, cruelty's corollary. Instead, Edward saw a man of authority, stern and just, challenging their right to appear before him.

He and Captain Pearse were now announced in their turn. Señor Chacón beckoned them forward and demanded to know why they had come. Edward translated the question and the answer. "We are here to acknowledge Your Excellency's communication to Rear Admiral Laforey and assure your Excellency no ship has been commissioned by him or his predecessor to prey on Spanish shipping."

"I sent my message via a neutral ship. A neutral ship could have delivered your Admiral's reply, not a man-of-war."

Although Pearse didn't understand the words, he reacted adversely to the tone. "The Admiral ordered me to place myself and my ship at Your Excellency's disposal, to prove England's desire to avoid hostilities. If such a ship exists, we will bring her crew to justice."

Edward barely had time to translate before Chacón snapped, "If such a ship exists? Do you think me a fool? You not only question my veracity, but hope to use your presence here to gauge the preparedness of His Catholic Majesty's ports against English attacks, perhaps even seize a ship or two on your own. Go back! Tell your Admiral Trinidad is prepared to fight, Spain is prepared to fight! We have no need of English ships nor do we fear them."

Even as Edward translated, his mind exulted, *War*.

"England has no desire to start a war. If Spain persists in making unreasonable demands," Pearse added, "she has only herself to blame if war in fact breaks out."

"Spanish ships will hunt the English pirate down," Chacón replied. "If England considers that an act of war, so be it. The Captain has until sunset to remove himself and his ship from the harbor and return to English waters."

Shallow and stiff, their parting bows were themselves opening shots. Pearse's broad shoulders and rigid back retreated to the antechamber. Guards were fanning out around the Governor. Edward realized why. He had paused in front of the portrait that had caught his attention upon entering. Lamely trying to cover his blunder, Edward said, "Your Excellency, allow me to congratulate you on the possession of an exceptionally fine Velásquez."

The technique strongly resembled the one in the portrait he'd long admired at his grandfather's London house. Edward prayed it was a Velásquez.

The Governor countered with more questions. Upon what did the young señor base his judgment? Could the painting not be a Vermeer, a Caravaggio, a Hals? Or perhaps Zurbarán? Edward replied in the negative to the first three. He omitted Zurbarán, an unfamiliar artist.

"You have travelled to Spain, then, that you recognize a Velásquez?" Señor Chacón asked more easily.

"No, Your Excellency, an ancestor. He returned with his portrait done by Velásquez."

"So an Englishman went to Spain."

"And lived to tell of it, Your Excellency."

Governor Chacón ordered the soldiers back to their places. He walked over to a small pencil sketch and pointed to it. "Tell me, do you recognize this?"

The study echoed Velásquez's treatment, but the subject's expression was brutally frank and the style too informal. "No, Your Excellency."

"Ah, but then it was your ancestor who visited Spain. This is a Goya." His Excellency's reverence for art yielded to duty. More sternly he continued, "Have you been long in the service of your King? Enough to recognize a merchantman from a man-of-war?"

He was testing him again. "Yes, Your Excellency."

"And to disbelieve in the existence of an English pirate?"

"I have insufficient knowledge to believe or disbelieve it."

"If you hear more, then would you believe, and your Captain also?"

Edward momentarily had forgotten Pearse. He whirled to find him standing beside him. "I – er – your pardon, sir." Angry shadows darkened the Captain's face.

"*Señor Capitán*, over a month ago, a chapman making its way from the mainland to Puerto de España came upon a wreck. Her master found two survivors clinging to a grating, both Spaniards. He took them aboard his ship and dressed their wounds, for they were badly burned, and questioned them as much as he could. A schooner flying Spanish colors had hailed them under the pretense of a friendly exchange. Once aboard their ship, they attacked the crew. These two hid in the lazaretto, piling foodstuffs over them to hide from the pirates, for so they proved. Only when smoke choked the forecastle did they venture out. The attackers had fled, but the fires they'd set spread rapidly. The older sailor wrenched loose a hatch cover and flung it into the sea. Engulfed by flames, they jumped in after it." The Governor's face was grim. "The older one died aboard the chapman. Before he did, he swore his murders were English. The other swore also."

Unimpressed by Edward's shaky translation, Pearse asked to question the survivor, but Señor Chacón shook his head. He, too, had since died of his burns.

"Admiral Laforey's offer stands."

Governor and Captain said nothing more. During the uncomfortable interval, Edward wondered whether their mission had failed. Then Señor Chacón spoke.

"You have a fortnight to find the pirate and bring him to justice – Spanish justice, not English. If at the end of that time you do not return here, Spanish men-of-war will seek you out."

It was the final word, almost. Edward translated the Governor's ultimatum, simultaneously framing Pearse's acceptance as he did. However, the Captain had a surprise of his own.

"Request permission to take on water before we set sail. We're running low, and I don't wish to waste time returning to Grenada."

Señor Chacón agreed, stipulating that Edward personally oversee it. His parting dismissal was, "Remember – two weeks."

They left through the same series of doors through which they'd entered. Edward and Pearse retreated to their own worlds during their return to *Blanche*. Expecting to receive orders to oversee the watering detail, Edward obeyed his captain's curt command to accompany him to his cabin.

Unbuckling his sword belt with a series of disjointed movements, Pearse slammed the ornate presentation sword onto his dining table. The impact jarred the blade out of its scabbard.

"What did you say to him?"

"I – just translated, sir."

"The hell you did! I understand a little of their tongue, enough to know the Governor spoke of merchantmen and men o' war."

"His Excellency was leading up to the pirate, asking me whether I believed he existed."

"Pirate? Damned nonsense! And now, thanks to you, we are committed to cruising for two weeks on a fool's errand, entirely at the mercy of the dons!

"The survivors swore it was an English ship, sir," Edward said sullenly.

"You believe a second hand report rather than your Captain's judgment?"

"I... think the Governor spoke sincerely."

"Damn you! It's not service aboard a King's ship you want, but your precious Eton. Directly we finish this sorry affair, you're going home with Ricketts and the convoy."

"And the watering detail, sir?"

"The Governor said you were to oversee it. I cannot alter that."

"Aye, sir."

Edward took the long route to the quarterdeck. Face to shore to hide his flaming cheeks, he fought for self control. Until today, he'd thought Pearse the finest officer in the Service. The only difference between him and Neville, though, was that Neville publicly humiliated his officers while Pearse did it privately.

CHAPTER FORTY-ONE

Do what you like.

François Rabelais, *Gargantua*, lvii

Louis paced the mole until his shoes burned. The English boy had returned to his ship, only to bring with him his captain. Both had returned unharmed to their frigate. How dare the Governor allow this! He wasn't the only one watching the ship. The crowd which had gathered when the English brat first disembarked still milled about the waterfront, whites mostly. The majority of blacks were slaves, and slaves were not allowed to wander aimlessly.

Despite heightened worries about war, the harbor was filled with merchantmen. The English frigate lay at anchor like a cat among mice. Fools, Spaniards and Frenchmen alike, to idly stand by and do nothing.

With a "*Merde*," Louis turned seaward. He didn't doubt the frigate and its crew cared a finger's snap what he thought of them. As for his compatriots, how he could persuade them to do something other than nothing? A land breeze from the Ventilla hills cooled him. The hills rose above the channel designed by the royal engineer, Pozo y Sucre, to allow the Santa Ana River to flow more easily. The river, Louis had been told, supplied water for many, including visiting ships.

The breeze's soothing affect didn't last long. The English ship was a sore he could not let go. Even as he watched, two boats put

275

out, heading for the waterfront. The audacity of the English was matched by the cupidity of his countrymen. Louis could contain himself no longer.

"Citizens," he began, but when that word drew negative responses, Louis changed his tack. He wanted to persuade the French loiterers, not antagonize them. "Frenchman, why do you idly watch the English pollute these shores? Is it not enough they threaten not only Trinidad but all Spanish possessions? Nay, not only Spanish possessions, but French as well? Early this year, the National Assembly debated whether France, too, should war against England." Louis omitted the trivial details, namely that the Assembly opposed the King's arming fourteen ships of the line to go to Spain's aid. "Even now, Frenchmen may be girding for war."

The murmurs which greeted his oratory were not altogether hostile. Taking this as encouragement, Louis continued. "What Frenchman does not burn to avenge the Seven Years' War and its shameful concessions? What man here has not heard of daring Kersaint? Have not such as he proved the English are not invincible?"

Louis paused for breath. Reminded of naval victories during the American War, his countrymen seemed eager to hear more. What Frenchman did not thrill to *la glorie*? In the meantime, he'd acquired a second set of listeners. The boats had landed now, and the English were floating empty water casks toward shore. Louis couldn't believe his good fortune. The English brat led them.

To Louis' annoyance, though, the youth took care to bypass him and the crowd. He consulted a Spanish soldier posted at the waterfront, who indicated the river. The boy gave an order. English sailors began landing casks.

Beckoning his "men" – the crowd – Louis dogged the sailors' steps. "Wherever the English go, they cause trouble," he said, pointing to them so that none could mistake who he meant. "Do you think they come peaceably? No! They come to take what they can. They are so greedy they must even take our water."

An angry undertow of French muttering followed his speech. Louis thought the English boy cocked his head slightly. So he'd heard, this one who speaks such excellent French. Well and good. "They are dumb, the English," Louis said, louder still to ensure the brat could not but help hearing. "Can they think, can they reason like a Frenchman? No! They cannot even understand our language. They are dumb, just as the bull which personifies them."

B. N. Peacock

The watering party sank the casks in the river. The young officer moved aside for the first filled barrel but did nothing more. Hoots had replaced muttering. Louis watched contemptuously. It was as he had said; the brat heard but was dumb as a bull.

A filled water cask obscured the lower half of the young officer's body. The boy didn't appear to move, but the cask did. Quickly, quickly, it rolled, sending men crashing into each other as it rumbled down on them. As if the thing had been imbued with a life all its own, the cask malevolently closed in on Louis. With a cry, he scrambled out of the way.

A triumphant laugh rang high and clear. In perfect French came, "Monsieur jumps well – for a frog."

Wood crashed and splintered uncomfortably nearby. Cold water splashed all over him. Louis swore. The cask had met a bad end. So, too, would the Englishman who'd propelled it.

Contorted expressions showed Louis his fellow Frenchmen were as irate as he. The time was ripe for something more than insults. "Friends," he shouted, "shall we let the English mock us?"

"No!" returned the roar from every French throat.

"To arms!"

Louis seized a splintered stave and brandished it over his head. A battle before the actual battle ensued. Frenchman fought madly with Englishmen for staves, their sole weapons. What was left intact of the shattered water barrel was soon demolished. When that didn't suffice, the combatants demolished another cask. Both sides now armed as much as they were able, Louis urged his compatriots onward. As for him, he sought out the young officer. First, though, Louis had to push his way through the foremost of his countrymen, for many seemed much more accustomed to brawling than he. Whacking a stout man on the head, he got his attention and pushed him toward the rear. Then, he pulled another not as well fed aside. At last, Louis gained the front ranks. Before him were the English themselves, held at bay by his French hounds like so many bulls.

The English brat also had a piece of stick. He'd already engaged a Frenchman, and, to Louis's dismay, drove him back. He slashed and prodded, now forward, now backward, with consummate skill. Louis suddenly realized what he was doing, fencing. It was an art in which Beldoque had yet to instruct him.

277

The boy's eyes flashed as he spotted him. He evidently was as eager to find Louis as Louis was him. Louis drove toward him, but an English sailor blocked his path. The sailor, too, knew how to handle his "sword." Louis choked down a curse as the stave came viciously down on his wrist. But Beldoque's training had not been in vain. Louis steeled himself to his hurt and retrenched. Soon, his assailant was the one to cry out and fall back.

They were face to face, now, he and the boy. Cold blue eyes bored into his, testing him, seeing what he was worth. Louis lunged, but it was for nothing. The brat danced aside.

"Does Monsieur wish another cask sent his way – to lend wings to his feet?"

That laugh. Let the impudent brat savor his small triumph while he could. Louis charged again, but the brat again sidestepped, whacking him with his stave as he shot past. Smarting, Louis twisted in place rapidly and faced his opponent. How like an *aristo* to gloat too soon. Louis knew he could not hope to win at a game whose rules were unknown to him. So he changed the game. He employed his stave like a bayoneted musket. This time, it was the boy who was surprised. He wished Beldoque could have seen it.

Taller, stronger, Louis pressed his advantage. The brat's expression changed. No laughter now, just dogged concentration as Louis drove him back step by contested step. Glorying in what now could only end in victory, Louis shouted encouragement to the others. Not that they needed it. They outnumbered the English three to one.

"*¡Basta, basta!*"

Spanish orders flew thick and fast, followed by musket fire. An imbecile in a green and white uniform used his musket to separate Louis from the Englishman. The English boy initially reacted as hostilely as he. Just as they were about to clash again, a Spanish officer with a real sword upraised addressed the boy in Spanish. The brat drew back and answered – in Spanish. Louis' Spanish was limited. He didn't need to understand the words, for the brat's subsequent actions told the tale. He called his sailors to him. Battered and bruised, they returned to their original task. The soldiers, however, were not so patient with Louis. With shouts and curses, not to mention the occasional thrust of a musket butt, they made the French surrender their staves. Enraged that his victory had been snatched from him, Louis loosed a volley of impotent swearing.

"Do you wish to even the score, my friend?" asked a familiar voice.

De Mendoza stood enigmatically nearby. Where he'd come from or how long he'd been there, Louis didn't know. "Were you with us?" Louis demanded.

"Do you not mean instead, am I a lover of freedom?"

"A hater of the English as well?"

"Not every Englishman is to be hated. Listen," de Mendoza said, virtually whispering in his ear. "I know where to find the prize they seek, and how to rob them of it."

"Tell me," Louis said, dropping his voice likewise, "and I will help you every way I can."

"I have already arranged the first part. The pilot sent to guide the English ship out of the harbor is a former English slave. He will feed them a false tale as to the lair of the "pirate.""

"And – my part?"

"Come with me. We will alert their prey, so that they flee in time."

"Come with you? But –"

"You want revenge, don't you? Then take it. Freedom, too, if you dare."

Easy for him to speak, he who could come and go as he pleased. But for Louis, there was the small matter of Caron, the friend of the Marquis. Yes, friend of the Marquis and his Prussian discipline.

"Now?"

"No, my lover of liberty. When I send for you. But be of good cheer, I will not absent you long from your beloved plantation and its slavery, this I promise you."

Louis gave no answer, for de Mendoza left abruptly. Louis sensed, however, the Spaniard had no doubt but that he would comply.

For the present, there was nothing more to do. Never one to return to La Belle Aurore any sooner than he had to, Louis turned his attention back to the English. The casks at last filled, the boats made for the mother ship. The boy officer sat stiffly upright in the back of one of the boats, probably already suppressing the memory of his near defeat. Revenge. The thought cheered Louis. Humming, he made his way back to the *Gazetta's* office. No figures showed through the shattered panes. No matter. Perhaps it was better they wait a few days before publishing anything more. It was sunset before Louis returned to the plantation. Out of the slave's huts floated part of a song sung in patois.

"Hang the aristocrats!"

Revenge.

CHAPTER FORTY-TWO

The name of the slough Despond.

John Bunyan, *The Pilgrim's Progress*, pt. i

The larger river was the Thames; the smaller, the Hogsmill. Kingston lay just over the hill. Fearing recognition, Jemmy traveled by night. It had been a dark and lonely road, all the darker because of the dream.

The night gone, he had to risk going about by day. It was the only way to find the jail where they'd taken Dad. Pulling his cap low and holding his head down, Jemmy mingled with those entering the town. He hoped none were from Dorking.

No one challenged him as he wandered unknown streets. In time, he paid more attention to the surroundings. Fine carriages with servants lined a street overflowing with people. They boded him no good. His apprehension returning, Jemmy inquired the reason from a man holding a staff.

"That there's the County Building. There's murder trial going on, one the quality got an interest in. Lord Onslow hisself changed the calendar, so's to get it through the Assizes early."

Please God, Jemmy prayed, don't let it be Dad. "Who be the murderer?"

"Some foreigner," said a burly man.

A foreigner. The reply offered a shred of hope. "Foreigner? From what parts?"

"Dorking."

Jemmy's throat felt as if he'd swallowed a stone. "Dorking?"

"Aye, Dorking," said the man with the staff. "And foreign enough is its folk for me. He's a bad 'un, they say."

"Can – anyone see the trial?"

"If they can gets in," said the burly man.

"He being a boy, he just might squeeze by," said the first.

"Squeeze by" precisely defined Jemmy's progress. At length, he gained the door and then the entrance hall. If the going was difficult outside, inside was worse. Standing on tiptoe and still unable to see, Jemmy asked what was happening. He asked repeatedly before the man standing in front of him replied, "Jury's out, but won't be long 'fore they finds him guilty, not with the Lord Lieutenant of Surry wanting him hanged."

"They've come back!" shouted a female voice.

A fierce buzz drowned the verdict. For a moment Jemmy held his breath. Perhaps the people were angry because the jury found Dad innocent. Then someone said, "Serves him right, dirty bugger." What little hope Jemmy had nursed fled.

The flow from the courtroom threatened to overwhelm him. Intent on at least glimpsing his father, Jemmy doggedly fought to maintain his place. Dad, however, didn't appear. Who did appear were two finely dressed personages, preceded by lackeys clearing their way. The smaller one was a lady in black; the taller, a well-fed gentleman in scarlet. The going slow even for them, Jemmy caught part of their conversation.

"The children will be taken, too, Lady Elizabeth, any day now, so the bailiff says. Do you stay the night at East Dene?"

"No, I return directly to London. I have hopes of hearing something of Edward."

"What! Is your son still in the Indies?"

The crowd pressed hard. Jemmy caught a flash of dark blue eyes. Let her be annoyed. He had no time for the gentry's fine airs. Dad. Where were they taking him?

Unable to get out the front door, Jemmy discovered people were leaving by a side entrance. Desperate, Jemmy decided to follow. Once he was outside, he might be able to work his way to the front of the building and see Dad. The door led to a small courtyard. Jemmy's heart sank at what he saw. People jeered as a man in chains stumbled into a cart. An egg smashed into the back of his head. Yolk dribbled down his red hair. Someone in the crowd yelled, "Dirty Murderer!" and picked up a stone. Hating the man for trying to hurt his father, Jemmy acted quickly. He pushed the person next him, who jostled the thrower. The stone went wide. But more, many more followed. Try as he might, Jemmy was unable to deflect them. Choking, wretched, he went his way. Whatever he could do for Dad, it wouldn't be here.

CHAPTER FORTY-THREE

My salad days,
When I was green in judgement.

William Shakespeare, *Antony and Cleopatra*, I v

Nothing had gone right since Port of Spain. First, there had been the falling out with Captain Pearse. Based on the pilot's tip, *Blanche* had zig-zagged the Gulf of Paria for a week-and-a-half with no pirate in sight. Previously trusting the Governor's tale, numerous doubts now clouded Edward's mind. None of the ships they'd hailed had anything to report, not coastal schooners carrying vegetables and fruit or pit-pans, flat-bottomed canoes peculiar to the Spanish Main, paddling the inner currents. Nor a *guarda costa* – a warship which patrolled the coast for smugglers – which had challenged their right to cruise Spanish waters with open gun ports.

Had Señor Chacón been mistaken about the identity of the marauder or had Edward been mistaken about Chacón? Edward's soured relationship with Pearse was a direct result of that business. As for that the set-to with the Frenchman, Edward definitely didn't regret that. He and his men would have rallied, he was firmly convinced, and won the battle of the water barrels had it not been for Spanish interference. He would have taught that damned Frog his manners. At least Pearse hadn't reprimanded him for the fight or the two ruined casks. He had old lady Stark do

285

the job for him. When the watering party returned, the first lieutenant lit into him, publicly accusing Edward of deliberately trying to start trouble, not even asking Edward what had happened first.

A bo'sun's mate bawled at one of the impressed men. He was sullen, like Jake had been. Jake. Where were they now, Edward wondered, Jake and the fiddler boy? As for Jake, he might yet be taken and hanged, and it would serve him right. But Jemmy, if only he'd spoken out when he'd had the chance, perhaps the lad wouldn't have deserted. *Mea culpa.*

Spray plumed; white froth dissolved into air. Aloft, the royal yards had been sent down, topgallants set, and topsails single reefed. Underneath the mizzen course, Trewethey and Molloy stood a trick at the helm. Molloy was their best helmsman, the one responsible for training the reefers. It was almost dinner, but Trewethey stayed at the wheel. That much, at least, was well. The older mid lately had been sulky to the gills, taking his ill humor out on Edward whenever he could. Perhaps he sensed the coolness between Edward and the Captain. Edward doubly damned Trinidad and Port of Spain.

Their schoolmaster arrived promptly the first bell in the forenoon watch. He ordered Edward, Barnes, and Farnsworth to open their texts. Their teacher was a young man in his twenties, an uninspiring lecturer who substituted rigorous discipline for lack of experience. His monotone setting Edward's mind adrift, he aimlessly doodled in the margin of his copybook. Black lines became a recognizable figure and circular strokes a ship's wheel. He gave Trewethey an extra large head. Barnes, who sat on Edward's left, angled his copybook. Edward read the words "He's a pig!" underlined three times on a page all its own. Edward readily obliged, adding pig's feet and a curly tail to the caricature. Farnsworth laughed aloud.

The schoolmaster demanded their copybooks. He had no need to flip through them; the offending pages were all too evident. All three were caned, six cuts each to their backsides. Nor was that the end of it. After he'd gone, the school master must have related the tale to some of the older mids. Breathing fire, Trewethy charged into the berth, followed by his friends.

"So I'm a pig, am I?" he said, jabbing his forefinger into Edward's breastbone. "We'll see about that!"

Cowdry leisurely rolled up his sleeves. "Wicked, wicked children. A little cobbing appears to be in order. Deveare, belly down on the table. Barnes, you're next. You youngsters have gotten entirely out of hand."

It did no good to remonstrate they'd already been punished. Trewethey, as the offended party, got to administer justice. Edward was held spread eagle, stomach down, on the mess table and beaten with a stocking filled with sand from the fire bucket, Barnes after him. Farnsworth, who'd only laughed, got off with having his supper docked, for him a fate worse than cobbing.

Trewethey laid into Edward with a will. A point of honor, Edward refused to cry out. He'd not give his tormentor further satisfaction. After it was over, Edward sought the Cannonball. But if he'd expected sympathy, he was mistaken. Willoughby firmly sided with the oldsters. The youngsters had committed an act of *lése-majesté*.

Edward's sore back kept him awake that night, as did his thoughts. How could he repay Captain Pearse the money he owed him before returning to England, including the cost for the two spoiled water barrels? Unable to sleep, unwilling to dwell on his worries, Edward padded up the ladder. The slant of her yards indicated *Blanche* was on a starboard tack. That much was per usual. But not the figure in the shrouds, spy-glass to eye.

"Two sail, Mr. England, close-aboard, the one to weather showing no lights."

War! Prize money! Release from his debts! Edward wanted to whoop as the Captain re-examined the lee quarter. Tucking the night glass under his arm, he said, "Put the helm over to port," and climbed down.

The lieutenant repeated the order to the helmsmen, adding, "hard over," at an impatient move by Pearse, to swing the ship more quickly.

"Steady, Mr. England."

"Steady, there at the helm."

"Steady she is, sir."

Pearse trained his glass on the horizon. "Keep her so."

Blanche had been put on a course designed to get windward of the sighted ships. She responded to the helm like a mettlesome thoroughbred, eager to show her paces. Edward noted the wind hit his cheeks from a different angle – the Captain felt it too. He had her tacked, so that her head came up into the wind, yards swinging quickly to allow the wind to fill them from the opposite side, to bring her around. In deep channel and the wind freshening, her topsails single reefed and the topgallants set over, half the crew could work her. The veering wind would ally itself with the ship, bringing her sharply about, almost by her own accord. Good old *Blanche*, she was smart in her stays.

Edward rehearsed the orders with Mr. England as the watch ran to their stations, clearing rigging, making sure braces and bowlines, both leeward and windward, were ready for running, throwing off the pins. Others looked after the ties and halliards. The quartermaster conning the helm relieved the weather helmsman. He eased the spokes, moving *Blanche* along more briskly. At the same time he checked the weather leeches, making sure they didn't luff. Edward moved to where he could better feel the wind and study the sails. He anticipated the exact moment when the lieutenant would cry, "Ready! Ready! Ease down the helm!" and the helmsmen began putting the wheel down spoke by spoke. To his pleasure, he and Mr. England sang it out together. He caught the Captain's attention.

"You're up, are you? Get dressed, then. I may have need of you."

With an, "Aye, aye, sir," Edward bounded below. He returned to see *Blanche* nearly head to wind. A sharp flapping erupted overhead. The main topsail was aback, its center concave to the mast. Edward's lips formed the order. Mr. England bellowed it. "Mainsail haul."

The wind was now a point, or point-and-a-half at most, on the weather bow. All foresails were aback, their yards slanted on the original starboard tack. The main and mizzen yards swung round to the opposite tack, the men easily running away with braces and bowlines. The captains of the first and second quarter afterguard had seen to it the main clew garnets had been let go and overhauled, leaving the lower edge of the mainsail running free. Wind filled the canvass on the larboard side. Edward gave the final order before the lieutenant. "Haul taut! Let go and haul!"

"If anyone questions you on tacking when you stand for your lieutenant's examination, Mr. Deveare, you'll do well. Save for one thing."

"Sir?"

B. N. Peacock

"That after having successfully tacked, the lee side becomes the weather."

In his excitement, Edward had invaded the Captain's preserve by not moving. He faded back to where he belonged, but Pearse's comment haunted him. When you stand for your lieutenant's examination. Not if, but when. Had Pearse changed his mind?

The Captain issued orders for general chase. Mr. England called up the starboard watch, and with it came, Mr. Stark, pulling on his coat. *Blanche* hoisted her ensign as soon as it was light enough to see. There was only one ship now, and she tried to escape. Too late and too slow she hoisted sail and steered for the coast. *Blanche* fired a shot from her bow chaser. It sped in front of the barque's bowsprit and entered the water to leeward, sending up a harmless sheet of water. A yellow flag with two horizontal red bars ran up the stern flag staff and, even more hastily, ran down. The Spaniard hove to as awkwardly as she'd made sail.

Pearse ordered Edward to board her and bring back her master. Edward promoted himself to lend additional weight to his words. "I'm Mr. Midshipman Edward Deveare, of his Britannic Majesty's frigate, *Blanche*. We've come to aid you, not wage war."

He learned the barque had indeed been attacked. The master was angry and suspicious, all the more so because some of his crew had been wounded. Using all the diplomacy he could muster, Edward at last persuaded him with, "You've my word we mean you no harm. For the sake of your people, please come."

Aboard *Blanche*, they discovered the barque belonged to the Compañía Guipuzcoana, the Caracas Company, a trading monopoly sanctioned by the Spanish crown. Rigorous questioning by Pearse via Edward didn't shake the Spaniard's claim. The attackers were English. Their leader said he had a letter of marque. No matter how hard the Captain pressed him, the Spaniard stuck to his claim, the attacker had been an English privateer. An exasperated Pearse sent him back to his own ship, sending over the surgeon with him.

Edward stayed behind. From Willoughby he learned one of the lookouts claimed the fugitive had raked masts, a foreign-built schooner. This was in contradiction to what the pilot at Port of Spain had claimed, that the pirate was a brig.

Blanche's pinnace hoisted in, Pearse ordered Mr. Stark to steer west south by west, the last known course of the unknown ship.

A Tainted Dawn

Pirate or privateer, peace or war, they were going after her.

CHAPTER FORTY-FOUR

Big fires flare up in a wind...

St. Francis de Sales,
Introduction à la vie dévote, pt. III, ch. 31

Louis gloried in the "battle" at Port of Spain. Beldoque had been skeptical, but Lecluselle had laughed until his sides hurt. Gasping for breath, he demanded Louis repeat the part about how the English were spluttering at the water's edge when the Spanish came to their rescue. Louis gleefully obliged. This time, the English were up to their knees in water before they were saved. With the third telling, they were up to their necks.

But that was then, and this was now. The days ticked by; no word from de Mendoza. There were no more excursions to town either. Doubtless, Caron had learned of what he'd done. Louis hoped he had. It would show him how true Frenchmen dealt with the English. The three friends, however, found their work increased to the point where they often collapsed into their cots at night without undressing. If de Mendoza sent for him at night, he'd have a difficult time rousing him from sleep.

With just four days left until the two weeks' grace period expired – house slaves had supplied them that information – the promised messenger came. Not late at night, as Louis had feared and expected, but in the early morning, when he and his slaves made their way to a fresh work site. Louis had said nothing of de Mendoza's offer to Beldoque and Lecluselle. He hadn't wanted them to be blamed for his absence, or wanted, either, for them to try to dissuade him from going. Telling the slaves to begin work while he spoke to the visitor, he slipped after him. Hidden now from the clearing, Louis debated whether he should risk going back to tell one of the slaves. Beldoque must be told somehow, surely. But in the brief time Louis pondered, his companion forged far ahead. Louis had no choice except to catch up.

De Mendoza awaited them aboard a sloop, or some such small ship. No sailor, Louis neither knew nor cared her true designation. He was thankful, though, that the voyage was a brief one. Even a short voyage was to be dreaded, for Louis' stomach, like its owner, rebelled at the slightest up-and-down, side-to-side motion. They made land somewhere on the Venezuelan coast, an abandoned Dutch trading post, de Mendoza informed Louis when he was at last able to respond. Aware they were alone, Louis pressed de Mendoza for explanations. "This, my friend, is a rendevous point for other lovers of freedom."

"I believe in freedom with all my heart," Louis said, looking around at the encroaching vegetation and whatever beasts it hid with not a little displeasure.

"I do not just 'believe' in freedom," his friend said. "I fight for it! I and my brothers wish to throw off Spain's yoke from our necks. There are not many of us, that is true, but our numbers are growing. And we are grateful for such help as we receive, regardless of the source. A revolt requires guns, and we have found someone to supply them. He robs the ships that carry arms to the Spanish, to kill us. This is the man the English seek, the one the Viceroy and his governor decry. He is the one we have come to warn."

"Why have you waited so long? The English soon must return to Trinidad."

"Long? He has other cargoes as well, for he must appear to be an honest trader. We shall have a good laugh with him, when we tell him how the English chased him uselessly."

"But – they call him a murderer."

"You, who helped take the Bastille, did you weep at the sight of de Launay's head?"

De Mendoza had a point there. Impure blood must be shed. Before Louis could tell his companion so, one of the crew approached.

"*Capitán,* he said, "they have arrived! The lookout you posted has seen them."

Anxious to meet an Englishman who aided freedom fighters, Louis watched as a small ship hove into sight and anchored close to their ship. De Mendoza and an officer, the other captain, Louis surmised, greeted each other. The Englishman, however, soon did most of the talking. What exactly he said, however, was a mystery. Both men spoke Spanish, the Englishman's heavily accented. Louis could only guess one word in three. From that little he was able to understand, he deduced that another ship had followed the Englishman's here, a bad thing evidently, for both men's faces were grave. The conversation went on for a considerable time. When it finally ended, de Mendoza turned to Louis, his expression one of displeasure.

"Well, my friend, it appears you will get more than I promised."

"We must do something about the ship which followed his?" Louis asked, awkwardly embarking the boat back to their ship.

"You understood what we said?"

"Not everything. There was a fight, there was a ship, and it came here. A *guardacosta*?"

"Would the good God that it were! No, the English frigate from Port of Spain, the very one we came to warn him of. It seems they found him by chance, just as he was attacking another arms shipment, or so he says. He could not elude them thereafter, the devil English!"

Louis wisely held his tongue. So far as he was concerned, the English were all devils, de Mendoza's friend included. Hadn't he botched the affair? "What now?" he asked, after a decent interval had passed. "Do we attack?"

"Did you take no note of the size of that ship when she lay at Port of Spain? She is a frigate, a man-of-war! No, first we must move our ships to a different anchorage, the other side of this place. Once safely there, we will take further counsel."

Moving the ships meant waiting for high tide. From their disjointed talk and gestures, it was plain the crew feared the English would capture them before they were able to escape. Nor did their fears seem assuaged when they finally wore the ship to a more secure and vastly more secluded refuge. Louis was left to eat his supper in solitude, as de Mendoza left for another visit with the English captain. When he returned, he was plainly worried. He called his men together on the deck.

"We have been deceived!" he said, pacing up and down. "I thought it strange when Captain Wilkins said another ship had set out, bearing muskets to La Guaira. I'd heard of no such vessel, nor was there one. When I pressed him hard, he admitted he attacked, or tried to attack, a simple merchantman. The English frigate stopped him. She now blocks the main channel. Worse, the English sent out a landing party. They know we are here."

The English boy. He was aboard that ship. All these days, Louis had thought of nothing else, just him – and revenge. "We shall fight them. And win!" Louis said.

"We may well have to fight," de Mendoza said with undisguised displeasure. "One of Wilkins' scouts overheard the officer commanding the reconnoitering party say a night sortie might succeed. We cannot make sail until the next high tide, else we risk running aground. This will occur only well after midnight. I do not wish to fight, but we have no choice if they attack. The English will not distinguish between us and their pirate. And even if they did, they would still hand us over to the Governor, who would hand us over to the Viceroy. We would be hung as rebels instead."

De Mendoza gave orders to prepare, then sequestered himself in his cabin. Louis, on the other hand, eagerly helped ready weapons, muskets, swords, and bayonets. The English brat, would he be there? Or would he remain cowering aboard his ship? A reminder to take his plate brought him back to the present. He needed to eat, to be ready for what ever happened.

The weather changed late afternoon. Clouds blocked out the sun. If it stayed this way, the night would be impenetrable, an unhealthy place for a landing party with only minimal knowledge of the terrain to be; an excellent place for their side, familiar as they seemed to be with the old town and its outlying area. All the better to set a trap.

They waited until the last shred of daylight expired before setting out. Wilkins and de Mendoza ordered their men to spread out around a clearing, along a path the intruders must take to reach to deserted town. Night became deep night. Louis tensed as distant thunder sounded. He clutched his musket, thankful Beldoque had taught him well. Then, a whispered command brought them to the alert. Dark forms moved stealthily down the path. A flash of sheet lightning briefly illuminated the cleared space among the trees. There was another flash of light, this time followed by a report that could only have come from a musket, from which side, Louis couldn't tell. He discharged his own, then others, many others, did also. Shouts, rallying cries from both sides, or rather, the three groups, vied with the reports. Louis found himself moving forward, slowly at first, meeting with resistance from whomever it was who stood before him. There were more shots, a cry in a foreign tongue. English. Suddenly, Louis was running down the path after the others. The English had been driven back to their boats and were doing all they could to get them off. They had them! He had them! This was his last opportunity to close with the English brat, if he was there. Louis was among the foremost of the pursuers. He reached the point where the river widened into a deep channel, and shouted imprecations. The English were now too busy getting off their boats to answer. Louis went after a straggler, using his musket as a club. The man cursed but didn't turn. Splashing wildly, he clambered into one of the boats.

Louis was about to go after him when de Mendoza recalled his men. Wilkins also, but not before letting loose a last ragged volley. Once again his prey was escaping just as he was ready to pounce. Flouting orders, Louis had a close view of oars splashing confusedly in the water. Wishing for more sheet lightning, he squinted. One sailor appeared to be wading beside one of the boats rather than getting into it. A slight figure. Could it be...? Ignoring yet a third command from de Mendoza, Louis splashed out toward that boat. The English, though, had begun to come to their senses. Hands helped pull the slight figure into his boat. Too close for his own good, Louis just barely dodged a swipe from a sword from another boat.

It was too late to do anything other than watch. The water was quickly deepening beyond the capacity to wade, and he couldn't swim. Then, too, the boats were making rapid progress down channel. Out of range of their muskets probably. Begrudgingly, Louis was forced to admit to himself there was nothing more he could do. The English brat, he consoled himself, would never have risked his precious *aristo* self on such a dangerous expedition.

Finally heeding de Mendoza, he slogged through river water. He must go back, not only to shore, but to the ship and Trinidad. He'd left hot work here. When he returned, he'd no doubt face hot work again, in the form of Caron and Beldoque.

CHAPTER FORTY-FIVE

Duty sometimes requires more than our utmost.

Evington Papers, 7759/9

They'd chased the schooner along the Venezuelan coast. For a night and a morning they'd lost her. Once she appeared again, Captain Pearse set studdingsails and staysails, risking sandy shoals and currents to overtake her. A swift ship well-handled, the schooner eluded capture. In the end, they'd tracked her to one of the many inlets in the Orinoco delta. A place where a shallow-draft schooner could shelter, and a frigate, draft almost seventeen feet bow and stern, could not.

Edward restlessly paced the slash of mud beach beside the boats, their safety his part in the landing party. Overhead sheet lightning occasionally illuminated the clouds. He listened intently. Was that faint popping musket fire? He cocked a pistol.

"You might as well be in on this." The coxswains were already lowering the boats when the Captain ordered Edward into the launch. Stark hadn't been pleased. He commanded the launch. The reconnoitering party had located the raider's base earlier, an abandoned town on the other side of an island in the river channel. Captain Pearse had decided to attack from behind.

There was no mistaking it now. Flashes of light, the smell of black powder. Shouts and yells, growing ever louder and more urgent until the men who made them bolted out of the undergrowth. It might be a trick of hearing, but he thought he could pick out some French. Remembering that damned Frenchman, Edward aimed his pistol. It might not be such a bad thing to shoot a Frenchie. But the shadows of friend and foe were too much alike. He held his fire.

"*Blanches*, to me!"

Something whizzed past Edward's ear.

"Get the boats off, God damn you!"

Stung by the first lieutenant's cursing, Edward uncocked his pistol and stuffed it into his waistband. With help, he got the large pinnace afloat, the Captain's boat. A sailor got the small pinnace afloat. They'd barely gotten off the launch when a chaos of arms and legs, cutlasses and muskets, ran, vaulted, and scrambled past. Unshipped oars beat water in a way no coxswain would long tolerate.

"Ned, for God's sake, get in!"

Willoughby leaned out and grabbed his sleeve, the coxswain his coat. Musket balls kicked up water spouts around them. Edward reluctantly let them pull him headfirst into the launch.

Trewethey bawled at the large pinnace's crew as it shot past. Pearse wasn't in it.

"Where's the Captain?" Edward demanded of Willoughby.

"Shot, in the clearing near the –"

"Put your backs into, you buggers." A fresh volley was the cause of Stark's urgency. The boats flew toward the channel's mouth where *Blanche* lay anchored in deep water. They'd be safe there. With Pearse gone, Edward might not even have to return to England. But Pearse had said "when" he stood for his examination, not "if."

"Ned, come back!"

The flat-bottomed launch skimmed on without him. River water lapped his shoulders. His sword belt and pistols weighed him down. Too late now to hold them over his head. Too late to save his powder from the water. He hadn't considered the possibilities.

Mud sucked his feet, but he managed to wade ashore. Nothing moved on the narrow beach.

"Look! One's come back!"

Edward's pursuers were far enough away to allow him a slight lead. He crashed into entwined vegetation, twisting and turning like a rabbit in a thicket. Mangroves grew enormous roots above ground. He fell over a root as large as a giant's knee – and crawled underneath.

His cheeks stung where stems scratched them. His sword dug into his ribs; his brace of pistols jabbed his stomach. A frond tickled his nose. Feet stamped mere inches away.

"A mid runned in here somewheres, damn 'im."

"Leave off, Jake."

Jake? Steel slashed fronds. Edward held his breath.

"To camp! With the others gone, we'll have to wait till morning."

"He's right here, I tell ye!" Someone viciously hacked the mangrove where Edward hid. Yes, Jake Cairns.

The voices and squelching steps receded. Edward waited an eternity before sticking his head from under the mangrove root. Satisfied no one remained, he fought plant life to gain his footing. The vines were the worst; they twined like ropes around him. Imitating the men who'd hunted him, he devastated vines, leaves, branches – anything that hindered him. Sweat made his mosquito bites burn; his dirty, soaked uniform encumbered him. He accomplished one thing, though; he found the path.

The darkness was profound. Using his hanger like a blind man's cane, Edward worked his way forward. Pearse was in there somewhere, alive perhaps. Or had the pirates found him and finished him, even if he'd initially survived? Edward bit his lip and moved on.

He groped his way to a clearing. The Cannonball had said Pearse had been shot near a clearing. Edward slowed. Was that a log over there? He inched forward. Breeches and stockings showed dimly white. Edward lowered his sword and bent over.

The form burst into life. Edward fell backwards and dropped his sword. A hand closed around his throat. Flinging up his left arm to shield himself, Edward choked.

"My God, what are you doing here?"

"Cap – tain."

"I ordered you to stay with the boats."

Pearse relinquished his hold on his throat. "They've gone," Edward gasped.

"Stark ordered them away?"

"Yes, sir."

"My First outdoes himself this night." Pearse slumped against the log.

"Are – you wounded, sir?"

"Yes. Play surgeon. See if the ball came out my back."

Edward eased him out of a frock coat sticky with blood. Edward probed the indicated shoulder and back. "Nothing, sir."

"Damn. Jameson will have to dig it out. Here, what are you doing?"

"Using my shirt for bandages, sir," Edward said, slipping his shirt over his head.

"Not one I paid for, I trust."

"I'll make good the debt, Captain. Somehow."

"Perhaps you already are," Pearse said. "Perhaps you are."

Edward tore his shirt into strips, then helped the Captain out of his waistcoat and shirt. In doing so, he brushed against a sticky crust on Pearse's left temple. The head wound might have left him temporarily unconscious, giving the impression in the darkness and confusion that he'd been killed. Edward stubbornly maintained it still didn't excuse Stark's abandonment.

"You know, you could be sleeping in your hammock right now."

"I don't think I would," Edward said, tying the ends of the makeshift bandage together.

"No?" Pearse said, his head disappearing into his shirt. "I'll do that." He took the waistcoat from Edward. "What made you come back?"

"I... had to."

His prolonged pause convinced Edward of the lameness of his explanation. When the older man spoke, his voice rasped.

"My coat, Mr. Deveare."

The Captain's wounds must pain him. Edward carefully draped the stiff woolen coat over Pearse's shoulders and collected his sword belt and pistols. The weapons recalled the fugitives.

"When I came searching for you, I heard one of the pirates say they'd return in the morning."

"The island's not very large."

"We could return to the shore. It would be closer to *Blanche*." Not where Jake had almost found him, but down from where he'd kept watch over the boats.

"Alright then, lead on."

Edward alternately worried about being attacked because of their slow progress and the Captain's wounds. Under his own sail, though, Pearse reached the place Edward led. There, he sank to the ground while Edward hacked branches to form a lean-to. There was room for only one. Helping Pearse in, Edward made him as comfortable as his wounds allowed. Hanger on his knees, Edward kept watch outside.

Daylight heightened their risk of discovery, but Edward couldn't bring himself to waken Pearse. Morning haze softened the harsh greenery of the mangroves and obscured the mud beach. It was difficult to see at a distance.

"Any sign of the scoundrels, Mr. Deveare?"

Edward tried to penetrate the haze. No figures were visible, only footprints, their footprints leading here. He shook his head.

"We need to find fresh water. The river's too muddy."

Their progress was unsteady. Coercing will and body, Edward guided them to the path, and there, in the protection of the trees, collapsed beside Pearse.

The Captain needed food, water, and a surgeon. Edward glanced seaward. He might be able to swim out to the frigate, but that meant leaving Pearse. He hadn't been able to do that last night. He refused to do it now.

The discovery he dreaded occurred. A band of men raced down the path towards them.

Edward barred their way with his sword.

Ten or twelve men armed with pistols and cutlasses surrounded them. Sailors all, Edward concluded, from their dress and deep tan. A man demanded in broken English that Edward surrender his sword and pistols. Edward looked at Pearse, who nodded. Wanting to fight, but fearing what might happen to Pearse, Edward pulled his sword belt over his head and threw it at his feet, then his pistols. Pearse clumsily drew his hanger out of its sheath. One of the renegades, misinterpreting the action, cocked his pistol. A command delivered in Creole scattered the gang. The man for whom they parted stared down at Edward and Pearse. Another trailed behind him. Edward had no problem identifying either: Captain Wilkins from St. John's and Jake Cairns.

"One for you, Jake," Wilkins said. "You not only did wound an officer, but you were right about a mid coming back as well."

Cairns spit tobacco juice toward Edward. "He's a *Trite*, Cap'n."

"Your acts of piracy won't go unpunished," Pearse said.

"Oho, so it's the gallant Captain Pearse, is it? Your servant, sir."

"If you're such a servant, return us to our ship."

"Don't be so hasty, Captain. Allow me to extend our hospitality first. You look in need of it. Jake, take our guests back to the town. Give them my medical chest and some food and drink. We must show them we are honorable men."

"Honorable men don't attack ships in time of peace."

"Nor do I."

"You attempted to raid a Spanish barque off Cape St. Roque. Before that, you –"

"Captain, Captain, your wounds cloud your reason. You sighted me off Point Foleto, mistaking me for another, I don't doubt. As for last night, your men owe me their lives. Do you think I didn't know about the reconnoitering party? Yet you attacked under the cover of darkness. It is you, not I, who must bear responsibility for last night. Jake, escort them to town."

Jake and five Creoles fanned out on either side of them. Edward kept close to Pearse. Everything Wilkins had said was plausible. Too plausible and too glib. A pack of lies.

By stops and starts they reached a deserted town the other side of the island. Barrels lined the quay's better side. The town, like the quay, had been patched up after a fashion. The one room structure to which he and Pearse were escorted had a window with a heavy drop shutter. It and the door were the most substantial things about the hut. Bad as it was, Edward was thankful they'd come to the journey's end. Pearse sagged heavily on him. He was even more thankful when Pearse voluntarily eased himself onto the cot.

"Bring the medicine chest. Quickly!" Edward ordered. "And some vinegar and water."

"Be damned to you," Jake snarled." You don't give no orders here."

"Your captain ordered you to provide us with food, drink, and the medicine chest. Do it!"

Away from Wilkins, Jake obeyed only himself. Edward repeated what he'd said in Spanish, ending with, "¡Pronto!" One of the Creoles went running.

When he returned with the desired items, Edward tended Pearse as best he could. The Captain's pallor decided him against trying to get off his shirt the usual way. Edward instead cut the sleeve from the shoulder. Removing the bandage proved more difficult. Dried blood glued the strips to each other and to the wound. Dipping a cloth in the bowl of vinegar water, Edward moistened them. Soaked, they separated. He removed them and rinsed the cloth in vinegar and water and cleansed the wound. Pearse told him through clenched teeth to find some lint. Edward did, re-bandaging Pearse's shoulder as gently as he could. When he finished, Pearse lay back on the cot and closed his eyes. Edward covered him with his coat to keep off the insects.

With Pearse at rest, Edward was free to sit down. He buried his head in his hands and damned old lady Stark. Were Mr. England in charge aboard *Blanche*, he'd find a way to rescue them. Some time later the door banged open. Startled awake, Edward groggily observed two Creoles carry a tray with beans and rice and a bottle of wine into the hut. They scolded him off the table and deposited their burden on it.

Edward bristled when Wilkins sauntered in and picked up a discarded strip of last night's bloodstained bandage. He looked from it to Edward. "The shirt off your back. How touching."

Pearse hugged his coat to him and sat up. "Restore us to our ship."

Captain Wilkins oozed the same false geniality he'd exhibited at St. John's. "You know, your first lieutenant is most accommodating. He accepted my apologies for our mutual misunderstanding. I granted his request your body be returned for proper burial. He also mentioned a mid had disobeyed orders to run off and find you. A pity, I said, for these inlets teem with crocodiles. I assured Mr. Stark, I believe that's his name, I'd search for any remains."

"You won't get away with this," Pearse said.

"I think I shall, Captain. I think I shall." Wilkins smiled benignly. "Oh, and being a good officer, I know you worry about your ship. Well, you needn't. By tomorrow, she'll be mine."

CHAPTER FORTY-SIX

One woe doth tread upon another's heel,
So fast they follow.

William Shakespeare, *Hamlet* IV.vii

Jemmy swept the bow across the stings to test the pitch and adjusted the pegs. Satisfied the fiddle was in tune, he took off his cap and laid it upside down on the cobblestones. Although it wasn't market day, many hurried through Kingston's Market Square. A bronze disc flashed into his cap. The livelier his music, the more coins flashed. He played until a food stall's savory smells made his stomach rumbled unmercifully. He glanced at his cap. Coins, mostly pennies and half-pennies, lined the bottom. Would they be enough?

He'd keep none for himself. Bartering his playing for a place at the Castle Inn's stable loft, he sheltered in fragrant straw. All night he plotted how he'd gain entrance to where Dad was imprisoned.

The next morning, he stashed his hat and coins underneath his coat and ran down the street. He didn't slacken his pace until he found the jail. The gate was closed; no guard hovered protectively nearby. Jemmy eyed the wall. He'd shinned up higher trees.

"What you want here? Lodging, maybe?" The guard was inside his box after all.

"I, I come to see the murderer."

"He's quite the prize. Entrance fee's high."

Trembling, Jemmy took out the coins and showed them to the guard. He'd worked so hard to get them, come so far. Surely...

The pits in the man's face deepened. "I don't do no favors."

"I must see him." Jemmy shook the coins.

Greed, not mercy, triumphed. "Come along, then. But mind, you only get a peep."

Door hinges groaned before and after them. The sounds were as dismal as his mood, but he nevertheless wedged between the door and the frame. He saw a third of the room, the part directly in front of him. Kingston gaol was crowded with men chained to the floor by their legs. Desperate to see his father, Jemmy pushed inside. One unwashed and unshaven form stood out from the rest because of his red hair.

Jemmy stifled his cry of recognition and tried to go to Dad. The guard grabbed him and pulled him back. "You promised I'd see him!" Jemmy shouted, struggling.

"And so you did. What did you think you get for pennies? The King?"

"You cheat! Let me be with my dad!"

The guard gaped. He'd said too much. To make matters worse, Dad's voice pierced the door. "Jemmy! Take care of Nan."

"They's looking for two children. Might be there's room for you on the special gibbet they's fixed for him!"

Jemmy raised his hand to hit the jeering guard, but a feeling that all this had happened once before stayed him. This was how all their troubles had started, with Dad striking the agent.

Yet Jemmy couldn't allow himself to be taken. Without him, Dad was doomed. Jemmy took desperate measures. He jammed his knee into the man's crotch. The guard cried out and let go of Jemmy. Jemmy seized his chance and ran.

In his initial panic, Jemmy ran far enough away to temporary safety. Pain slowed him. Where was the special gibbet to hang his father? Who could tell him where? The Castle. People were always coming and going there. Someone must know.

A groom undid the traces on a tired horse in the yard. Jemmy breathlessly questioned him about the proposed hanging.

"Ye want to see it, do ye? A hanging, 'tis a grand sight."

"Yes."

"Well, tis a far way, surely. The gentlemen hiring this chaise don't know how to drive it, and our boy's gone out with another party. The long and the short of it, is we need a postillion."

"I never – "

"Tush! The beast's a quiet one. Just keep to the road, and ye'll do fine."

"But where be the hanging?"

"Where? Why, glory be! The very place this chaise is bound. Dorking."

Dorking. The dream. He should have guessed. Jemmy had little experience with horses, but this gave him a way to get there quickly. A way, perhaps, to yet save Dad.

B. N. PEACOCK

CHAPTER FORTY-SEVEN

If, in the course of a lifetime, a man finds in the friendship of another, guidance, acceptance, and likeness of mind, then he is rich indeed.

Evington Papers, 7759/10

The food, such as it was, brought little relief. Edward made sure Pearse had the larger share of rice and beans and all of the dubious wine. They'd been given no forks or knives, only spoons. Edward studied his. One side had been worn so thin it was sharp like a knife.

Jake came by later with a Creole to see to them. The Creole wielded a pistol, its hammer cocked. Jake carried some ropes.

"You bloody little bastard, you're as rotten as your father afore you! I mightn't wait till Cap'n says it's time to kill you!"

Pearse's order to "Belay that!" went unheeded. Angrier at his captain's treatment than Jake's insults to him, Edward said, "You dog, I'll see you flogged!" and meant it.

Jake grabbed Edward by his coat and flung him against the wall. Before Edward could recover, Jake stripped off his shirt. Amazingly, he turned his back to Edward.

"Flogged? Like your father done!" Discolored knobs jutted through the skin's surface. Bones.

"My father never –"

"The bloody hell he didn't!" Jake thrust his head back into his shirt and rounded on Edward. "Midshipman of top gived wrong order. Would've meant foret'gallant mast going over. But he were counted an officer, though he knowed nought. Wrong or right, we were to obey. Right or wrong, we'd be flogged, and we was. I got worst, for speaking out. Brighty were bo'sun's mate back then. He kept me from you 'board *Phitrite*. He can't do nothing now."

Edward went numb from what he heard. He offered no resistance when Jake pulled the rope so tight around his wrists the ropes bit the flesh. Forcing Edward into a sitting position, he tied his wrists behind his back, then his ankles. From his place in the dirt, he watched Jake shove Pearse into the chair and tie him to it. Dejected, Edward rested his head in the dirt. His cheek stung from something slick and sharp: the dropped spoon.

Their job done, Jake and the Creole left. Edward lay still, guarding the spoon. When he was certain they weren't coming back, he crawled close to Pearse.

"Is anyone outside, sir?"

"Not that I can see. Why?"

"My spoon had a sharp edge. It's possible, with enough effort, it could cut through rope. I'm going to take it in my mouth and put it in your hands. I'll rub my wrists against it while you hold it. When my hands are free, I'll untie you. Whistle a tune if anyone comes."

When Pearse grunted assent, Edward carried out his plans. He settled into position and began working his ropes.

It was like trying to build a ship with twigs. Edward's back felt the strain. His coat irritated the places where he'd scratched mosquito bites raw. As many times as he rubbed the rope against the spoon, he rubbed his skin. When a guard poked his head into the window to check on them, Pearse started "Hearts of Oak." Edward rolled onto his back, glad for the chance to rest.

Jake's accusations haunted Edward. The physical resemblance between his father and grandfather had bothered him from the start. What had Brighty said? *You're like yourself, Mr. Deveare. Be glad of it.* Brighty had served under both his father and grandfather. He'd kept Jake from harming him. He'd also kept the truth from him: his father had been as brutal as his grandfather. Yet hadn't that been a thought which had long chipped at the edges of his mind?

Darkness came. The tingling in his arm, long absent, returned with a vengeance. Unable to move any longer, Edward toppled onto his side. Then it happened. The ropes parted.

He lay still until his circulation returned. Not waiting to untie his ankles, he tackled the ropes binding Pearse to the chair. A second piece of luck, Jake carelessly had used reef knots. A few determined tugs and Pearse was loose as well.

"Damn me, but that feels good! And you? You've borne the brunt of this."

"I'm fine, sir. Shouldn't you rest?"

"I'll rest when I'm back in my own cabin." Pearse cautiously checked the window. "They'll be clearing out about now, if I miss my guess."

"Who, sir?" Edward asked, untying his ankles.

"The cutting-out party, that's who. We've got to warn the ship. Get the chair and stand behind the door. When I call the guard in, give it to him! Quickly!"

They positioned themselves either side of the door. Pearse cursed the guard in his limited Spanish. The effect was magical. The man came, cursing them. Edward felled him with the chair. Pearse wrested the pistols away and clubbed the Creole again. They then tied and gagged him.

They slipped out the door and barred it. Voices rose and fell like breakers on a reef. Constantly alert for renegades, they crept from shadow to shadow to avoid being seen until they came to the quay.

When the last boat rounded a point of land, Pearse beckoned Edward into the open. "We need some powder. Are you up to finding some?"

"Aye, sir."

"Good. Find her powder locker and help yourself to a keg. And some slow matches as well."

There was no time for fear or hesitancy. Edward checked several dilapidated buildings before he found had any success. In their haste to capture *Blanche*, the pirates had left the door to their make-shift powder locker ajar. Edward ducked inside. He had little problem locating a powder keg. The slow matches, however, eluded him. His ship's welfare uppermost in his mind, he left without them. He did, though, help himself to a stray cutlass.

He found Pearse also had been busy. The Captain had found some embers, which he scraped into a cooking pot. Their escape had not yet been detected, but their situation was perilous. Pearse ordered him to run for it.

Hugging the canister much the way the way he'd watched the powder monkeys aboard ship practice, Edward sprang down the path. But not hearing Pearse, he slowed. The Captain's wounds had left him struggling many steps behind. Edward refused to budge until he caught up. He answered Pearse's disapproving growl with "Powder's no good without fire."

At the edge of the mangroves, Edward rested the keg on the silt bank, Pearse likewise the cooking pot. After several trials, Pearse managed to smash a hole in the keg's top with the butt end of the pistol. Edward anxiously looked down channel. No sight of the cutting-out party.

But they weren't alone. The whine of a ball followed the crack of musket fire. Others, beside their guard, must have stayed behind. Two men burst out of the thicket. Pearse waited until the first one was in good sight and fired. The fellow cried out and fell. The other man attacked Edward with a cutlass. Strong and having the high ground, he and Edward contested their footing inch by inch. When Edward tried to get in under his guard, his adversary nearly knocked the cutlass from his grip. Desperate, Edward's mind salvaged a piece of single stick instruction. *Slash an arm or leg.* Edward brought his blade down on the man's arm. His opponent's swipe faltered. Before he could regroup, Edward this time successfully got in under his guard. The cutlass blade entered his throat and exited. There was no need to do more. Grasping his throat and gurgling, the figure staggered in place.

"To the trees!"

Edward swiftly heeded the Captain's order. They'd barely gained the safety of the thicket when an explosion rocked the muddy shore. After their eardrums stopped ringing, Pearse slumped against the base of the tree against which he'd been flung. "You forgot the slow matches. I had to rip out the lining of my coat to fashion one. No matter. *Blanche* has warning enough to wake the dead."

Despite his flippant words, Edward knew Pearse was spent. His sole concern now was for his captain. As gently as he could, he helped Pearse ease into the crook of a mangrove knee. He'd stand guard as he had last night. But when he reached for his cutlass, it

312

wasn't there. Asking Pearse's permission, Edward went in search of some weapons. He warily approached the first body. Bracing himself, Edward turned it over to claim its sword. He was glad it was too dark to see who it was. Edward relieved the other body of its weapons also. He spread the cache between himself and Pearse before sinking to the ground. Above, he saw pinpoints of light. The clouds were clearing to let the stars free. Something the schoolmaster had said during an astronomy lesson came to mind. The primovant. The ancients believed one sphere controlled the movements of all the others. *Blanche* was their primovant. What happened aboard her tonight controlled the destinies of England, Spain, and France. Of him and Pearse as well.

The grey light of dawn wasn't kind to captains or corpses. Pearse's frock coat was askew. A fresh stain covered most of his left shoulder. Heavy whiskers covered the lower half of his haggard face. The brown eyes which regarded him thoughtfully, however, were clear.

"What made you fight?"

"Sir?"

"What made you fight?"

"I – They would have killed us."

"No, not last night. That day I met you. You knew what faced you, didn't you?"

"This. They stole it from me." Edward drew the portrait from its hiding place.

"A sweetheart?"

"My father."

"Ah."

One word rife with many undercurrents. Edward put away the miniature. Without Edward's help, Pearse struggled to his feet. Then he saw what Pearse had seen. One after another, ship's boats rounded the bend. Uncertain whose they were, Edward moved forward to see better, but one of the corpses stopped him. Insects swarmed the face. Something, land crabs perhaps, had already eaten pieces of exposed flesh. Yet it was the face which most disturbed Edward. Not even death could dim the hatred in those eyes, hatred for him and his father. Shaken, Edward recognized the dead thing was Jake. *A good son.* Jake's bloating corpse bore witness to the sort of man his father had been. Edward no longer wanted to be a good son.

Pearse draped his good arm around Edward's shoulder. "It had to be," he said. "It had to be."

The bond which had been forged between them last night transcended time and place. Never again need Edward imagine his father's approval now that he had Pearse's.

"Sir, the boats! They're *Blanche's*!"

Mr. England commanded the launch. The Cannonball stood up in the jolly boat, waving his hat for all he was worth. They'd been sighted.

The launch touched land first. Mr. England jumped out before she'd even been secured.

"Captain! Thank God, you're alive!"

"Any callers, Mr. England?"

The second lieutenant fell in with Pearse's banter. "A varied lot, sir."

"They enjoyed their visit?"

"They were so taken with our hospitality, none went home."

"Butcher's bill?"

"Six or seven dead, including their leader. Fourteen wounded, two ours. Jameson was up to his elbows last night, but he'll find time to tend you. Mr. Deveare, too, if he needs it."

Six or seven dead, not including Jake. Was the fiddler boy one of them? But that was as much conjecture as Edward was capable. He'd come to his hole in the wind: that strange place where the wind no longer blew.

"Search the island for any stragglers, though I don't think you'll find any. Then find and secure their ship and bury the dead. After you've finished, I want a detailed report of last night's work."

"Mr. Stark —"

"I said *you*, Mr. England. Mr. Stark is relieved of his duties as of this instant."

"Aye, aye, sir."

"Edward."

Pearse had never called his by his Christian name. "Sir?"

"We'll send for the barber directly Jameson's finished with us."

Edward doubly doubted his hearing. Were the Captain's wounds exacting their toll?

B. N. Peacock

Pearse fingered his chin. "I think we could both use a good shave, don't you?"

CHAPTER FORTY-EIGHT

... the inevitable hour.

Thomas Gray,
"Elegy Written in a Country Churchyard"

With minimal difficulty, Jemmy shepherded his gentlemen to the White Horse stable yard in Dorking. The gentlemen's leisurely stop and go on the downs, which so galled him before, had worked to his advantage. It was past sunset, and Dorking had no street lights. Less chance for anyone to recognize him. Jemmy slid off the horse. With a deliberately inaudible farewell, he gathered his bundle from under the box and left the lights of the Inn behind.

He'd planned what he'd do along the way. Cautiously making his way to the head of the lane leading to the tannery, he stashed his things behind the pottery works. Despite the night, many still milled about in the street. They behaved as if on holiday, the holiday being Dad's hanging. Pretending not to hear, Jemmy set his course for the gaol.

Market House, the decrepit old building which also served as the gaol, stood in the middle of East Street in plain sight. Jemmy hesitated. Contrary to custom, locals with muskets guarded the ramshackle place. Jemmy sized them up. They weren't much. He might be able to get by, if he was quick. Then he saw the small crowd congregated near the door and heard his name mentioned. His heart beat so hard it threatened to exit his chest. Someone said the guard was being doubled to prevent any rescue attempts. Nor were they long in coming. A squad of militia men marched in tight formation. The bumpkins were given a curt dismissal.

The officer in charge positioned part of his men at each end of the building. The rest were deployed a short distance away, within sight of both it and the outlying area. Whatever hopes Jemmy had of seeing his father, much less freeing him, were over.

Nevertheless, he stayed as long as he dared. He owed Dad that much. The moon and its treacherous light finally chased him away. He couldn't risk being taken. Safe in the fields away from town, Jemmy struggled with what he should do next. He rebelled against hiding in the caves again, like a hunted animal. But that was just what he was, he thought bitterly. The countrymen would turn him over to the soldiers if they found him, and the soldiers over to the executioner. The farmer? He and his wife sheltered Nan. With many a backward look, Jemmy picked his way to their home.

It was some time before anyone answered his knocking. Finally, the door cracked a little. Jemmy glimpsed a grumpy, tousled figure in a nightshirt. His words tumbling out so as not to leave room for refusal, Jemmy pressed his case.

"Where they be taking Dad?" Another dim figure stirred behind the farmer. Jemmy guessed it was the man's wife, the better head and heart of the pair. "Where?" he yelled at her.

"Poor, orphaned childers," was all she said.

The farmer shook himself awake. "He's at the Mar –"

"I know that! Where?"

"Hush, Jemmy," the women softly chided. "They take him early, to Box Hill. We let on none of this to Nan."

"Help me to see him. I must –"

"Jemmy come. Daddy come." Nan wove between the pair and clutched at him.

"Now see what you've done," the woman said, pulling Nan away.

"They be looking for a boy, not so much a maid," the farmer said speculatively. "Might be –"

"There's an old shawl folded up in the press. And a dress I was going to cut up for rags. With that and a mobcap, his hair all down, he might just pass for a maid."

318

As he'd said, the wife had the better head. Nan wailed and threw her arms around Jemmy, crying for their dad. Visualizing her by that lord's lake, Jemmy roughly pushed her away.

They gave him the clothes and fed him. Both, however, insisted he leave before dawn. Nan tried to follow, but the woman gently but firmly held her back. Relieved to be free of her, to be away from them, Jemmy raced down the lane.

He'd had no sleep last night, and little the night before. Sleep was something he'd shunned. The dream, not ever again, the dream. Only now he was living its reality. Even at this early hour, people were filling the streets. They laughed and jeered at someone ahead. Reckless, Jemmy openly sought Market House. Not caring who he shoved out of his way, he stopped just short of caring if he were recognized. With great difficulty, the throng parted to allow passage of an open cart pulled by a single horse. Mounted militiamen escorted it. The soldiers guarding the gaol had their muskets at the ready as they herded Dad into the cart. Jemmy clawed to secure a place behind it.

His father looked dazed. Jemmy's movement, his desperate attempts to get closer to his last remaining parent, kindled a light in Dad's dulled eyes. Gazing over the throng, as if speaking to it in general, he said, "I ain't been the father I might, but I cared for my children. They ain't done no one no harm. My little maid especial needs looking after."

Couldn't Dad understand Jemmy needed someone to look after him? That he desperately needed his father, too? As quickly as the thoughts surfaced, shame and guilt quashed them. Dad was the one who needed help most of all. And Jemmy had failed him.

The dream. Burford Bridge was a bottleneck at the foot of Box Hill, but nothing stayed the inexorable climb. Up, up, to the thing atop the hill: the gallows. Never once did Jemmy relinquish his place behind the cart until soldiers finally dislodged him at the foot of the scaffold.

Even so, Jemmy remained as close as was possible.

As the hangman draped the noose around Dad's neck, he spoke one last time. In a clear, loud voice that projected well, he said, "I die with a clean conscience! And a cleaner heart!"

A man in a black gown ascended the steps of the gallows. He read to Dad from a book and stepped back down again. The hangman checked to make sure the noose was tight, then stepped back. The platform underneath Dad's feet gave way.

Unable to watch his father's final sufferings, Jemmy tottered down the hill. Laughter and catcalls, insults and cursing, rose on every side. He had failed Dad. He'd come home to save him, and what had he done? Had he not wanted that knife, Dad would be safe now.

Amidst the madness, a pocket of tranquility of sorts lured him out of himself. The men nearest him had broken off their conversation. They wore blue uniforms, uniforms which bore an awful significance. Out of the silence came a whisper even the dream had spared him.

"I'm sorry, Jemmy lad."

CHAPTER FORTY-NINE

This animal is very bad; when attacked, it defends itself.

Théodore P.K., *La Ménagerie*

Beldoque, not Caron, had been livid when Louis returned to La Belle Aurore. Where had he been, how could he be so foolish, nay, wicked, as to have left without telling anyone where he was going? To have dared to leave at all? At first they'd all feared slaves had killed him, even though it had been a slave who'd taken it upon himself to seek them out and tell them Louis had gone off with another white man. They'd searched everywhere for his body, Madame Caron hysterical a slave uprising was in the making. Then he'd returned, behaving as if he'd never been away at all. Beldoque had clouted him.

But Caron? He had done nothing, said nothing. Louis attributed his good fortune to Caron's pre-occupation with the upcoming party he was giving in honor of the Marquis. The Chevalier du Caron had spared no expense in his efforts to ingratiate himself with a real *aristo*.

Beldoque and Lecluselle were not so sure. They made inquiries among the friendly slaves.

Still, nothing ominous had happened then, nor today, the day of the *fête*. Only the singing, or rather the absence of slaves singing, was unusual. Caron's guests compensated for their silence. Eventually the many white voices died away. Then, urged on by the whites, a black voice sang, punctuated by shrieks.

Charlevilles at the ready, Louis, Beldoque, and Lecluselle moved closer to the "party." The shrieks issued from a slave hanging from the limb of an ancient tree. He cried out because the skin was being ripped from his back in long strips. Louis recognized the victim as one of his charges, the one who'd learned "Ça Ira." The same one whom Beldoque said had alerted them Louis had gone. He gripped his musket tighter. He'd not considered the full impact his teachings might have, the ferocity with which they would be opposed.

Before another piece of flesh could be torn from the wretched slave's body, Beldoque roared for Caron to stop. Bottle in hand, the planter played flunkey to the Marquis. Caron's self-satisfied smirk deepened at the sight of the three.

"So you have come at last. Do you wish to join us – or him?"

"I come in the name of humanity," Beldoque said, his eyes burning. "Cut him down!"

"Men, to arms! The 'citizens' threaten us."

The would-be militia ran for the muskets piled at the foot of the veranda. But for Beldoque's previous injunctions, Louis would have laughed aloud at their clumsy maneuvers. As it was, he just stood his ground as Caron gave the order to fire. Nothing happened. This time, Louis did laugh. Never had he seen such stupid expressions. Caron ordered the ragtag group to reload. Still no flash, no fire. Last night, when all slept, the three had removed the flints. Encouraged by Lecluselle's cajoling and the little money they jointly had to offer, Lecluselle's black mistress had stolen the key to the armory – and given it to them.

"Friend Caron, can your men not fire? Shall we show them how?"

Beldoque's words were a pre-arranged signal. Louis discharged his Charleville in unison with his comrades. Three musket balls whizzed over the heads of the would-be soldiers. The beasts exchanged glances, broke, and ran. All this, neatly timed to the discharge of another overhead volley.

"Traitors!"

Whether he meant the militia or the three, Caron no longer stood idly by. He drew his sword and tried to rally the poor whites. They merely changed route and kept on running. The planters in the group initially halted, until a third volley, aimed in their midst, sent them in hot pursuit of the rest.

"Beldoque, I have nothing against you. He," Caron shouted at Louis, "he is the one I want!"

The Marquis stood aloof. It was he Louis wanted to fight, he and the diseased ideals he represented. But if his puppet Caron, challenged him, so be it. "Let us decide the fate of this poor wretch. Now!"

The bayonets had been stored near the muskets, on Caron's side of the lawn. Some of his former training resurfaced. Caron abandoned his sword, the emblem of an officer, in favor of bayonet and musket. When he charged, Lecluselle ran in and grabbed one of the bayonets, but there was no time to throw it to Louis.

Louis blocked the bayonet thrust with his musket barrel. Caron thrust again. Louis felt a sharp pain in his right arm. Beldoque shouted something, what or to whom Louis couldn't tell. He focused on Caron. Changing tactics, Louis swung his musket by its barrel. The stock caught Caron on the temple. He groaned and fell.

"Murderer!"

Caron inert, Louis looked up. Madame stood on the verandah. The Marquis tried to restrain her, but she ran to where her husband lay. Kneeling, she called his name and caressed his brow. Getting no answer, she screamed "Murderer!" again and again.

Louis stood gazing uncomprehendingly down at her. Madame must be mistaken. She had a tendency to overreact. Her husband was hurt, not dead. He'd only meant to defend himself. But Caron's eyes began to cloud over. He had indeed killed Caron.

He didn't like Madame Caron and her airs, but he felt responsible for her wild grief. Clumsily, he stooped to give what comfort he could. She was on him like a tigress, pounding his chest with her fists, calling him obscenities. Beldoque and Lecluselle tried to restrain her but to no avail.

The Marquis intervened. His method of "comforting" succeeded. Without bothering to check the prone figure of the planter, he turned accuser. "It is as Madame says. This man is a murderer. I myself shall report him to the Governor."

His arrogance, the self-righteousness, exceeded anything Louis had experienced in Paris. "The laws of Spain are more merciful than those of France," he said, every bit as haughtily as the

Marquis. "We will plead our cause – and this slave's – before Governor Chacón."

CHAPTER FIFTY

There are but few things of which we may give a sincere
judgment: for there be very few wherein in some sort or
other we do not have a personal or material concern.

Michel de Montaigne, *Essays* III.vii

Edward's hair at last had grown long enough to club into a
queue. The ribbon he'd borrowed from the Cannonball to dress it
lay on the top tray of his sea chest, curled around Knoles' razor
and the miniature of his father. He snatched the ribbon and shut
the lid.

"The people are hoisting out the Captain's barge."

The great Trewethey had come in person to fetch him. Acting
as Pearse's aide, Edward was to request another audience with
Governor Chacón. He had no time to spare nor desire to spare it.
Edward hurredily tied the ribbon around his stub of a queue. To
his annoyance, the Welsh mid lingered.

"Deveare – I, I was wrong about you. Hallard said you were a
troublemaker, a rabble-rouser, like those Frogs running amuck.
We'd been shipmates once, he and I. I, I'm sorry."

That Hallard had given him the worst possible character
Edward didn't doubt. To be accused of being a radical, though...
Knoles, his eyes filled with awe. *You called me a man.* Jake, his
dead eyes filled with hatred. *Your father done this.* His mind full

of these things, Edward's fingers barely brushed Trewethey's outstretched hand. And another whose eyes he'd never again see, Jemmy. Edward wavered. Of the two, somehow it was Jemmy's death which now bothered him most. He was so young.

In the barge, Edward kept his eyes from the crew, focusing instead on the quay of Port of Spain. They'd accomplished their mission, found and captured the pirate. The other ship had eluded them, whatever she was. Only it had been an English pirate. Was that why he felt so dirty? His countrymen had committed murder on the high seas. He'd killed Jake. The the fiddler boy had joined with the pirates and had died as a result. Edward felt a bitter pang. Jemmy.

The same officer who'd previously escorted him waited with a spare horse. They both knew the drill. This time, though, the Spaniard was less hostile. He chatted about some affair the Governor presently was judging. Did the young *Señor* wish to view it?

Edward nodded. In truth, he'd heard little. When the aide led him to a building other than the Governor's residence, he expressed surprise.

"No, *Señor*. Judgments are never given at His Excellency's home. The English hate the French, no? Well, this should amuse."

Curious as to what he alluded, Edward followed his guide into an official room. Governor Chacón sat on a carved wooden chair on a dais. Two groups faced him. The larger: an aristocratic man, a distraught woman, and what Edward assumed were their followers. The other: four men and a mutilated slave. On closer examination, Edward recognized one: that damned Frenchman again. He served as spokesman for his companions.

"Your Excellency, the laws of Spain require just treatment of all, including slaves. This man was being cruelly tortured. His crime? Singing."

Man. Only a rabble-rouser would use that term. Edward flushed uncomfortably.

"Your Excellency, the song in question was '*Ça Ira*'. The insurgents sing this in France, inciting the mob against their betters. This criminal taught it to the slaves, wishing to foment rebellion here also. And murder. I sent my men also for Villoux, who though not there, is one with these dogs."

"Dogs? I was attacked and defended myself!"

326

"You came armed to a party –"

"Flaying a man alive is a party to you?"

"A piece of property, to be disciplined."

"See" said the young Frenchman, pivoting the slave's back to the Governor, "what Frenchmen do to their 'property!'"

Edward blanched at what he saw. Had Jake's back looked as bad when his father finished with him? Anger welled up inside him. Who was this Frenchman to twist the knife of guilt in his conscience? Who was he to sway the Governor?

"Your Excellency," Edward said, coming forward, "forgive my intrusion. I came as a spectator, but my experience with this fellow necessitates comment."

"What has he –"

"Silence! He has our permission to speak."

"When last I was here, this fellow accosted me and my watering party. He urged the crowd to attack us, which they did. I agree with the honorable gentleman," Edward said, bowing to the Marquis. "This person is a dangerous radical. He is not fit to dwell among enlightened men."

The Marquis acknowledged Edward's aid and resumed his case. "Even so, Your Excellency," he said. "Perhaps the means by which French planters control their slaves is repugnant to Spanish palates, yet it has proven effective in France's colonies. Monsieur Caron prospered. He was loyal to both his own king and later, his new Spanish lord. He, and others like him, myself for one, wish to increase the wealth of this island, to the glory of Spain and her present governor. Refuse like these, the printer most assuredly included, strive to overthrow the rightful government here, as do their counterparts in France."

"Present" governor. Was the slight emphasis a dig that Chacón could be replaced if he didn't see things the way the wealthy planters did? Although Edward disliked the inference, he bowed his approval in return. Between them, they must make Señor Chacón see these men were dangerous.

"Your Excellency," Louis began, "these Englishmen ran like –"

"Enough! I will consider my decision."

Señor Chacón retired to an inner room. The Governor had impressed Edward as a fair man, too fair, perhaps? Swayed by pity for the torn slave? Would he decide that the Frenchman had been right to interfere, even when death was the result? Trade with the English island of Grenada argued he was a realist, not an idealist. Yet Edward hoped the latter side of his character would prevail. And that his decision would not add an additional burden to Edward's conscience.

His Excellency gone, the Frenchmen conversed among themselves. The rabble-rouser glared his way. Edward returned hate for hate.

Governor Chacón didn't keep them waiting long. "Madame, it grieves me you have lost your husband, but based upon the witnesses questioned, I cannot rule his death a murder." Madame cried out, but the Governor held up his hand. "Neither do I condone what these men have done. They have proven themselves unfit to dwell here. Therefore, I banish them. A ship now lies in our harbor bound for Tobago. I intend they shall be sent aboard, with a letter from me requesting the Governor of Tobago to send them back to France in chains. As for this misguided slave, I give him to your keeping. See to his wounds. He has been punished enough."

The aide-de-camp nudged Edward. "A good show, eh, *amigo*? Wait here, while I inform His Excellency of your purpose."

A show? Was that all it had been? Edward shifted from one foot to another as he awaited the aide's return. The Frenchmen deserved more than exile, although what exactly he couldn't say. Something, though, even if it wasn't hanging. The judgment not only dissatisfied Edward, it increased his dissatisfaction with himself.

The principal players dispersed. The Marquis gave the lady his arm. Edward thought Madame leaned a little too heavily on his arm for one so recently bereft. Their followers collected the poor slave and hustled him away.

After the prosecution filed out, armed soldiers surrounded the four. They shrugged and joked, three of them did, that is. The fourth marched rigidly by, until he came to Edward.

"*Aristo*," he said, through guards, "there will yet come a day when none separate us. Then I will deal with you as you deserve!"

"Is France so shorn of glory she sends her galley slaves to war?"

Edward drew his ceremonial sword as the Frenchman broke though the guard. The youth's friend's however, succeeded in restraining him before the guards could. They chided him, warning him to bide his time. War would come, and they would see to it he was ready.

Edward grimly echoed their promise. War would come, and he would be ready.

CHAPTER FIFTY-ONE

Can a woman forget her sucking child, that she should
not have compassion on the son of her womb?

Isaiah 49:15

The Spanish crisis had played neatly into Pitt's hands. He'd
been handily re-elected, and Fox soundly defeated. After all that
talk of both sides running two candidates, Leicester politics had
settled into the old, familiar pattern, each side running only one.
Despite business as usual, unease lingered. The riots in Leicester,
for example. The 11th Dragoons had put them down, shedding
blood in the bargain, after radical Whigs dissenters attacked the
Assembly rooms and destroyed the music library. A barbarous
affair; Whigs, no less. Elizabeth sighed. What was the world
coming to?

Then there was father. He'd openly avoided her since that
failed trip to Portsmouth. What had he to be angry about? Edward
was her son, not his. More peculiar, relations between him and
Portland also were strained. Now, though, he seemed totally
immersed in some other affair, the Spanish Crisis she supposed,
although she could be wrong. He also avoided discussing his
concerns with her. On top of it all, the newssheets hadn't come
today. Father was reading the *Leicester Journal*, a Tory paper,
another bad sign.

"Well, how was it?"

He hadn't raised his head, but at least he'd acknowledged her existence. "It? Oh, the trial. The fellow was convicted and hanged. The children are still at large, but Lord Onslow assured me they'll be found soon."

"I saw Lady Onslow in Town."

"Really? Was she well?"

"Don't play coy with me. We had rather an interesting discussion, enlightening I might say. About you and Charles James Fox."

"Fox? Well, what of it? He's an old family friend."

"Lady Onslow intimated you and he dined together at the Crown in Guildford, and that at least one letter from him to you was delivered to East Dene. Rumors about you two have been circulating."

"Rumors? What rumors? Don't tell me people have been saying things about us, based on such flimsy facts?"

"Is there anything between you and him?"

"I enlisted his aid in helping about Edward, that's all. Not that he succeeded in doing anything. Besides, he has Mrs. Armistead to amuse him, as well you know."

"Speaking of Edward –"

"With Pitt calling up the fleet, I can see no remedy for him."

"He writes he owes his captain and officers money."

"Then I suggest he find a way of repaying them."

"For clothes and outfitting."

"That is not my concern."

"Some of our set are on station there. You don't want people saying we're having difficulties, do you?"

"Elizabeth!"

He was definitely angry, using her Christian name. But she was ready for him. "Well, I suppose we must let matters be, then."

"Precisely."

"If he has no money, he must come home."

* * * *

B. N. Peacock

The chicken was excellent, the herbs enticing. The cook had prepared a special sauce for the vegetables. They even had fresh bread, expensive these days. Albertine picked at her plate.

"I shall summon Dr. Portier if you get any thinner."

"Portier? He cannot cure what ails me."

"Well, then," Jean-Claude said, laying down his knife and fork. "Who can? Surely not I."

Albertine looked across the table at her husband of eighteen years. His hair had gotten greyer. His paunch was less, too, he who complained of her thinness. Did he worry about her, or Louis?

"The Fête went well."

"Bah! The rabble have not all gone home."

"The Guard units? Some. The city is not as crowded."

"You cannot get him out of your thoughts, can you? You insist on having his ghost here, at every meal, at every hour. Well, he is gone! Had you not indulged him so, he might still be at his studies."

"I indulge him? Was it not more a case of you hounding him?"

"I was right to do what I did. What would my patrons think, what would they do, if they knew my son were a revolutionary?"

"What I think, what I feel, is that nothing to you?"

Jean-Claude rose. "I see Michaud today. Pardon, Madame, I do not wish to be late."

She let him go without a good-bye or Godspeed. Another day and no letter from Louis. Husbands were cruel, but sons crueler still. She'd have the serving man pack the food in a hamper. The little one, Marie-Rose, would welcome it. The tiny garret room had become more of a home to her than this. They'd comfort each other and talk of Louis as they ate.

CHAPTER FIFTY-TWO

And this was the price of my manhood: the loss of all innocence and the burden of blood.

Evington Papers, 7759/9

"You have the ship and its miscreants, Captain Pearse?"

The Governor's English was slightly accented, but good English nonetheless. Pearse and Edward simultaneously stiffened.

His translating no longer needed, Edward faded to the sidelines. He was being paid back for his actions at the trial, during and after. He listened while a terse Pearse and a terser Governor negotiated. The schooner's papers listed her as *Perdita*, out of La Guaira. (Pearse had destroyed the duplicate set, listing her as English.) And here also, the letter of marque from the non-existent country of Venezuela, giving him license to prey on Spanish ships. (Edward had translated it for Pearse's benefit.) Yes, *Perdita's* Captain had been English and one or two of his men, but that was all. Pearse would be pleased to hand both ship and remaining captives over to His Excellency. No mention of the fugitive ship. For his part, Señor Chacón commented dryly that the Viceroy would be duly informed.

No prize money, no war. Edward and Pearse were about to depart when the Governor called them back. He wished a word in private with the young *señor*.

335

Edward turned helplessly to Pearse. He didn't want another round of accusations, especially as he was likely to receive a reprimand from the Governor. Pearse waved him back.

Señor Chacón sat with his head bent in thought until all others left the audience chamber.

When he spoke, Edward strained to hear.

"I counted myself a fool for letting you weigh anchor, never really believing you'd return, and if you did, with a story of how you could not find the pirates. You not only kept faith with me, but you brought your own to justice. You, my friend, are responsible. Had I been your Captain, I would not have credited my story either. You alone saw with clear eyes. Again, just now, you showed me an honorable way out of a dilemma."

Uncertain what to make of this, Edward let Señor Chacón guide him to where the Goya hung. He took it down and held it out to Edward.

"Your Excellency, this is too great a gift."

"Peace is an even greater gift."

Edward reluctantly accepted the study. It would serve as a lesson to him. Much as he still respected the Governor, he'd never blindly trust anyone again.

With the Governor as his escort, he rejoined Pearse. Unlike their last visit, Pearse proved talkative on the ride back to the quay.

"You came out of this well."

"The drawing? It really should go to –"

"No, damn me, keep it. I approve the Governor's opinion of you. If you must know, I have an even higher one. Just no paintings to bestow."

Blanche's masts rose straight and clean. Somehow, some way, he'd atone for the things that had gone wrong, for Jake, even more, for Jemmy. Looking at the Goya, Edward realized with a pang the face was that of a peasant. A man. Would he never be allowed to forget?

He forced his attention back to his ship. Over dinner last evening, Pearse had outlined his plans for getting Edward the funds he needed. He'd authorize his agent back in England to get Edward's due from the Portsmouth property. Not a bad plan, actually. His eyes lovingly roved his ship, his wooden world. He was proud to serve in her, prouder yet to serve under Pearse.

* * * * *

"That Englishman! Because of him, we are being sent back to France!"

"Saulnier," Beldoque said, with exaggerated weariness, "is returning to France such a bad thing? Think!"

Lecluselle eyed their guards warily. "We are fortunate not to be hung for what you did."

"You blame me?" Louis said, rounding savagely. After the initial shock, he had no regrets about Caron's death. The man had chosen the wrong side. It was the slave's fate which troubled him, for which he was responsible. Madame, egged on by the Marquis, would find a way to mutilate him further, Louis had no doubt. And kill him. As for the Marquis, he lived and prospered, with the Governor's blessing.

There was no justice on this earth.

"For Caron? But no! For shooting off your mouth, but yes!"

"Citizens," Villoux said, "hear me. Even if we are sent back to France in chains, does that mean we will remain in them? A sailor on the very ship that will carry us to Tobago told me all France plans to celebrate its brotherhood. Ah, to be there! Just think what Paris must be now."

To Louis, Villoux daily sounded more like Bertrand. With any luck, he might be detained in Tobago, maybe. But Louis did long for Paris. There, he would do his utmost to spread the ideals of liberty and equality, to bring those like the Marquis to their knees.

"I, too, have heard rumors," Beldoque said, dodging a musket butt herding them down a different street. "Not of brotherhood, but unrest among the regiments. Soldiers chafe under the heavy hands of their officers, of *aristos*. The time is ripe for our return."

"As for the English," Lecluselle said, snapping his fingers gaily, "so much for them. We will yet bloody *les goddams* noses. Let us sing!"

"*Ça Ira?*"

"Are you mad? That is what got us into this trouble," Lecluselle said.

"A good marching song," Beldoque said. "You know the one."

In defiance of the guards and as a personal insult to the English ship in the harbor, the three strode abreast, Villoux bringing up the rear. In perfect step, in perfect tune, they chanted "Malbrook Goes Off to War."

Louis sang loudest. With all his heart, his soul, his being, he'd devote himself to creating a new France, one whose glory would never fade. As he belted out the refrain, it struck him that no matter how much it taunted the English, the song belonged to the *ancien régime*. Some day, he assured himself, Frenchmen would march to a better tune.

* * * * *

The British navy has a long arm. Throughout that long day, Jemmy alternated between this thought and anguish over his father. He'd easily eluded Brighty, up there on Box Hill. He'd become familiar with Dorking, after all. Or had the bo'sun been so sure of capturing him he hadn't bothered to immediately follow?

Jemmy forced Nan to keep pace. Last night, he'd stayed in the cave until well after midnight. Only then, had he dared make his way to the farmer's home. He demanded they hand Nan over to him. Sleepily, the farmer and his wife complied. The farmer complained that there had been talk of a strange girl on the hill. It was too dangerous for them to keep Nan now.

Jemmy was glad he hadn't slept. Never again would his dreams be innocent. The gift? No, the curse. From now on, he'd always wonder what and how his dreams would unfold. Yet as much as he dreaded the night, he feared the day. He didn't want anyone to see him, to recognize him. Them, he corrected himself, for he now was responsible for Nan. Traveling with her made recognition and capture much more likely.

For all his haste, it was nearly daybreak. He identified the road on the right as the one leading to the lord's estate. Of a sudden, a thought struck him, or rather, recognition. That lady at Kingston. She talked of going up to London to see about her son. He was in the Indies. The dark blue eyes! She was Mr. Deveare's mother, the one he'd seen in front of that fancy shop. Mr. Brighty was here, so must be *Amphitrite*. The lady was seeing about her son because he was home. Mr. Deveare had told his mother about him. That's why everyone had been so keen to take him and Nan. If only he'd been able to understand that Frenchie the day in London. He must have tried to warn him they were both no good.

They had to get away. Nan whimpered they needed to wait for Daddy. Daddy was here, by the lake. Jemmy broke into a run, dragging her after him. Let her dare try to stray.

Even as he ran, memories seared him. Albury. The only place he'd ever call home. It was lost to him forever. Where to go? Not London, for someone might recognize them. Not anywhere in England. Liberty. The Americans boasted of their freedom and their rights. Every man was as good as another there. The quality couldn't trample all over them like they had here. Like Mr. Deveare had, and his mother, and Captain Finch.

He'd work his passage, maybe to New York. It seemed a likely place from what he'd seen. Nan tripped over his foot. What was he to do with her?

The horizon glowed red. A bad sign, Jemmy recalled from shipboard lore. More awful was the picture that tore into his mind. Was it the gift, even though he was wide awake? As clearly as he saw Nan panting beside him, he saw their father. Jemmy gouged his eyes with his fists, but he couldn't erase the vision.

Against a livid sky a dark figure hung in chains, the body tarred to preserve it as a warning for all who passed. A tainted death and a tainted dawn.

HISTORICAL NOTE

The summer of 1789 witnessed two significant events. The first, the opening stages of the French Revolution, requires no explanation. The second, however, is lesser known. Spanish ships seized four British merchantmen trading for sea otter pelts in Nootka Sound, in what is now British Columbia. Spain interpreted this as an attempt by England to establish a strategic trading and naval base in a vulnerable Spanish colony. Spain and England nearly went to war over what was then termed the Spanish Armament or Crisis, and what is now called the Nootka Crisis. Both sides mobilized their fleets and set their colonies at high alert. As related here, France, via the Family Compact of the Royal House of Bourbon between her and Spain, also considered war. The Nootka Crisis was in some ways a dress rehearsal for the long series of wars which were to begin in 1792, wars the British would later refer to as "The Great War," until a more cataclysmic struggle – World War I – took over that title. William Pitt the Younger eventually settled the Nootka Crisis through diplomatic means. The crisis was also significant in that it played a role in securing his 1790 re-election.

England also sought to increase her prestige by taking advantage of France's burgeoning revolution by sending a secret embassy to Vienna. Lord Evington is a fictional character, as are the Evington Papers, but a delegation did conclude a secret pact with the Austrian government. Like Evington, cool heads not only played power politics on an international scale, but also sought to keep England from war a long as possible, that she might gain precious time to recover politically and economically from the American War.

Amphitrite was a real ship but not on station as mentioned here. Her real life counterpart, HMS *Blanche* dropped anchor in Carlisle Bay, Barbados on 29 June 1789. Her actual captain was Robert Murray. I used literary license in having her come on station some months later, as well as giving her a different captain. Charles Hunt was *Blanche's* actual first lieutenant. He bears no resemblance to the character of Mr. Stark. *Blanche's* other officers, except for the midshipmen, are as listed.

Trade between Trinidad and Grenada flourished, to the benefit of both islands. Don José María Chacón was Trinidad's last, and best loved, Spanish colonial governor. As mentioned in the book, the Spanish government encouraged French settlers to establish plantations there. He did indeed have to look the other way at the way French planters treated their slaves. French cruelty to slaves later played a significant role in triggering the violent uprisings in the French West Indies, as did the concepts of liberty and equality.

Jean Villoux did indeed publish inflammatory articles praising the revolution in France in his *Gazetta*. As in the book, Governor Chacón deported him to Tobago for sedition.

Other famous historical figures play walk-on roles, such as those mentioned in the National Assembly and Parliament. Not so famous was Marie-Rose Barré, Louis' sweetheart, an actual lace maker who served as part of the deputation to the King during the October Days. The others are figures of romance, patterned on people who lived during those times, doing deeds they might have done.

About the Author

B. N. Peacock has had a life-long passion for history. Her childhood hero was Lord Nelson. In school, she won an honorable mention in a national *READ* magazine contest for a short story about Bunker Hill, written from the viewpoint of a British correspondent. College and career later shifted to economics. She worked for the USDA's Economic Research Service and wrote for several of their publications. Busy raising a family and caring for her mother, her interests returned to her original loves. It was at that time she began researching and writing *A Tainted Dawn,* and also contributing to local papers and book reviews. She is currently at work on the next volumes in the Great War Series.